Steventon Parsonage

Chawton Cottage

Countryside near Lyme Regis

The house on College St. in Winchester where Jane Austen passed away

(Photographs by Li-Ping Geng)

The Roman bath house

The Upper Rooms at Bath

The Cobb

The stone steps (Granny's Teeth) at the Cobb

Progressive States of Mind

Progressive States of Mind

Dialectical Elements in
the Novels of Jane Austen

Li-Ping Geng

北京大学出版社
PEKING UNIVERSITY PRESS

图书在版编目(CIP)数据

与时俱进的思维:简·奥斯汀小说的辩证观＝Progressive States of Mind：Dialectical Elements in the Novels of Jane Austen/Li-Ping Geng. —北京:北京大学出版社，2006.12

（外国文学研究丛书）

ISBN 7-301-11157-6

Ⅰ. 与… Ⅱ. L… Ⅲ. 奥斯汀，J.（1775～1817）—小说—文学研究—英文 Ⅳ. I561.074

中国版本图书馆 CIP 数据核字(2006)第 125426 号

书　　　名：**Progressive States of Mind：**
　　　　　　Dialectical Elements in the Novels of Jane Austen

著作责任者：Li-Ping Geng

责 任 编 辑：孙凤兰

标 准 书 号：ISBN 7-301-11157-6/H · 1703

出 版 发 行：北京大学出版社

地　　　址：北京市海淀区成府路 205 号　　100871

网　　　址：http://www.pup.cn

电 子 邮 箱：zpup@pup.pku.edu.cn

电　　　话：邮购部 62752015　发行部 62750672　编辑部 62767315
　　　　　　出版部 62754962

印 　刷 　者：三河市新世纪印务有限公司

经 　销 　者：新华书店

　　　　　　650 毫米×980 毫米　16 开本　19.25 印张　彩插 4 页　325 千字

　　　　　　2006 年 12 月第 1 版　2006 年 12 月第 1 次印刷

定　　　价：38.00 元

For John D. Baird who guided me
from 1998 to 1999

Contents

Preface

In the past thirty years or so, historical studies of Jane Austen tend to characterize her novels as either conservative or radical. Marilyn Butler's *Jane Austen and the War of Ideas* (1975) argues that Austen's "morality is preconceived and inflexible," that she is reacting against the English Jacobin novelists of the 1790s such as William Godwin and Robert Bage. On the other hand, *The Proper Lady and the Woman Writer: Ideology as Style in the Works of Mary Wollstonecraft, Mary Shelley, and Jane Austen* (1984) by Mary Poovey and *Jane Austen: Women, Politics and the Novel* (1988) by Claudia L. Johnson contend that Austen is a feminist writer who operates in "a largely feminine tradition of political novels" (Johnson) and "both completes Wollstonecraft's analysis of female inhibition and perfects Shelley's attempt to make propriety accommodate female desire" (Poovey).

These divergent and seemingly irreconcilable views, reflecting two important aspects of Austen's literary relations with her contemporaries and immediate predecessors, reveal nevertheless two disconcerting tendencies: the tendency to highlight one narrow aspect while ignoring others, and the tendency to be prescriptive rather than descriptive. It is the view of this study that the alternatives represented by these two camps are "neither mutually exclusive nor collectively exhaustive" (Fischer), for tendencies in Austen's work seem to indicate that the author does not see her world in terms of oppression or conformation.

This book traces and identifies dialectical elements in Jane Austen's six completed novels and analyzes the working of these elements in the learning process of the protagonists. It investigates and makes clear the extent to which contrary if not contradictory elements function in her fiction, especially in the moral education of her protagonists. In doing so it aims to offer a comprehensive view of Jane Austen's novels.

The introductory chapter first outlines the generic change of dialectic both as an approach to and as an integral part of discourse, logic and knowledge; it then sketches relevant aspects of the political, social and literary scene in England about the time of the French Revolution; finally, it characterizes the dialectical stance taken by Austen which enables her to learn from both the conservative and the reform-minded writers of the time. Chapter 2 analyzes the dialectical nature of the plot and argues that Catherine Morland's learning experience in Volume 2 of the novel is organically connected with and significantly affected by her learning experience in Volume 1. Chapter 3 investigates the way in which the dichotomous subject matter is affected and undermined by the presence of dialectical elements in the narrative. Chapter 4 describes the role which dialectics plays in the moral transformation of Elizabeth Bennet and Mr Darcy. Chapter 5 illustrates the dialectical essence in the moral growth of Fanny Price. Chapter 6 examines the dialectical process wherein Emma's moral judgment is made, and Chapter 7 dissects a series of dialectical twists that lead to the eventual reunion of Anne Elliot and Captain Wentworth.

The book concludes by stressing that Jane Austen is concerned with a moral and philosophical regeneration of the mind of individuals within existing social structures, that she diligently communicates such concern through the deployment and development of dialectical elements in the fabric of her narrative art, and that the resulting interplay of conservative and progressive tendencies contributes to the intellectual complexity of Jane Austen's novels.

Acknowledgements

I would like to thank the people who helped me while I was writing an early version of the manuscript. Professor J. D. Baird of the University of Toronto guided me through the entire study; I am deeply indebted to him. Professors G. E. Bentley, Jr. and F. T. Flahiff of Toronto read the early drafts and gave judicious advice; I am grateful to both of them. Zhang Bing and Sun Feng-Lan of the Peking University Press offered valuable assistance while I was getting this study ready for print; to both of them, I express sincere gratitude.

Finally, I thank my wife Gu Li-Ya and daughter Geng Hui, whose cheerfulness is exemplified in their joint 1997 Christmas present, a rock-shaped paperweight, bearing the inscription: Whether you think you can or you can't, you're right.

LPG
Weihai
Oct. 2006

Editions and Abbreviations

Austen, Jane. *The Novels of Jane Austen*, ed. R. W. Chapman, 3rd
ed. 5 vols. (London: Oxford UP, 1932–1934; rpt. 1988)
—. *Minor Works*, ed. R. W. Chapman, vol. 6 (London: Oxford UP,
1954; rpt. With further revisions B. C. Southam, 1988)
—. *Jane Austen's Letters*, collected and ed. Deirdre Le Faye (Oxford:
Oxford UP, 1995)
Locke, John. *An Essay Concerning Human Understanding*, ed. Peter
H. Nidditch (1690; Oxford: Clarendon, 1975; rpt. with correc-
tions 1979)
—. *Of the Conduct of the Understanding* in vol. 3 of *The Works of
John Locke* (1707; London, 1823; rpt. Aalen: Scientia Verlag,
1963)

E	*Emma*
MP	*Mansfield Park*
MW	*Minor Works*
NA	*Northanger Abbey*
P	*Persuasion*
PP	*Pride and Prejudice*
SS	*Sense and Sensibility*
Conduct	*Of the Conduct of the Understanding* (cited by section)
Essay	*An Essay Concerning Human Understanding* (cited by book, chapter, and section)
Letters	*Jane Austen's Letters* (cited by date)

1　Introduction

In the past thirty years or so historical studies of Jane Austen have tended to fall into one of two camps. Marilyn Butler's *Jane Austen and the War of Ideas* (1975; reissued with a new introduction in 1987) describes Austen as a "conservative" novelist whose "morality is preconceived and inflexible,"[1] who is reacting, much in the vein of Mrs Jane West, against the English Jacobin novelists of the 1790s such as William Godwin and Robert Bage. On the other hand, Claudia L. Johnson's *Jane Austen: Women, Politics and the Novel* (1988) portrays Austen as a progressive feminist, in the vein of "Wollstonecraft and Hays," who "center[s] her novels in the consciousness of unempowered characters—that is, women" and "exposes[s] and explore[s] those aspects of traditional institutions—marriage, primogeniture, patriarchy—which patently do not serve her heroines well."[2] "In endowing attractive female characters like Emma Woodhouse and Elizabeth Bennet with rich and unapologetic senses of self-consequence," Johnson argues, "Austen defies every dictum about female propriety and deference propounded in the sermons and conduct books which have been thought to shape her opinions on all important matters."[3]

Johnson's feminist-oriented critical position is in fact a variation of

---

[1]　Marilyn Butler, *Jane Austen and the War of Ideas* (Oxford: Clarendon, 1975) 298.

[2]　Claudia L. Johnson, *Jane Austen: Women, Politics and the Novel* (Chicago: U of Chicago P, 1988) xxiv. Johnson's more recent book: *Equivocal Beings: Politics, Gender, and Sentimentality in the 1790s: Wollstonecraft, Radcliffe, Burney, Austen* (Chicago: U of Chicago P, 1994) is a continuation of the same discussion.

[3]　Johnson xxiii. Butler, by contrast, contends that Jane Austen's "reading, in sermons and conduct-books, must have given her old-fashioned notions of social cohesion and obligation" (*Romantics, Rebels and Reactionaries: English Literature and Its Background: 1760 – 1830* [Oxford: Oxford UP, 1981] 102).

Mary Poovey's feminist theorizing in her book *The Proper Lady and the Woman Writer: Ideology as Style in the Works of Mary Wollstonecraft, Mary Shelley, and Jane Austen* (1984), in which Poovey views Austen as a sophisticated feminist who "both completes Wollstonecraft's analysis of female inhibition and perfects Shelley's attempt to make propriety accommodate female desire."[1] The sophistication chiefly lies in the fact that Austen, according to Poovey, is able to introduce "the ideal of romantic love in a socially realistic fiction" by creating an alluring but ultimately pernicious illusion: "[F]reezing the narrative at the climactic moment of marriage—as Austen always does."[2] Such illusion "promises women emotional fulfillment and the legitimation of their autonomy, their intensity of feeling, and even their power," making "women dream of being swept off their feet;" but it always "ends by reinforcing the helplessness that makes learning to stand on their own two feet unlikely."[3]

The characteristic views of these camps, needless to say, are divergent and even seemingly irreconcilable; however, they both point to directions in which a productive investigation of Jane Austen's novels may be conducted.[4] At the same time, though, they reveal certain disconcerting tendencies: the tendency to highlight one narrow aspect while ignoring others, and the tendency to be prescriptive rather than

---

[1]   Mary Poovey, *The Proper Lady and the Woman Writer: Ideology as Style in the Works of Mary Wollstonecraft, Mary Shelley, and Jane Austen* (Chicago: U of Chicago P, 1984) 173.

[2][3]   Poovey 243.

[4]   The directions are as many as they are varied. D. D. Devlin, for example, places Jane Austen's fiction in the educational environment of the eighteenth century, especially in relation to John Locke and Lord Chesterfield (*Jane Austen and Education* [London: Macmillan, 1975]). Roger Sales reads her fiction against such matters as domestic instability and military miscalculation that happened during and after the second Regency Crisis (*Jane Austen and Representations of Regency England* [London: Routledge, 1994]). Gene Koppel explores the religious aspect in Jane Austen's novels in terms of the religious environment of the author's time (*The Religious Dimension of Jane Austen's Novels* [Ann Arbor: UMI Research P, 1988]). Since the publication of Sandra M. Gilbert and Susan Gubar's ground-breaking, if also misleading , criticism of Austen's fiction in *The Madwoman in the Attic : The Woman Writer*

descriptive. Or in the words of Mary Waldron, the "tendency to prioritise what *we* think was important over the perceptions of the author working within the cultural parameters of his / her time."① Indeed some of these radically new departures in recent Austen criticism, judging the Regency author by today's critical sentiment or even by personal preferences, make their arrivals very much in doubt.

For example, Claudia L. Johnson's attempt to "reconceptualize the stylistic and thematic coherence of Austen's fiction by demonstrating how it emerges, draws, and departs from a largely feminine tradition of political novels" begins by accusing "historical and biographical Austenian scholarship" in general of being "sometimes merely methodologically naive and sometimes irrecoverably entrenched in logical fallacies"② and by attacking R. W. Chapman's edition of Jane Austen's novels in particular:

> *The Oxford Illustrated Jane Austen* is animated by an impulse markedly more Antiquarian than scholarly. Though acclaimed, one suspects, almost as a matter of convention, the editions themselves are hardly models of rigorous textual scholarship, and to all appearances they do not intend to be. ③

Johnson's depreciation of Chapman's scholarship is based on her belief that Chapman's edition of Austen creates the author it presumed, and the history it desired. Allusions to the riots in London, or the slave trade in Antigua, for example, are first passed over, and then believed not to exist at all. With their appendixes detailing Regency fashions in clothing, carriages, and modes of address, and their chronologies of events based on almanacs, Chapman's editions appear less to illuminate

---

and the Nineteenth-Century Literary Imagination (New Haven: Yale UP, 1979), a host of feminist-oriented critics have tried to read Austen's fiction in light of the essential argument laid out by Gilbert and Gubar. These critics will be noted and their ideas discussed in the course of this study.

① *Jane Austen and the Fiction of Her Time* (Cambridge: Cambridge UP, 1999) 12 – 13.

② Johnson xix. Johnson later names Lionel Trilling, Marvin Mudrick, Wayne C. Booth and Alistair M. Duckworth as the representatives in this category.

③ Johnson xvi.

and to honor Austen's compositional process than to preserve the novels in a museumlike world situated somewhere between fiction and real life. ①

Whereas Chapman's work speaks for itself, Johnson is mistaken to cite riot scenes or slave trade as the criteria for realism in Jane Austen's fiction. The quasi-criteria of realism remind one of Woolf's criticism of the masculine criteria that are transferred from life to fiction: "This is an important book, the critic assumes, because it deals with war. This is an insignificant book because it deals with the feelings of women in a drawing-room."② Moreover, there seems to be some inherent contradiction in the logic of Johnson's argument itself. A museum is a place where historical relics are preserved so that the living may go and see what their ancestors and their way of life were like; there is nothing fictional about it—it is real life at a temporal and spatial remove. Similarly, it is a serious misunderstanding to argue that Chapman's effort to establish the proper social, moral, and intellectual contexts of Jane Austen's writings "has implied that her novels are off limits to the ponderous diction of literary scholarship."③ Literary scholarship has not since been deterred either in the austere East or in the liberal West. In fact, Chapman's edition has facilitated, rather than deterred, all kinds of Austen criticism, including Johnson's own "ponderous" assessment which is based, ironically, on Chapman's edition.

For another example, Deborah Kaplan's 1992 book, *Jane Austen*

---

① Johnson xvii.

② *A Room of One's Own* (London: Hogarth, 1929) 111.

③ Johnson xvi. Johnson's criticism may, however, be appropriately applied to Leslie Stephen's comment on Jane Austen made in 1876: "I should dispute the conclusion that she was therefore entitled to be ranked with the great authors who have sounded the depths of human passion, or found symbols for the finest speculations of the human intellect, instead of amusing themselves with the humours of a country tea-table" ("Humour," *Cornhill Magazine*, 1876, xxxiii; B. C. Southam, *Jane Austen: The Critical Heritage*, rev. ed., 2 vols. [London: Routledge, 1968; rpt. 1986] vol. 2, 174). Notice the similarity in the tone of Stephen's reservation and Charlotte Brontë's indignation: "And what did I find? An accurate daguerreotyped portrait of a commonplace face; a carefully fenced, highly cultivated garden, with neat borders and delicate flowers" (Letter to G. H. Lewes [12 January 1848]; Southam, vol. 2, 126).

among Women, purports to give a "systematic consideration to those social and psychological supports that made Austen's writing possible and helped to enliven and extend her representational range," but she fails to mention the vital nurturing and encouragement which the fledgling Austen had received from her father and brothers (Jane had six brothers and one sister)① while stressing exclusively "[t]he impact of Cassandra Austen on the novelist's career" and "the wider social and cultural context of contemporary female friendship."② These are partial truths and may cause misunderstanding. Saying, as Kaplan does, that "Austen's close female friends formed her audience for work in draft and discussed it with her"③ potentially excludes, by a stroke of the pen, the great interest and valuable feedback which her male audience, especially her brothers (Henry in particular), had unfailingly shown and offered.

At the other extreme, there is Marilyn Butler who contends that "the Austen exemplary heroine is meek, self-disciplined, and self-effacing,"④ and concludes that "[w]omen in Austen don't age well—none is shown having grown to wisdom through experience, or even exercising authority over servants or children. Collectively, Austen's women are oddly and

---

① Mr George Austen, for example, wrote as early as 1797 to the London publisher Thomas Cadell to propose the publication of *First Impressions* (James Edward Austen-Leigh, *Memoir of Jane Austen*, intro. etc. R. W. Chapman [Oxford: Clarendon, 1926] 137). Henry Austen, according to Le Faye, perhaps encouraged his sister to make a second copy of *Susan* and then had his business associate Mr Seymour sell the manuscript on Jane Austen's behalf to Richard Crosby & Son for £10; furthermore, Henry later negotiated with the same publisher and retrieved the manuscript which was yet to be published (William Austen-Leigh and Richard Arthur Austen-Leigh, *Jane Austen: A Family Record*, rev. and enl. Deirdre Le Faye [London: The British Library, 1989] 127 – 128; 210). Park Honan suspects that Henry Austen might have advanced his sister the money to publish *Sense and Sensibility*, since Richard Egerton only agreed to publish the book on commission (i. e., the author was responsible for all the expenses, which would run in the range of one to two hundred pounds (*Jane Austen: Her Life* [London: Weidenfeld, 1987] 286). Also, young Jane may have contributed a burlesque letter to *The Loiterer* (January 1789 – March 1790), the weekly periodical run by James Austen at Oxford with the assistance of his brother Henry (for a detailed discussion, see pp. 12 – 17).

② Deborah Kaplan, *Jane Austen among Women* (Baltimore: Johns Hopkins P, 1992) 3.

③ Kaplan 4.

④ Butler 298.

even unnaturally ineffective. "[1]

1

I believe that the alternatives represented by these two camps of historical criticism are, to borrow David Hackett Fischer's words, "neither mutually exclusive nor collectively exhaustive. "[2] They certainly reflect two important aspects of Jane Austen's writings: her awareness of the social and political situations, and her response to what has been expressed by her contemporaries and immediate predecessors. However, what they both overlook is the tendency in Austen's fiction which indicates that the author does not see her world in terms of oppression or conformation. While it may be partially true, as Butler insists, that "at the period when Jane Austen began to write, literature as a whole was partisan,"[3] it does not necessarily follow that Austen herself was a partisan novelist pure and simple. While it is credible, as Poovey and Johnson argue, that Jane Austen echoed certain feminist sentiments, it is not convincing to explain Austen merely from the angle of "a largely feminine tradition of political novels"[4] and regard her fiction primarily in the context of male oppression of women. Obviously, not all political novels of the time were written by women; and equally obvious is the fact that Jane Austen did not appreciate many of the so-called political novels written by women. In actual fact Jane Austen seems to hold a dialectical point of view that enables her to see farther afield. To the credit of these modern scholars, their contradictory viewpoints delineate or identify an essential characteristic of Austen's novels: they constitute an arena within which ideas are contested.

As early as 1870, Richard Simpson, a Shakespearean scholar, touched

---

① Butler, Introduction (1987) xl.

② David Hackett Fischer, *Historians' Fallacies: Toward a Logic of Historical Thought* (New York: Harper, 1970) 11.

③ Butler 3.

④ Johnson xix.

upon these dialectical elements in Jane Austen's novels. Simpson's review article, occasioned by James Edward Austen-Leigh's *Memoir of Jane Austen* (1870), represents one of the early high points in Jane Austen criticism. ① Simpson offers many shrewd and perceptive observations. For example, he notes that Austen's characterization is complex: "She was too great a realist to abstract and isolate the individual, and to give a portrait of him in the manner of Theophrastus or La Bruyére."② He describes Austen's method of portraying a character as follows:

> She sees him, not as a solitary being complete in himself, but only as completed in society. Again, she contemplates virtues, not as fixed quantities, or as definable qualities, but as continual struggles and conquests, as progressive states of mind, advancing by repulsing their contraries, or losing ground by being overcome. Hence again the individual mind can only be represented by her as a battle-field, where contending hosts are marshalled, and where victory inclines now to one side, now to another. ③

This dialectical process, having the mind as the battlefield where conflicts of ideas provide the impetus for the "progressive states of mind," is precisely the subject of this book.

Jane Austen lived in an age of intense political, moral and religious debates provoked by the American and, more profoundly, the French Revolutions, and the content of these debates makes its way in various guises into her novels. The form of these debates, dialectic in nature and featuring sympathy and antipathy, manifests itself in the conduct of Austen's narrative which assesses and rationalizes the conflicting ideas. In

---

① Southam praises Simpson's review article as "the outstanding piece of nineteenth-century criticism" (vol. 1, 31). However, Simpson's comment that "Jane Austen has a most Platonic inclination to explain away knavishness into folly" (vol. 1, 249) makes one wonder if he had read *Mansfield Park* or *Persuasion*. A previous highlight occurred when Thomas Babington Macaulay became perhaps the first to "have no hesitation in placing Jane Austen" "nearest" to Shakespeare (*Edinburgh Review* [January 1843]; Southam, vol. 1, 122). Simpson followed suit by saying: "Within her range her characterization is truly Shakespearian" (*North British Review* [April 1870]; Southam, vol. 1, 243).

② Southam, vol. 1, 249.

③ Southam, vol. 1, 249 – 250.

other words, there exist in Jane Austen's novels dialectical tendencies fully and fairly rendered by a series of dialectical techniques. Through this dialectical process Austen's protagonists are able to reach a higher stage of understanding and achieve a moral synthesis, metaphorically represented by happy marriages at the end of each of her six completed novels.

The working of dialectics in Jane Austen's novels is consistent, prominent, and divergent. [1] Dialectical elements are to be found in many significant narrative aspects of Jane Austen's fiction such as theme, structure, character (and relations among characters), motif, action and dialogue. In *Northanger Abbey* (1818), [2] for example, Catherine Morland's attitude towards novel reading has gone through a dialectical process. She first "read all such works as heroines must read" (15) and acquired a superficial knowledge of the world. Then, affected by Isabella Thorpe's contagious enthusiasm for Gothic novels, she quickly becomes a committed Gothic-novel fan until John Thorpe's dislike of novels in general forces her to reconsider, and even conceal, her position. Then Henry Tilney's open-mindedness about novel reading, directly opposing Thorpe's opinion and therefore adding a new degree of difficulty to a problem which Catherine already finds hard to grapple with, compels her to adjust yet again the point of view which she has already adjusted a couple of times. But with her entry into the quasi-Gothic world of Northanger Abbey, Catherine's most recently obtained knowledge is to be put to further test. Catherine's changes of mind reveal her

---

[1] I have so far used such terms as "dialectic," "dialectical" and "dialectics;" whereas the first two are often interchangeable in their capacity to describe the concept or nature of logical inquiries into contradictory views and their solutions, the last refers to the development or process wherein such inquiries are carried out through systematic reasoning and rationalizing of opposed or contradictory ideas. I will elaborate on this provisional differentiation shortly in this chapter, and illustrate the usage of these terms through the rest of this study.

[2] The publication dates follow those given by R. W. Chapman; that is, the date on the title page of the novel rather than the actual date of publication, which was December 1817 for *Northanger Abbey* and December 1815 for *Emma* (see Le Faye, *Family Record* 207, 233). Books published in November or December were routinely dated the next year at the time.

susceptibility but they also point to her adaptability. The changes that occur are not simply the result of external influences, but are also the outcome of internal rationalization.

In *Sense and Sensibility* (1811) the seeming structural opposition of the two abstract qualities, respectively represented by the two older Dashwood sisters, is gradually but unmistakably subsumed by an interaction between the two sisters, in such a dialectical manner that conflict gives way to confluence. At the local level, dialectics informs significant dialogues which in turn help to enhance vivid characterization. For example, almost the entire second chapter of the novel is devoted to a dialectical debate, in the form of a conversation between John Dashwood and Fanny Dashwood. There it is not so much the financial meanness of the couple, reprehensible as it is, that appears extraordinary; rather, it is the dialectical exchange of words between them, gradually trimming away John Dashwood's obligation—reminiscent of the way Lear's train of one hundred knights are reduced by Goneril to fifty and then by Regan to five and twenty and finally by both to zero[1]—which he solemnly promised at his father's death-bed to fulfil towards his step-mother and sisters, so rationally calculating and so civilly brutal, that generates the most chillingly obnoxious effect.

In *Pride and Prejudice* (1813) the dialectical principle plays an even more significant role in that it not only undermines the structural line between pride and prejudice—the behaviour patterns of both Darcy and Elizabeth cut right through them—but also underscores the motif of appearance versus reality, or, more appropriately, reality by virtue of appearance. Both Darcy and Elizabeth change as each comes to recognize merit as well as fault in the other. This very successful novel reflects a significant step forward in the development of Jane Austen's art of dialectic, in that the heroine's process of change is rendered with marked subtlety and complexity. Elizabeth does not realize, nay, will not even acknowledge, her error in judgment in spite of, indeed because of, Mr

---

[1]   *King Lear*, 2.4.

Darcy's criticism; in fact she strongly resists such criticism during the entire first volume and much of the second, and rather justly at times at that. It is not until Elizabeth has reflected upon the evidence which has been presented to her in a series of face-to-face encounters or gathered by herself through her scrupulous and purposeful investigation during her visit to Pemberley that she begins to admit her ignorance about the complexity of moral issues.

In the sequence of *Northanger Abbey*, *Sense and Sensibility* and *Pride and Prejudice* each succeeding novel shows greater complexity and maturity than its predecessor, as the increasingly evenly matched protagonists gradually give up playing ethical roles that are juxtaposed against one another, and become instead struggling human beings embodying a wider spectrum of genuine moral qualities. ① In the three later novels there is a progressive concentration of dialectical exchanges in the internal experience of the protagonist, coinciding with a perceptible change, already seen in *Pride and Prejudice*, from straightforward ethical contrasts to complicated moral and psychological debates. This inward turn of dialectics marks the maturity and sophistication in the development of Jane Austen's art of fiction.

In *Mansfield Park* (1814) Fanny Price's moral growth follows the pattern of moral naivety, moral consciousness and conscious morality, as her initial reliance upon Edmund Bertram, as well as Sir Thomas, for moral guidance gradually shifts to self-reliance and independent decision-making. Many critics, including R. W. Chapman, have failed to appreciate the moral message and the artistic achievement of the novel precisely because they have failed to see the dialectical process in which the moral shaping of the heroine takes place. Fanny's morality is not pre-conceived nor is she morally inactive, though she is never overtly censorious owing to her inferior social position. She has weaknesses, and

---

① Robert Nordell rightly notes that in *Pride and Prejudice* "Elizabeth expects to be, and is, treated as a rational and intelligent opponent—and often more than holds her own as such" ("Confrontation and Evasion: Argument Scenes *in Mansfield Park* and *Pride and Prejudice*," *English Studies in Africa* 36 [1993] 17).

not infrequently feels morally and psychologically insecure. Fanny copes by constantly conducting criticism and self-criticism in the privacy of her own mind; ultimately, she benefits from her own mistakes and those of others.

In *Emma* (1816) the heroine's virtue is nearly offset by her conceit; the two qualities are interlocked to form the character of this morally. complex heroine. Emma's weaknesses are never exposed without a confirmation of certain positive aspects of her character. In fact there is a perpetual struggle within Emma's mind as she goes about her business at Highbury. For example, even when she is coaching Harriet to refuse Robert Martin's marriage proposal, Emma is never unaware of her own prejudices; her superior understanding somehow always questions her own judgment even as her judgment is in the making. It is this kind of dialectical thinking process that makes the young woman interesting and convincing in spite of, even because of, her insufferable wilfulness and reckless imaginings.

Persuasion (1818) represents the culmination of Jane Austen's creation of psychological interest that had been manifest since the early days of her writing. Anne Elliot's seven-year reflection on turning down the marriage offer from Frederick Wentworth is still being carried on when the story unfolds. Although her refusal of Wentworth is not morally wrong, it has proved nonetheless psychologically damaging, even devastating at times. Throughout the novel it is apparent that the earlier decision, painful as it is, is only the beginning of a long process of dialectical deliberations. Anne has to weigh her earlier decision not only against what has happened since but also, and more importantly, against what is rapidly and dramatically taking place in front of her eyes or within her hearing, once Captain Wentworth returns. Thus the central interest of the novel is the dialectical debate constantly going on in Anne's mind. Her usually calm and unruffled manner, for the sake of decorum, hides but also emphasizes the intense emotional and intellectual turmoil raging behind the serene façade.

Jane Austen's novels give full play to dialectic both directly and indirectly, broadly and subtly. It is often the case that, while we are preoccupied with, or distracted by, the dialectical activities at the surface level, we miss the dialectical nuances quietly working away in the depth of the narrative. For example, in *Emma*—reputed to be Austen's most finished novel—there is an apparent dialectical struggle in the foreground, within the consciousness of Emma as well as in her relationship with Harriet Smith. In the background, however, there throbs an almost imperceptible dialectical tension between Emma the most consequential personage of Highbury and Miss Bates the least important, which is obliquely yet frequently hinted at by the narrator. Eventually, at Box Hill Miss Bates turns out to be one of the two people who understand the malicious nature of Emma's apparently harmless joke. That Miss Bates should become the moral touchstone up on the Hill is no accident. It is rather the culmination of a persistent albeit unacknowledged relationship subsisting in many seemingly trivial and irrelevant incidents and details. Therefore Jane Austen's dialectic is not something monotonous and inept that plods through her narrative; it is a chameleon-like phenomenon that blends with its surroundings while maintaining its distinct presence.

Such a philosophical style is partially the result of sibling influence. Two of Jane Austen's brothers, James and Henry, went to Oxford, where the former, with the assistance of the latter, edited a college periodical. The periodical appeared every Saturday in 1789 and early 1790 for almost fourteen months until James wound it up on 20 March 1790. In total sixty weekly issues had been published. [1] From its very beginning, *The Loiterer*, as a literary enterprise, is markedly more ambitious than all the other college periodicals; it distinguishes itself by being consistently elegant and relatively free from verbosity. James Austen's Oxford publishing adventure was consistent with his literary disposition and his reputation as the scholar in the family. Mrs Austen

---

[1] For a full discussion of *The Loiterer*, see my article "*The Loiterer* and Jane Austen's Literary Identity" (*Eighteenth-Century Fiction*, 13. 4 [2001]: 579 – 592).

deemed this son of hers to possess "Classical knowledge, Literary Taste, and the power of Elegant Composition in the highest degree."[1] As a young man James wrote poetry,[2] organized amateur theatrical performances at Steventon when he was home on vacations, and wrote his own prologues and epilogues for the plays which the Austen clan enthusiastically staged at home.[3] *The Loiterer* earned James praise from the *Critical Review*, which commended the periodical on its "easy and elegant style" and its "faithful descriptions of life and manners"—"the pictures are sketched correctly, and coloured naturally"—and also on its "judicious precepts and apposite examples."[4]

These words remind us of the similar praise which Jane Austen received from her contemporaries. For example, Walter Scott was impressed by Jane Austen's "art of copying from nature as she really exists in the common walks of life, and presenting to the reader, instead of the splendid scenes of an imaginary world, a correct and strong representation of that which is daily taking place."[5] In Scott's words, Jane Austen's novels have "a great deal of nature in them—nature in ordinary and middle life to be sure but valuable from its strong resemblance and correct drawing."[6]

Jane Austen's novelistic realism can be traced to the objective and

---

　①　*Austen Papers, 1704 - 1856,* ed. R. A. Austen-Leigh (London: Spottiswoode. 1942) 265.

　②　Among other poems. James wrote an elegy for Jane upon her death, praising her "wit," her "clear good sense," and her "mental eye" that is "quick and keen," qualities which his own *Loiterer* essays embody as well. See "Venta! Within thy sacred fane," *The Poetry of Jane Austen and the Austen Family,* ed. David Selwyn (Iowa City: U of Iowa P, 1997) 48 - 50.

　③　It is known that *Matilda, The Wonder, The Chances, The Sultan, High Life below Stairs,* and *The Rivals* were performed in the Austen household, and in all likelihood young Jane either acted in them or helped with sets and costumes. The vivid description of Fanny Price's theatrical experience in *Mansfield Park* seems to have derived from personal knowledge.

　④　*Critical Review* 70 (1790): 376, 375.

　⑤　Walter Scott, unsigned review of *Emma, Quarterly Review* (1815); quoted in *Critical Heritage,* 1:63.

　⑥　*Letters of Scott 1821 -1823,* ed. H. J. C. Grierson, 7:60; quoted in *Critical Heritage,* 1:106.

balanced literary representation in *The Loiterer*, whose motto, appearing on the title page of each of the sixty issues, reads: "Speak of us as we are." Indeed Jane Austen's relation with her Oxford brothers was a very close one. James Austen had "a large share in directing her reading and forming her taste," according to his son. ① Henry Austen, on the other hand, was Jane's favourite brother, who encouraged his sister to make a transcript of *Susan*, which his business associate Mr Seymour sold on Jane's behalf to Richard Crosby and Son for £ 10. ② Henry later deftly retrieved the manuscript from the same publisher at the behest of his sister after the publication of *Emma* (1816), "and arranged for the posthumous publication of the book as *Northanger Abbey* (1818), together with *Persuasion* (1818), which was left in his care by the dying Jane, having chosen both titles himself." ③

While reading the *Loiterer* essays written by James and Henry Austen, one cannot help noticing the remarkable similarities in style and subject matter between their writing and Jane's juvenilia—written at about the same time—as well as some of her later writings. Jane Austen was then fourteen (the same age as James when he matriculated at St John's College), and she must have read eagerly at least the contributions by both James and Henry. ④ It is likely that the literary tastes and elegant style of the two Oxford brothers, especially that of James, had exerted strong influence on Jane's own critical judgment and method of composition.

Issue no. 9 of the weekly periodical features an impudent letter "To the author of the *Loiterer*" which seems full of young Jane's tone and voice. In this letter a fictitious "Sophia Sentiment" tells James the editor:

---

① *Memoir*, 12.

② *Family Record*, 127 – 128, 120.

③ See Mary Augusta Austen-Leigh, *Personal Aspects of Jane Austen* (London: Murray, 1920) 126.

④ A. Walton Litz astutely pointed out that "Since the life of *The Loiterer* spanned several Oxford vacations, some of the numbers may have been planned and executed at Steventon" ("*The Loiterer*: A Reflection of Jane Austen's Early Environment," *Review of English Studies* 12 (1961): 251 – 261.

"You must know, Sir, I am a great reader, and not to mention some hundred volumes of Novels and Plays, have, in the two last summers, actually got through all the entertaining papers of our most celebrated periodical writers." The author then challenges the editor to publish more sentimental stuff such as a "sentimental story about love and honour" or an "Eastern Tale full of Bashas and Hermits, Pyramids and Mosques" or at least "an allegory or dream": ①

> In short, you have never yet dedicated any one number to the amusement of our sex, and have taken no more notice of us, than if you thought, like the Turks, we had no souls. From all which I do conclude, that you are neither more nor less than some old Fellow of a College, who never saw any thing of the world beyond the limits of the University, and never conversed with a female, except your bed-maker and laundress. I therefore give you this advice, which you will follow as you value our favour, or your own reputation. —Let us hear no more of your Oxford Journals, your Homelys and Cockney; but send them about their business, and get a new set of correspondents, from among the young of both sexes, but particularly ours; and let us see some nice affecting stories, relating the misfortunes of two lovers, who died suddenly, just as they were going to church. Let the lover be killed in a duel, or lost at sea, or you may make him shoot himself, just as you please; and as for his mistress, she will of course go mad; or if you will, you may kill the lady, and let the lover run mad; only remember, whatever you do, that your hero and heroine must possess a great deal of feeling, and have very pretty names. If you think fit to comply with this my injunction, you may expect to hear from me again, and perhaps I may even give you a little assistance;—but, if not—may your work be condemned to the pastry-cook's shop, and may you always continue a bachelor, and be plagued with a maiden sister to keep house for you.

This letter is a perfect specimen of the kind of family joke which the Austens were known to enjoy among themselves. Of course what is urged in the letter—the false tastes of Gothicism and sentimentalism currently in

---

① The sharp contrast in sentiment and style seems to exclude James from the authorship of the letter. The letter's crude irony resembles very much that seen in Henry Austen's essays, but the charming exuberance and feminine tone suggest that it was the hand of Jane Austen, who was more than capable of it at the age of fourteen.

vogue—is precisely what the fourteen-year-old Jane Austen was satirizing,
along with her brothers, at about the same time, in her juvenilia
(especially the stories in "Volume the First" and the story of "Love and
Freindship" in "Volume the Second). "①"Sophia" is the name given to a
protagonist in "Love and Freindship," whom the sentimental Laura—
possessed with "A sensibility too tremblingly alive"—recognizes as "most
truly worthy of the Name,"② because she has "A soft Languor spread over
her lovely features," which is "the Charectarestic of her Mind." Sophia,
who is herself "all Sensibility and Feeling," decides with Laura that the
best way to punish the sensible Mr Macdonald is to deprive him of his
banknotes without his knowing it. ③

James, the editor, of course refuses to grant Sophia's wishes, stating
that he is not at all sure that "our female readers would be much amused
with Novels, Eastern Tales, and Dreams," "For the fine ladies of the
present age are much too wise to be entrapt into virtue by such underhand
means, and I should fear would turn in disgust from an Eastern Tale,
when they know that a Dervise and a Mosque mean, in plain English, a
Parson and a Church, two things that have been so long and so justly
voted *bores*."

The play on the name of Sophia was obviously relished by Jane, who
also gave the name to one of the dramatis personae in "The Visit, A
Comedy in 2 Acts," and dedicated the play, meaningfully enough, "To
the Revd James Austen. "④ In the play the good-humoured "Sophia" offers
to seat her host-cum-lover, Lord Fitzgerald, in her lap, owing to the fact
that there are more people than chairs in the drawing room, generously

---

① Judging "from stylistic and internal evidence," Southam assumes that "Love and
Freindship" was written in 1790: see "The Juvenilia," *Minor Works*, I. See also Southam's
discussion of the factors in dating the juvenilia in chapter 2 of *Jane Austen's Literary
Manuscripts: A study of the Novelist's Development through the Surviving Papers* (London:
Oxford UP, 1964).

② The irony of the name arises, of course, from its etymology: "Sophia" derives from the
Greek for "wisdom."

③ *Minor Works*, 78, 85, 96.

④ *Minor Works*, pp. 49 – 54.

observing in the meantime that his lordship is "very light."

The literary collaboration between Jane Austen and her Oxford brothers is such that many interesting episodes in *The Loiterer* foreshadow their more developed versions in Jane's novels. Indeed the kinship between the brothers' writing and that of Jane Austen goes as far as specific words and phrases. For example, in *Sense and Sensibility* (begun in 1797 and published in 1811), Fanny Dashwood and her mother, Mrs Ferrars, try insolently to belittle the pair of pretty screens which Elinor has painted. Their insolence makes Marianne indignant, whose pointed remarks to the snobbish pair draw out the "bitter phillippic" from the class-conscious matriarch— "Miss Morton is Lord Morton's daughter." "Bitter phillippic" is a quaint phrase, seldom seen in the fiction of the time, but James used it in one of his concluding essays (no. 58), and Henry put it to good use in one of his essays too (no. 37).

But the literary relation between the brothers' *Loiterer* essays and Jane Austen's own fiction extends well beyond the apparent resemblance in narrative voice, tone, and sentiment, beyond the same linguistic preferences. There is an apparent social, intellectual, and even philosophical bond between the writing of James and Henry and that of Jane. Henry's quick wit and tongue-in-cheekiness shed light on our understanding of the caustic prowess of his precocious younger sister, yet James's balanced point of view and critical sophistication seem to intimate the direction of his sister's literary development. James shows no lack of the comic vein which Henry ardently displays, but his *Loiterer* essays, upon close reading, reveal an unmistakable superiority in critical and rhetorical sophistication. Whereas Jane Austen's juvenilia may suggest that her art had, at the time, more in common with that of her favourite brother, Henry, her completed novels show that she shared much of her subtlety and complexity with her eldest brother, James, whose essays have clearly the advantage of age, education, and experience.

Being aware of the sibling influence helps us to trace and identify dialectical elements in Jane Austen's six completed novels, especially the working of such elements in the learning process of the protagonists. The rest of this study will continue to investigate and make clear the extent to which contrary, if not contradictory, elements function in her narrative. The goal is to offer a comprehensive view of Jane Austen's novels, especially in regard to the philosophical and moral education of her protagonists.

In the remaining sections of this introductory chapter, I will discuss the generic change of "dialectic" both as an approach to and as an integral part of discourse, logic and knowledge. I will then sketch relevant aspects of the political and literary scene in England about the time of the French Revolution, and characterize Jane Austen's dialectical stance which enables her to learn from both conservative and reform-minded writers of the time. [1] In the six chapters that follow, one for each novel, I will focus on how the dialectical elements affect aspects of character, plot and structure in Jane Austen's fiction, how they generate the intellectual complexity therein, and how they challenge our understanding of her vigorous and comprehensive intellect. These analyses will show that Jane Austen is concerned with a moral and philosophical regeneration of the mind of individuals living in well-defined yet nonetheless evolving social structures. Moreover, they will demonstrate how the presence of dialectics informs the interplay of conservative and progressive tendencies and hence gives Austen's fiction its intellectual, even philosophical, richness and complexity.

---

[1]   I use "reform-minded" here in lieu of the trenchant but imprecise "Jacobin" (derived from the most famous of the political clubs of the French Revolution whose members include, among others, Robespierre), which I use tentatively elsewhere in this introduction. The partisan word enjoyed a wide currency probably owing to the powerful parody of the short-lived (20 November 1797 – 9 July 1798) but provocatively satirical magazine, *The Anti-Jacobin; or, Weekly Examiner*, which was set up in the wake of such liberal magazines as Richard Phillips' *The Monthly Magazine* (1796 – 1843), which had Godwin among its many liberal-minded contributors, and Samuel Taylor Coleridge's *Watchman* (1 March – 13 May 1796). See Walter Graham's *English Literary Periodicals* (1930; New York: Octagon, 1966) 187 – 190.

2

According to Aristotle, the word "dialektike" was coined and given its purport about the fifth century BC by Zeno of Elea, ①"the author of the famous paradoxes,"② whom Timon speaks of thus:

> Great Zeno's strength which, never known to fail,
> On each side urged, on each side could prevail. ③

The word denotes the form of paradoxical defence by Zeno of Parmenides' argument against its detractors. ④ However, this rhetorical phenomenon was soon transformed by Socrates, through his technique of question and answer, into the philosophical method which is recorded in Plato's dialogues. It was Plato who promoted the method as a useful tool in any investigation of truth. Although there are a number of variations to the meaning of "dialectic" even in its Greek sense, ⑤ its basic meaning is clearly defined by Plato and, afterward, by Aristotle.

Plato's notion of dialectic is largely laid out in *Phaedrus*, one of his most important dialogues, where Socrates engages Phaedrus on the question of love and rhetoric. Phaedrus approaches Socrates with a speech by Lysias, the famous rhetorician, who contends that non-lovers should be favoured over lovers in daily life. The reason is that love is fickle and therefore potentially harmful: "injury" will be done "to the old love if

---

① "Aristotle says that Zeno was the inventor of dialectic, as Empedocles was of rhetoric" (Diogenes Laërtius, *Lives of Eminent Philosophers*, trans. R. D. Hicks [1925; rev. and rpt. London: William Heinemann, 1959] vol. 2, ix, 25).

② *The Encyclopedia of Philosophy*, ed. Paul Edwards et al. (New York: Macmillan, 1967) vol. 2, 385, "DIALECTIC."

③ Laërtius, vol. 2, ix. 25.

④ See *Parmenides*, trans. F. M. Cornford, *The Collected Dialogues of Plato, Including the Letters*, ed. Edith Hamilton and Huntington Cairns, Bollingen series 71 (New York: Bollingen Foundation, 1963) 127e – 128e, 135e – 136c. All references to Plato are to this edition.

⑤ See, for example, F. E. Peters, *Greek Philosophical Terms: A Historical Lexicon* (New York: New York UP, 1967) 36 – 37; or *The Encyclopedia of Philosophy* 385 – 387.

required by the new," whereas "one who is not a lover will not be jealous of others who seek your society."[1] Besides "a lover commends anything you say or do even when it is amiss, partly from fear that he may offend you, partly because his passion impairs his own judgment."[2] Phaedrus is convinced that Lysias has offered the best possible dissertation on the subject of love, and he embraces his view with "frenzied enthusiasm." [3] Socrates, however, discredits the speech as "a piece of rhetoric," "an extravagant performance," and a show of Lysias's "ability to say the same thing twice, in different words but with equal success."[4]

Socrates contends that what Lysias demonstrates is "not invention" but "arrangement,"[5] and he proves the point by first offering an equally, if not more, impressive speech on the vices of love, and then an entirely different, in fact opposite, argument favouring love and, simultaneously, showing the inferiority of rhetoric to dialectic. In so doing Socrates advocates "a certain pair of procedures" which he regards as "scientific:"

> The first is that in which we bring a dispersed plurality under a single form, seeing it all together—the purpose being to define so-and-so, and thus to make plain whatever may be chosen as the topic for exposition. For example, take the definition given just now of love. Whether it was right or wrong, at all events it was that which enabled our discourse to achieve lucidity and consistency. [T]he second procedure [is] [t]he reverse of the other, whereby we are enabled to divide into forms, following the objective articulation; we are not to attempt to

---

① Plato, *Phaedrus*, trans. R. Hackforth, 231c, 232d.

② Plato, *Phaedrus* 233a.

③ Plato, *Phaedrus* 228b.

④ Plato, *Phaedrus* 235a. Plato is perhaps treating rhetoric unfairly here, as he obviously does in *Gorgias*, which causes Brian Vickers to dub him "rhetoric's most influential enemy" (*In Defence of Rhetoric* [Oxford: Clarendon, 1988] vii); Vickers elsewhere refers to Plato as the one exemplifying Cicero's paradox that "it was when making fun of orators that he himself seemed to be the consummate orator" (*Rhetoric Revalued: Papers from the International Society for the History of Rhetoric* [Binghamton: Center for Medieval and Early Renaissance Studies, 1982] 250).

⑤ Plato, *Phaedrus* 236a. The word "invention" denotes the ability to bring up essential points in arguments or analyses.

hack off parts like a clumsy butcher, but to take example from our two recent speeches. The single general form which they postulated was irrationality; next, on the analogy of a single natural body with its pairs of like-named members, right arm or leg, as we say, and left, they conceived of madness as a single objective form existing in human beings. Wherefore the first speech divided off a part on the left, and continued to make divisions, never desisting until it discovered one particular part bearing the name of 'sinister' love, on which it very properly poured abuse. The other speech conducted us to the forms of madness which lay on the right-hand side, and upon discovering a type of love that shared its name with the other but was divine, displayed it to our view and extolled it as the source of the greatest goods that can befall us. ①

Clearly, what is of primary significance here is not any *one* actual analysis of love and rhetoric, either for or against, but a dialectical approach that considers both sides of the subject. The "divisions and collections" which Socrates is "a lover of" give him, as Socrates himself claims, "the power to speak and to think."② Socrates concludes that this "art of dialectic" enables the "dialectician"③—"the pure and rightful lover of wisdom"④—to spread "words which instead of remaining barren contain a seed whence new words grow up in new characters, whereby the seed is vouchsafed immortality, and its possessor the fullest measure of blessedness that man can attain unto."⑤

Aristotle's theory of dialectic is principally explained in *Rhetoric*, *Topics* and *Sophistical Refutations*. Although Aristotle's notion of dialectic differs somewhat from that of Plato, chiefly in his view of its

---

① Plato, *Phaedrus* 265d – 266b.

② Plato, *Phaedrus* 266b.

③ Plato, *Phaedrus* 276e.

④ Plato, *Sophist* 253e.

⑤ Plato, *Phaedrus* 276e, 277a. Overall, the contrast between the views held by the two speakers is pervasive; in fact the two figures form a physical contrast by themselves: Phaedrus is young and handsome whereas Socrates is old and lacks external beauty (*Phaedrus* prays at the end of the dialogue that he "may become fair within" [279b]).

relationship with rhetoric,① there is no fundamental difference between them in regard to the nature of dialectic. Aristotle recognizes Plato's dialectic as "a mode of examination"② that "asks for a choice between two contradictories"③ and, more importantly, as "a process of criticism wherein lies the path to the principles of all inquiries"④ even though its "argument is not concerned with any definite genus."⑤ Aristotle stresses that dialectic enables one "to reason from reputable opinions about any subject,"⑥ be it "ethical, e.g. 'Ought one rather to obey one's parents or the laws, if they disagree?'" or "logical, e. g. 'Is the knowledge of opposites the same or not?'" or physical, i.e., in the field of "natural science," "e. g. 'Is the universe eternal or not?'"⑦ And he emphasizes that a person who practises dialectic "regards the common principles with their application to the particular matter in hand."⑧

Aristotle's refinement of the concept and function of dialectic confirms the status of dialectic as a vital philosophical instrument in reasoning and understanding.

3

In the later Middle Ages, "dialectic," according to Peter Mack, "was

---

① Aristotle declares in the opening sentence of *Rhetoric* that "[r]hetoric is the counterpart of dialectic" (*The Complete Works of Aristotle*, ed. Jonathan Barnes, Bollingen series 71. 2, 2 vols. [Princeton: Princeton UP, 1984] vol. 2, 1354a1; all references to Aristotle are to this edition). Plato (through Socrates) on the other hand defines "rhetoric" as "the counterpart in the soul of what cookery is to the body," which is "a form of flattery that corresponds to medicine" (*Gorgias* 465e, 465b).

② Aristotle, vol. 1, *Sophistical Refutations* 172a22.

③ Aristotle, vol. 1, *Prior Analytics* 24b10.

④ Aristotle, vol. 1, *Topics* 101b3 – 4.

⑤ Aristotle, vol. 1, *Sophistical Refutations* 172a13.

⑥ Aristotle, vol. 1, *Topics* 100a21 – 2.

⑦ Aristotle, vol. 1, *Topics* 105b22 – 25.

⑧ Aristotle, vol. 1, *Sophistical Refutations* 171b6 – 7.

the most important subject in the university arts course,"[1] and by the Renaissance period more attention than before was paid to it as the primary tool for reasoning. Gabriel Harvey, the Cambridge University praelector in rhetoric, urged his students to

> Pay attention not only to the brilliant greenery of words, but more to the ripe fruit of meaning and reasoning ... Remember that Homer [*Iliad* I. 201] described words as *pteroenta*, that is, winged, because they easily fly away unless they are kept in balance by the weight of the subject-matter. Unite dialectic and knowledge with rhetoric. Keep your tongue in step with your mind. Learn from Erasmus to combine an abundance (*copia*) of words with an abundance of matter; learn from Ramus to embrace a philosophy which has been allied to eloquence; learn from Homer's Phoenix to be doers of deeds as well as writers of word. [2]

In the 1555 version of his *Dialectique* the above-mentioned Peter Ramus argues that dialectic functions in the same way as logic " 'because it proclaims to us the truth of all argument and as a consequence the falsehood, whether the truth be necessary, as in science, or contingent, as in opinion, that is to say, capable both of being and not being. [S]o the art of knowing, that is to say, dialectic or logic, is one and the same doctrine in respect to perceiving all things. ' "[3]

The increasing emphasis on the affinity of dialectic with logic coincides with the arrival of the Age of Enlightenment. Whereas the growing number of followers of Bacon, who recommended empirical enquiries into the natural world, tended to reject the Scholastic philosophizing associated with the universities, they did not abandon the Aristotelian methods of thinking and argumentation on which university curricula were founded. Thus John Locke, though a very conscious

---

[1] "Humanist Rhetoric and Dialectic," *The Cambridge Companion to Renaissance Humanism*, ed. Jill Kraye (Cambridge: Cambridge UP, 1996) 83.

[2] Gabriel Harvey, *Ciceronianus*; quoted by Peter Mack, *Cambridge Companion* 82.

[3] Quoted by Wilbur Samuel Howell in *Logic and Rhetoric in England, 1500 – 1700* (Princeton: Princeton UP, 1956) 154 – 155. I follow in general Howell's assessment of the philosophical trends in the modern age both in this book and in its sister book: *Eighteenth-Century British Logic and Rhetoric* (Princeton: Princeton UP, 1971).

innovator, did not ignore the valuable part of the philosophical tradition in his enquiry into the methods of discovering the nature of reality. Locke, the most prominent and influential English philosopher of the modern age,① published in 1690 *An Essay Concerning Human Understanding* and, sixteen years later and posthumously, *Of the Conduct of the Understanding*.② Although Locke does not use the word "dialectic" in his exposition, his major epistemological writings describing how knowledge was to be sought, tested and understood were informed by an unmistakable dialectical spirit which makes him the chief architect of what Wilbur Samuel Howell calls "the new logic"③ in the dawning modern age.

Locke in his *Essay* argues that knowledge begins with sensory experience in particular instances; then the initial perception goes through a series of mental operations such as retaining (contemplation and memory), discerning and distinguishing, comparing, composing (turning simple ideas into complex ones), and abstracting (generalizing), so that simple ideas based on initial sensory experiences will develop into complex ideas or general principles. But these complex ideas or general principles do not enjoy a permanent status, since they must be tested and proved by further trials and examinations conducted against an ever-changing reality.

Locke is well aware that the "very Substances" of all objects in the world are "in a continual flux."④ Human understanding must therefore

----

① Locke was very much a product of the enlightenment environment boasting such philosophical and scientific theories as Francis Bacon's scientific enquiry, Thomas Hobbes' political philosophy and Descartes' rational thinking; however, Locke distinguished himself by subsuming all those theories in a dialectical manner, and in doing so became, in the words of Peter Nidditch, "a firm spokesman for all these currents at once, in association with an elaborate philosophy of mind and cognition" ("Foreword," *Essay* xvii).

② The latter was originally intended as an additional, probably the concluding, chapter to the former; see his letter to William Molyneux dated April 10, 1697 (*The Correspondence of John Locke*, ed. E. S. De Beer, vol. 6 [Oxford: Clarendon, 1981] 87).

③ Howell, *Eighteenth-Century British Logic and Rhetoric* 284.

④ Locke, *Essay* 2.21.4.

make adjustments relative to those changes. In "Of Power," one of the chapters in his *Essay*, Locke observes:

> The Mind, being every day informed, by the Senses, of the alteration of those simple *Ideas*, it observes in things without; and taking notice how one comes to an end, and ceases to be, and another begins to exist, which was not before; reflecting also on what passes within it self, and observing a constant change of its *Ideas*, sometimes by the impression of outward Objects on the Senses, and sometimes by the Determination of its own choice; and concluding from what it has so constantly observed to have been, that the like Changes will for the future be made, in the same things, by like Agents, and by the like ways, considers in one thing the possibility of having any of its simple *Ideas* changed, and in another the possibility of making that change; and so comes by that *Idea* which we call *Power*. [1]

Locke's style is a little awkward, if only because the thought-forming process is dialectically complicated. What he stresses here, in a nutshell, is the active power of the thinking mind. Ideas of primary qualities go through changes as they transform into ideas of secondary qualities, and conclusions based on simple ideas of sensations are constantly modified through the operations of the mind.

The thinking process is not only sustained but also broadened constantly to take in new aspects because, Locke reasons, "in many cases it is not one series of consequences will serve the turn, but many different and opposite deductions must be examined and laid together, before a man can come to make a right judgement of the point in question."[2] Even after a man has constructed a theory or formed a principle or an argument, he should still critically "examine his own principles, and see whether they are such as will bear the trial,"[3] for "Trial and Examination must give [Truth] price, and not any antick Fashion."[4] Locke, using mathematical demonstration as an analogy, stresses that "it is not enough

---

[1] Locke, *Essay* 2. 21. 1.

[2] Locke, *Conduct* 6.

[3] Locke, *Conduct* 10.

[4] "The Epistle Dedicatory" (To the Earl of Pembroke and Montgomery), *Essay* 4.

to trace one argument to its source, and observe its strength and weakness, but all the arguments, after having been so examined on both sides, must be laid in balance one against another, and, upon the whole, the understanding determine its assent."[1] In short, Locke's theory of human understanding is not simply a *tabula rasa* whereupon the mind, as a passive receptacle, gathers sensory data; nor is it simply a process from simple ideas to complex ones; it is indeed a dynamic and dialectical process in which the operations of the mind, accompanied by tests and trials of reality and experience throughout, ideally never cease.

4

The most systematic and theoretical discussion of dialectic as the philosophical method by which knowledge is to be acquired was by G. W. F. Hegel. Much in the vein of Locke, Hegel in his *Phenomenology of Spirit* (1807) bases his philosophical exposition of dialectics on the existence of the two modes of knowledge: one dominated by apprehension, the other by comprehension. Like Locke he emphasizes that "sensuous apprehension"—that is, "tasting, smelling, feeling, hearing and seeing"—serves as "the source of truth" only in part; the other part is the process conducted by "Consciousness" to seek the "*universal*" through the "*sensuous particular.*" [2] The process of understanding, or the "activity of *describing* things," is an inexorable one (having a "restless, insatiable instinct"); it continuously engages the object ("divide and analyse") in order to seek the "*universal*" out of the "*sensuous particular.*"[3] Hegel is in agreement with Locke when he makes clear that "immediate knowledge"

---

[1] Locke, *Conduct* 7.

[2] G. W. F. Hegel, *Phenomenology of Spirit*, trans. A. V. Miller, analysis and foreword by J. N. Findlay (Oxford: Clarendon, 1977) 244, 245. Unless noted otherwise, subsequent references to *Phenomenology* are to this edition and are accompanied by section, instead of page, numbers.

[3] Hegel, *Phenomenology* 245, 244; notice how closely the process of dividing and analyzing echoes Plato's "divisions and collections" or Locke's five steps of mental operations.

("what simply *is*"), or "sense-knowledge," is not true knowledge. ①
Sensuously apprehended objects merely initiate the process of
understanding. Knowledge will not be achieved until comprehension, as a
scientific sequel, dissolves apprehension, namely, "*that from which it
results*—a result which contains what was true in the preceding
knowledge.*"*② In this dialectical process of human understanding, the
primary mode, apprehension, duly informed by the secondary mode,
comprehension, raises the level of interaction by making available what
fresh information it now has, until consciousness embodying the two
modes of knowledge identifies itself completely with the object. "[T]his
dialectical movement which consciousness exercises on itself and which
affects both its knowledge and its object," Hegel maintains, "is precisely
what is called *experience.*"③

　　Elsewhere, in his commentary upon Sophocles's tragedies, Hegel
points out the dire consequences of allowing oneself to be swayed by
pathos alone and closing one's mind to an alternative point of view. ④
Hegel thinks that the lack of dialectical thinking is the vital source of the
Sophoclean tragedy. He cites the conflict between Creon, who forbids
anyone to bury the corpse of Polyneices (brother to Antigone), and
Antigone, who insists on carrying out her duty of interment, in
Sophocles's *Antigone*. Here "the political authority of Creon" clashes
with Antigone's respect for "the sacred ties of relationship.*"*⑤Antigone,
as a subject of the city state of Thebes, is obliged to abide by the state law
declared by the king, whereas Creon, as uncle and would-be father-in-law
of Antigone, is honour-bound by the blood relationship to protect

　　① 　Hegel, *Phenomenology* 90, 91.

　　② 　Hegel, *Phenomenology* 87.

　　③ 　Hegel, *Phenomenology* 86.

　　④ 　A. C. Bradley regards Hegel as "the only philosopher who has treated [tragedy] in a
manner both original and searching ... [s]ince Aristotle dealt with [it]" (*Oxford Lectures on
Poetry* [London: Macmillan, 1909; rpt. 1926] 69).

　　⑤ 　*Hegel on Tragedy*, ed. Anne and Henry Paolucci (Garden City: Doubleday, 1962) 73.

Antigone. [1] Tragedy occurs as each refuses to acknowledge the legitimacy of the argument of the other. Antigone is executed before her marriage to Haemon (Creon's son); Creon pays for his intransigence by losing first his son and then his wife. The moral of the tragedy is complex, but Hegel's dialectical analysis is enlightening:

> In this case, family love, what is holy, what belongs to the inner life and to inner feeling, and which because of this is also called the law of the nether gods, comes into collision with the law of the State. Creon is not a tyrant, but really a moral power; Creon is not in the wrong; he maintains that the law of the State, the authority of government, is to be held in respect, and that punishment follows the infraction of the law. Each of these two sides realizes only one of the moral powers, and has only one of these as its content; this is the element of one-sidedness here, and the meaning of eternal justice is shown in this, that both end in injustice just because they are one-sided, though at the same time both obtain justice too. Both are recognized as having a value of their own in the untroubled course of morality. Here they both have their own validity, but a validity which is equalized. It is only the one-sidedness in their claims which justice comes forward to oppose. [2]

Hegel's philosophical understanding of the human problems in Greek

---

　　[1]　Similar situations abound in Sophocles's plays; for example, in *Oedipus at Colonus* the titular hero responds to Creon's glib accusation of his being "a father-killer" (1076) and "the unholy husband of his own mother" (1078) with:

> ... If,
> here and now, a man strode up to kill you,
> you, you self-righteous—what would you do?
> Investigate whether the murderer were your father
> or deal with him straight off? (1132 – 1136)

Similarly, in *Oedipus the King*, Jocasta cynically advises her husband-son not to fear:

> What should a man fear? It's all chance,
> Chance rules our lives. Not a man on earth
> Can see a day ahead, groping through the dark.
> Better to live at random, best we can. (1069 – 1072)

(*The Three Theban Plays*, trans. Robert Fagles, intro. and notes Bernard Knox [New York: Penguin, 1984; rpt. with revisions, 1984]. Subsequent references to Sophocles's plays are to this edition).

　　[2]　*Hegel on Tragedy* 325.

tragedies draws our attention to what A.C. Bradley summarizes as Hegel's focal point: "The end of the tragic conflict is the denial of both the exclusive claims. It is not the work of chance or blank fate; it is the act of the ethical substance itself, asserting its absoluteness against the excessive pretensions of its particular powers."[1]

The above survey of dialectic(s) both as an approach to and as an integral part of discourse, logic and knowledge is meant to provide a philosophical basis upon which will rest the dialectical principle, or method, which I propose to use in my analysis of Jane Austen's six completed novels. Such principle or method is one by which a rational and critical investigation of a phenomenon, considering multiple, especially, contrary perspectives, assuming a continuous and reflective process, aiming at understanding and knowledge, may be carried out. It is my belief that Jane Austen's fiction was composed with a keen sense of the dialectical nature of reality in mind. Hence discovering and digesting the dialectical elements in her fiction will help us appreciate the complexity of her mind and also the complexity of her work.

Despite the pervasiveness of dialectical elements in her fiction, one should not be persuaded that Jane Austen had any hidden philosophical agenda. Indeed there has been no documented evidence indicating that she had read any philosophical work by any of the philosophers surveyed above.[2] On the other hand, she can hardly have escaped the influence of Locke's conception of the human mind and its operations. Austen may not have been a reader of philosophy, but she could not have helped being exposed to the kind of pervasive philosophical influence exerted by the

---

[1]　Bradley 72.

[2]　Conspicuously absent in Jane Austen's writings of any kind is the name of John Locke, whose *Essay* was banned at Oxford, where Austen's father and two of her brothers went, in the early eighteenth century (see Kenneth MacLean's *John Locke and English Literature of the Eighteenth Century* [New Haven: Yale, 1936] 6), after his expulsion from the University on suspected complicity in Shaftesbury's plots. However, Locke was taught extensively at Cambridge in the eighteenth century (see Hans Aarsleff, *From Locke to Saussure: Essays on the Study of Language and Intellectual History* [Minneapolis: U of Minnesota P, 1982] 123 – 124).

movement of the new logic set in motion since the Renaissance. Jane Austen had lived the formative part of her life in the eighteenth century, in which Locke's works had remained highly accessible as a result of the many editions and printings. Addison, who was an ardent lover of Locke and whose essays in the *Spectator* Austen must have read,[1] warmly recommended Locke (sometimes down to a specific chapter in a particular volume of his work).[2] Many of the major eighteenth-century authors with whom Austen was familiar, such as Pope, Richardson, Hume, Gray, Goldsmith, and Sterne, had read Locke and referred to him in their writings. Doctor Johnson, one of Austen's "favourite moral writers ... in prose,"[3] cited Locke 1,674 times in the first volume alone of his *Dictionary* (1755).[4]

Indeed, Jane Austen's novels indicate a firm grasp of many of the important Lockean epistemological principles. Her protagonists often seem to illustrate the different stages of mental operations and the various tendencies of faulty thinking which Locke methodically identified in his writings. Thus Jane Austen does not seem to be unfamiliar with the mainstream eighteenth-century Enlightenment philosophy. In that sense she is neither particularly radical nor conspicuously conservative in both the philosophical and the political senses of the day.

---

[1]　Austen referred to *The Spectator* in Chapter 5 of *NA*, albeit not in entirely flattering terms. Also, according to James Edward Austen-Leigh, Austen "was well acquainted with the old periodicals from the '*Spectator*' downwards" (*Memoir* 89). See also the letter by "Sophia Sentiment" to James Austen, the editor of *The Loiterer*.

[2]　See No. 37 (Thursday, 12 April 1711), No. 110 (Friday, 6 July 1711), and No. 413 (Tuesday, June 24, 1712) of *The Spectator*, ed. Donald F. Bond, 5 vols. (Oxford: Clarendon, 1965).

[3]　Henry Austen, "Biographical Notice of the Author," *The Novels of Jane Austen*, vol. 5, *Northanger Abbey and Persuasion*, 7.

[4]　Lewis Freed, "The Sources of Johnson's *Dictionary*," diss., Cornell U, 1939, 67. Freed's findings were based on his compilation of the instances in the first volume of Johnson's *Dictionary*.

5

As noted at the beginning of this chapter, Marilyn Butler's *Jane Austen and the War of Ideas*, which defines Austen in terms of her "reaction" both to the sentimental tradition and to the French Revolution of 1789, focusing in particular on the context of "the Jacobin novel" and the "Anti-Jacobins," inevitably draws the conclusion that "Jane Austen's novels belong decisively to one class of partisan novels, the conservative."[①] In her new introduction to the 1987 reissue of her book Butler reiterates her opinion that "despite Austen's own superior artistry and overt reluctance (part feminine, part aesthetic) to state opinions, she participates in a conservative reaction against more permissive, individualistic, and personally expressive novel types of earlier years."[②] Butler's point is well taken, but Jane Austen may not be such a die-hard conservative as Butler has confidently painted her.

Part of the reason is that the historical situation in England at the time, both political and literary, was more complicated and less clear-cut than Butler's formulation might suggest.[③] On the political side, the attitude of the British public towards the French Revolution was divided from the beginning, and there were subsequent shifts within the main partisan groups. When Louis XVI on 23 June 1789, under the political pressure of both the privileged Orders and the Third Estate, agreed to a series of reform measures, including parliamentary control of taxation,

---

① Butler 3.

② Butler, Introduction (1987) xv.

③ G. E. Mingay's *English Landed Society in the Eighteenth Century* (London: Routledge, 1963) offers a comprehensive view of the economic, social and political structure of eighteenth-century England; Warren Roberts' *Jane Austen and the French Revolution* (New York: St. Martin's, 1979), especially the chapter on "Politics," is also generally informative. More recently, Emma Vincent Macleod's *A War of Ideas: British Attitudes to the Wars Against Revolutionary France 1792 – 1802* (Aldershot: Ashgate, 1998) discusses in detail the intricacies of "popular pro-war, anti-war and uncommitted opinion and behaviour" in Britain during the first ten years of the war against revolutionary France (180).

the abolition of *lettres de cachet*, the freedom of the press, internal free
trade and the reform of the law, the British public in general responded
positively,[1] remembering their own not-so-distant Glorious Revolution
of 1688 and the necessary and beneficial constitutional changes that had
been brought about as a result. Dr Richard Price, for example, compared
what was unfolding in France to the English Revolution a century earlier
in his sermon *A Discourse on the Love of Our Country* (1789). The sermon
drew a rebuttal from Edmund Burke, whose *Reflections on the French
Revolution* (1790) expressed conservative sentiment.[2]

But when the nature of the French Revolution changed, when
Robespierre and Saint-Just introduced radical political reforms and drastic
administrative measures and later conducted a full-scale war in the name
of ideology, many ardent English supporters such as Mary
Wollstonecraft,[3] Arthur Young[4] and William Wordsworth were unable

---

[1]   Norman Hampson, *The Enlightenment*, The Pelican History of European Thought,
vol. 4 (Harmondsworth: Penguin, 1968) 256.

[2]   In 1790 Burke's conservative views were distinctly in the minority (see James T.
Boulton's analysis of the printed replies to Burke in *The Language of Politics in the Age of
Wilkes and Burke* [London: Routledge, 1963], especially Chapter 6 of "Part Two: Political
Controversy 1790 – 1793"). That situation changed after the execution of Louis XVI on 21
January 1793 and after France declared war on Britain on 1 February 1793, which led to bitter
disappointment among many English sympathizers.

[3]   Wollstonecraft represents an interesting case in that her political sentiment was
adulterated with her romantic love affair with Imlay, the American trader. As Richard Holmes
points out, "her deepest understanding of what the Revolution meant was produced by the
emotional changes in the 'little kingdom' of her own heart. She gave an entirely new importance
to instinctive feeling, and sincerity of emotions" (*Footsteps: Adventures of a Romantic
Biographer* [London: Hodder, 1985] 109).

[4]   Young, an agriculturist and publicist who was appointed Secretary to the Board of
Agriculture of Britain in 1793, was on the whole a reliable witness and judge of the French
Revolution which he had foreseen before it was made. In his journal entry for 22 September
1788, he wrote: "The American revolution has laid the foundation of another in France, if
government do not take care of itself." As late as 1792 Young was still positively assessing the
reforms that had been brought about in France, observing that "[t]he true judgment to be
formed of the French Revolution, must surely be gained, from an attentive consideration of the
evils of the old government: when these are well understood—and when the extent and
universality of the oppression under which the people groaned—oppression which bore upon them
from every quarter, it will scarcely be attempted to be urged, that a revolution was not absolutely
necessary to the welfare of the kingdom" (*Travels in France during the Years 1787, 1788 and
1789*, ed. Jeffry Kaplow [1792; Garden City: Doubleday, 1969] 98, 447).

to continue to offer their sympathy. But even then, Opposition writers and MPs accused the government of practising "'Pittism,'" that is, "kindling a blaze of deceived popular hysteria for a war in order to corrupt the liberal British constitution for their own personal gain" and with a view to "robbing the British people of their civil liberties."[1] The colourful R. B. Sheridan mocked ministers in the Commons even as late as 1801:

> You have gagged the people, and bound them hand and foot; and then you say, look how quiet they are.[2]

Mary Wollstonecraft, who went to Paris in December 1792 and stayed there until April 1795, witnessed the ups and downs of the Revolution first-hand and wrote about it in her book: *An Historical and Moral View of the Origin and Progress of the French Revolution and the Effect It Has Produced in Europe* (1794). She abhorred the apparently indiscriminate and excessive guillotinings and she despised "the despotism of licentious freedom."[3] Arthur Young also saw the destructive side of the French Revolution and conceded that "[i]t is impossible to justify the excesses of the people on their taking up arms."[4] The change of mood of the former supporters of the French Revolution is faithfully traced in Wordsworth's narrative poem, *The Prelude*, where the poet is seen to turn from "a patriot" (that is, one who pledges allegiance to the Revolution) whose "heart was all / Given to the people," celebrating "France standing on the top of golden hours" because "human nature seeming born again," to a crestfallen detractor who "suffered grief / For ill-requited France" and is "distressed to think of what she once /

---

①　Macleod 97, 98.

②　William Cobbett, ed. *The Parliamentary History of England from the Earliest Period to the Year* 1803 (London, 1806 – 1820); quoted in Macleod's *War of Ideas*, 98.

③　*The Works of Mary Wollstonecraft*, ed. Janet Todd and Marilyn Butler (New York: New York UP, 1989) vol. 6, 85. All references to Wollstonecraft are to this edition.

④　Young 446.

Promised, now is. "① Wordsworth, like the other two supporters just mentioned, had spent time in France in the early 1790s. His anguished change of sentiment chronicled in *The Prelude* must have expressed the feelings of a generation of like-minded English reformers.

At the other end of the political spectrum, however, there was Edmund Burke, who believed in "rational liberty,"② that is, an orderly and gradual improvement. ③ Burke acknowledged unhesitatingly in his *Reflections on the Revolution in France* (1790) that "[a] state without the means of some change is without the means of its conservation,"④ but he disagreed fundamentally with the programme of the revolutionaries. What he objected to in particular was putting the individual above the state: "We are afraid to put men to live and trade each on his own private stock of reason; because we suspect that the stock in each man is small, and that the individuals would do better to avail themselves of the general bank and capital of nations and of ages."⑤ This is the point which Butler emphasizes when she formulates her criteria for literary Jacobinism. In short, Burke was a progressive conservative, so to speak, guarding against "[t]he *extreme* of liberty" which "obtains nowhere, nor ought to obtain anywhere,"⑥ while sympathizing with such justified freedom movements

---

①   All references are to the 1850 version in *The Prelude: 1799, 1805, 1850,* ed. Jonathan Wordsworth et al. (New York: Norton, 1979) 9. 123 – 24, 6. 340 – 41, 11. 382 – 383 and 11. 385 – 386.

②   *Reflections on the Revolution in France and Other Writings*, pref. F. W. Raffety (London: Oxford UP, 1907; rpt., 1958) 95. All references to Burke's *Reflections* are to this edition.

③   Edmund Burke was a staunch defender of the English Revolution of 1688 when the Parliament dethroned a legitimate monarch and established itself as the power to be. He was also a champion for free trade and Catholic emancipation, and a very vocal abolitionist. His position in the *Reflections* was reminiscent of many of the points made in his *Speeches On American Taxation* (1774) and *On Conciliation with America* (1775), and in his *Letter to the Sheriffs of Bristol* (1777).

④   Burke, *Reflections* 23.

⑤   Burke, *Reflections* 95.

⑥   Edmund Burke, *A Letter to John Farr and John Harris, Esqrs., Sheriffs of the City of Bristol, on the Affairs of America* in *Burke's Speeches*, ed. F. G. Selby (New York: St. Martin's, 1956; Westport: Greenwood, 1974) 169.

as the American Revolution.

If the line between conservatives and liberals on the political front is less rigid than it sometimes appears, that on the literary front between the conservative and the reform-minded authors is not inflexible either. Mrs West's novels, which Butler singles out as the conservative specimen, qualify as much in the moral or religious sense as in the political sense. Vigorous promotion of traditional Christian values was logically viewed at this time as a safeguard against the godless and immoral revolutionaries across the channel; it became an integral and invaluable part of the concerted conservative resistance to the Revolutionary programme. Mrs West's *A Gossip's Story* (1796) was, for example, "intended, under the disguise of an artless history, to illustrate the advantages of consistency, fortitude, and the Domestick Virtues; and to expose to ridicule, caprice, affected sensibility, and an idle censorious humour."[1] Few English readers at the time, one suspects, would be confused as to where all those vices lay. Mrs Prudentia Homespun, the narrator of the novel, makes the subtext rather unambiguous as she cautions the reader that "the extreme of modern refinement" will not "improve upon the model which Christianity (our best comfort in this world and sure guide to the next) presents for our imitation."[2] Therefore Mrs West's conservative novels were politically motivated merely in the sense that advocating traditional "family values" in the 1790s was by itself anti-Jacobin.

As for the so-called Jacobin novels, their theme and content testify to various degrees of social, political, even religious, concerns as well. For example, if we try to apply the general Jacobin features which Butler has identified in such novels: "permissive, individualistic, and personally

---

[1] Jane West, *A Gossip's Story, and a Legendary Tale*, 4th ed., 2 vols. (1796; London, 1799) vol. 1, v.

[2] *Gossip's Story* vol. 1, 48. We remember that Henry Austen takes care to emphasize in his "Biographical Notice" his sister's "love of God" and the fact that "[s]he was thoroughly religious and devout" and "fearful of giving offence to God" in order to present a politically correct Austen to the postwar English public (*NA and P* 4, 8).

expressive"[1] and "steady championing of Individual Man against a corrupt society,"[2] we will soon find that some of the Jacobin novels do not exactly fit the description. According to Butler, Maria Edgeworth is "unquestionably a jacobin"[3] when she allows Belinda to form her personal view of moral standards by critically comparing and assessing the virtuous Percivals of Oakly Park and the depraved Delacours of London. However, Edgeworth also stresses in her "Moral Tale" the need for a rational control of mind and behaviour of the individual.[4] She does not simply endorse the individual and denounce the society, putting one above the other; she is more interested in changing the behaviour of an individual rather than that of the society. In fact Edgeworth is highly critical of forms of extreme individualism such as egotistic ambition, excessive sensibility and thoughtless sensuality, well reflected in *Belinda* as well as her earlier work, "Letters of Julia and Caroline" (1795).

In her late novel, *Patronage* (1814), Edgeworth describes patronage as a viable social phenomenon that should not be misused or abused. Mr Falconer seeks patronage and sinecures from Lord Oldborough for his three sons and is duly punished, along with his sons, whereas Mr Percy encourages his sons to seek professions and become useful members in the existing, rather than a brand-new, society. Indeed Edgeworth's individuals do not treat society with excessive "hostility," for it is a neutral space where good and bad things coexist (patronage, for example, has its good and bad effects). Even the traditionally notorious London society turns into a place where one can make one's mark without sacrificing one's conscience and becoming morally and financially bankrupt, or achieve notoriety by acting in devious and immoral ways, as Mr

---

[1]   Introduction (1987) xv.

[2]   Butler 32.

[3]   Butler 124.

[4]   Maria Edgeworth is so serious about the educational value of her writings that she refuses to call *Belinda* "a Novel" because that designation connotes if not denotes "folly, errour, and vice;" she insists on calling her work "a Moral Tale" ("Advertisement" to *Belinda*, ed. Kathryn J. Kirkpatrick [Oxford: Oxford UP, 1994] 3).

Falconer's ambassador-son, Cunningham, did.

One other major English Jacobin novel, Robert Bage's *Hermsprong*; *or*, *Man As He Is Not* (1796), displays similar complexity about the relationship between individual and society. [1] This novel in fact exposes the danger of excessive passion and extreme individualism no less vigorously than Mrs West's does, though in a different context and from a different perspective. Hermsprong's crusade is aimed not at the existing social system but at the misbehaviour of another individual, namely, Lord Grondale. Though Grondale may be seen as the epitome of the privileged and corrupt aristocracy, it does not follow that the whole society, consisting of various other classes, is condemned as a consequence. The fact that the panel of magistrates at the county court judge Hermsprong innocent of the charges concocted against him by Lord Grondale signifies that the system can and does function well. This impression is complemented by the fact that Hermsprong eventually becomes "Sir Charles" by reclaiming the family title and is subsequently given "a full title to his property" (i.e., to the magnificent Grondale Hall). [2] The switch of rank is suggestive. It connotes a change from extreme to moderation, already exemplified by the conduct of two completely different individuals. Such change, again, signifies that the basic social structure to which the hero submits himself is not intrinsically hostile or corrupt, and inheriting it actually makes moral and financial sense.

Yet another book that does not quite fill Butler's bill, so to speak, is *Nature and Art* (1996), a widely recognized Jacobin novel by Mrs Inchbald, [3] a close friend and associate of William Godwin to whom she

---

[1] Butler regards Bage as "revolutionary" and his work "radical" (57, 32).

[2] Robert Bage, *Hermsprong*; *or*, *Man As He Is Not*, ed. Peter Faulkner (Oxford: Oxford UP, 1985) 248. D. J. Gilson reports that a copy of *Hermsprong* that is housed in Henry E. Huntington Library has "Jane Austen's name ... written at the top of the front free endpaper in each volume" ("Jane Austen's Books," *The Book Collector* 23.1 [1974] 31).

[3] Gary Kelly thinks that Mrs Inchbald was one of the founders of the English Jacobin novel (*The English Jacobin Novel* [Oxford: Clarendon, 1976] 113).

related how she redrew the portrait of Lord Rinforth, a character that resembles George III in *A Satire on the Times*, "having Newgate before my eyes."[1] There the message, delivered through the words of the virtuous elder Henry sounds, and is, familiarly and even platitudinously Christian:

> How much indebted are *we* to providence, my children, who, while it inflicts poverty, bestows peace of mind; and in return for the trivial grief we meet in this world, holds out to our longing hopes the reward of the next![2]

And this after the narrator has ponderously satirized the moral sham of the corrupt judicial and ecclesiastic system exemplified by the elder and younger Williams (a bishop and a judge respectively), and after the virtuous characters, enjoying "a stinted repast of milk and vegetables, by the glimmering light of a little brush-wood on the hearth," had recited "numerous other examples of the dangers, the evils that riches draw upon their owner."[3] The religious imagery enhanced by the equally religious tone is too obvious for anyone to miss.

The review of the above novels covered by the epithet "Jacobin" suggests that certain common grounds are shared by authors of Jacobin or other persuasions, grounds such as the importance of the cultivation of the mind, the superiority of individual merits and the advocacy of gainful profession instead of hereditary privilege, and injudicious patronage. Jane Austen's novels reveal a close affinity with these and other novels, all within the same historical frame, in terms of theme, content and even technique.[4] What is perhaps unique about Jane Austen is that she has firmly maintained a dialectical attitude towards her contemporaries and

---

[1]   Undated letter to William Godwin, C. Kegan Paul, *William Godwin: His Friends and Contemporaries* (London: Henry S. King, 1876) vol. 1, 141.

[2]   Elizabeth Inchbald, *Nature and Art*, ed. Shawn L. Maurer (1796; London: Pickering, 1997) 133.

[3]   *Nature and Art* 133. I will discuss this novel in more detail in chapter 3.

[4]   Butler elsewhere suggests that "many of the techniques that Jane Austen later used so successfully ... were all to be found first in Maria Edgeworth" (*Maria Edgeworth: A Literary Biography* [Oxford: Clarendon, 1972] 328).

immediate predecessors.

Jane Austen is an open-minded novelist, and her non-partisanship—giving the impression that "the politics of the day occupied very little of her attention"[1]—frustrates any attempt to identify her with any political camp of the day, conservative or otherwise. Austen's attitude towards Evangelicalism is a good example. Her comment in 1809: "I do not like the Evangelicals"[2] did not prevent her from declaring in 1814: "I am by no means convinced that we ought not all to be Evangelicals, & am at least persuaded that they who are so from Reason & Feeling, must be happiest & safest."[3] Yet two years later she was rejecting the enthusiastic strain in Mr Cooper's "new Sermons," which are "fuller of Regeneration & Conversion than ever—with the addition of his zeal in the cause of the Bible Society."[4]

Jane Austen's adaptation of, rather than confrontation with, her contemporaries and immediate predecessors is a mark of her political and philosophical maturity. Such maturity makes it possible for her to nurse and cultivate a dialectical approach in her writing. Her protagonists have complex characters; their learning experiences are not linear but spiral. Gaining knowledge and self-knowledge is a process of making mistakes and learning from them, as her protagonists find out sooner or later. No one is infallible, morally or otherwise. Indeed Austen's trademark is not only the presentation of truths but also the dialectical process by which such truths are diligently sought and tortuously arrived at.

Aristotle once said that "the function of man is an activity of soul in accordance with, or not without, rational principle."[5] How Jane Austen's protagonists think and behave, dialectically (hence rationally) or one-sidedly, in their given roles in the novelistic world created for them will be the focus of the following pages.

---

[1]　Austen-Leigh, *Memoir* 89.
[2]　*Letters* 24, *January* 1809.
[3]　*Letters* 18 – 20, November 1814.
[4]　*Letters* 8 – 9, *September* 1816.
[5]　*Nicomachean Ethics*, trans. David Ross, rev. J. O. Urmson, vol. 2, 1098a 7 – 8.

2 *Northanger Abbey*: A Dialectical Plot

Northanger Abbey as Jane Austen's earliest completed novel exemplifies its author's attempt to incorporate established themes and conventions into a realistic representation of England in the 1790s by way of a dialectical plot. That is to say, although this first finished but posthumously published novel notably echoes the familiar plot of a young lady's entrance into the world typically represented by Fanny Burney's *Evelina* (1778) and the popular theme of a young heroine's adventurous experience in picturesque and Gothic milieux typically represented by Mrs Radcliffe's *The Romance of the Forest* (1791) and *The Mysteries of Udolpho* (1794), it conforms to neither the novel of sentiment in the Burneyesque tradition nor the novel of romantic mystery in the Radcliffean. In fact, it satirizes improbable situations and absurd sensibilities found in both of them. Jane Austen's fiction may be seen as embodying a "dialogic orientation" which, as M. M. Bakhtin says, "creates new and significant artistic potential in discourse" and "the potential for a distinctive art of prose."[1] The philosophical basis for such orientation is dialectical thinking and the *modus operandi* the deployment of dialectical narrative techniques.

The historically oriented criticism associated with Butler and Poovey, however, fails to address the distinct nature of the plot of *Northanger Abbey* in general and the development of Catherine Morland in particular. The main reason seems to be that both critics approach this novel with a more or less determined opinion as to which part of the novelistic tradition or what kind of political sentiment the novel responds to. In this

---

[1] *The Dialogic Imagination: Four Essays*, ed. Michael Holquist, trans. Caryl Emerson and Michael Holquist (Austin: U of Texas P, 1981) 275.

chapter I will first discuss how seeing one meaning in *Northanger Abbey*, as Butler's or Poovey's readings tend to do, reduces the complexity of Austen's nárrative to monologic, rather than dialogic, utterance, and hence misconstrues the moral implication of the Austenian discourse. I will then offer an analysis of the dialectical nature of the plot of the novel both as parts (two volumes) and as a whole, and make clear the dialectical relation among the narrative events contained in the two-volume structure, and, in particular, how certain important actions and dialogues may be understood dialectically as part of Austen's literary attempt to rein in some of the absurd tendencies in contemporary romantic and Gothic novels, while promoting what seems to her valid and commendable. This dialectical aspect of the plot is, I believe, one of the intrinsic and essential values of Jane Austen's *Northanger Abbey*.

1

In *Jane Austen and the War of Ideas*, Marilyn Butler observes that Catherine's character shows great inconsistency in the two volumes:

> In the first, it is the reader alone who is enlightened, by comparable dialogues between Catherine and the Thorpes, and Catherine and the Tilneys. During the same period the heroine neither learns to discriminate between her two groups of friends, nor to be discriminating about them. Although Henry Tilney has been setting her a good example for virtually a full volume, Catherine returns from her walk with him and Eleanor nearly as unenlightened as when she set out. ①

She then argues that it is "Jane Austen's reluctance to commit herself to her heroine's consciousness"② that makes Catherine stay unenlightened in the first half of the book. She goes on:

> From the consistent naïveté of her earlier thinking to her final state of enlightenment is a long step, but Jane Austen is not really concerned to examine it. Ultimately this is because, unlike Maria Edgeworth, she does not value the personal

---

① Butler 176.

② Butler 177.

process of learning to reason as an end in itself. What is required of Catherine is rather a suspension of a particular kind of mental activity, her habit of romantic invention; at the moment Jane Austen is not concerned to define positively what kind of regular mental process it is that will keep Catherine sensible. ①

    This is a disconcertingly inaccurate characterization of Jane Austen's art as well as her ideology. Jane Austen is a thinking individual, and so is Catherine Morland; "what kind of regular mental process it is that will keep Catherine sensible" is precisely Austen's business in *Northanger Abbey*. Butler, through her rather negative analysis of Austen's method, is expressing, if not imposing, a simplistic, conservative, even anti-Jacobin, reading of the book, in the same tune of *The New Morality*, ② which she has earlier summarized in her book as "[t]he best single poem" that criticizes "the indiscriminate, easy optimism of the friends of revolution" and "opposes a wary scepticism about human nature" to the "habit of easy forgiveness, or unwillingness to scrutinize."③ Indeed she

----

    ①   Butler 177.

    ②   A poem that appeared in the issue dated 9 July, 1798 in *The Anti-Jacobin ; or, Weekly Examiner.*

    ③   Butler 93. But "best single poem" is an ambiguous and dubious compliment, for the poem adopts the same theme, rhetoric and tone as the rest of satirical poems carried by the political magazine. For example, in the opening stanza, the poem declares that its task here is "To trace the deep Infection, that pervades / The crowded Town, and taints the rural Shades" and "To drive and scatter all the brood of Lies, / And chace the varying Falsehood as it flies" (3 – 4; 7 – 8). Of course all the bad things the poem attacks are French in origin, such as the hypocrisy of "O'er a dead Jack-Ass pour the pearly show'r;- / But hear, unmov'd, of *Loire's* ensanguin'd flood, / Choak'd up with slain;—of *Lyons* drench'd in blood" (143 – 145). The poem then looks at the British scene and ridicules the English Jacobins who tell "Of *acting foolishly, but meaning well*" (196) and accuses them of finding "BLACK's not so black;—nor WHITE so very white" (200) in spite of their "keen discriminating sight" (199). Sometimes the poem drops the already thin disguise and advises the reader "to fill up the blanks according to his own opinion, and after the chances and changes of the times" (note 17) in such lines as: "PAINE, W-LL-MS, G-DW-N, H-L-CR-FT-praise LEPAUX!" (345). The poem ends by urging the British to

    Guard We but our own Hearts; with constant view

    To antient Morals, antient Manners true,

    True to the manlier virtues, such as nerv'd

    Our father's breasts, and this proud Isle preserv'd

    For many a rugged age .... (450 – 454)

Otherwise "London may shine, but ENGLAND is no more" (463). It is fairly obvious that "New Morality" is more political than artistic.

tells us that "[a]fter reading *The New Morality* it becomes clear that Jane Austen's strong liking for the actual—that virtually moral distaste which she displays, from the juvenilia on, for the romantic gloss on truth—is a characteristic partisan position of the time."[1] As a result, Butler supposes that

> here we have to make do with facetious stylization, and allusion to a ready-made inner world acquired from reading other people's books. We are shown that Catherine has learnt a significant general rule, that human nature is worse than she first thought: for, apart from her aberration over the General, she has successively overrated the Thorpes, Frederick Tilney, and perhaps even Henry, with all the sentimentalist's optimism about human nature. [2]

Once again, Butler's analysis of *Northanger Abbey* is heavily weighted by her political assessment of Austen's ideology. We are given to understand that Austen's satire and burlesque and her "hurried treatment"[3] of Catherine Morland's interiority match the crude humour and trenchant satire of the reactionary *Anti-Jacobin*. That is why the reader, according to Butler, "sees little or nothing ... [o]f the actual change in her [Catherine's] habits of mind."[4]

Mary Poovey's analysis of *Northanger Abbey*, on the other hand, politicizes Austen's novel from the feminist perspective. Drawing on the *topoi* of "enclosure and escape" which Sandra M. Gilbert and Susan Gubar have identified as "so all-pervasive in nineteenth-century literature by women that [they] believe they represent a uniquely female tradition in this period,"[5] Poovey contends that one of the "strategies" which women writers employed as an alternative to "confrontation" with the "masculine authorities" is "in the form of enclosed episodes" where they "can explore material otherwise considered unladylike."[6] For example, "Austen's satirical *Northanger Abbey* contains a similar sequence of enclosed episodes, and the fact that Catherine Morland's perception of the

---

[1] Butler 93.

[2][3][4] Butler 177.

[5] Gilbert and Gubar 85.

[6] Poovey 44, 45.

tyrannical General Tilney is in many ways ratified by the outcome of the novel serves to highlight the importance of the imaginative freedom Catherine is momentarily granted. "① Poovey does not elaborate on what she means by "the outcome of the novel." If, presumably, she refers to the exposure of General Tilney's greed and vanity, her focus then seems to be on the events that happen in the last two thirds of volume 2 only, which arouse Catherine Morland's suspicion of General Tilney. Poovey subsequently quotes Gilbert and Gubar to clarify and substantiate her rationale: "'Trapped in so many ways in the architecture—both the houses and the institutions—of patriarchy, women expressed their claustrophobic rage by enacting rebellious escapes.'"②

The critical approaches adopted by Butler and Poovey are valid, but their analyses are less than convincing and their conclusions arbitrary. To begin with, Poovey's—and, by a logical extension, Gilbert and Gubar's—hypothesis that only physical entrapment allows Catherine the "imaginative freedom" is rather dubious, for it makes two assumptions that lack narrative basis:

1. Catherine Morland has not enjoyed "imaginative freedom," or has been unable to think for herself, until she is physically under the roof of Northanger Abbey;
2. Those so-called "enclosed episodes" where Catherine does enjoy "imaginative freedom" form a contrast to—shall we say—"open episodes" where her imagination must, by implication, have been inactive or stifled.

This suggestion of a schizophrenic Catherine, echoing, in a different sense, Butler's reading of two different Catherines in the two volumes, cuts the heroine's learning process in half. The arbitrary separation denies, therefore, that Catherine has gone through a series of mental operations while she is at Bath and has learned much from her association with the Tilneys, the Thorpes, and the Allens there. On the other hand, Catherine's imaginative act, or what Poovey calls "the imaginative freedom" that gives impetus to it, is not something that is really worth

---

① Poovey 45.
② Gilbert and Gubar 85; quoted in *Proper Lady* 45.

celebrating, as the heroine herself has painfully found out. Butler's assertion that Catherine "neither learns to discriminate between her two groups of friends, nor be discriminating about them" in the entire first volume of the novel while she is at Bath likewise ignores the fact that Austen's heroine, though not perfectly clear-eyed, does learn to distinguish Henry from Thorpe and Eleanor from Isabella. Her decisive conclusion about Catherine's failure to learn anything from the walk taken with the Tilneys "round Beechen Cliff" (106) in chapter 14 of volume 1 is as unfair as the evidence she provides is inappropriate. Catherine certainly has learnt a number of things while in the company of Henry and Eleanor. For example, she is reassured by Henry that novel reading is not something to be ashamed about, for Henry Tilney, whom Catherine admires as a gentleman, has no qualms about reading novels. In fact he has read "'hundreds and hundreds'" (107) of them, and told her rather pointedly that "'[t]he person, be it gentleman or lady, who has not pleasure in a good novel, must be intolerably stupid'" (106).

Catherine may be ignorant but is never stupid. In fact she has shown some quickness and tactfulness even in the early stage of her Bath experience. For example, Catherine has sense enough to feel, quite early in her acquaintance with Henry, that he is the type of man she wishes to fall in love with, which prompts her to observe him very carefully. She has even developed a little jealousy. Spotting him one evening "talking with interest to a fashionable and pleasing-looking young woman, who leant on his arm" (53), Catherine suddenly fears that Henry is married. Though she quickly dismisses the idea on the calculation that "he had not behaved, he had not talked, like the married men to whom she had been used; he had never mentioned a wife, and he had acknowledged a sister" (53), the unwarranted suspicion and the embarrassing thought process are given away by the change of colour in her cheek—"only a little redder than usual ... instead of turning of a deathlike paleness" (53).

Catherine also loses no time in tactfully yet thoroughly debriefing Mrs Allen about the Tilneys. Mrs Allen, who is more interested in talking about Miss Tilney's "'very pretty spotted muslin'" (68), is soon drawn into providing information more useful to Catherine, whose questions are quite specific, such as: "'Did she [Mrs Hughes] tell you what part of Gloucestershire they come from?'" (68), "'[a]nd is Mr. Tilney, my partner, the only son?'" (68 - 69). Catherine learns that the Tilneys "'are very good kind of people, and very rich,'" that "'Mrs. Tilney was a Miss Drummond'" who "'had a very large fortune,'" "'twenty-thousand pounds'" to be exact, "'and five hundred to buy wedding clothes'" (68). Although Catherine may not think in the same way as her bosom friend Isabella does—the narrator hastens to add that Catherine "had heard enough to feel that Mrs. Allen had no real intelligence to give" (69)—even though she probably knows more about Henry Tilney's worth (in both senses of the word) than he does about hers at this point. ①

Butler quotes the narrator's comment as evidence to back up her argument: "It was no effort to Catherine to believe that Henry Tilney could never be wrong. His manner might sometimes surprize, but his meaning must always be just:—and what she did not understand, she was almost as ready to admire, as what she did" (114). ② But this does not really support her flawed analysis and erroneous conclusion that Catherine fails to see the sterling example that Henry, in Butler's own words, "has been setting ... for virtually a full volume." In fact the opposite is true: Catherine has understood Henry's character well enough to be ready to exercise some willing suspension of disbelief. What Catherine does not understand, as the narrator explains, is Henry's "manner" of speaking, or his wit, which may "sometimes surprize" the ingenuous girl. ③

To clarify the point further, let us trace the sequence of the relevant speeches on this page. First, Henry Tilney gallantly but also slyly speaks

---

① John A. Dussinger takes the narrator's commentary at its face value and cites the instance as evidence in a chapter entitled: "Mrs. Allen: 'No Real Intelligence to Give'" (*see In the Pride of the Moment: Encounters in Jane Austen's World* [Columbus: Ohio State UP, 1990] 114 - 16).

② Butler 176.

③ In fact the narrator is more or less repeating the same point, which she has made earlier, when she points out that, although Henry Tilney's "fluency and spirit" engage Catherine's interest, his "archness and pleasantry" are "hardly understood" (25) by her.

to a credulous Catherine:

> Miss Morland, no one can think more highly of the understanding of women than I do. In my opinion, nature has given them so much, that they never find it necessary to use more than half. (114)

Catherine fails to register the humour but Eleanor does; the latter follows it up with a playful rejoinder:

> We shall get nothing more serious from him now, Miss Morland. He is not in a sober mood. But I do assure you that he must be entirely misunderstood, if he can ever appear to say an unjust thing of any woman at all, or an unkind one of me. (114)

The two humorous speeches are then followed by the narrator's amusing but meaningful comment quoted at the beginning of last paragraph. The sequence of the speeches (or events) shows that Butler's argument is strained, for what the narrator's comment does is extending to Catherine the feeling manifested in Eleanor's speech—love for Henry Tilney; it does not lend support to her argument that Catherine has not learned anything in volume 1 of the novel.

Let us visit one more time Butler's own sentence, which precedes the quotation ("It was no effort to Catherine") that she selects:

> Although Henry Tilney has been setting her a good example for virtually a full volume, Catherine returns from her walk with him and Eleanor nearly as unenlightened as when she set out. ①

We notice an incongruity in the discordant parallel of general and particular. Even if Catherine had not learnt anything from her engagement with the Tilneys during the delightful walk, returning "nearly as unenlightened as when she set out," this one particular instance happening in the brief span of shorter than one morning (114) should not be cited as evidence to prove or disprove something that has been unfolding over a good number of weeks or "for virtually a full volume." The urgency of Butler's criticism to prove that Catherine "has been

---

① Butler 176.

crossed with the burlesque heroine of the 'female quixote' variety"[1] and cannot, and is not supposed to, learn anything until a designed "suspension" of "mental activity" is lifted and she is given a new set of ideas to embrace, seems to cause her to miss the logic of the narrative evidence.

In a nutshell, the problem with these conservative and feminist readings is that they try to discover a particular moral or political inclination in Austen's fiction in terms of their respective critical persuasions, in order to prove that Jane Austen subscribes to either the conservative or liberal camp of the time. This kind of effort, as I have earlier observed, is likely to be futile, largely owing to Jane Austen's dialectical and non-partisan attitude which profoundly informs her novelistic writings. Jane Austen "shows us her mind" through the literary production of *Northanger Abbey*,[2] but that mind is not biased. In the following sections I will examine in more detail the ways Austen's heroine acts in the course of her continuous learning process, both at Bath and in the Abbey (the two parts of Catherine's development are intertwined), and demonstrate the consistently dialectical nature in the development of her moral character.

2

Catherine Morland is a heroine born, growing up and developing under a set of rules that are different from those of romantic or Gothic fiction. Her mother did not die at her birth, as a sentimental heroine's should have; in fact she went on to "have six children more" (13) and managed "to enjoy excellent health herself" (13). Nor did anything

---

① Butler 173.

② Jocelyn Harris, *Jane Austen's Art of Memory* (Cambridge: Cambridge UP, 1989) 33. Harris's chapter on *Northanger Abbey* demonstrates well Jane Austen's allusions to Locke. However, she seems to weaken her point a little by saying that the novel "shows a mind educating itself through innate powers" (1), and by commenting on Catherine's moral weakness favourably: "Free from the biases of traditional education, she courageously tests her hypothesis that General Tilney is a murderer" (1).

untoward happen to Dr Morland, her clergyman father. Both parents are alive and well. On the other hand, both as an infant and a pupil, Catherine lacks the qualities that are stereotypical of the common run of romantic heroines. She cuts "a thin, awkward figure" with "a sallow skin without colour, dark lank hair, and strong features" (13) and she does not have a quick mind either: Catherine "never could learn or understand any thing before she was taught" (14), and her talent for artistic accomplishments is all but non-existent: the "houses and trees, hens and chickens" that she draws are "all very much like one another" (14), and the day that her music master is dismissed is "one of the happiest of Catherine's life" (14).[①] The narrator informs us that at fourteen Catherine prefers "cricket, base ball, riding on horseback, and running about the country" to reading "books—or at least books of information" (15).

By constructing the childhood of such an atypical "heroine," setting her apart from the prototype of standard romantic fiction boasting beauty,

---

[①]   Mary Lascelles suggests that Austen likely had the titular heroine of Emmeline in mind when she prepared the draft of *Northanger Abbey*, but she concedes that "there is great similarity among the heroines of that age" (*Jane Austen and Her Art* [Oxford: Oxford UP, 1939] 60). However, we need to bear in mind the ironic nature in many of Jane Austen's echoings which undermine rather than uphold a common narrative identity. For example, Catherine's brief attempts at music and drawing seem to echo those of young Emmeline who endeavoured to cultivate a genius for drawing, which she inherited from her father; but for want of knowing a few general rules, what she produced had more of elegance and neatness than correctness and knowledge.

She knew nothing of the science of music; but her voice was soft and sweet, and her ear exquisite. The simple songs, therefore, she had acquired by it, she sung with a pathos which made more impression on her hearers than those studied graces learned by long application, which excite wonder rather than pleasure. (Charlotte Smith, *Emmeline, The Orphan of the Castle*, ed. and intro. Anne Henry Ehrenpreis [1788; London: Oxford UP, 1971] 41).

But in fact Catherine, "noisy and wild," hates "confinement and cleanliness" (14) and "greatly prefer[s] cricket" (13) and "rolling down the green slope at the back of the house" (14). If anything, Catherine is almost an anti-type of Emmeline.

knowledge and orphanhood,[1] Jane Austen is able at once to satirize the artificial traits of romantic heroines and to lay the groundwork for her dialectical scheme. As a young lady "in training for a heroine" (15) Catherine falls woefully short; but as an average apprentice about to embark on an educational journey, she is by no means inadequate. She has no serious character flaws such as "a bad heart" or "a bad temper" (14); she is "seldom stubborn" and "scarcely ever quarrelsome" (14); she becomes even "pretty" when "in good looks" (18) at the age of seventeen, and the backhanded compliment from the narrator: "her mind about as ignorant and uninformed as the female mind at seventeen usually is" (18) suggests that Catherine is in no way inferior, if not superior either, in terms of her learning and her ability to learn, to most girls of similar age.

These basic facts about the heroine of the novel, mostly humorous and ironic at this stage, are crucial to the dialectical art of Austen's fiction as they become increasingly meaningful both in the depiction and in the comprehension of Catherine's progress towards moral maturity. The nature of Austen's irony is dialectic. The fact that Catherine is presented as a heroine but, in Stuart M. Tave's words, "neither she nor her family will do the heroic thing 'as any body might expect,'"[2] points to the tension between Jane Austen's novelistic approach, even at this very early stage of her writing career, and the conventions of her literary milieu. Catherine has to play a heroine without becoming one. The series of dialectical engagements in which Catherine takes an active part gives

---

① *Emmeline* 2. Emmeline lost her mother soon after her birth and her father a few years later. Evelina lost her mother when she was very young (and effectively lost her father too because she had been switched with the nurse's own baby). Adeline in Mrs Radcliffe's *The Romance of the Forest* lost her mother soon after she was born and subsequently lost her father (murdered by the henchmen sent by his brother Phillip de Montalt). Emily in *The Mysteries of Udolpho* lost her mother when she was young and her father not long after. Interestingly enough, some of the reform-minded novelists also adopted this convention; for example, in Mary Hays's *Memoirs of Emma Courtney* (1796) the mother of the heroine died in child-bed and the father died when Emma was nineteen.

② *Some Words of Jane Austen* (Chicago: U of Chicago P, 1973) 36.

substance to the dialectical framework that Austen has set up. These engagements themselves will indicate the dialectical nature of Catherine's learning experience. She needs to gain knowledge and self-knowledge from interacting with other members of society, but she also runs the risk of being led astray by what she finds in society. This tension foreshadows the problematic nature of the epistemological process. The narrator's scrupulous documentation of the mental as well as physical states of the heroine at different age levels (pre-eight, eight, nine, ten, fourteen, fifteen and seventeen), apart from its general satirical purpose, guarantees beyond any doubt that the heroine is not going to be naturally smart and free from errors. ①

When Catherine enters the world of Bath, she is socially, intellectually and morally poorly prepared. At Fullerton she preferred books that were "all story and no reflection" to those that furnish "information" (15). The odd quotations from common-place books with which Catherine familiarized herself from the age of fifteen to seventeen (15)② are useless at Bath when she has to deal with real issues in life. Nevertheless, her warm personality, her artless nature and her ability to learn will prove valuable assets.

The juxtaposition of the naïve but sincere heroine with sophisticated Bath society creates a deliberate dialectical situation, which is epitomised by the first encounter between Catherine Morland and Henry Tilney. Mr Tilney, a clergyman who is socially experienced and intellectually

---

① The stratagem of furnishing early background information about a heroine in order to establish her ordinariness and open-mindedness will be adopted again to advantage in *Mansfield Park* when Jane Austen presents Fanny Price. This is a narrative strategy which many Austen critics and commentators tend to overlook when they comment on the heroine in that book.

② One of the quotations which Catherine had memorized is from James Thomson's *The Seasons* (1730), a poem which refers or alludes to Locke, his works or his ideas at least nine times on different occasions. For example, in "Summer" Locke is lauded as one of the English worthies "Who made the whole internal World his own" ("Summer" 1559, *The Seasons*, ed. with intro. and commentary James Sambrook [Oxford: Clarendon, 1981]). Austen's slight misquote here, like the ones of Shakespeare and Gray, does not alter the sense of the original; it rather suggests Austen's familiarity with the sources, since she seemed to have quoted from memory.

superior, takes Catherine, on their initial acquaintance, for one of the common run of female visitors to Bath, and he adopts the façade of a dandy and behaves somewhat like Sir Clement Willoughby in *Evelina*. Mary Wollstonecraft's criticism of men's sexist treatment of women— "flattering their *fascinating* graces, and viewing them as if they were in a state of perpetual childhood, unable to stand alone"[①]—seems to be ironically worked through Henry's knowing parody:

> I have not yet asked you how long you have been in Bath; whether you were ever here before; whether you have been at the Upper Rooms, the theatre, and the concert; and how you like the place altogether. I have been very negligent— but are you now at leisure to satisfy me in these particulars? If you are I will begin directly. (25)

Henry is not acting *in propria persona*; he is obviously performing, with irony, the Bath ritual on Catherine, complete with "a set smile," a softened "voice" and "a simpering air" (26). He has no doubt taken Catherine to be one of the wonted heroines that walk out of the romantic fiction that he reads, that he assumes she reads too.

But Catherine's serious and exact answers to Henry's formal, hackneyed queries puncture the romantic stereotype which Henry insists, in jest, on finding in Catherine. By giving true answers to ironically ceremonious questions, Catherine shows that she is no Isabella Thorpe (who, arriving soon, is an expert in managing double-talk). The sharp contrast between Catherine and Henry gradually moderates into a prevailing irony, but it is an irony that cuts both ways. Catherine's succinct acknowledgement of having been to the Upper Rooms last Monday, to the theatre on Tuesday and to the concert on Wednesday may seem mechanical and laborious, but it highlights the kind of routine that the watering place offers. It is not just Catherine who is boring by giving those answers but also Henry who solicits them without the real need of doing so. Henry is doubtless joking, but the joke is his assumed "foppishness." When he says, "'Now I must give one smirk, and then

---

① *A Vindication of the Rights of Woman*, *Works of Mary Wollstonecraft*, *vol.* 5, 75.

we may be rational again,'" Catherine is not sure "whether she might venture to laugh" (26)—which would be the correct response if she did.

The dialectical juxtaposition is continued when Henry assumes that Catherine, like every other heroine, keeps a journal and presumes to know what she will write in the journal, only to be told by Catherine: "'But, perhaps, I keep no journal'" (27). Henry is obviously parodying the romantic conventions, as he was just now the Bath conventions, but his listener's total lack of the little arts which Isabella will soon demonstrate so perfectly provides no proper response to his spirited ironic performance. He has found himself an awkward ironist frustrated by a simple provincial girl and a first-timer at Bath to boot, who disrupts his game plan, so to speak, and forces him to be less theatrical though no less ironic. He starts again:

> —My dear madam, I am not so ignorant of young ladies' ways as you wish to believe me; it is this delightful habit of journalizing which largely contributes to form the easy style of writing for which ladies are so generally celebrated. Every body allows that the talent of writing agreeable letters is peculiarly female. Nature may have done something, but I am sure it must be essentially assisted by the practice of keeping a journal. (27)

But Catherine, by treating the topic seriously (naïvely we might say), again prevents Henry's irony from taking hold and achieving its intended effect. As a consequence the parody seems to have been turned on the parodist.

Catherine's candid doubt about the validity of Henry's assessment: "'I have sometimes thought whether ladies do write so much better letters than gentlemen! That is—I should not think the superiority was always on our side'" (27) proves to be the last straw, inducing Henry, finally, to come to terms with Catherine and take her seriously in the conversation. The irony is gone because it has been ineffective. But Henry now presses his case with the help of hyperbole. He begins to elaborate, apparently in the capacity of an acknowledged linguistic expert, on the "'three particulars'" (27) in "'the usual style of letter-writing among women'" (27), i.e., "'A general deficiency of subject, a

total inattention to stops, and a very frequent ignorance of grammar'"
(27). The element of parody has all but disappeared as Henry's
seriousness comes close to, even exceeds, that of Catherine. But, yet
again, and indeed a little humiliatingly for Henry, Catherine will not go
to the other extreme with him; she tells him directly, even ironically:
"'Upon my word! I need not have been afraid of disclaiming the
compliment'" (27). Catherine holds on to her own belief and
understanding and refuses to bow to any stereotypical view of women,
real or ironic. Tara Ghoshal Wallace aptly points out that Henry's
subsequent dispassionate remarks:

> I should no more lay it down as a general rule that women write better
> letters than men, than that they sing better duets, or draw better landscapes. In
> every power, of which taste is the foundation, excellence is pretty fairly divided
> between the sexes. (28)

are "derivative."[1] Or, as another critic rightly comments in a different
context, Henry Tilney himself "'is guided by second-hand conjecture'"
(152), which is, in his own words again, "'pitiful'" (152).[2]

   In this first encounter, the unequal intellectual capacities of the two
speakers have not decided the outcome of the engagement. At the surface
level Henry certainly appears to be eloquent and effective with his faint
praise of women. However, he seems to be too clever by half. It is
Catherine, whose mind is pure and whose speech unprejudiced, who is
able to argue convincingly, if unknowingly, even unconsciously.
Catherine's balanced, dialectical vision, a result of her natural sincerity
and moral seriousness rather than her mastery of rhetoric or depth of
philosophical deliberation, has clearly won over Henry's witticism and
mockery, if not the man himself as well.[3] By not pretending to know
more than she does, she has made him appear to know less than he

---

[1]   *Jane Austen and Narrative Authority* (New York: St. Martin's, 1994) 21.

[2]   Alison G. Sulloway, *Jane Austen and the Province of Womanhood* (Philadelphia: U of
Pennsylvania P, 1989) 124.

[3]   This reminds us of the discovery which Lord Orville makes in *Evelina*. At one point he
takes her hand and declares: "'My dearest Miss Anville ... I see, and I adore the purity of your

pretends. Catherine is learning about the world, but obviously not quite in the way expected of her. Her responses are spontaneous, which fact shows that she is discriminating in her own way. In fact she soon suspects that Henry "indulged himself a little too much with the foibles of others" (29). Thus the learning mode at Bath, even at this early stage, appears to assume a dialectical nature.

Catherine's engagement with Henry, however satirical or naïve he or she may be, often occurs in the form of discussions on worthwhile subjects, such as the institution of marriage, the character traits of women, the correct usage of words, and the reading of Gothic fiction. Needless to say, Henry has been bent on teasing Catherine on a number of occasions, but, as we have already seen, the irony does not always succeed, or it succeeds in more ways than one. The dialectical nature of their discussions means that both of them have to adjust their views as they come to know each other better and see the virtues and weaknesses in each other. If Henry exposes Catherine's faults in linguistics, such as her misuse of the word "nice" (107 – 108) and her tautological expression of "'promised so faithfully'" (195), Catherine shows Henry that his opinion is not always just, nor is his wit always witty—not when he is being witty for the sake of being witty. Eleanor must be right when she comments derisively that Henry's vigilance over "'[their] faults in the utmost propriety of diction'" (108) exudes as much pedantry as rational thought.

Another example that illustrates the dialectics in their relationship is their debate about the quality of life at Bath. In chapter 10 of the first volume Henry, not without justice, asserts that Bath is "'the most tiresome place in the world'" (78); but he forgets that he is arguing from the vantage point of having lived in both the watering place and the

---

mind, superior as it is to all little arts, and all apprehensions of suspicion; and I should do myself, as well as you, injustice, if I were capable of harbouring the smallest doubts of that goodness which makes you mine for ever'" (301).

cosmopolitan city. ① If he has good reasons to be tired of Bath, Catherine has equally good reasons to be fascinated by it. Henry speaks from experience, comparing Bath with London; so does Catherine, comparing Bath with Fullerton. She has been living in "'a small retired village in the country'" (78) and suffered from such "'intellectual poverty'" (79) as Henry can hardly picture—"'I can only go and call on Mrs. Allen,'" who is endowed, we are told elsewhere, with "vacancy of mind and incapacity for thinking" (60). If Bath is for Henry where "'papas and mammas, and brothers and intimate friends are a good deal gone by'" (79), it is for Catherine a place where "'honest relish of balls and plays, and every-day sights'" (79) is still a luxury.

Therefore, on the whole, Catherine's association with Henry as well as his sister Eleanor constitutes a learning experience beneficial to her in terms of intellectual (aesthetic, linguistic, etc.) stimulation and in terms of moral education. To say nothing else, her association with the right company facilitates her attempt to identify the wrong. For example, the comfortable ride in Tilney's curricle at once demystifies Thorpe's legend about his "neatest" gig (65); likewise Thorpe's self-styled driving prowess pales quickly in comparison with Henry's ease and competence: "Henry drove so well,—so quietly—without making any disturbance, without parading to her, or swearing at them; so different from the only gentleman-coachman whom it was in her power to *compare* him with!" (157; emphasis added). Indeed, to Catherine, Thorpe's persistent "sexual hazing" (frightening her, lying to her, swearing before her, and even trying to control her physical movement), so to speak, raises daily her admiration of Henry, who is better looking, better mannered, and better principled. Catherine's comparison of her two sets of friends, the Tilneys and the Thorpes, helps her to read people's characters with

---

① Dr Johnson, upon hearing Boswell's doubt: "if I were to reside in London, the exquisite zest with which I relished it in occasional visits might go off, and I might grow tired of it," replies: "No, Sir, when a man is tired of London, he is tired of life, for there is in London all that life can afford" (*Boswell's Life of Johnson*, ed. George Birkbeck Hill, rev. and enl. L. F. Powell, 6 vols. [1934; Oxford: Clarendon, 1971] vol. 3, 177 – 178).

increasing accuracy.

But it is precisely this kind of dialectical process that the Thorpes attempt to disrupt. They want to sever the link between Catherine and the Tilneys, who are superior to them in appearance, conduct and speech as well as wealth and social position. They resort to various unethical means to prevent her from meeting Henry and Eleanor, thus depriving Catherine of opportunities to learn from their good examples, though in the meantime setting bad examples for her. One evening in the Upper Rooms at Bath, there occurs an awkward situation when Catherine, who wants to dance with Henry and become better acquainted with his sister's "real elegance" and "good sense and good breeding" (56), is frustrated because John Thorpe has spoken for her first and because "[t]he two dances were scarcely concluded before Catherine found her arm gently seized by her faithful Isabella" (56). On another occasion, just as Catherine is happily—with "sparkling eyes and ready motion" (75)— engaged with Henry for the country-dance, John Thorpe, who "stood behind her" (75), exclaims: "'Heyday, Miss Morland! what is the meaning of this?—I thought you and I were to dance together'" (75). Catherine's first attempt to keep her promise with the Tilneys for a country walk is foiled by Thorpe's deliberate misinformation about Henry and Eleanor's activity (85). Her second attempt is almost scuttled by John Thorpe's misinformation (100). Just as she in desperation tries to "'run after Miss Tilney directly and set her right,'" she finds herself physically restrained by the Thorpes: "Isabella ... caught hold of one hand; Thorpe of the other" (100). Ironically, by trying to enforce Catherine's separation from the Tilneys, and thus preventing her from making comparisons, the Thorpes have inadvertently, yet also inevitably, made themselves objects for comparison, and unfavourable ones at that.

3

Catherine's learning experience is spatially divided between Bath and Northanger Abbey, but that does not result, as Butler explicitly and

Poovey implicitly suggest in their analyses discussed at the opening of this chapter, in two different Catherines, each of a different character and with a different mode of thinking. It is not the case that she has remained stupid, insensitive, unimaginative and unimproved in the first volume and then turned around and become intelligent, sensitive, imaginative and improved in the second. Indeed Jane Austen seems to pre-empt precisely such schizophrenic analysis of her heroine by organizing her narrative structure in such a way that the Bath section begun in the first volume extends well into the second—Catherine's departure from Bath and her subsequent arrival at Northanger Abbey takes place in chapter 5 of the second volume. ① The truth is that the two stages of Catherine's learning are not only structurally but also thematically and thus dialectically intertwined. Bath is where Catherine has learned bad or misleading lessons as well as good ones. If anything, Bath is where she has learned most, if only because the opportunities for learning are most abundant, whereas Northanger Abbey is where her learning is most dramatic, if only because what she has learned must be challenged. Without her apprenticeship at Bath Catherine would not have learned the way she did at Northanger Abbey; without her experience at the Abbey her knowledge accumulated at Bath would not have been tested and evaluated.

When she first arrives at Bath Catherine mostly uses her eyes and ears: she listens, she sees and she files away her impressions: "[H]er eyes were here, there, every where" (19). She is not fit to judge yet: partly because of her generous and trusting nature, giving everyone the benefit of the doubt, but mostly because of her sheer ignorance. Catherine's experience with people, let alone their characters, is very limited, and her practical knowledge of the world is limited too. She is not sure whether John Thorpe has got a good bargain by spending fifty guineas on a second-hand curricle (46); she is equally uninformed about the rule of female

① There has been no evidence to suggest any tampering with Jane Austen's manuscripts of *Northanger Abbey*.

propriety regarding riding in an open curricle in the company of a young male. Catherine is not sophisticated; a "simple praise" of her "pretty" look (24) satisfies her "humble vanity" (24), and makes her content to be part of the Bath crowd.

In this initial stage of learning about the world, Catherine mainly reacts to what she sees and hears. Henry Tilney's "tall" figure, "pleasing countenance" and "very intelligent and lively eye" (25), and his general agreeableness impress her favourably, though his intimate knowledge about women's clothing in general and muslin in particular puzzles her and makes her think him "strange" (28). Isabella's wide knowledge about "dress, balls, flirtations, and quizzes" (33) secures Catherine's "admiration" (33); by contrast her brother's rough talk and ill manners leave her with an unfavourable first impression of the "stout young man of middling height with a plain face and ungraceful form" (45). She is quite put off by all that animal talk about "horses" and "terriers" (55) in general and the wrangling about the "forehand" and "loins" (46) of his horse in particular.

Even in this early stage of apprehension, however, Catherine's mind is already diligently working, processing the sensory data she receives with a view to converting them into meaningful messages. Through her association with John Thorpe, for example, Catherine begins to form opinions about his character: she starts to wonder if his *Abuse of Words*," which produces "Noise" and "Wrangling" without conveying "Information,"[1] is a sign of irrational thinking, however rational it may seem to him. Thorpe's gallantry towards Catherine is spurred by his misguided impression that she is, or will be, an heiress to Mr Allen who "owned the chief of the property about Fullerton" (17). Thus he sets his sights on Catherine and is determined to win the hand of this provincial but "wealthy" girl. This is why he is always flaunting his knowledge, prowess and generosity in the presence of Catherine, regardless of the truthfulness, propriety or even consistency of the swaggering. He assures

---

[1]   Locke, *Essay* 3. 10. 22.

Catherine that Blaize Castle is "'[t]he oldest in the kingdom'" (85) even
though it was built in the eighteenth century; [1] he boasts about the speed
of his horse—forgetting that "[t] he speed of the horseman must be
limited by the power of his horse"[2]—by losing one hour in the count
while calculating the travelling time; and he claims that he "'threw down
the money'" (46) for a used curricle without "'haggling'" (46) though
he knew that he "'might have got it for less'" (46).

Catherine, completely oblivious to Thorpe's ulterior motive, does
not, however, discriminate against Thorpe on the ground of his linguistic
confusion. She thoughtfully reserves her judgement of his character when
James, her brother, asks her how she likes his friend. At this point she
respectfully submits her private opinion to the judgement of her
university-trained brother (who is however hardly impartial): a valued
friend of James's cannot be entirely worthless. In fact her judgment is
"further bought off" (50) by Thorpe's compliment, conveyed by Miss
Thorpe, that she is "the most charming girl in the world" (50).
Catherine keeps taking Thorpe's words for truth—she is frightened when
Thorpe says that his horse "should dance about a little at first setting off"
and "will, most likely, give a plunge or two" (62)—until his action, or
that of his horse, has given the lie to his words. Indeed he lies so casually
and so confidently that at one point Catherine is unable to trust him even
when he is telling the truth (Thorpe did give Miss Tilney the message that
Catherine could not make the planned walk [102]). The contradictions in
John Thorpe's language and behaviour force Catherine to ponder about his
meaning and, more importantly, to be wary about his character. At one
point she wants to request from the man "a clearer insight into his real
opinion," but she refrains from doing so because "it appeared to her that
he did not excel in giving those clearer insights, in making those things
plain which he had before made ambiguous" (66). Catherine eventually

---

[1] See note 32 of Anne Henry Ehrenpreis's edition of *Northanger Abbey*
(Harmondsworth: Penguin, 1985) 251.

[2] Samuel Johnson, *Lives of the English Poets*, ed. George Birkbeck Hill (Oxford:
Clarendon, 1905) vol. 1, 99.

realizes that John Thorpe acts on no other principle than rude, irascible selfishness. Instead of respecting his opinions, Catherine begins to resist them. She even defies the authority of James so long as he sides with Thorpe against her (99 – 100).

Catherine Morland has learnt much, and quickly,[1] within her seven-week stay at Bath by meeting and associating with diverse parties. That Catherine has been in contact with both Henry Tilney and John Thorpe, not to mention other sets of characters, is greatly to her advantage. By comparing the speech and behaviour of the two gentlemen, unconsciously at first, Catherine is able to turn her valuable sensory experience into even more valuable perceptual experience. Her newly acquired knowledge has enriched to a great extent her moral and social awareness. She has seen through John Thorpe and is beginning to suspect that his sister is equally "ungenerous and selfish, regardless of every thing but her own gratification" (98). Catherine starts to disregard "such tender, such flattering supplication" (98) from her "'particular friend'" (112), and refuses to let "Isabella's opinion of the Tilneys" (131) sway her own judgment when she feels herself to be in the right. Catherine will not even allow James's opinion, to which she has been deferring all along, to dictate her action now. This marks a significant change in her own character, which makes her concerned but also confounded Oxford brother wonder aloud: "'I did not think you had been so obstinate, Catherine . . . you were not used to be so hard to persuade; you once were the kindest, best-tempered of my sisters'" (99 – 100).

One clear sign of Catherine's growing maturity presents itself when Captain Tilney arrives at Bath and makes his appearance at the evening

---

[1] The narrator reports a speedy and drastic change of feeling in Catherine within a fortnight of her meeting Henry and Thorpe:

> She entered the rooms on Thursday evening with feelings very different from what had attended her thither the Monday before. She had then been exulting in her engagement to Thorpe, and was now chiefly anxious to avoid his sight, lest he should engage her again; for though she could not, dared not expect that Mr. Tilney should ask her a third time to dance, her wishes, hopes and plans all centered in nothing less. (74)

dance that Catherine attends. She quickly sizes him up and judges him to be "a very fashionable-looking, handsome young man" (131). However, to Catherine's now experienced eye Frederick Tilney's "air was more assuming, and his countenance less prepossessing," and "[h]is taste and manners were beyond a doubt decidedly inferior" (131) to his younger brother's. Catherine may admire Frederick's appearance—perhaps "handsomer than his brother" (131)—and look at him "with great admiration" (131), but she positively has doubts about his character, especially after she has heard his raucous scoffing at "every thought of dancing himself" and his inordinate laughing at his brother's "finding it possible" (131), a morally questionable behaviour which Darcy will be guilty of at the Longbourn ball. We recall that, when Catherine met John Thorpe for the first time, his "plain face," "stout" figure, "middling height," and "ungraceful form" (45), not to mention his rash, crude horse talk, did not draw any morally negative criticism from Catherine— her displeasure was with his "manners" (50); in fact Catherine considered it "her own felicity" in being "engaged for the evening" by the ill-mannered yet extremely gallant Thorpe. But on this occasion Catherine is simply glad that Captain Tilney's "admiration of her" is "not of a very dangerous kind" (131).

4

Notwithstanding her marked moral and intellectual improvement, Catherine's learning process will remain dialectical. The all-round progress that the heroine has made at Bath does not erase the weaknesses she still has. In fact her gain is not without some loss. As her knowledge about people and things increases, so does her level of over-confidence. She appears eager, though not ready, to play an active moral role in the social world. If Catherine normally will not judge a person's character without seeing a substantial amount of evidence, she is beginning to shed that habit now. While this may be a sign of her increased power of discernment, it is also a sign of overweening vanity. Catherine's experience at Bath has opened her eyes to many things, but she must realize that her eyes can and must open still wider, because there are still more things to be seen and to be known. Catherine has yet to recognize the characters of two of her acquaintances: Isabella Thorpe, who mouths fine words and fills her ears with excessive endearments, and General Tilney, who habitually smiles at her and behaves handsomely by her. Catherine has yet to learn to judge the former in spite of her sweet talk and her capacity as James's fiancée, and the latter despite his civil façade and his being Henry's father. Above all, she must distinguish fictional reality, especially that portrayed by Gothic romances, from life's own reality. Unless the proper distinction is made, Catherine runs the risk of misreading and hence losing touch with the reality she has only just come to behold.

Reading is always important in Jane Austen's novels. [1] Two essential questions in that regard are what to read and how to read. In Catherine's case the problem is not the reading material itself, nor the act of reading, but how to read. Jane Austen's narrator makes it very clear in chapter 5 of the first volume that it is hypocritical for writers of novels to censure their own heroines for reading novels. [2] The narrator further cites Fanny Burney's *Cecilia* (1782) and *Camilla* (1796), and Maria Edgeworth's *Belinda* (1801) as sterling examples showing that "the greatest powers of the mind," "the most thorough knowledge of human nature, the happiest delineation of its varieties," "the liveliest effusions of wit and humour"

---

[1]   Elizabeth Bennet, for example, loves reading whereas Miss Bingley makes a show of it. Mr Darcy is "'always buying books'" to consolidate the family library at Pemberley; in his own words: "'I cannot comprehend the neglect of a family library in such days as these'" (*PP* 38). Fanny Price, we are told, has "a fondness for reading," which, "properly directed, must be an education in itself," and Edmund Bertram "recommended the books," "encouraged her taste," and "made reading useful by talking to her of what she read" (*MP* 22). Anne Elliot advises Captain Benwick to add more "prose" to his reading in order to "fortify" a mind skewed by "tremulous feeling" as a result of indulging himself in romantic poetry (*P* 101, 100).

[2]   Jane Austen's notion of the novel differs significantly from Johnson's evaluation of the "fictions" in 1750 when they were more or less a novelty; *see Rambler* 4, *The Yale Edition*, vol. 3.

are in the possession of novelists who deliver them "to the world in the best chosen language" (38).

Clearly, Jane Austen has very positive views about the novel as a major literary genre, even though she does not condone what seems to her the blemish of the profession and weaknesses in writing. Austen judges novels from the circulating library by the criteria of probity and probability. She may not have a high opinion for *Tom Jones* (1749)[1] or *The Monk* (1796)—both fancied by Thorpe—but *The Romance of the Forest* and *The Mysteries of Udolpho* are a different matter. Jane Austen was cool to Gothic novels, but she was interested in reading them and appreciated the well-written ones such as those by Mrs Radcliffe.[2] She was impatient with the inferior ones, however, and satirized their obsession with mysteries and ruins and their promotion of sentimentalism, sensationalism and supernaturalism in her own novel.[3]

Catherine's attitude towards novel reading goes through a dialectical

---

[1]   Henry Austen mentions in his "Biographical Notice" that Austen "did not rank any work of Fielding quite so high" (7), and this seems consistent with Austen's nonchalant remark about Tom Lefroy's weakness for Tom Jones in her letter to Cassandra (*Letters* 9 – 10, January, 1796).

[2]   One reason why Jane Austen likes Radcliffe's novels is that Radcliffe defers to the domestic and social realism practised by Richardson, Burney and Edgeworth. Radcliffe does not spare the mystic and turbulent promptings of imagination, and her sensational scenes, usually explainable, are incorporated by design into the main theme of moral education. In fact certain scenes in Radcliffe may have provided inspiration for Austen. For example, Adeline was perpetually imagining to have heard sighs at night, wind or no wind, while residing in the Abbey of St Clair, especially when reading a mysterious manuscript; and then she would awake in the morning to "the cheerful sun-beams play [ing] upon the casements," which "dispelled the illusions of darkness" (*The Romance of the Forest*, ed. Chloe Chard [1791; Oxford: Oxford UP, 1986] 134). For another example, M. St. Aubert warned his daughter just before he died: "Above all, my dear Emily, [...] do not indulge in the pride of fine feelings, the romantic error of amiable minds. Those, who really possess sensibility, ought early to be taught, that it is a dangerous quality, which is continually extracting the excess of misery, or delight, from every surrounding circumstance" (*The Mysteries of Udolpho*, ed. Bonamy Dobrée, intro. Terry Castle (1794; Oxford: Oxford UP, 1998] 79 – 80).

[3]   According to Cassandra's brief memorandum (*MW* facing page 242), *Northanger Abbey*, or its early version *Susan*, was composed between 1798 and 1799 when the rage of Gothic fiction was at its height.

process, influenced in turn by the views of Isabella, Thorpe and Tilney as well as her own reflection and empirical experience. Isabella's acquaintance with Catherine has not been made by chance: she is daughter of Mrs Allen's old friend and sister of James Morland's friend. Like her brother, she is an interested party and has her own ulterior motive for coming to Bath to meet Catherine and strike up an instant friendship. In fact introducing Catherine to Gothic plots is an integral part of her thoughtfully designed mercenary plot. Isabella, ironically described by the narrator as being "at least four years better informed" by virtue of her "being four years older" (33) than Catherine, wants to catch James, a "rich" heir. By converting Catherine into an avid Gothic fan and by arranging "to read novels together" (37) with her, Isabella wishes to achieve a bonding with one Morland, which she hopes will lead to engagement with another. While Catherine takes reading as an end, succumbing to the illusion and suspense of Gothic fiction, Miss Thorpe uses it as a means to an end. She disguises reality with fiction whereas Catherine takes fiction for reality. They may read the same book together but their minds are world apart.

A sure sign of Isabella's success in tightening her grip on James's sister is found at the linguistic level: Catherine is starting to recycle some of the Thorpean tics such as "'exceedingly'" (50) and "'amazingly'" (107). In time Isabella's strong expression of friendship—"'I have no notion of loving people by halves'" (40)—and her lavish praise of Catherine—"'the highest things that could possibly be'" (50)— mesmerize her and make her believe that Miss Thorpe is her best friend indeed. When Isabella professes to Catherine her romantic sentiment towards James—"'Had I the command of millions, were I mistress of the whole world, your brother would be my only choice'" (119)— Catherine's vision of fiction and reality begins to blur. The charming sentiment sounds familiar to her; in fact it evokes "a most pleasing remembrance of all the heroines of her acquaintance" (119). That acquaintance is made, of course, through the reading of Gothic novels. Isabella's conscious self-presentation reflects sentimental fiction in general, where it is dramatized as an index of virtue.

Jane Austen, as early as "Love and Freindship," satirizes pretentious sentimentality as something inherently selfish, as Isabella reveals rather fully here. For example, in "Letter 3d" Laura tells Marianne what sensibility it is in which she has been immersed: "A sensibility too tremblingly alive① to every affliction of my Freinds, my Acquaintance and particularly to every affliction of my own" (*MW* 78). Laura would indulge her anarchic impulse to the point of removing "Bank notes" from Macdonald's library and feeling offended when caught red-handed and taken to task (*MW* 96). As Marvin Mudrick points out, Jane Austen demonstrates that "sensibility and passionate love" are "liable in themselves to turn the individual obsessively inward away from all social participation or responsibility."②

John Thorpe's approach to Catherine is like his horse talk, considerably less subtle than his sister's, but the hard-headed Thorpean realism is the same. He is preoccupied with the materialistic aspect of the world in general and the estate value of Catherine in particular. When Catherine, who is brimful with Gothic ideas, attempts, tentatively, to discuss her reading experience of *The Mysteries of Udolpho* with John Thorpe, the "self-assured" (48) man declares that he "'never read[s] novels'" because they are "'all so full of nonsense and stuff'" (48). Catherine becomes disorientated by this unexpected attack on novels by Thorpe. She is so "ashamed" (48) of the fact that she loves reading novels, whereas the Oxford man, to whom she looks up, does not, and has such negative sentiments about it, that she tries to "apologize" (48) for her foolish question. Thorpe's seemingly authoritative assessment of novels makes Catherine pause and ponder her own position. But then the situation changes. Catherine discovers that Thorpe's knowledge of fiction is not only very limited but also quite unreliable: he has never read *The*

---

① The phrase might have come from Mrs West's *A Gossip's Story* where Marianne, at nineteen, was "tremblingly alive to all the softer passions" (vol. 1, 19); but it is probably a catch phrase used routinely to describe the sentimental heroines of that age.

② *Jane Austen: Irony as Defense and Discovery* (Princeton: Princeton UP, 1952) 16.

Mysteries of Udolpho, or any other work by the same author, though he assures her that he enjoys reading Radcliffe (48 – 49). His credibility as a novel critic is further dented when he condemns *Camilla* as "'that other stupid book'"—containing "'the horridest nonsense'" one can imagine—that "'would not do'" (49), without being able to name either the book or its author, and without finishing, as he indirectly admits, the first volume of the five-decker. The clear evidence from his own mouth can only serve to undermine Thorpe's forceful albeit vague, frothy and stupid denunciation of novels. In this brief but interestingly dialectical conversation, Catherine's idea of the novel zigzags. Her earlier shame must have been eased considerably by her later perception of Thorpe's shameless double-talk.

Catherine's belief in novel reading will be strengthened when she learns, on the way from Bath to Northanger Abbey, that Henry Tilney not only reads novels, even Gothic ones, but has actually read more than she has. Henry's open-mindedness about novel reading will be sufficient to offset John Thorpe's bad-mouthing of novels. Catherine is startled, yet not at all convinced, by Thorpe's inane, unfair and downright ridiculous comments on novels. John Thorpe's moral authority suffers another blow when the narrator describes his meeting with Mrs Thorpe right after his criticism of novels:

> This critique, the justness of which was unfortunately lost on poor Catherine, brought them to the door of Mrs. Thorpe's lodgings, and the feelings of the discerning and unprejudiced reader of *Camilla* gave way to the feelings of the dutiful and affectionate son, as they met Mrs. Thorpe, who had descried them from above, in the passage. "Ah, mother! how do you do?" said he, giving her a hearty shake of the hand: "where did you get that quiz of a hat, it makes you look like an old witch? Here is Morland and I come to stay a few days with you, so you must look out for a couple of good beds some where near." (49)

Jane Austen's controlling irony sideswipes Thorpe's impertinence and rudeness, and exposes further his general ignorance as well as obnoxious character. [1]

Henry Tilney's affirmation of novel reading, however, does not come as exactly the opposite view. This is a juncture which calls for a dialectical attitude, which Catherine Morland has not yet acquired. During the rather lively conversation between Henry and Catherine while they are riding in a curricle towards Northanger Abbey, Henry demonstrates his intimate knowledge of Gothic fiction by mixing his account of the interior of Northanger Abbey with some of the most memorable, if not the most easily remembered, scenes from *The Romance of the Forest* as well as *The Mysteries of Udolpho*. In doing so Henry hopes to kill two birds with one stone. First he wants to reiterate the point, which he has made earlier while walking with Catherine and Eleanor around Beechen Cliff near Bath, that "'[t]he person, be it gentleman or lady, who has not pleasure in a good novel, must be intolerably stupid'" (106).

Second, he cannot help satisfying his urge to tease Catherine, as he has done at Bath, on her unquenchable Gothic aspirations, which he has noticed for some time, by vicariously acting out their folly. Henry pretends to make things more Gothic than they are in order to expose the fact that Catherine is more Gothic-struck than he pretends. Unfortunately, his "Gothic" performance has turned out to be an act of double irony, achieving very limited success. Listening to his dramatized description of the Abbey, Catherine cries: "'Oh! Mr. Tilney, how frightful!—This is just like a book!'" (159). Catherine's terror and, a little later, her desire for more reflect the characteristic emotional response of the Gothic heroine and the readers of Gothic novels, a narrative phenomenon which Chloe Chard calls, in a shorthand, "collapse and recovery."[2]

This is yet another sign that Catherine is in danger of tangling fiction

---

[1]   It is also revealing that Mrs Thorpe accepted it all cheerfully. This scene forms a sharp contrast with the reception of Catherine by her family when she returns home later in the novel (233).

[2]   Introduction to her 1986 edition of *The Romance of the Forest*, xviii.

with reality. Although she is "ashamed" (160) of losing her composure to Henry's vivid oral rehearsal of what is to become of her once she gains entry to the Abbey, she remains unconvinced of the Gothic novel's fictitiousness. Her Gothic credulity does not recede in spite of, or perhaps because of, Henry's tongue-in-cheek fictionalization of Northanger Abbey. That she is at once frightened and fascinated by Henry's makeshift fiction is clearly seen in her seemingly conflicting remarks: "'Oh! No, no—do not say so. Well, go on'" (160); that she "earnestly" assures Henry that she is "'not at all afraid'" (160) betrays her conjured-up imagination and uncalled-for agitation.

Henry reads Gothic romances for pleasure (so does Eleanor, apparently); Catherine, for "instruction." Henry knows that a novel is fiction no matter how real it seems, whereas Catherine falls victim to the deliberately contrived sentimentalism as well as sensationalism such novels furnish, and takes great pleasure in being shocked. We recall that when Isabella promises Catherine a list of ten or twelve more Gothic romances to read, all of which are of the calibre of *The Mysteries of Udolpho*, the latter pleads with the former to make sure that "'they are all horrid'" (40). We recall also that when Henry's talk of politics fails to interest the ladies he is accompanying and a "silence" sets in (111),① Catherine tries to start a new topic by supplying the information that "'something very shocking indeed, will soon come out in London'" (112). Catherine's Gothic news follows on the heels of Henry's discussion of politics, so closely that Eleanor, who presumably cannot imagine, in her right mind, that any prospective fiction, Gothic or not, is worth being announced in such "a solemn tone of voice" (112) or capable of generating such massive shocking effects, becomes confused and alarmed. Clearly, in Catherine's case, it is not so much the novels that are to blame but her single-minded approach and infatuated response to them. From this point on, what has hitherto been part of the narration merely starts to become part of the

① Feminist critics tend to make an issue of the "silence;" for example, Claudia L. Johnson thinks that Henry's talk of politics is intended "in part to bring Catherine to 'silence'" (39).

story; what has been merely verbal starts to become "real," just as the story invented by Henry on the drive to Northanger starts to come true when Catherine reaches her bedroom.

5

If, in the realm of Bath of the first volume, Catherine is mainly engaged in gaining knowledge about the world, absorbing impressions and trying to digest them, in Northanger Abbey of the second she is preoccupied with discerning how she is to function as a moral agent in the world. She is particularly excited about the opportunity of seeing a real Gothic building and applying her special knowledge to it. Her eagerness to explore the Gothic phenomenon is in fact part of the reason why she leaves Bath behind "without any regret" (156), considering that only six or seven weeks ago she assured Henry that she should not be "'tired'" of Bath even in "'six months'" (78). The unobtrusive imagery of water which Jane Austen employs in presenting Catherine's arrival at Northanger Abbey in late March—the "sudden scud of rain driving full in her face" (161), blurring her vision of the Abbey—may be read as a sort of symbolism signalling the clear and present conflict between Gothic eagerness and sober reality. The process of laying the Gothic ghost is to be tortuous and dialectical as Catherine, armed with her knowledge of Gothic, which she holds as truth or touchstone, prepares to perform her practicum.

Catherine first puts to use her knowledge of Gothic architecture as soon as she is inside Northanger Abbey. She keenly looks for such primary Gothic features in the Abbey as "the pointed arch" (162). Catherine is disappointed to see that what remains of the old abbey has been extensively renovated and substantial additions have been made to it, but she notices that "the form" of windows, with their pointed arches, is "Gothic" (162); yet, again to her disappointment, "every pane was so large, so clear, so light!" (162). The contrast is "distressing" indeed for "an imagination which had hoped for the smallest divisions, and the heaviest stone-work, for painted glass, dirt and cobwebs" (162). Catherine's determination to supplant the entity of Northanger Abbey with her Gothic notions reveals the extent of her harmful addiction to misconceived romantic ideas. Nothing short of an object lesson can awaken her from her Gothic imaginations, from her mistaken assumptions about reality.

The geographical shift from the dazzling buzzing city of Bath, where visitors "remember the difficulties of crossing Cheap-street" (44), to the quiet and private Northanger Abbey in Gloucestershire brings with it other changes, both visible and invisible. At Bath Catherine is seldom at liberty: she is chaperoned by Mrs Allen, manipulated by Isabella and coerced, if not controlled, by the aggressive and possessive John Thorpe. When she is able to assert herself and fulfil her promise to be with the Tilneys, she is usually in a learning mode: either absorbed in Henry's eloquent "lecture on the picturesque" (111): the "fore-grounds, distances, and second distances—side-screens and perspectives—lights and shades" (111) that underlie the striking landscape around Bath or learning "to see beauty in every thing admired by [Henry]" (111).

At Northanger Abbey, however, Catherine is more or less left on her own. Her privacy is emphasized: she seems to reflect or imagine more in her own space in quietude; and she seems to be able to roam in and out of the Abbey inspecting the rooms and viewing the grounds at leisure. She is not imposed upon in general, nor is she obliged to do things that she does not want to. As a matter of fact all three Tilneys try to please their guest, for different reasons of course, and Catherine, taking full advantage of their hospitality, is not shy about telling them what she wants them to do for her. For example, Catherine, deeming it "highly expedient that Henry should lay the whole business before [General Tilney] as it really was" so as to "prepare his objections on a fairer ground than inequality of situations," should Captain Tilney apply to him for permission to marry Isabella, subsequently "proposed it to him accordingly" (208 – 209). In addition Catherine insists on venturing into that part of the Abbey which she knows clearly General Tilney does not wish to be visited (185). Indeed Catherine's role seems to have been reversed; even she herself "sometimes started at the boldness of her own surmises, and sometimes hoped or feared that she had gone too far" (188).

The successive enquiries that Catherine has carried out soon after her arrival at Northanger Abbey involve investigating an ancient chest and a black cabinet in her bedroom and stealing into the private bed-chamber where she fancies that Mrs Tilney may have been murdered by her husband. ① The subsequent failure to locate any evidence embarrasses Catherine and forces her to confront her own folly. Her delusion begins to turn into disillusion. But Catherine's persistent attempts to conceal her snooping and her keen effort to appear as if she had been thinking and behaving quite normally indicate that she is not prepared to come clean with her vision of non-reality. Having penetrated the "mystery" of Mrs Tilney's apartment and seen with her own eyes a neat, well-furnished and brightly-lit room, Catherine is astonished. Whereas earlier the Gothic windows letting in so much light (162) disappointed Catherine, now "the warm beams of a western sun [that] gaily poured through two sash windows" have brought her "some bitter emotions of shame" (193). Nevertheless, no sooner had "a shortly succeeding ray of common sense" (193) taken hold than Catherine's insurgent Gothic imagination revives, only more unnerving. It begins with "the sound of footsteps" which makes her "pause and tremble" (194). Admittedly, Catherine is worried about being discovered loitering in that sequestered part of the house, but the lingering Gothic effects cannot be entirely ruled out. Hearing some "swift steps," Catherine is instantly transfixed by "a feeling of terror not very definable" (194).

Good-natured Eleanor is not sensitive to Catherine's Gothic aspirations (165), but astute Henry is who has been aware of Catherine's

---

① Incidentally, two murders did occur, according to David Nokes' research, in 1775 and 1790 respectively, in and near Chawton Cottage, where the manuscripts of *Susan* would be revised for publication as *Northanger Abbey*, although Jane Austen was not there then (see *Jane Austen: A Life* [New York: Farrar, 1997] 359, 550).

Gothic psychology for some time. The conversation between Henry and Catherine, leading to Henry Tilney's climactic rhetoric featuring the famous phrase of "'a neighbourhood of voluntary spies'" (198),[1] contains an element of dialectics.

The initial part of the conversation resembles, without too much exaggeration, an intense interrogation with Henry trying, skilfully, to draw out the information which Catherine's countenance—she "blushed deeply" (194)—intimates but "her lips did not afford" (194), and Catherine struggling to fend off his probing and withdrawing into a state of denial. Except the reluctant admission, under Henry's close questioning (195), that she has been to see Mrs Tilney's room, Catherine's answers, as we will see, are marked by a series of negatives:

> No, nothing at all.—I thought you did not mean to come back till to-morrow.
>
> No, I was not.—You have had a very fine day for your ride.
>
> Oh! No; she shewed me over the greatest part on Saturday.
>
> No, I only wanted to see—Is not it very late? I must go and dress.
>
> No, and I am very much surprized. Isabella promised so faithfully to write directly. " (195)

---

[1] The business of spying must be something rather tame and commonplace for the readers of the time, given the historical background. Gripped by the fears of a French invasion and domestic insurrections, the British government took various measures, such as "the Alien Act (1793), the creation of the Alien Office (1794), the Traitorous Correspondence Act (1793; extended in 1798), the 'Two Acts' against treasonous Practices and Seditious Meetings (1795), and the Newspaper Act (1798)" (J. Ann Hone, *For the Cause of Truth*: *Radicalism in London*, *1796 – 1821* [Oxford: Clarendon, 1982] 47, 78). In fact spies and espionage are common occurrences in novels of the time. Hermsprong, the hero in Bage's novel, is suspected by the rioters to be one of King George's spies, yet he is charged and tried as a French spy (see *Hermsprong* 219 – 26). In the words of one of the trial justices, "'In these suspicious times we think circumspection with regard to strangers necessary'" (226). M. de Tourville, a chargé d'affaires in Edgeworth's *Belinda* is a spy whose encrypted papers are intercepted and deciphered by Lord Oldborough; so are Count Altenberg and Cunningham Falconer. Mary Wollstonecraft's letter from Paris to her friend Eliza in London carefully says nothing about the political affairs there for fear of serious consequences on either side of the Channel (Holmes 107). The Treason Trials of 1794 of some of the sympathizers of the French Revolution obviously contributed to the heightened fear of French infiltrators. For an extensive discussion of espionage of the time see Mary A. Favret's chapter, "Letters or *letters*? Politics, interception and spy fiction" in *Romantic Correspondence*: *Women*, *Politics and the Fiction of Letters* (Cambridge: Cambridge UP, 1993) 38 – 52.

Catherine is trying to divert Henry's attention. Her words suggest that
she is not in the least interested in the enquiry Henry is making in regard
to the "'extraordinary" route that Catherine has chosen to follow "'from
the breakfast-parlour to [her] apartment'" (195) even though her mind is
precisely occupied with what the investigation intends to find out.

It is rather significant that, at this point, surfaces her tautology:
"'Isabella promised so faithfully'" (195). The confusion in terms
reflects faithfully the confusion in thought, and it links a wayward
Catherine to the ignominious Thorpes. Henry, ever sensitive and alert,
notices the ill logic of Catherine's rhetoric and slowly but surely zeroes in
on the afflicted mind of Catherine. Haltingly, she admits that she has
harboured some dark suspicions about General Tilney's treatment of his
wife: "'Her dying so suddenly,' (slowly and with hesitation it was
spoken,) 'and you—none of you being at home—and your father, I
thought—perhaps had not been very fond of her'" (196). When Henry
has fully explained the circumstances under which his mother died,
Catherine feels immensely relieved: "'I am very glad of it . . . it would
have been very shocking!'" (197). The subjunctive mood here is not
simply correct grammar; it reveals to Henry the instigating Gothic
thoughts in the mind of Catherine.

It is clear that one has the facts whereas the other does not. Only at
this point, when the two opposed positions engage and sort out the
ambiguities, converging all the while on the moral issue of unrestrained
mental dissipation, does the Rev Mr Tilney feel completely justified in
giving Catherine Morland an eye-opening sermon, so to speak. Only now
does Catherine acknowledge the ludicracy of cherishing those dark
thoughts in her contaminated mind; the tears in her eyes vouch for her
shame and self-reproach.

6

The discussion above shows that the plot of *Northanger Abbey* may,
and even should, be understood from the point of view of dialectics.

Indeed the novel is dialectical not only in structure but also in action and characterization; indeed the plot as a whole is dialectical. The significant changes in the character of the heroine do not happen overnight; they are the results of a series of mental operations over moral, social and intellectual issues. Catherine has not won all the moral battles, but her good nature and authentic character, her willingness, and her ability to learn, have eventually turned the tide and enabled her to gain knowledge and self-knowledge. Catherine's Gothic experience, begun earnestly in delusion at Bath and ending abruptly in disillusion in Northanger Abbey is central in the shaping of Catherine's mind. It constitutes an integral part in her general learning about the facts of life and the complexities of society. The progress that she has made, from general ignorance to vicarious experience, to felt and lived experience, is of a dynamic and dialectical nature.

Catherine is now able to think dialectically and conceive "a general though unequal mixture of good and bad" in things and people (200): she correctly assumes that even virtuous people like Henry and Eleanor may have "some slight imperfection" (200), and she has judiciously sensed that "the character" of General Tilney, though not "grossly injurious," does have "some actual specks" (200), to say the least. When Isabella's long-expected letter has finally arrived at the Abbey, Catherine is able to read its contents not literally but between the lines. She has become a rational and sophisticated reader as a result of her dialectical experience, both empirical and perceptual. She recalls what she saw at Bath, she remembers what her brother James told her in his letter from Oxford, and she detects the "shallow artifice" and "falsehood" camouflaged in the fine words (218). Catherine knows what ugly thoughts are hidden in the mind of her beautiful friend. The same grand hyperbole—"you are dearer to me than any body can conceive" (216) "—and the same superlative endearments—"my dearest, sweetest Catherine" (218)—have lost their enchanting touch and can no longer extract their desired romantic, sentimental effects. In fact Catherine is wise enough to think her former friend's professions of love "disgusting" and her request for her to act as a go-between—"Lose no time, my dearest, sweetest Catherine, in writing to him [James] and to me" (218)—"impudent" (218). These epithets are pertinent and apt, for they express precisely the feelings of someone who has been played for a fool by the shameless fortune-seeker and whose brother's genuine affection and whose family's handsome endowment are rewarded by wickedness and contempt. Catherine does not reply to Isabella's impudent letter, breaking off what is left of their dialectical relationship.

If *Northanger Abbey* bears testimony to the deployment of a dialectical plot featuring a dialectical process in the heroine's learning experiences both at Bath and at Northanger Abbey, the final act of its heroine becomes highly symbolic of what such plot is supposed to achieve. By the end of the novel the young, healthy and curious Catherine, who left Fullerton "ignorant and uninformed" (18), returns to her home village in a hack post chaise, depressed emotionally but seasoned morally and intellectually. Though not much older—in less than three months—she is no longer "free from the apprehension of evil as from the knowledge of it" (237); she has learned to base her judgment upon close observation and "serious consideration"(200). It is not Catherine's fault that she fails to comprehend why she has been mistreated by General Tilney,① because she does not have all the relevant information surrounding the event. The General has taken care to present—throughout the first volume and at least one third of the second—a gay, courteous and gallant appearance to her: "perfectly agreeable and good-natured, and altogether a very charming

---

① There is a tendency to misread the nature of General Tilney's abrupt expulsion of Catherine, which Maria Edgeworth thinks "'quite outrageously out of drawing and out of nature'" (Butler, *Maria Edgeworth* 445). Gilbert and Gubar, for example, regard the General as "a modern inquisitor" (*Madwoman* 136), even though he does not really inquire nor torture. Similarly, Johnson thinks that Austen "emphasizes the political subtext of gothic conventions: her villain, General Tilney, is not only a repressive father, but also a self-professed defender of national security," and that "Austen may dismiss 'alarms' concerning stock gothic *machinery*— storms, cabinets, curtains, manuscripts—with blithe amusement, but alarms concerning the central gothic figure, the tyrannical father, she concludes, are commensurate to the threat they actually pose" (Johnson 35). It is plain that General Tilney is no Montoni and Northanger Abbey no Udolpho. Catherine's suspicion and imagination are objects of Austen's satire.

man" (129). It is to Catherine's enormous credit that she avoids a Gothic interpretation of General Tilney's uncouth domestic conduct towards his children and his hypocritical and then abominable treatment of herself, even though she is in possession of a fair amount of concrete evidence that indeed suggests that he resembles some sort of a Montoni figure. Catherine prefers to form her judgement not only on the basis of her empirical evidence, but also on the logic of such evidence. She has learned to think, not merely to imagine. Her good sense and rational sensibility are implicit in her thought to write Eleanor "a letter which might at once do justice to her sentiments and her situation, convey gratitude without servile regret, be guarded without coldness, and honest without resentment" (235). The Johnsonian style is the narrator's, but the collected poise is that of Catherine.

Jane Austen's dialectical dialogue with the themes as well as forms of the late eighteenth-century novels, irrespective of implicitly or explicitly expressed political leanings embodied in them, is continued in *Sense and Sensibility*. Whereas *Northanger Abbey* is not informed by dialectics in a formally systematic manner, *Sense and Sensibility* apparently is, where dialectics intrudes into the narrative events almost from the very beginning and interferes with the narrative statement throughout.

3 *Sense and Sensibility*:
Dialectics vs. Dichotomy

The schematic and antithetical structure of *Sense and Sensibility* is reminiscent of such late eighteenth-century English fiction as Maria Edgeworth's "Letters of Julia and Caroline" in *Letters for Literary Ladies* (1796), Elizabeth Inchbald's *Nature and Art* (1796) and Jane West's *A Gossip's Story* (1796),① in that two conflicting moral positions have been set up to carry the weight of the narrative and move the plot forward. While infusing diverse moral sentiments into two young persons, either siblings or close friends, for the purpose of ethical contrast is nothing new—Fielding's *Tom Jones* (1749) comes naturally to mind, which pairs off the virtuous but imprudent Tom with his mean-spirited and hypocritical step-brother Blifil—the practice seems to have gained such popularity by the middle of the last decade of the eighteenth century, the political situation of the time being particularly propitious for its employment, that it had become a convention and was exploited by novelists of various political persuasions: conservative, moderate, and radical.②

---

① Kenneth L. Moler's chapter on *Sense* and *Sensibility* in his *Jane Austen's Art of Allusions* (Lincoln: U of Nebraska P, 1968) explains the contextual background of the novel. For other commentaries on the same subject see J. M. S. Tompkins's "Elinor and Marianne: A Note on Jane Austen," *The Review of English Studies* 16 (1940): 33 – 43; A. Walton Litz, *Jane Austen: A Study of Her Artistic Development* (New York: Oxford UP, 1965) 73 – 78; Alistair M. Duckworth, *The Improvement of the Estate: A Study of Jane Austen's Novels* (Baltimore: Johns Hopkins, 1971) 103; and Marilyn Butler, *Jane Austen and the War of Ideas*, 182 – 183.

② Jane Austen attempted something like it in the early 1790s in *Catharine, or the Bower*, in which two girls, one silly (Camilla), one sensible (Catharine), interact with each other and show their moral and intellectual differences.

Jane West's novel, *A Gossip's Story*, for example, features two sisters, Louisa and Marianne, who develop different moral characters due to different modes of early education. Louisa, the elder child, who grows up with her father, Mr Dudley, receives useful "instructions" which are "enforced by example" and shows "from her earliest years a disposition to improve both in moral and mental excellence."[1] Marianne, on the other hand, is raised after her mother's death by her maternal grandmother, Mrs Alderson, who envelops her granddaughter with "all the fond indulgence of doting love" and regards her as "possessing a kind of hereditary claim to perfection."[2] While Louisa has "an informed, well-regulated mind"[3] and shows "intelligence and ingenuous modesty,"[4] her younger sister has grown "tremblingly alive to all the softer passions"[5] by reading romances.[6] Their differences are ultimately reflected in their respective choices of husbands. Marianne makes her choice on the basis of "extreme sensibility,"[7] and Louisa on the basis of "kindred minds."[8] The outcome is not unpredictable: Marianne's marriage quickly turns sour, and she lives "unhappily" and in "sorrows,"[9] whereas Louisa's is nothing but happiness.

Maria Edgeworth's "Letters of Julia and Caroline" delivers a sharper contrast between two close friends (who almost become sisters-in-law) holding two different sets of values. The opening lines of Julia's first letter make clear where she stands: "In vain, dear Caroline, you urge me

---

[1]   Jane West, *Gossip's Story* vol. 1, 15.

[2][3]   *Gossip's Story* vol. 1, 18.

[4]   *Gossip's Story* vol. 1, 17 – 18.

[5]   *Gossip's Story* vol. 1, 19.

[6]   *Gossip's Story* vol. 1, 39, 80.

[7]   *Gossip's Story* vol. 2, 41. Marianne's first meeting with Mr Clermont, her future husband, is described in the following terms: "Never was such a wonderful coincidence of opinion! Both were passionate admirers of the country; both loved moonlight walks, and the noise of distant waterfalls; both were enchanted by the sound of the sweet-tone harp, and the almost equally soft cadence of the pastoral and elegiack muse; in short, whatever was passionate, elegant, and sentimental in art; or beautiful, pensive, and enchanting in nature" (vol. 1, 205).

[8]   *Gossip's Story* vol. 2, 201.

[9]   *Gossip's Story* vol. 2, 220.

to *think*; I profess only to *feel*."① In reply to Caroline's request that she explain her system, Julia emphatically retorts: "But I have no system: *that* is the very difference between us. My notions of happiness cannot be resolved into simple, fixed, principles."② Julia, like Marianne in Jane West's story, indulges her "taste for romance and poetry" and embraces "the exquisite sensibility of enthusiasm."③ Caroline, unmoved by Julia's "*lively nonsense*,"④ explains to Julia that her so-called "nature" is in fact one form of "art"⑤ because she acts according to some particular principles based on a particular "philosophy."⑥ In the end Julia's suffering is in direct proportion to the firmness of her belief: her marriage to Lord V—breaks down; she is separated from her husband and shortly after dies in illness and disgrace. Caroline, however, is happily married and enjoys domestic felicity.

Elizabeth Inchbald's portrayal of the contrast between the Henrys and the Williams in her novel *Nature and Art* is even more thorough and startling: for one thing she relates the moral issue to social class by placing the protagonists into the social categories of rich and poor; for another she allows the distinct moral traits to become hereditary and persist through two generations. Henry and William are the sons of a deceased English country shopkeeper. They go to London and try to make a living there. Henry, the younger brother, plays the violin and uses this skill to earn what he can. He brings food home, he supports William while he is at university, and he even manages to find him a patron when he graduates. But William is ungrateful. He becomes arrogant and grows disdainful of his musician-brother, especially after he has secured a deanery for himself. The relationship between the two brothers becomes strained, and they finally drift apart when William marries a wealthy but haughty and

---

① *Letters for Literary Ladies*: *To Which Is Added*, *An Essay on the Noble Science of Self-justification*, 4th ed. (1795; London, 1799) 115.

② *Literary Ladies* 115.

③ *Literary Ladies* 117, 118.

④ *Literary Ladies* 120.

⑤ *Literary Ladies* 124, 125.

⑥ *Literary Ladies* 127.

snobbish *Lady Clementina and Henry one in "his own rank in life."*[1]

The children of William and Henry inherit the moral traits of their parents. The young William seduces a pretty cottage girl, Hannah, at the family's country estate and subsequently deserts her. Hannah gives birth to William's child and is forced to abandon it, and later she becomes a prostitute in town and commits fraud. The climax arrives when William, the presiding judge at the assize, sentences his sometime beloved to death, and Hannah "with a scream exclaims—'Oh! Not from *you*!'".[2] By the end of the story, the elder William, now a bishop, is killed by a raging fever; his aristocratic wife also dies; his guilt-ridden son is divorced and suffers from sleep deprivation. By contrast both the elder Henry and the younger Henry (who marries a curate's daughter), though still poor, live happily to tell the moral of the story.

Generally speaking, the dichotomous structure is an ideal vehicle to convey morally contradictory subject matter compelling an unmistakable and uncompromising moral vision. In the above instances, however, such narrative tendency is ritualized by allowing the morally superior to always survive and live happily, though not necessarily prosperously, and the morally inferior to always live in misery or simply perish. Jane Austen's announced motifs in the title of *Sense and Sensibility* seem to promise more of the same, i.e., what the major authors of the 1790s had done with such traditional motifs as "nature and nurture," or "head and heart," using a polarized narrative structure complete with antithetical character types.

Yet a close reading of *Sense and Sensibility* reveals that Austen does not exactly follow in the footsteps of her predecessors either in form or in content; in fact she uses the convention in a selective and innovative way. Jane Austen has revamped the convention by adding to it an element of dialectics which allows the developing of a moral and philosophical complexity beneath a seemingly familiar black-and-white surface.

---

[1]   *Nature and Art* 10.
[2]   *Nature and Art* 116-17.

Whereas in earlier examples the characters were conceived and fixed in Fielding's sense in order to teach a simple moral lesson, in *Sense and Sensibility* the relationship is truly dialectical in that opposites are not immutable, and may shift in the course of the novelistic action. In other words Jane Austen's pair of heroines do not operate within a stiff antithetical structure or conform to a rigid dichotomy.

This dialectical aspect of the narrative, either implicit or explicit, informs the entire novel. The phenomenon is thought-provoking since it turns simple contrast into nice comparison. It alerts the readers to the potential complications in the relationship between "sense" and "sensibility," and, at the same time, compels them to pay special attention to the interaction not only between "sense" and "sensibility" but also within each of "sense" and "sensibility." The work is no longer a mere allegorical enactment of a routine dichotomy which serves a particular brand of ideology, relying on its sheer power of contrast for the purpose of explicit moral instruction, but a philosophical entity that offers a complex psychological process and demands scrupulous analysis and measured response. It is the aim of this chapter to investigate and report how dialectics undercuts the dichotomous structure in this deceptively conventional novel, what beneficial results the undercutting produces in deepening our understanding of the moral connotations of "sense" and "sensibility," and how Jane Austen has reformed, so to speak, the convention of dichotomy in general.

1

The first sign of dichotomous convention is of course intimated by the alliterative title; then, as if to set the scene for contrast, the narrator offers portraits of Elinor and Marianne in the opening chapter right after the preamble:

> Elinor, this eldest daughter whose advice was so effectual, possessed a strength of understanding, and coolness of judgment, which qualified her, though only nineteen, to be the counsellor of her mother, and enabled her

frequently to counteract, to the advantage of them all, that eagerness of mind in Mrs. Dashwood which must generally have led to imprudence. She had an excellent heart;—her disposition was affectionate, and her feelings were strong; but she knew how to govern them: it was a knowledge which her mother had yet to learn, and which one of her sisters had resolved never to be taught.

Marianne's abilities were, in many respects, quite equal to Elinor's. She was sensible and clever; but eager in every thing; her sorrows, her joys, could have no moderation. She was generous, amiable, interesting: she was every thing but prudent. The resemblance between her and her mother was strikingly great. (6)

There are three character profiles here, but they fall into two categories. Elinor Dashwood appears a paragon: more mature than her nineteen years both morally and intellectually. Marianne, who is sixteen as we learn in chapter 3, is, on the other hand, less able and less mature. There is some qualified praise of her at first—"in many respects, quite equal"—but that soon gives way to candid criticism—"but eager in every thing," "no moderation," "every thing but prudent." She is eventually relegated to her mother's company—"The resemblance between her and her mother was strikingly great." Both Mrs Dashwood and Marianne are stigmatized as imprudent, in both the moral and economic senses of the word.

Such exposition seems to promise a strict contrast between the camp of right and that of wrong, much like that between Elizabeth Inchbald's Henrys and Williams in *Nature and Art* or Jane West's Louisa and Marianne in *A Gossip's Story* or Julia and Caroline in Edgeworth's "Letters from Julia and Caroline." Apparently, Elinor has much to offer but little to learn; Marianne has much to learn but refuses to learn it. However, on close reading, we notice that neither of the two sisters monopolizes a set of values signifying purely either "sense" or "sensibility."[1] Marianne is after all "sensible," "generous," and "amiable," whereas Elinor has "an excellent heart:" she is not only "affectionate" but her "feelings" are "strong." The distinction is that Elinor knows how to

---

[1]　Unsigned review, *Critical Review* (Feb. 1812) n. s. 4, i, 149 – 57; quoted in Southam, vol. 1, 36.

govern her feelings, which Marianne refuses to do, and Mrs Dashwood has never learned to do. Thus by endowing her protagonists with mixed qualities, Jane Austen is able to establish the necessary conditions under which dialectics may operate in *Sense and Sensibility* as an essential narrative ingredient.

As a matter of fact the earliest reviewer of *Sense and Sensibility* recognized, with considerable perspicacity, that Miss Dashwood, though "possessing great good sense," also has "a *proper quantity of sensibility*," and that Marianne has "an equal share of the sense which renders her sister so estimable," which is however blended with "an *immoderate* degree of sensibility." Indeed the line that is drawn between "sense" and "sensibility" in the first chapter of the novel seems to have been quickly and evidently readjusted, if not redrawn, in a conversation between the two heroines a couple of chapters later. As a result, each half of the dichotomy seems to generate a new dichotomy within itself, which induces readers to reconsider the full spectrum of the meaning and implication of the terms "sense" and "sensibility."

The rigid antithetical structure begins to be undermined when Edward Ferrars becomes the object of a *tête-à-tête* between the two sisters in chapter 4, and Elinor is found to behave in much the same way as Marianne would. An observation from Marianne at the opening of that chapter about Edwards's lack of taste for drawing sparks a long and passionate torrent of apology from her elder sister:

> "No taste for drawing," replied Elinor; "why should you think so? He does not draw himself, indeed, but he has great pleasure in seeing the performances of other people, and I assure you he is by no means deficient in natural taste, though he has not had opportunities of improving it. Had he ever been in the way of learning, I think he would have drawn very well. He distrusts his own judgment in such matters so much, that he is always unwilling to give his opinion on any picture; but he has an innate propriety and simplicity of taste, which in general direct him perfectly right." (19)

Marianne's remark originates from her single-minded appreciation of all that is visible in a person such as appearance and accomplishments, but

Elinor's unanswerable reply cannot be more astounding, coming the way it does from a "counsellor" supposedly possessing "coolness of judgment." That Edward "'does not draw himself'"—which prevents him, as far as Marianne is concerned, from acquiring a real taste for drawing—is the only point Elinor reluctantly concedes in her 105-word-long defence of her particular friend; the rest is refutation. The rhetorical question "'why should you think so?'" and the conviction "'I assure you he is by no means deficient in natural taste'" and the subjunctive mood "'Had he ever been in the way of learning, I think he would have drawn very well'" and the repetition of the conjunction "'but'" which indicates an impatience to express a contrast, capped by the almost ludicrous adulation of Edward's "'innate propriety and simplicity of taste which in general direct him perfectly right,'" all portray a warmly incensed Elinor who fights tooth and nail, so to speak, in defending her man.

Elinor's heated assertion is the natural, spontaneous reaction of a young lady who is deeply, if not passionately, in love, but all that ammunition fired in defence of Edward seems to have been wasted, because it is mistargeted. Marianne's fault is her failure to observe the inner quality of people such as Edward Ferrars, who is "not handsome" and has no "peculiar graces of person or address" to recommend him (15). Elinor, if she must fight back, should have tackled the root problem that has given impetus to Marianne's comment. Instead she is seduced by Marianne's aesthetic approach and plays into the hands of her romantic sister. Elinor focuses her attention narrowly on a concrete issue, i.e., whether Edward has the artistic talent, about which she, though talented in that respect herself, obviously does not have anything concrete to say to change the fact that "'[h]e does not draw,'" except by changing the subject and talking about the man's potentialities.

Marianne at once senses that it is Elinor's "blind partiality to Edward" (19) that has caused this vigorous defence. The adjective "blind" is a strong qualifier which discloses Marianne's emotional tendency to overstate, but the stative noun of "partiality" is factual. Marianne quickly drops the subject as she is "afraid of offending" (19) her elder sister. Although Elinor is to serve as a judicious and cool-headed heroine, there is little doubt that she has a considerable capacity for emotions and is also capable of releasing those emotions in a way which is, properly speaking, characteristic of Marianne. This instance of Elinor's sensibility confirms the narrator's point that Elinor's "feelings" are every bit as "strong" (6). Nevertheless, Elinor's emotional upsurge does not and should not obscure the fact that Marianne is wrong on both counts: she has misjudged Edward as well as Elinor.

Marianne's estimation of Edward Ferrars is based on two things, one seemingly objective, the other purely subjective. Edward's plain physical appearance, his awkward shy manners and his lack of charm altogether— "He was not handsome, and his manners required intimacy to make them pleasing" (15)—fail to impress her; but, more importantly, he fails to meet her highly romantic criteria that identify "taste" with "rapturous delight" (19) or with the capacity of being ostensibly animated by Cowper (18). Edward just does not demonstrate sensibility enough to satisfy her narrowly and strictly defined taste. Plainly, Marianne does not see beyond what meets the subjective eye: she conceives one's inner worth by extrapolating one's outward form according to her stringent sentimental standards.

This is why she later falls in love, almost instantly, with Willoughby after he rescues her in dramatic fashion, and after she notices "[h]is manly beauty and more than common gracefulness" (43) and what appears to be "the perfect good-breeding of the gentleman" and "frankness and vivacity" and a passion for "music and dancing" (46). Marianne is even attracted by his "name" and the geographical location of his "residence" (43). She does not take time to become really acquainted with "the hero" who almost literally walks out of "a favourite story" of hers (43); she is simply happy that this man can provide her with "all that her fancy had delineated" (49). We are told that "long before his visit concluded, they conversed with the familiarity of a long-established acquaintance" (47). This reminds one of the "sudden intimacy" (*NA* 33) between Catherine Morland and Miss Thorpe, and of the first meeting *between Jane West's Marianne and Clermont.* [1] In all three cases the familiarity is unwarranted because it is the result of alluring manners, sentimental address and deceptive charm, made familiar by romantic reading rather than mutual understanding—in short an outcome of apprehension rather than comprehension.

By contrast, Elinor's response to Willoughby is cautious (though no less cordial); she makes inquiries: "'But who is he? ... Where does he come from?'" (44). When she notices the inordinate warmth between Willoughby and Marianne, she cautions her sister with gentle irony:

> Well, Marianne for *one* morning I think you have done pretty well. You have already ascertained Mr. Willoughby's opinion in almost every matter of importance. You know what he thinks of Cowper and Scott; you are certain of his estimating their beauties as he ought, and you have received every assurance of his admiring Pope no more than is proper. But how is your acquaintance to be long supported, under such extraordinary dispatch of every subject for discourse? You will soon have exhausted each favourite topic. Another meeting will suffice to explain his sentiments on picturesque beauty, and second marriages, and then you can have nothing farther to ask. (47)

This friendly admonition is, however, misinterpreted by the enthusiastic Marianne, who takes it as her sister's attempt to apply the conduct-book strictures to her, "an unnecessary effort" and "a disgraceful subjection of reason to common-place and mistaken notions" (53).

The two sisters' reactions to Edward and Willoughby, to their appearance and inner-quality, constitute a dialectical tableau where confronting attitudes engage and try to convince each other. There is a subdued but persistent suggestion that Marianne merely reacts to the surface whereas Elinor tries to grasp what is beneath the surface. If Edward is an ambiguous case where a less than dazzling surface hides a decent depth, Willoughby's sparkling surface is all there is. If Marianne hesitates in her overall evaluation of Edward's worth because of his ambiguity—we later learn that there is an ambiguity of a different kind

---

[1] *Gossip's Story* vol. 1, 205.

too—she embraces all that Willoughby is worth at its face value. Claudia
L. Johnson sympathizes with Marianne's position, contending: "Far
from basing her actions on impulsive, purely subjective feelings,
Marianne employs a rational argument to justify her behaviour, one that
illuminates the essential arbitrariness of established standards."① She goes
on to quote from Elizabeth Hamilton's novel, *Memoirs of Modern
Philosophers* (1800), to demonstrate how we may, through comparison,
"appreciate the sympathy Austen evinces for Marianne's position:"②

When Bridgetina's friend urges her to restrain her tender effusions
about Henry Sydney until they can discuss them in private, Bridgetina
bursts out:

> You would have me basely conceal my sentiments, in conformity to the
> pernicious maxims and practices of the world. But what so much as the dread of
> censure has cramped the energy of the female mind? . . . What are the censures of
> the world to me? . . . Do you think I have not sufficient philosophy to despise
> them?③

Mrs Hamilton, conservative and anti-jacobin as Mrs West is, though less
fervently religious than the latter, is in fact poking fun at the
Wollstonecraftian heroine, which is more or less what Austen does to
Marianne:

> "Elinor", cried Marianne, "is this fair? is this just? are my ideas so scanty?
> But I see what you mean. I have been too much at my ease, too happy, too
> frank. I have erred against every common-place notion of decorum; I have been
> open and sincere where I ought to have been reserved, spiritless, dull, and
> deceitful:—had I talked only of the weather and the roads, and had I spoken only
> once in ten minutes, this reproach would have been spared." (47 – 48)

In both cases the heroine's response to the cautionary advice is very
similar, even down to the tone of voice, and so is the satire! Therefore it
is curious to hear Johnson argue that "Austen has omitted in Marianne's
case the prohibited protofeminist emphasis, but the principled

---

① Johnson 60.

②③ Johnson 61.

determination to scorn the unworthy practices of the world stays the same."[1]

Marianne's surmise of Elinor's sentiment towards Edward is based on her mother's ill-advised prediction that "'[i]n a few months ... Elinor will in all probability be settled for life'" (17) and on Elinor's privately acknowledged favourable opinion of him. Mrs Dashwood, who cannot distinguish between "'like,'" "'love,'" and "'esteem'" (16), "evidence of moral confusion" as Norman Page points out,[2] clearly jumps to conclusions; but Elinor has taken pains to explain to Marianne why she thinks Edward is "'worthy and amiable'" (20):

> Of his sense and his goodness ... no one can, I think, be in doubt, who has seen him often enough to engage him in unreserved conversation. The excellence of his understanding and his principles can be concealed only by that shyness which too often keeps him silent. You know enough of him to do justice to his solid worth. But of his minuter propensities as you call them, you have from peculiar circumstances been kept more ignorant than myself. He and I have been at times thrown a good deal together, while you have been wholly engrossed on the most affectionate principle by my mother. I have seen a great deal of him, have studied his sentiments and heard his opinion on subjects of literature and taste; and, upon the whole, I venture to pronounce that his mind is well-informed, his enjoyment of books exceedingly great, his imagination lively, his observation just and correct, and his taste delicate and pure. His abilities in every respect improve as much upon acquaintance as his manners and person. At first sight, his address is certainly not striking; and his person can hardly be called handsome, till the expression of his eyes, which are uncommonly good, and the general sweetness of his countenance, is perceived. At present, I know him so well, that I think him really handsome; or at least, almost so. (20)

The dialectical process which Elinor goes through, testing the inside as well as assessing the outside of Edward, trying to learn as many aspects of him as is morally prudent, ensures that her character reading is as fair and objective as possible. She hopes that her younger sister will see the moral

---

① Johnson 61.
② Norman Page, *The Language of Jane Austen* (Oxford: Basil, 1972) 21.

underpinning of her approach and judgment.

However, Marianne's preoccupation with sensibility renders her incapable of truly understanding Elinor. Once she realizes that her elder sister likes Edward, of whom she herself actually has a low opinion, she switches gear. Marianne assures a surprised Elinor: "'I shall very soon think him handsome, Elinor, if I do not now. When you tell me to love him as a brother, I shall no more see imperfection in his face, than I now do in his heart'" (20 – 21). Marianne's change of mind is the result of her interaction with Elinor, but the interaction is not dialectically beneficial. She sacrifices her judgment, however partial it is, for the sake of assenting to what she perceives to be a romantic relationship involving her sister; she is being generous or selfless for the wrong reason. Elinor's assessment of Edward's handsomeness follows, as she explains, her appreciation of the man's inner worth: "'I know him so well, that I think him really handsome; or, at least, almost so.'" There is no intention whatsoever on her part to coerce Marianne into the same acknowledgement. Edward's appearance is not charming (the narrator has made this abundantly clear on several occasions), but that is beside the point. The point is that Elinor's "inside out" approach suggests that Edward's beauty is internal rather than external. Marianne, on the other hand, adopts an "outside in" approach; she has been indifferent to Edward because "'his figure is not striking'" and "'[h]is eyes want all that spirit, that fire, which at once announce virtue and intelligence'" (17). Clearly, Marianne does not intend to give up her own "principle" even as she enthusiastically but mistakenly submits herself to Elinor's assessment of Edward. Her shift of position is not a leap of faith but an act of convenience; she merely trades one form of sensibility for another.

It is this kind of intricate and intertwined dialectical engagement between the two conflicting dispositions as per "sense" and "sensibility" (not necessarily always represented by the two heroines), effectively loosening the rigid antithetical dichotomy, that proves to be most interesting and also most educational. In the next two sections I will look into the actions of the two sisters in more depth and detail in light of Jane

Austen's dialectical conception and technique.

2

As the above examples illustrate, Elinor is a character capable of showing strong emotions even though she is also capable of controlling them. To put the matter in another way, there is a conflict between "sense" and "sensibility" within the mind of this character. Each and every stage in the process of her thinking sees one tendency militating against another and each step taken constitutes a serious moral consideration. Elinor is often strapped with difficult tasks such as divining the real intent of Edward Ferrars, discovering the nature of the relationship between Marianne and Willoughby, and keeping Lucy Steele's unsolicited confidence to herself under trying circumstances. Essentially, Elinor's morality is not a given. It is not that she does not err but that she detects her errors early and corrects them, at some sacrifice, quickly. Three examples, the lock of hair at Barton, the relationship between Marianne and Willoughby, and the surprise evening call by Willoughby at Cleveland, will illustrate the point.

The scene at Barton Cottage where a plait of hair is discovered in the middle of the ring which Edward is wearing proves once more a test of Elinor's "sense" and "sensibility." Marianne, who has made the discovery, ventures to guess that the hair belongs to Edward's sister Fanny Dashwood:

> "I never saw you wear a ring before, Edward," she cried. "Is that Fanny's hair? I remember her promising to give you some. But I should have thought her hair had been darker." (98)

It is typical of impetuous Marianne to ask such forward and awkward questions, but her enquiry makes Edward doubly embarrassed since he has a secret to hide not only from Marianne but also from her elder sister— "giving a momentary glance at Elinor" (98)—who is also listening. He colours "very deeply" (98) and begins to lie (as we later learn[①]): "'Yes; it is my sister's hair. The setting always casts a different shade on it you know'" (98).

At this point, Elinor "met his eye, and looked conscious likewise" (98), as if she had understood Edward's unexplained uneasiness about the real donor of the lock of hair:

> That the hair was her own, she instantaneously felt as well satisfied as Marianne; the only difference in their conclusions was, that what Marianne considered as a free gift from her sister, Elinor was conscious must have been procured by some theft or contrivance unknown to herself. (98)

Elinor seems to have arrived at a premature conclusion, as her sister undoubtedly has, but she is hardly to blame. She does not have the necessary information to make the correct finding under the given condition; she knows that Edward has affection for her, but she does not know why he has procrastinated about his visit, nor indeed can she detect the subtext of his self-analysis: "'Shyness is only the effect of a sense of inferiority in some way or other'" (94). Similarly, none of the Dashwood women had earlier realized that Edward's "surprise and concern" (25) upon hearing that they were moving to Devonshire were sympathetic in appearance but selfish in nature. He was in fact worried about the mother-in-law of the lord of the manor, Mrs Jennings', who is related to his fiancée (115).[②]

In spite of the tricky circumstances Elinor catches herself in time and urges her mind to stay open and consider other scenarios. To be sure, her affection for Edward is a factor that tends to influence her judgement, but she exerts herself to draw the most objective conclusion that she can. It is clear to Elinor that Edward should not have taken a lock of her hair without her permission, and she is "internally resolved henceforward to

---

① On hindsight Edward's lie is quite elaborate, quite inconsistent with his well advertised ineptitude and shyness.

② Although there is no direct evidence, it is highly conceivable that Lucy, given her character, would have told Edward about such an important connection.

catch every opportunity of eyeing the hair and of satisfying herself, beyond all doubt, that it was exactly the shade of her own" (99). It is to Elinor's credit that she attaches importance to concrete evidence and refrains from speculating on plausible signs.

In the case of Marianne's relationship with Willoughby, Elinor exercises the same kind of caution and dialectical thinking. Elinor is the first and the only one who has detected that "want of caution" (49) in Willoughby, even as others are dazzled by his charm. Willoushby is able to seek "the enjoyment of undivided attention where his heart was engaged" (49) while "slighting too easily the forms of worldly propriety" (49). However, when Elinor overhears the conversation between Willoughby and Marianne about giving and accepting a horse (which Elinor later asks her sister to decline), she gathers that there is "a perfect agreement between them" (60). Further evidence of "his manner of pronouncing it" and "his addressing her sister by her christian name alone" (59 – 60). gives Elinor the notion of "their being engaged to each other" (60), which is further supported by Margaret's eye-witness report that Willoughby has cut off "'a long lock of [Marianne's] hair,'" "'kissed it, and folded it up in a piece of white paper, and put it into his pocket-book'" (60). Still, Elinor's curiosity about their need for secrecy is not satisfied; and Willoughby's abrupt departure for London without offering a plausible explanation turns her curiosity to suspicion: "'I confess ... that every circumstance except *one* is in favour of their engagement; but that *one* is the total silence of both on the subject, and with me it almost outweighs every other'" (80). Elinor, unlike her mother, focuses on the substantial evidence of engagement rather than on the circumstantial evidence of affection. She questions Willoughby's motive in not making "'a plain and open avowal of his difficulties'" (81) even though she is reluctant to embark upon raising "'objections against any one's conduct on so illiberal a foundation'" (81). This is an intricately dialectical situation where the lack of a declared engagement creates an ambiguity which can be interpreted as either strong evidence or the very lack of it. Elinor rises to the occasion by taking into account the duplicity of the evidence that she has, carefully weighing the meaning of each remark, each gesture.

Indeed Elinor is acutely aware of the danger of making hasty judgment and openly acknowledges the problem, almost as a precaution to herself, in the presence of both Edward and Marianne:

> I have frequently detected myself in such kind of mistakes ... in a total misapprehension of character in some point or other: fancying people so much more gay or grave, or ingenious or stupid than they really are, and I can hardly tell why, or in what the deception originated. Sometimes one is guided by what they say of themselves, and very frequently by what other people say of them, without giving oneself time to deliberate and judge. (93)

Elinor's self-criticism reflects her keen awareness of the difficulty in avoiding errors of judgment owing to "haste and impatience of the mind," and she tries hard not to be one of those who "see a little, presume a great deal, and so jump to the conclusion."①

Elinor's ability to study evidence and make a rational finding is once again the focus of the narrative the night Willoughby pays his surprise visit to the Palmers' house in Cleveland. The event occurs while an evening storm is raging outside and while a physically and psychologically stricken Marianne is just beginning to recover her health, and while Elinor is anxiously expecting the arrival of her mother in the company of Colonel Brandon. So the visit from the man who is responsible for the fall of Colonel Brandon's niece and Marianne's mental breakdown, is unpropitious in more senses than one. Elinor's "look of horror" (317) when encountering Willoughby in the drawing-room announces the deep gulf and the absolute antagonism between the two parties. But the meeting is soon to take a dialectical turn.

Willoughby's avowal of his sincere love for Marianne, in spite of, or rather because of, his marriage to the rich but inelegant Miss Grey, reconstitutes in a backhanded way Marianne's character. It lends support to Marianne's own claim that " 'I felt myself to be as solemnly engaged to

---

① Locke, *Conduct* 16.

him, as if the strictest legal covenant had bound us to each other'" (188) and that "'[h]e *did* feel the same'" (188). However, Willoughby's eventually declared love can justify neither Marianne's moral imprudence nor his romantic feeling. It however shows how morally weak he is, succumbing to the attraction of both beauty and money and making choices according to the dictate of his sensual but ultimately selfish inclination. In fact the very act of his declaration is contrary to moral prudence. As a newly-married man Willoughby is already betraying the marriage vow he has solemnly and recently made, as Elinor rightly and quickly reminds him (325). Consequently, the more he wishes to correct one error—professing genuine love for Marianne—the closer he is to committing another, which will be even more serious in nature. Nevertheless, the fresh information enables Elinor to regard Willoughby in a new light. She will not condone his villainous behaviour, or Marianne's imprudence for that matter, but she is beginning to understand why things happened the way they did at Barton Cottage. Willoughby is unprincipled and devious, but he is not dishonest in terms of his feelings towards Marianne. He may be more of "'a fool'" than "'a knave'" (318), but "'a cunning fool'" (321) nonetheless, who calculates himself into unhappiness and moral bankruptcy by advertising his "'honour'" without delivering his "'faith'" (321).

By questioning Willoughby closely, by listening carefully to his explanations and by observing his facial expression and body language, Elinor is able to follow the psychological swings of the greedy and dissolute young man who wants the best of both worlds. Indeed Willoughby has done some dialectical thinking himself. He started out by designing to marry a woman of fortune and therefore had no thought of "'returning'" Marianne's affection (320) even as he was trying to "'engage her regard'" (320). But the "'selfish vanity'" (320) soon gave way to genuine attachment, and he would not even give up love for money when Mrs Smith, with her financial clout, pressured him to marry Eliza (323) to avoid a scandal. But when he was "'formally dismissed from [Mrs Smith's] favour and her house,'" the prospects of poverty loomed too large for him to bear. Eventually, "'that dread of poverty'" (323) induced him to choose money over love.

Willoughby's thinking process is tempered by selfish considerations. It is true that he did not break any engagement, for he had never proposed marrying Marianne (though she imprudently writes to him, giving Elinor the impression that an engagement has been in place), as Marianne later admits in well-balanced Johnsonian style: "'It was every day implied, but never professedly declared'" (186). Nevertheless, the technicality does not excuse his rapacious dissolution and gross immorality. By doting on the girl in order to gratify his pleasure of the moment and by abandoning her when she is unable to satisfy his greed for money, he has demonstrated a juggling of "sense" and "sensibility" in their lowest and most despicable form.

The revelation of Willoughby's negatively dialectical calculation allows Elinor to judge the messy relationship between Marianne and Willoughby more objectively. Willoughby's apology for his partial responsibility in the sordid affair with Eliza, whom he had impregnated and subsequently deserted, citing "'the violence of her passions, the weakness of her understanding'" (322), may have caused Elinor to imagine what Lucy Steele might have done with young Edward. Willoughby's grumbling about the unfairness of the argument that "'because she was injured she was irreproachable, and because *I* was a libertine, *she* must be a saint'" (322) may well remind the readers of a parallel in reverse in Edward's imprudent engagement with Lucy Steele, who has since demonstrated her inferior character.

By arguing his case in person, by showing his "open, affectionate, and lively manner" (333), and by asserting his "still ardent love for Marianne" (333), Willoughby almost achieves the purpose of making his listener, Elinor, consider "circumstances which ought not in reason to have weight" (333). Her heart is "softened" (321) and "softened again" (325), she cannot help "pitying" (325) him, and her "voice, in spite of herself, betrayed her compassionate emotion" (329). Eventually, Elinor allows herself to call him "'poor Willoughby'" (334), as her mother did, naïvely, earlier (78). It is to Elinor's credit that she is now able to appreciate how Marianne's romantic entanglement with Willoughby could have happened so imprudently fast. She has experienced first-hand how her own moral views have been influenced—modified though not altered—by Willoughby's impressive talk within "only half an hour" (333). Such direct and frank moral engagement affords the thinking heroine a precious opportunity to receive and digest new information and consequently to make a more objective and balanced character judgement.

Elinor's sympathy for Willoughby is not a form of moral capitulation. On the contrary, it is a sign of the improvement of her moral and philosophical understanding. Elinor sees the harm which "too early an independence and its consequent habits of idleness, dissipation, and luxury, had made in the mind, the character, the happiness, of a man who, to every advantage of person and talents, united a disposition naturally open and honest, and a feeling, affectionate temper" (331). At the same time she sees that "[e]xtravagance and vanity had made him cold-hearted and selfish. Vanity, while seeking its own guilty triumph at the expense of another, had involved him in a real attachment, which extravagance, or at least its offspring, necessity, had required to be sacrificed" (331). The emotional power which Willoughby has unleashed remains potent even "after the sound of his carriage had died away" (333). Yet Elinor stays morally focused and reminds herself that Willoughby's "open, affectionate, and lively manner" constitutes "no merit," that his "still ardent love for Marianne" is "not even innocent" (333). Therefore, the moral gulf that has existed between Willoughby and Elinor before the interview takes place is not bridged, but a better understanding of his wicked act and weak mind has been achieved, which has brought her closer, as a fellow human being, to the fallen man even as they have parted "for ever" (333). Elinor's "pang for Willoughby" (339) after their parting indicates the extent of her balanced view, which offers a contrast to Mrs Dashwood's about-face once her imagined "son-in-law" is exposed.

These instances of Elinor's dialectical handling of "sense" and "sensibility" indicate clearly that even for the rationally-minded heroine correct responses to real-life situations, especially those that touch one's own heart-strings, do not come effortlessly. Sometimes even as people try hard not to be emotional and not, as Locke says, to "put passion in the place of reason,"[1] it is all they can do to control their emotions and suppress their irrational urges.

3

In the case of Marianne such emotions and urges are nearly uncontrollable. Marianne judges others by her subjective and arbitrary criteria, which are essentially whatever she likes and dislikes. Her highly subjective approach to reality even extends to natural elements. She will declare that "the day would be lastingly fair" (41) even when "threatening" (41) clouds are clearly seen hovering over the hills at Barton.[2] She loves Willoughby because his interest in every point— especially "dancing and music" (47)—coincides with hers and because he shares "all her enthusiasm" and because "the same books, the same passages" charm them both (47). In contrast, those who do not succumb to Marianne's romantic and sentimental notions fall victims to her excessive sensibility. Edward would not suit her, not because he does not have enough virtues but because he is sedate and reads Cowper's "'beautiful lines'" with "'so little sensibility'" (18)—the same lines that "'have frequently almost driven [her] wild'" (18). Mrs Jennings "common-place raillery" (34) disqualifies her as a friend; Colonel Brandon's "silent and grave" (34) manner and his "old" age (34) put him beyond the pale of Marianne's matrimonial consideration—"'thirty-five

---

①   Locke, *Conduct* 3.

②   Both Marianne and her like-minded younger sister, Margaret, choose to pursue "the partial sunshine" (41) and ignore the "threatening cloud" (41); both prove their recklessness by taking a dangerous shortcut, "running with all possible speed down the steep side of the hill" (41) after they have been caught in the rain. It is interesting that Willoughby has also ignored the possibility of bad weather and come out hunting.

has nothing to do with matrimony'" (37). [1] Locke advises that anyone who seeks truth "suffers not his assent to go faster than his evidence, nor beyond it;"[2] Hume echoes the same point by saying that "[a] wise man, therefore, proportions his belief to the evidence."[3] But Marianne's wilfully subjective mind does not follow such basic epistemological rules. The mere mention of "'flannel waistcoats'" (38) induces in her thoughts of "'rheumatism'" (37), which in turn prompt her to infer that Colonel Brandon must be a case of "'infirmity'" (37).

Marianne's general imprudence in the company of Willoughby is exemplified in her visiting Allenham while its mistress, Mrs Smith, is not on the premises (67) and her accepting a horse from him (58) without considering the financial burden it would add to the Dashwood household. What strikes us, however, is the way Marianne rationalizes her indulgence in sensuous delight as a moral act adhering to the supreme principle of nature, or the way she makes sensibility the ultimate measure of propriety, even of morality. Countering Elinor's argument that "'the pleasantness of an employment does not always evince its propriety'" (68), Marianne asserts:

> On the contrary, nothing can be a stronger proof of it, Elinor; for if there had been any real impropriety in what I did, I should have been sensible of it at the time, for we always know when we are acting wrong, and with such a conviction I could have had no pleasure. (68)

Marianne's sentimental assertion of the infallibility of the individual feeling, accompanied by her corollary rejection of external standards of conduct and good behaviour, is a kind of secular imitation of a type of seventeenth-century "enthusiasm." To be more exact, her argument for

---

[1] Marianne also asserts that "'[a] woman of seven and twenty ... can never hope to feel or inspire affection again'" (38). Anne Elliot, as we know, both feels and inspires affection after she has turned twenty-seven.

[2] Locke, *Conduct* 34.

[3] David Hume, *An Inquiry Concerning Human Understanding* in *Enquiries Concerning the Human Understanding and Concerning the Principles of Morals*, ed. L. A. Selby-Bigge, 2nd ed. (Oxford: Clarendon, 1902; rpt. 1927) 106.

the authority of the heart is a variation of what the Cambridge Platonists urged, about one and a half centuries earlier, who dissented from the orthodox notion that man, who was born in original sin, must suppress his evil nature in this life in order to preserve the purity of his soul for the next. ① But, more probably, it is an echo of the very popular Shaftesburian philosophy in the first half of the eighteenth century. Walter Francis Wright thinks that Shaftesbury and Richardson are chiefly responsible for the spread of the ideal of sensibility in England. ② Shaftesbury in his often printed and widely read *Characteristics of Men, Manners, Opinions, Times, etc.* (1711) stipulates:

> [T]he sum of philosophy is, to learn what is just in society and beautiful in Nature and the order of the world. 'Tis not wit merely, but a temper which must form the well-bred man. In the same manner, 'tis not a head merely, but a heart and resolution which must complete the real philosopher. ③

The problem with this brand of philosophy is that it confidently puts nature before society and feeling before thinking, so that man, the social animal, must seek inspiration from woods, field, and river by yielding to every stimulus they provide. As a result, it blurs, even blocks, the moral perspective, reducing it to emotional impulses and individual satisfaction. Common sense has it that individual happiness and societal good are two sides of the same coin; therefore a balance must be struck betwixt them. In the middle of 1790s in England such balance seems

---

① The group of philosophers, consisting of Ralph Cudworth, Henry More, John Smith and Nathanael Culverwell, advocated the goodness of human nature: since man was made in the image of God he must have retained something of that image. Therefore man's nature was not, as the Calvinistic doctrine would have it, totally depraved. Henry More in *Enchiridion Ethicum* (1656) wrote: "[T]o attain this perfection in virtue is to attain the most perfect happiness that man's nature is capable of" ([New York: Facsimile Text Society, 1930] 242).

② See *Sensibility in English Prose Fiction 1760 –1814: A Reinterpretation* (Urbana: U of Illinois P, 1937) 14 – 15. Alistair M. Duckworth similarly observes that the "philosophy of sentiment ... was generally considered to have begun in the *Characteristics of Men, Manners, Opinions, Times* (1711) of the third Earl of Shaftesbury" (106).

③ Anthony Earl of Shaftesbury, *Characteristics of Men, Manners, Opinions, Times, etc.* (Gloucester, Mass.: Peter Smith, 1963) vol. 2, 255.

particularly necessary. ① The urge of individualism in some Jacobin novels reflects, apparently, a political continuation of the same philosophical trend. In Marianne's case the loss of balance has definitely led to a loss of moral focus; she is, by all counts, at the mercy of erratic emotional swings.

There seems to be a general pattern in the behaviour of the heroines believing in the superiority of nature and heart in many novels of the time: a sudden loss of spirit usually occurs in the wake of a spurt of emotional exuberance. The same pattern manifests itself in *Sense and Sensibility*. After Willoughby leaves Marianne in the lurch at Barton (in the middle of their reading *Hamlet* together [85]), the latter is launched into a trance-like melancholy. "Marianne's *mind* could not be controuled" (85), and she begins to hallucinate about reality. When a gentleman is spotted riding towards the Dashwood sisters as they walk near Barton, Marianne madly clings to her intuition that it is Willoughby coming back to fetch her: "'It is he; it is indeed;—I know it is! ... I knew how soon he would come'" (86). But the rider turns out to be Edward. Later, in London, having sent a note to Willoughby, Marianne begins to expect every knock on the door to be the signal of the arrival of Willoughby. When a loud, long-expected rap is finally heard, Marianne cries out rapturously: "'Oh! Elinor, it is Willoughby, indeed it is!'" (161); only this time it turns out to be Colonel Brandon. Giving free rein to her emotion and fancy has fatally affected Marianne's ability to think and distinguish.

Marianne's subjective thinking is at odds with Elinor's dialectical thinking. The clash between the two philosophical tendencies inevitably results in frequent misunderstandings between the two sisters. Two episodes—one in chapter 17 of volume 1 (briefly touched upon earlier), the other in chapter 13 of volume 2—give us insights into the nature of

---

① Jane West's narrator, Mrs Prudentia Homespun, attacks the "Parisian enthusiasts" as one of the sources of "the wiles of systematic depravity" (*A Tale of the Times*, 2nd ed., 3 vols. [London, 1799] vol. 1, 5, 6).

their ideological differences as reflected in their cross-purpose conversations. In the first instance, as we recall, Elinor mentions her occasional inability to read people's character correctly and she wonders where things could have gone wrong: "'Sometimes one is guided by what they say of themselves, and very frequently by what other people say of them, without giving oneself time to deliberate and judge'" (93). At this point comes Marianne's sarcastic rejoinder:

> But I thought it was right, Elinor ... to be guided wholly by the opinion of other people. I thought our judgements were given us merely to be subservient to those of our neighbours. This has always been your doctrine, I am sure. (93 – 94)

Marianne's attitude shows clearly that her morality is personal and not principled. It also reveals her grossly impercipient understanding of Elinor's moral and philosophical position; her parodic view of it shows her mistaking it for a mere accumulation of surfaces rather than an indication of significant depth. Thus in a different way she manifests the same persistent desire to act according to her own sensibility.

Marianne is apparently protesting against Elinor's moral exhortation to her in general and her recent criticism of her unfair judgment of the Middletons (88) in particular. However, she fails to see that her excessively sentimental conduct is at fault, and that the root problem is her idealistic individualism. Willingness to consider alternative views and opinions is a sign of maturity and dialectical thinking; it prevents one from becoming self-centred and opinionated. But the central purpose of Elinor's suggestion is to help Marianne open her mind to a point of view which privileges depth and conscience over surface and sentimentality, instead of stubbornly clinging to the idealistic notion of following one's own natural judgement and acting on the recommendation of one's heart. It is not that Marianne is unable to be polite and respectful, but that she thinks it is wrong not to speak and act instinctively and wilfully.

Elinor quickly realizes that Marianne is confused about the difference between keeping an open mind so that one can think dialectically in order to draw the most objective conclusion under any given circumstances, and surrendering one's judgment and desisting from using one's faculty of thinking; so she admonishes her:

> No, Marianne, never. My doctrine has never aimed at the subjection of the understanding. All I have ever attempted to influence has been the behaviour. You must not confound my meaning. I am guilty, I confess, of having often wished you to treat our acquaintance in general with greater attention; but when have I advised you to adopt their sentiments or conform to their judgment in serious matters? (94).

Elinor's admonition is reasonable, serious and forthright, but Marianne's mind seems closed.

Evidence of that closed mind presents itself in the London scene where Lucy will not leave before Edward is gone. When the two are eventually both gone, Marianne exclaims: "'Could she not see that we wanted her gone!—how teazing to Edward!'" (244). Elinor, who knows by this time why Lucy chooses to tarry, offers the most rational, generous, and appropriate explanation that she is able to think of under the circumstances:

> Why so? —we were all his friends, and Lucy has been the longest known to him of any. It is but natural that he should like to see her as well as ourselves. (244)

Marianne, whose narrow belief in romantic sensibility causes her to mistake mutual affection for grounds of exclusion, cannot perceive the plain truth in Elinor's remarks. She is mistakenly annoyed by what she perceives as Elinor's romantic gamesmanship. She looks at Elinor "steadily" (244) and reproves her sister:

> You know, Elinor, that this is a kind of talking which I cannot bear. If you only hope to have your assertion contradicted, as I must suppose to be the case, you ought to recollect that I am the last person in the world to do it. I cannot descend to be tricked out of assurances, that are not really wanted. (244)

Marianne's accusation is groundless. Elinor does not need any of her "'assurances'" about Edward's preference for her, and this not just because she knows Edward's plight or Lucy's motive in outstaying

Edward. Marianne's insensitive sensibility proves to be painfully frustrating to Elinor as well as to her true friends, such as Colonel Brandon and Mrs Jennings.

4

That "sensibility" is meant to be a foil to "sense" is plain; however, a careful reading of the novel reveals that the narrative does not always bear it out that way. "Sensibility" itself has a duality that must be recognized. In point of fact the lexical definition of the word "sensibility," even in its eighteenth-century sense,[1] does not indicate that it has an exclusively pejorative meaning. Interestingly enough, the eighth definition of "sense" in the *OED* (marked obsolete, however), which can be traced to the fourth definition of the word in Johnson's *Dictionary*, is "sensibility."[2] In this novel "sensibility," while being examined as an imprudent, selfish, even intrinsically immoral human attribute, likewise retains at least a tinge of its positive purport. Jane Austen seems to suggest that certain sets of circumstances in human life warrant the exercise of well-measured sensibility. There are times in *Sense and Sensibility* when "sensibility" is not just about lachrymation and sentimentality but also about sympathy, honesty, and morality. The concept is not original. As a matter of fact Maria Edgeworth's Caroline

---

[1] The *OED* offers two definitions of "sensibility" relevant to the period under discussion, with illustrations from, among others, Cowper, Sterne, Johnson, Godwin, Byron and Austen:

> 5. a. Quickness and acuteness of apprehension or feeling; the quality of being easily and strongly affected by emotional influences; sensitiveness. Also, with const., sensitiveness *to*, keen sense *of* something.

> 6. In the 18th and early 19th c. (afterwards somewhat *rarely*): Capacity for refined emotion; delicate sensitiveness of taste; also, readiness to feel compassion for suffering, and to be moved by the pathetic in literature or art.

(*The Oxford English Dictionary*, prep. J. A. Simpson and E. S. C. Weiner, 2nd ed. 20 vols. [Oxford: Clarendon, 1989] vol. 14, 982).

[2] See *OED*, vol. 14, 978; for comparison, see Samuel Johnson's *A Dictionary of the English Language* (London, 1755) vol. 2. See also Chapman's discussion of the word "sensible" in "Miss Austen's English," *SS*, 413.

has come very close to defining it dialectically for Julia in "Letters of Julia and Caroline:"

> I, Julia, admire and feel enthusiasm; but I would have philosophy directed to the highest objects. I dread apathy, as much as you can; and I would endeavour to prevent it, not by sacrificing half my existence, but by enjoying the whole with moderation.
>
> You ask why exercise does not increase sensibility, and why sympathy with imaginary distress will not also increase the disposition to sympathize with what is real? —Because pity should, I think, always be associated with the active desire to relieve. If it be suffered to become a *passive sensation*, it is a *useless weakness*, not a virtue. ①

Caroline emphasizes the duality of "sensibility:" a good thing if it serves a positive purpose, and bad if it is " *passive*," i. e., indulged merely gratuitously. An individual who can exercise sensibility properly will not be in the wrong. In *Sense and Sensibility* Jane Austen seems to echo this point as she tries to keep that positive aspect of Marianne's sensibility in full view of the readers. ②

On several occasions Marianne has indeed exercised her sensibility to moral advantage, if against the rules governing propriety. For example, when Edward Ferrars at last comes to Barton Cottage for a visit, he babbles self-consciously about his shyness: " 'If I could persuade myself that my manners were perfectly easy and graceful, I should not be shy'" (94). Marianne, who does not know (nor does Elinor or the reader) that Edward is secretly engaged to Lucy Steele, offers him a pointed rejoinder: " 'But you would still be reserved ... and that is worse'" (94). When Edward, staring at her, retorts: " 'Reserved! Am I reserved, Marianne?'" (94), Marianne emphatically replies: " 'Yes, very'" (94). Marianne is not going to mince her words about what seems to her to be Edward's unnatural coolness towards Elinor, whom he has indeed come to know so well that there is little excuse but plenty of irony to his

---

①   *Literary Ladies* 133 – 134.

②   Tave comments judiciously on Marianne's sensibility in the first half of his chapter on *Sense* and *Sensibility* (74 – 96).

pathetic self-pitying: "'I am so little at my ease among strangers of gentility'" (94). [1]

Again, it is typical of Marianne, who is guided by her sensibility, to be inordinately straightforward, to the point of being rude, even though Edward, as her sister-in-law's brother, is no stranger. But Edward's feeble defensive sparring: "'I do not understand you. Reserved! —how, in what manner? What am I to tell you? What can you suppose?'" (94 - 95) does not help to clear up the issue. Unbeknownst to all present except himself, Edward has formed a secret engagement with the ill-educated Lucy Steele, [2] though he realizes that Elinor is superior both morally and intellectually, if not also physically. [3] He is having a hard time reproaching himself and trying to walk a fine line. Therefore he cannot help "colouring" (94), nor can he help becoming grave and thoughtful. In fact we are told that his "gravity and thoughtfulness returned on him in their fullest extent—and he sat for some time silent and dull" (95).

Obviously, neither Marianne nor Elinor can tell correctly at this juncture what Edward really means by turning red-faced and "silent and dull" at Marianne's verbal assault. However, there is no doubt that Jane Austen intends the readers to review this brilliant act of double, nay, triple irony once they have read the novel. Marianne's outburst of sensibility is in part intended to clarify rather than smooth over the issue that puzzles her, and in that sense she is not entirely at fault. If she is emotionally charged, that part of sensibility should be dealt with; but it is not her fault that she is speaking truer than she knows, whereas

---

[1]   However, from Edward's point of view, there may be some truth to the statement. Edward has lived in a middle class family and then at Oxford; therefore he has had little contact with ladies of "gentility" as is assumed the norm in *Sense and Sensibility*.

[2]   Lucy's grammatical errors in writing as well as speech suggest her intellectual and moral inferiority.

[3]   We may compare the narrator's description of Elinor: "Miss Dashwood had a delicate complexion, regular features, and a remarkably pretty figure" (46) with that of Lucy Steele: "[h]er features were pretty, and she had a sharp quick eye, and a smartness of air, which though it did not give actual elegance or grace, gave distinction to her person" (120).

Edward knows more than he speaks.

Similarly, and perhaps more clearly in her favour as well, Marianne pursues Willoughby in London, which results in a surprising showdown. She wants the man to make a clean breast of the state of affairs between them. As a result of her effort, she has the satisfaction of discovering the true character of the personable Willoughby, whom she has fantasized as a sentimental knight but who actually turns out to be a practical knave. Marianne's bold act contributes in a large measure to the exposure of the profligate, greedy and selfish villain not only among her family circle but also, thanks to the garrulous but principled Mrs Jennings, among the London social circle. The way Marianne relentlessly executes her wishes may seem, in fact it is, scandalous—losing her composure in the middle of an evening party against Elinor's repeated exhortation: " 'Pray, pray be composed' " (176)—but it is also the expression of sensibility at its moral best. Ironically, the action brings the moral issue to the fore even though Marianne's intention is to pursue the sentimental dream. In a way it is poetic justice for both Willoughby and Marianne.

However, there is no mistaking, at least to the readers if not to the bystanders at the evening party, who is the more reprehensible. The real scandalous act has been committed by Willoughby, who by this time has demonstrated his lack of integrity, to say the least, by fostering a romantic relationship with an ardent and ingenuous young lady, and then reneging on his commitment.

One last example of the worthy aspect of Marianne's "sensibility" occurs in John and Fanny Dashwoods' London house on Harley Street, where the heroine bursts out indignantly, in defiance of social etiquette, against the moral impropriety of Fanny Dashwood and Mrs Ferrars. If Mrs Ferrars is, as Butler puts it, "the false idol compounded of materialism, status-seeking and self-interest,"[1] then Marianne, rather

---

[1]   Butler 193.

than Edward,[1] in challenging all that is base and insidious, is the Christian moralist who sees evil and calls it evil. At the dinner party Elinor is "pointedly slighted" (233) by both Mrs Ferrars and her daughter Fanny, who take her as the ambitious girl who shamelessly seeks to marry into the rich Ferrars family. When the "very pretty pair of screens" (234), generally admired by the dinner guests, meets the misfortune of being snubbed, as it were, by Mrs Ferrars, upon the insidious prompting of her daughter—"that they were done by Miss Dashwood" (235) and then "'something in Miss Morton's style'" (235)—for whom these screens had been painted in the first place, Marianne's sense of moral decency is outraged. Although Elinor has carefully kept a smile on her face (232, 233) because she does not want to show any sign of pain to Lucy, who is also present, she is nonetheless silently but "thoroughly despising" (233) the mean-spirited Mrs Ferrars and Fanny Dashwood, who are determined to distinguish "particularly" (232) the fawning Lucy Steele at the expense of her. Marianne, unaware of Elinor's predicament and of "what was principally meant" (235) by Mrs Ferrars's "ill-timed praise of another" (235), but conscious of the unfair inconsistency nonetheless, boldly acts out Elinor's well-disguised moral indignation. She snatches the screens out of her sister-in-law's hands and rightly takes both Mrs Ferrars and Fanny to task:

> This is admiration of a very particular kind! —what is Miss Morton to us? —who knows, or who cares, for her? —it is Elinor of whom *we* think and speak. (235)

In this incident Marianne shows the purity of her "sensibility;" she has quite naturally sensed the injustice being done to Elinor and does not hesitate to express her sentiment. She is on the whole beyond reproach here because her sensibility is not self-centred, nor is it self-indulgent—it is provoked by prejudice and insidiousness. It is for a just cause and is justly recognized as such by Colonel Brandon, who endorses it with the

---

[1] Butler thinks that the "enduring qualities of his mind and spirit, his 'sense' and 'goodness'" make him "the Christian" figure in the novel (186).

expression of his "eyes" (236). The narrator's scrupulously precise description of the dramatic tableau illuminates once again the dialectical nature of her discerning narrative:

> Fanny looked very angry too, and her husband was all in a fright at his sister's audacity. Elinor was much more hurt by Marianne's warmth, than she had been by what produced it; but Colonel Brandon's eyes, as they were fixed on Marianne, declared that he noticed only what was amiable in it, the affectionate heart which could not bear to see a sister slighted in the smallest point. (236)

There are four types of well differentiated reactions here. Fanny's anger and John's fear are in character and therefore more or less taken for granted. Elinor's complex internal turmoil should be well understood. She distinguishes her sister's behaviour, which is socially unacceptable on such an occasion, from her understanding, with which she must be in sympathy—as she has been truly hurt, though not wounded, by the calculated slight. Nevertheless, Elinor does not condone Marianne's imprudence, which hurts "much more" because of the jeopardy to which Marianne has subjected her; Elinor alone is aware of the precariously complicated situation and the potentially dire consequences, what with Lucy's presence and her secret, which Elinor has promised to keep, and the delicate relationship between her and the John Dashwoods and Mrs Ferrars.

But it is the Colonel's action that is most interesting. Brandon has been hopelessly in love with Marianne for some time and the recent dissolution of the affair between Willoughby and Marianne has given him renewed hope. In fact he has received encouragement in the form of Marianne's "pitying eye" and "the gentleness of her voice" (216) when he lately shares his "past sorrows and present humiliations" (216) with her and her sister. It is only too natural that his eyes are, and in all likelihood have been, "fixed" (236) on the girl whom he perseveres in cherishing and loving. Although he is equally conscious of the inappropriateness of Marianne's outburst, as a lover he is more than ready to overlook or forgive the imprudent part of the behaviour and think "only" of the moral value of Marianne's sensibility. At the same time he must have recognized that her indignant outburst has been touched off by a slight "in the smallest point" (236).

Marianne's sharp tongue draws out Mrs Ferrars's "bitter phillippic"—"'Miss Morton is Lord Morton's daughter'" (236), which diminishes the class-conscious patriarch into an object of irony, sarcasm, and amusement. In short, the kind of sensibility which Marianne has displayed on the above occasions should be distinguished from that indulged in over the "'dead leaves'" (87) at "'dear, dear Norland'" (87) or in "seeking increase of wretchedness in every reflection that could afford it" (7) when she loses a father or a lover, or on other occasions discussed elsewhere in this chapter. The point is that Marianne's "sensibility" should not be censured indiscriminately; instead, its positive and negative ingredients should be separated and weighed on the strength of their intrinsic merit.

5

In *Sense and Sensibility* dialectics, as a technique, is not confined to the depiction of the two heroines; it is employed in the portrayal of characters and actions of secondary characters as well, not only positive but also negative ones. The dialectical treatment of the dubious characters, especially of their thinking process, prevents them from dwindling into two-dimensional puppets with nothing but evil to show. Nevertheless, this does not mean that they will appear less evil and less vicious than they actually are; on the contrary, their evils will be more palpably felt because the readers are able to see in what a calculating manner those evils are committed.

We have already seen the brief example of John Willoughby's deliberation about the question of to be or not to be Marianne's fiancé, but there is a more striking and more extended example involving the John Dashwoods, which is of greater significance as it is conspicuously placed right after the opening chapter of the novel. Jane Austen here presents us with a dialectical deliberation between John Dashwood and his wife Fanny Dashwood over the issue of financial assistance to their relations which takes up almost the entire second chapter. During their discussion we experience a dialectical reversal of John Dashwood's position as it is gradually but inexorably subsumed by that of his wife. Both demonstrate a good deal of sense and sensibility as they rationalize their despicable act of abandoning their financial responsibilities for the Dashwood women. ①

The discussion begins with two contrasting views held respectively by John Dashwood who is determined, at least seemingly so, to fulfil his solemn promise to his dying father, Henry Dashwood, to " 'assist his widow and daughters' " (9) by giving the Misses Dashwood "a thousand pounds a-piece" (5), and Fanny Dashwood who "did not at all approve of what her husband intended to do" (8). Fanny's rhetoric in response is conveyed in indirect, or reported, speech, whose grammatical function is to distance the speaker from what is spoken. But the contrast she makes between "their poor little Harry" and those who are related to her husband "only by half blood" (8), the hyperbolical image she creates— "impoverishing him to the most dreadful degree" (8)—and the pointed rhetorical questions in indirect speech: "How could he answer it to himself to rob his child, and his only child too, of so large a sum?... And why was he to ruin himself, and their poor little Harry, by giving

---

① This domestic consultation scene echoes, as I have earlier mentioned, the scene in *King Lear* where Lear is methodically stripped of his privileges by his two elder daughters, but it also echoes that in *Nature and Art* by Elizabeth Inchbald, where the affluent yet imprudent Lord and Lady Bendham give their opinions about the "needless" poor:

The wages of a labouring man with a wife and half a dozen small children Lady Bendham thought quite sufficient, if they would only learn a little oeconomy. You know, my lord, those people never want to dress—shoes and stockings, a coat and a waistcoat, a gown and a cap, a petticoat and a handkerchief, are all they want—fire, to be sure, in winter—then all the rest is merely for provision. "

... [Lord Bendham] "you must add to the receipts of the poor my gift at Christmas— Last year, during the frost, no less than a hundred pounds. " (43)

away all his money to his half sisters?" (8) make her argument sound
much more forceful and direct than the tepid linguistic medium which carries
it.

Fanny's indirect speech is immediately followed by her husband's
direct speech, but there is really nothing direct about it. Instead of
remembering that "he promised to do every thing in his power to make
them comfortable" (5), John Dashwood recalls: "'It was my father's last
request to me that I should assist his widow and daughters'" (9). The
shift of focus is unobtrusive but disconcerting: it shifts the active duty of
a living man to the responsibility of a dead man and transforms the close
mother-and-sister relationship to that of remote relatives. His direct
speech distances the matter from him, it conceals his acknowledged
obligation, and it relieves him of the duty to honour his own pledge. In
fact John Dashwood limits his role to the minimum by creating the
impression that he was going through the motions of passively complying
with a dying man's wish: "'[A]s he required the promise, I could not do
less than give it'" (9). His direct speech has in effect been transformed
and eventually consumed by his wife's indirect speech that precedes it.

As the discussion between the couple goes on, it begins to take
another dialectical turn when a twist of logic yields the notion that more
means less, and less more. John Dashwood supposes that "'it would be
better for all parties if the sum were diminished one half. —Five hundred
pounds would be a prodigious increase to their fortunes!'" (9). While
making up his mind to reduce the level of assistance, Mr Dashwood
shamelessly pronounces that "'[o]ne had rather, on such occasions, do
too much than too little'" (9-10). Fanny quickly echoes by eulogizing
her husband's meanness as demonstrating "'such a generous spirit!'"
(9). Further reduction from five hundred to "'[a] hundred a year'"
while the mother lives (10), and then down to "'[a] present of fifty
pounds, now and then'" (11), and from that to "'sending them presents
of fish and game'" (12) is likewise perceived as a painful process of
sinking their own fortune, making Mrs Dashwood and her three

daughters, with their £ 500 a year,[1] "'much more able to give [them] something'" (12), who have at least 5000 a year.[2] At the end of the discussion the two initially diverging opinions have merged into one: John Dashwood " finally resolved, that it would be absolutely unnecessary, if not highly indecorous, to do more for the widow and children of his father, than such kind of neighbourly acts as his own wife pointed out" (13).

This rather civil, deliberate and amusing dialogue between the Dashwood couple exudes every intention of brutally expropriating financial comfort to which the Dashwood women are entitled by virtue of their situation and John Dashwood's death-bed pledge. The brilliant use of dialectical procedure here is much like that used in John Willoughby's deliberation about how best he can advance his own interests while ignoring and damaging those of others. Jane Austen uses the neutral method of dialectics to highlight the inner workings of the mind of those very human characters who follow merely their selfish impulses and whose actions are directed solely by pecuniary considerations. They engage in what Aristotle terms "sophistical refutations," which display "the semblance of wisdom without the reality,"[3] and "deduce or appear to deduce to a conclusion from premises that appear to be reputable but are not so."[4]

---

[1]   In chapter 1 of volume 1, the narrator informs us that at the death of Henry Dashwood "ten thousand pounds, including the late legacies, was all that remained for his widow and daughters" (4). In chapter 6 of the same volume, the narrator mentions the "income of five hundred a-year" (29)—five per cent interest on £10,000—in relating Mrs Dashwood's ambition to renovate Barton cottage in the coming spring.

[2]   This is a most conservative estimate; John Dashwood had "four thousand a-year" from his estate, in addition to the inherited fortune of his mother, "which had been large," and his wife's fortune which was £10,000 (374).

[3]   *Sophistical Refutations*, vol. 1, 164a20, 165a21 – 2.

[4]   *Sophistical Refutations* 165b8 – 9.

6

In summary, *Sense and Sensibility* is permeated with dialectical elements. The novel begins with all the indications of a conventional story, only to be told in an unconventional way, largely due to the dialectical interest which the narrative generates. Although Elinor is set up as the representative of the traditional moral values in contrast to the sentimental and enthusiastic ideal embodied by Marianne, the working out of the dichotomy has yielded something more complicated. Alistair Duckworth justly comments that "[b]y choosing sense as her point of view over sensibility, Jane Austen has made a statement about the priority of discipline to freedom, and of social principles to individual propensities."①"[P]riority" is definitely the right word, because it is clear that Jane Austen does not denounce "sensibility" as something that has no intrinsic value, nor does she deny that it has no place in human life. In fact she seems to intend a degree of transmutation of the two diverging qualities. "Sensibility," like "sense," has an important role to play in one's life, but consideration must first be given to time, place, degree and, above all, purpose. Jane Austen's ideological outlook in this respect seems close to that of Maria Edgeworth, but her literary expression of the ideology, while treating similar subject matter, is rich and subtle. The complexity of Jane Austen's fictional world matches that of the real world, which means that the dichotomy of "sense" and "sensibility" will not be an adequate literary form for the complex human matter.

Not only is there a dialectical interaction between "sense" and "sensibility" which modifies the meaning of both, but there is a whole range of other social and moral significations associated with the two words. For example, to Elinor's surprise, John Dashwood describes Mrs

---

① Duckworth 113.

Ferrars as "'one of the most of affectionate mothers in the world'" (296), despite her rather high-handed treatment of Edward. On the other hand, Mr John Dashwood, who identifies "sense" with financial gain, fails to grasp the motive behind Colonel Brandon's generosity of presenting the rather decent Delaford living to Edward: "'Really! — Well, this is very astonishing! —no relationship! —no connection between them! —and now that livings fetch such a price! ... a man of Colonel Brandon's sense!'" (294 – 295). As Myra Stokes has rightly stated: "sense" is indeed "an elastic word."①

It is apparent that "sense" and "sensibility" in Austen's narrative are complementary human qualities that co-exist in the same social system. As value signifiers, "sense" and "sensibility" have managed to acquire, to a substantial extent, open identities at the hand of Jane Austen, resembling the Blakean use of such words as "innocence" and "experience." They are faculties of human beings to be used or abused.

Jane Austen's first published novel is an admirable example of incorporating traditional motifs creatively into a fresh mode of dialectical narrative,② in order to reflect her own moral experience of changing realities. Despite some awkwardness in the novel, the complexity of reality is truthfully represented by an equally complex mimesis with dialectics as a chief component. *Sense and Sensibility* bespeaks a marked difference of Jane Austen's work from those of her predecessors. The innovative spirit, already germinating in *Northanger Abbey*, gains confidence here in *Sense and Sensibility* as it successfully escapes what A. Walton Litz dubs the "tyranny of antithesis."③ The narrative complexity, where dialectics militates against dichotomy, compels the readers to take a

---

① *The Language of Jane Austen: A Study of Some Aspects of Her Vocabulary* (Houndmills: Macmillan, 1991) 128.

② Litz describes the novel as one of "the transitional works of a great artist;" but an unsuccessful one in that it shows Austen's "inability to transform the conventions inherited from other writers and embodied in the novel's original versions" (74, 81).

③ Litz 76.

hard and careful look at the meaning of the two nominal attributes as they are dialectically presented. The novel proves more complicated and suggestive than its deceptively conventional title and opening seem to pronounce. Jane Austen's dialectical approach cuts across the boundary between "sense" and "sensibility," resulting in the two sisters' sharing, albeit to different degrees, in both "sense" and "sensibility." Such treatment breaks down the barriers between the two seemingly irreconcilable moral positions and creates a middle ground wherein different aspects of human nature may be shown in action by an apparently neutral narrator.

However, the confluence of the moral and psychological makeups of the two sisters does not obscure, in fact it often highlights, the essential difference between them. For example, both Marianne and Elinor keep secrets, but they do so for different reasons which set them apart morally. Elinor's decision to keep Lucy's secret is the result of careful consideration; it is a balancing act designed as much for the sake of Edward as of Lucy, and also, indirectly, for the sake of Marianne and Mrs Dashwood. The lack of disclosure should not nullify the existence of a covert dialectical reflection on the part of Elinor. The fact that Elinor keeps secrets just as Marianne does[1] does not settle them on the same moral stratum, because the nature of their practice and the contingency that is involved are different enough to keep them widely apart.

Sense and Sensibility demonstrates how Jane Austen has brought her individual talent to tradition and in so doing proves that "her relation to tradition is," in F.R. Leavis's words, "a creative one."[2] Indeed she maintains a dialectical approach to existing conventions and uses them to suit her own literary construction. Suffice it here to give one more

---

[1]   The word "secret" is used more often in *Sense and Sensibility* than in any other novel by Jane Austen; see Peter L. De Rose and S. W. McGuire, *A Concordance to the Works of Jane Austen*, 3 vols. (New York: Garland 1982) vol. 2, 1006.

[2]   *The Great Tradition: George Eliot, Henry James, Joseph Conrad* (1948; Harmondsworth: Penguin, 1962) 13.

example of her adaptation. One of the stock-in-trade devices to attach a heroine to a hero is "accident and rescue," which usually involves horses. For example, in Mrs Radcliffe's *The Romance of the Forest* (1791), M. Verneuil, who catches the bridle of Clara's runaway horse, is accurately described as "her preserver" (266 – 271); the two young people eventually get married. In Jane West's *A Gossip's Story*, Marianne's horse is running wild when Mr Clermont appears and catches its bit and subsequently captures the rider's heart (201). In Bage's *Hermsprong*, the hero performs a similar act of chivalry by seizing the reins of the chair horse carrying the fair Miss Campinet, and her aunt, and thus saves them from dashing down the Lippen Crag with the horse (17 – 18); he and Caroline Campinet are married at the end of the novel.

Jane Austen, however, manipulates the conventional device in an ironic manner. She will not allow the allegorical schema of romance to run its own course. There are horses and a "rescue" in her novel, but Willoughby the "preserver," as Margaret "with more elegance than precision" (46) calls him, fails to preserve his romantic relationship with Marianne because of his pecuniary consideration; and Marianne who has mistakenly regarded him in hackneyed romantic and sentimental terms, is given the opportunity (she is not conveniently killed off to complete the moral allegory) to adjust her ideology and eventually to marry the upright Colonel Brandon, a match suitable at least from the dialectical point of view. ①

The next chapter discusses *Pride and Prejudice*, where "pride" seems opposed to "prejudice" at the beginning. Then the dividing line between them begins to fade as the engagement between Elizabeth and Darcy starts

---

① Another such match is made between the morally strong Elinor and the morally weak Edward. However, many critics are unhappy about Marianne's match: Tony Tanner, for example, regards it as "punitive" and "certainly the weakest part of the book" (*Jane Austen* [Houndmills: Macmillan, 1986] 100); Margaret Kirkham, for another, sees Marianne's marriage as "a betrayal of the developed character she has become" (*Jane Austen*, *Feminism and Fiction* [London: Athlone, 1997] 87).

to produce dialectical effects. As a result, the work is not only "light &
bright & sparkling"[1] but also, according to one of the most informed
readers of the time, "the most probable."[2]

---

① *Letters* 203 (4 February 1813).

② From Miss Anna Isabella Milbanke's letter to her mother; the passage from which it is
culled reads:

> I have finished the Novel called *Pride and Prejudice*, which I think a very superior
> work. It depends not on any of the common resources of novel writers, no drownings, no
> conflagrations, nor runaway horses, nor lap-dogs and parrots, nor chambermaids and
> milliners, nor rencontres and disguises. I really think it is the most probable fiction I have
> ever read. (Quoted in Southam, vol. 1, 8)

The would-be Lady Byron was the only daughter of Sir Ralph Milbanke, Bart., and the Hon.
Judith (born Noel), daughter of Lord Wentworth; she was highly educated, a mathematician and
a poetess (*The Encyclopædia Britannica*, 11th ed. [Cambridge: Cambridge UP, 1910 – 1911]
vol. 4, 900). The *DNB*, which does not notice Miss Milbanke separately (incorporated into the
Byron biography), mentions that she was "on friendly terms with Mrs. Siddons, Miss Baillie,
Miss Edgeworth, and other literary persons who frequented her mother's house" (ed. Leslie
Stephen [London, 1886] vol. 8, 140).

4 *Pride and Prejudice*:
The Dialectics of Moral Transformation

Much has been, and should be, made of the alliterative title of *Pride and Prejudice*, for it is only in grasping the dialectical relationship between the two human qualities, synthesized by the two abstract nouns, that a keen understanding of Jane Austen's philosophical motif as well as her artistic execution in this novel may be achieved. Indeed the celebrated opening of the novel at once delimits the field in which pride and prejudice will be brought into full play, even as it foreshadows the complexity of the game and the seeming unpredictability of its outcome. The complexity lies in the fact that, of the tripartite opening sentence, only the middle section is unironic:

> It is a truth universally acknowledged, that a single man in possession of a good fortune, must be in want of a wife. (3)

The emphatic modal verb "must" together with the ambiguous "want" in the last section must have suggested something quite different to its Regency readers, thus handily subverting the sonorous claim of "a truth universally acknowledged."

Claudia Brodsky Lacour raises an interesting question in her article on *Pride and Prejudice*:

> Critics and admirers of the novel tend to characterize its unparalleled first sentence as "ironic," without, however, ever specifying precisely what or who the object of its irony is. No critic, to my knowledge, has raised the immediate and pragmatic question of what the sentence actually *means*, although all, I

think, would universally acknowledge it cannot mean what it says. ①

As a matter of fact the object of the irony is defined somewhat generally in the second sentence—which is also the second paragraph—of the novel, which serves as a transition, namely, those "surrounding families" with "fixed" ideas on the issue of matrimony. Then a particularized form of the object is presented in the third paragraph through that lop-sided dialogue between Mr and Mrs Bennet. The vignette has a double function: it illustrates the dialectic even as it drives home the irony. This extended example, consuming most of the chapter, brings the settled past into the vibrant present as if to see if history is going to repeat itself. It dissects in vivid human terms what the universally acknowledged truth is really about in its most basic and crassest formulation.

Whereas the opening sentence constitutes a dialectical maxim that catches the attention of the readers, what follows immediately not only keeps the dialectical essence and construct intact but also invigorates them by introducing the male and female points of view over the jubilantly claimed universal truth. Apparently, the universally acknowledged truth is being illustrated in human terms, but the illustration actually deflates it. If the male party's "feelings or views" on the issue of matrimony are "little known," the applicability, if not the validity, of the truth becomes doubtful. It would be a partial truth at best, and at worst a fondly indulged delusion. Indeed the truth is in danger of becoming merely hope or wishful thinking, however "well fixed" it is "in the minds of the surrounding families" (3), which turn out to be mothers of nubile daughters.

From this point on, what appears to be simple irony begins to acquire a double perspective. If the issue of matrimony appears ironically facile according to the initial claim made in the first sentence, subsequent efforts—second and third paragraphs—to support the claim complicate the

---

① "Austen's *Pride and Prejudice* and Hegel's 'Truth in Art': Concept, Reference, and History," *ELH* 59 (1992): 621 (note 24). Lacour herself thinks that "[Austen's] point seems to be to move on from the quizzical sentence quickly."

matter, turning a maxim into a point at issue, by introducing different, even opposite, views, which in turn create, as if unwittingly, fresh points of irony in the very process of their introduction. It looks as if they jointly deconstruct, rather than support, the opening paragraph, and are determined to bring into uncertainty the claim it has so confidently made.

The opening lines of the dialogue between Mr and Mrs Bennet offer a glimpse of the kind of dialectic that is implicit, even explicit, amidst the rhetoric of courtship and matrimony:

> "My dear Mr. Bennet ... have you heard that Netherfield Park is let at last?" Mr. Bennet replied that he had not.
>
> "But it is," returned she; "for Mrs. Long has just been here, and she told me all about it."
>
> Mr. Bennet made no answer.
>
> "Do not you want to know who has taken it?" cried his wife impatiently.
>
> "*You* want to tell me, and I have no objection to hearing it." (3)

Here we see a couple holding completely contrasting views about the issue of courtship and marriage: while Mrs Bennet is profusely positive about the "truth universally acknowledged," Mr Bennet is persistently negative and refuses to have anything to do with the universally acknowledged truth. Not even the affirmative sentence structure of the last reply can disguise Mr Bennet's vigorous rebuff and utter disavowal.

Yet Mr Bennet has very good reason not to accommodate Mrs Bennet's enthusiasm about the possibility, nay probability as far as she is concerned ("'it is very likely that he *may* fall in love with one of them'" [4]), of marrying off one of their daughters to the newly arrived, well-heeled bachelor. As "a single man in possession of a good fortune" himself "three and twenty years" (5) ago,[①] he had the misfortune of marrying "a woman of mean understanding, little information, and uncertain temper" (5). Such hard evidence bears out the trumpeted truth

---

① Mr Bennet's fortune, however, was an entailed one, as the narrative will soon make clear.

about matrimony. If anything, there seems to be a direct correlation between the amount of folly the man commands and the extent of the foolishness his wife exhibits. Who indeed can fault Mr Bennet for being cool to a possible repetition of "a marriage of such minds," in the words of Lacour paraphrasing Shakespeare, " as are each other's true impediment?"①

The dialectical dialogue, mirroring the dialectical circumstances, demands a dialectical outcome. Despite the moral non-sense the marriage convention makes, it makes perfect economic sense for Mrs Bennet to conceive the arrival of "'a young man of large fortune'" (3) in view of the glaring fact that the Bennets have "'five grown up daughters'" (4). Even Mr Bennet, despite his teasing of Mrs Bennet and his ambivalent feeling about the propriety of the connection, does not necessarily disfavour it.

The situation here is rather like that in *Northanger Abbey* where Catherine is engaged in a dialogue with Mrs Allen during which she draws out every bit of useful information about Henry Tilney—place, birth and wealth—from her dumb, garrulous guardian, even though the narrator hastens to remind us that Catherine feels " Mrs Allen had no real intelligence to give" (*NA* 69). By seemingly making a game of Mrs Bennet's "stock-taking" of the new-comer's name and status, Mr Bennet is actually able to line the quarry up in his sights. The difference in narrative discourse is that, whereas in *Northanger Abbey* Jane Austen's narrator has to come out and make the authorial comment from time to time (which reduces moral ambiguity even as it is creating one), in *Pride and Prejudice* the narrator is mostly content to stay behind the scene and let the characters' speech and, more importantly, their action make the point.

Readers may have the impression that Mr Bennet is indeed behaving in a rather irresponsible manner, but it would be an insult to his intelligence if they thought the full implications of having five daughters

---

① Lacour 612.

and no sons were lost on him. Mr Bennet knows full well that his silly, loquacious wife thrives on excitement or stretched nerves, and he duly delivers just that by playing the game properly and in its entirety, complete with his blasé posture, levity of wit and scathing sarcasm. Mrs Bennet is absolutely right in accusing him of taking delight in vexing her (5), but she is absolutely wrong in criticizing him for not respecting her "'poor nerves'" (5). She is simply not sophisticated, or dialectical, enough to see that he, like herself, is governed by the "truth universally acknowledged," that the very fact of his being married to her speaks volumes. Mr Bennet's genuine belligerence is a sort of psychological exercise which aims at displacing his regret and frustration. What he hates to acknowledge openly to the immodest victor who made a conquest of him, he cannot help embracing surreptitiously in letter and spirit. The fourth, and also the final, paragraph of the opening chapter evaluates what has proceeded so far and concludes on a cheerful note of "visiting and news" (5), thus indirectly, or even directly, complimenting Mrs Bennet and signalling perhaps yet another victory for her.

That she is again victorious is confirmed by the opening sentence of the following chapter: "Mr. Bennet was among the earliest of those who waited on Mr. Bingley" (6). Thus a balancing act seems to have been performed. While marriage should not be "'a commercial exchange'" (*SS* 38), financial independence is important,① and the economic aspect of marriage should not be treated cavalierly or cynically. In Jane Austen's view, marriage is about the matching of two minds that understand the significance of their union above, though not beyond, worldly considerations. In *Pride and Prejudice* the protagonists, along with a group of secondary characters, will illustrate, through their courtship and marriage, the difficulty as well as the desirability of achieving such a union. Their chequered experiences suggest that a dialectical engagement

---

① In her letter to Fanny Knight, who is hesitating about accepting John Plumptre, Jane Austen points to the fine line between love and independence: "Years may pass, before he is Independent. —You like him well enough to marry, but not well enough to wait" (*Letters* 30 November 1814).

of ideas contributes significantly to a healthy relationship, especially a romantic courtship, for it stimulates the moral as well as the intellectual capability of the parties involved and, at the same time, exposes their woeful inadequacies in those respects.

The difficulty of achieving such compatible marriages is seen in the serious confusion about the personal worth of the heroine even between her parents. Mrs Bennet thinks her second daughter, Elizabeth, "'not half so handsome as Jane" (4), their first daughter, whereas Mr Bennet strongly advocates her ability at the expense of all other children of theirs—"'I must throw in a good word for my little Lizzy'" (4) for "'she has something more of quickness than her sisters'" (5). Therefore the real character of the heroine is cast into obscurity by the diverging views of her own mother and father, and clarification is contingent upon the narrative events to come, and upon the dialectical discourse informing those events in the context of the declared motifs of courtship and marriage. This is yet another broad hint that dialectics will be a crucial mediating factor not only in terms of general thematic crystallization but also in terms of individual moral transformation.

In light of the narrative information that has already been transmitted, it is apparent that any one-sided view on the complex issue of courtship and marriage is going to be as false as it is true. In the remaining space of this chapter I will continue the dialectical investigation of the interplay between motif and moral transformation, paying special attention to the moral, intellectual and romantic engagement between the two protagonists, namely, Elizabeth Bennet and Fitzwilliam Darcy.

Whereas the elder Bennets have been stuck in a dialectical bind for more than twenty years, because they communicate without mutual understanding (Mr Bennet of course understands Mrs Bennet very well), Elizabeth and Darcy will show how true dialectical interchange can lead to mutual understanding, satisfactory courtship and compatible marriage.

1

When Darcy and Elizabeth first see each other, they, like others, rely on personal appearance as the basis of moral judgment. It seems a cliché in Austen criticism today to talk about this novel, and others for that matter, in terms of appearance and reality, but the apparent cliché has its own reality since the key issue constitutes a dialectical understanding of appearance of reality. Indeed the issue of appearance versus reality is essential to the moral transformation of the protagonists. It is so very important that it was actually set forth by the title of the earlier version of *Pride and Prejudice*, that is, *First Impressions*. [1] In *Pride and Prejudice* all the characters attach importance to appearance, for the simple reason that one's appearance—stature, dress, countenance, manner, conversation, look (especially eyes) and facial expression, etc.—offers the readily available evidence which others can record and work with in their effort to assess the character of the person in question. Well-trained eyes often catch the most significant details, however small they are, and well-trained minds often quickly process those details, generalize them and yield first impressions that may serve as informative labels. [2] For example, at the Meryton assembly where the Hertfordshire locals first meet the illustrious Netherfield party, appearances work vigorously on the minds of those present and rapidly produce impressions leading to

---

[1] The book with this title was offered to and rejected by the London publisher Thomas Cadell by return of post in 1797 (see Chapman's "Introductory Note to *Pride and Prejudice*," *PP*, xi; see also Le Faye's *Family Record* 94 – 95).

[2] Hegel in his *Phenomenology* offers an analogy to explain the dialectics of appearance. If a man with sight is placed in pure darkness, he sees as much or as little as a blind man does, even if a world of wealth is before him. Hence while it may be true that the man with sight sees nothing, it is not true that there is nothing to be seen. Once the "curtain of [appearance] hanging before the inner world is ... drawn away," "the inner being [the 'I']" will be "gazing into the inner world." "It is manifest that behind the so-called curtain which is supposed to conceal the inner world, there is nothing to be seen unless *we* go behind it ourselves, as much in order that we may see, as that there may be something behind there which can be seen" (146, 165).

moral judgments.

The first half of the evening sees Darcy's fame rising high on account of his "fine, tall" figure, his "handsome" features and his "noble mien," and on the report that his income is "ten thousand a year" (10); the second half, however, quickly sinks his reputation below that of Bingley. The reason for Darcy's loss of popularity is that "his manners gave a disgust which turned the tide of his popularity" (10)—he has been "discovered to be proud, to be above his company, and above being pleased" (10). Darcy has not undergone a personality change in the course of one short evening, nor has there been any change to his person. He is still tall, fine and no less handsome; and his manners remain what they have always been. What has changed is the perception of the people at the assembly whose company has not been sought, whose wish to dance with him has not been fulfilled, and whose pride and vanity have been injured, such as Mrs Bennet in particular. She is amongst "the most violent against him," and holds "particular resentment" because "one of her daughters" has been "slighted" (11) by him. She concludes that Darcy is "'a most disagreeable, horrid man'" who is "'so conceited that there was no enduring him!'" (13).

But the perception is the result of prejudice on the part of the Hertfordshire locals, for their conclusion is not derived from insights or experience: Mr Darcy has never mingled, hardly talked, with any one of the locals throughout the evening,[1] and he "danced only once with Mrs Hurst [Bingley's elder sister] and once with Miss Bingley, declined being introduced to any other lady, and spent the rest of the evening in walking about the room, speaking occasionally to one of his own party" (11). The spectators have only seen the outside of Darcy; his inner self remains to be seen. Mrs Bennet, whose mind is dominated by the "truth universally acknowledged," takes Darcy's appearance at its face value and

---

[1]   Miss Lucas tells the Bennet women that Mrs Long has told her that Mr Darcy "'sat close to her for half an hour without once opening his lips'" (19). Although the authenticity of the report is cast in doubt by Jane's cross-examination (19), it is probably true that Darcy never initiated any conversation with the locals.

judges him harshly on the basis of his failure to promote the "business of her life" (5). Elizabeth Bennet seems to have maintained a neutral position until she has overheard Darcy's comment on her: "'She is tolerable, but not handsome enough to tempt *me*'" (12). She is "delighted" by what she regards as perfectly "ridiculous" (12) and at once spreads what she has just overheard "with great spirit" (12). Although Elizabeth does not seem to take offence at being personally slighted by Darcy at the moment, she agrees totally with the conclusion of the Merytonians that Mr Darcy is unbearably arrogant. Her memory is imprinted by his arrogant manners and insulting remarks; her emotional reaction is delayed rather than dissolved. A hint of her grudge is perhaps dropped shortly afterwards during tête-à-tête between the two eldest Miss Bennets when Elizabeth tells Jane: "'Compliments always take *you* by surprise, and *me* never'" (14).

The assembly scene in fact conducts the dialectical juxtaposition of appearance and reality in terms of pride and prejudice; however, the boundary between pride and prejudice becomes blurred when we consider some of the facts of that night. It is apparent that the local group has its own pride, potent if less visible, manifested in its negative reaction to what it perceives to be the obtrusive pride of Mr Darcy. On the other hand, Darcy's serious, disagreeable mien has been inopportunely highlighted by Bingley's easy, pleasing manner. The unfair comparison of manners favours the outward appearance and discounts the inner quality. Bingley's good nature makes him think almost every girl in the room "'pleasant'" and "'several of them,'" such as Jane, even "'uncommonly pretty'" (11). Darcy's cautious and discriminating nature directs him to the quick detection of such vulgar people as Mrs Bennet and her younger daughters, who will be later described by the Netherfield people as either "intolerable" (21) or "not worth speaking to" (21). Bingley is as satisfied with the appearance he sees as Darcy is dissatisfied with it. Darcy refrains from making real contact with the local group whereas Bingley embraces it all warmly.

Darcy refuses to socialize with any of the strangers at the assembly because he believes he has seen "a collection of people in whom there was little beauty and no fashion, for none of whom he had felt the smallest interest, and from none received either attention or pleasure" (16). He quickly brushes them into the category unworthy of his attention and society. Bingley, on the other hand, is too friendly to think anyone unpleasant, and his warmth and friendliness are repaid in kind. Neither Darcy nor Bingley is completely right, for there is beauty as well as vulgarity among the people at the assembly. If Mr Darcy is right about Mrs Bennet and her younger daughters, Mr Bingley is right about her elder daughters, Jane and Elizabeth. To be sure, it is not that people are not allowed to judge from appearances but that their first impressions of appearances should be understood as what they are and be supplemented and complemented by their second, third, fourth, and further impressions. People should understand that first impressions are likely to be tainted by personal emotion, opinion or prejudice.

The same problem exists in the conduct of the understanding of the Bennets. Mrs Bennet, for example, detests Darcy for not dancing with her daughters and for slighting one of them. Miss Bennet, for that matter, falls for Mr Bingley because of his display of "'such happy manners! —so much ease, with such perfect good breeding!'" (14). Her good feelings for him even extend to his sisters, who, she believes, are "'very pleasing women'" (15). Elizabeth Bennet seems the better judge, if only because her "judgment [is] too unassailed by any attention to herself" (15). She does not approve of the Bingley sisters, who, she thinks, are "proud and conceited" (15). However, like Mr Darcy, Elizabeth is likely to misjudge in spite of her ability to judge correctly. Because she is right about many she is wrong about few—significant few, though—namely, Darcy and Wickham.

Locke in his *Of the Conduct of the Understanding* analyzes this kind of error at the epistemological level:

> many men give themselves up to the first anticipations of their minds, and
> are very tenacious of the opinions that first possess them; they are often as fond
> of their first conceptions as of their first-born, and will by no means recede from

the judgment they have once made, or any conjecture or conceit they have once entertained. This is a fault in the conduct of the understanding, since the firmness or rather stiffness of the mind is not from an adherence to truth, but submission to prejudice. ①

Both Darcy and Elizabeth are victims of their own prejudices; their confidence in their ability to judge prevents them from judging fairly. It is important to recognize that even if one's first impressions turn out to be right, they are never intrinsically right; rather, they are proved to be right by later events.

What we have seen so far in the opening sections of *Pride and Prejudice* suggests a marked difference in terms of dialectical sophistication in this novel over the earlier *Northanger Abbey* and *Sense and Sensibility*. We recall that when the seventeen-year-old Catherine first arrives at Bath she engages in a number of conversations with Henry Tilney and opposes his half-serious ritual mannerisms without comprehending them fully. Her seriousness and ardour enable her to counter several of Henry's witty arguments, and in the process a number of seemingly unintended dialectical situations have been created. In *Sense and Sensibility*, however, Marianne, who is also seventeen years old, consciously engages her elder sister's point of view with well-articulated, albeit erroneous, opinions of her own. The set of values that she upholds exude visible traces of Shaftesburian "enthusiasm" or what Walter Francis Wright calls the "super-rational experience"② advocated by Shaftesbury, among others. But Marianne's moral position is clearly untenable throughout the course of the novel (except for a few specific scenes where her sensibility serves a useful purpose), due to its excessiveness and extremity, and for the most part it is displayed to be censured. But here in *Pride and Prejudice*, from the very beginning, we are presented with a series of situations which defy measurement by any one-sided moral judgment since the two epithets—pride and prejudice—are imbued with a fair amount of moral

---

① Locke, *Conduct* 26.
② Walter Francis Wright 15.

ambiguity. Both Darcy and Elizabeth think they have recorded a tell-tale moral impression of each other, even though those first impressions are potentially problematic as they are only partially reliable. Indeed the moral and artistic sophistication of *Pride and Prejudice* far exceeds not only what Austen's earlier works have shown but also what other contemporary works have managed to achieve.

Let us make two comparisons and see how Jane Austen and Fanny Burney treat similar situations. When Darcy "coldly" (12) observes at the assembly ball, after evaluating Elizabeth with his connoisseur's eye, that she is merely "'tolerable'" but "'not handsome enough to tempt *me*'" (12), Elizabeth's reaction is by all accounts extraordinary. She is bemused rather than embarrassed by what she has overheard.

We recall that in Burney's *Evelina*, when told by Maria Mirvan (who has heard Lord Orville's conversation with Sir Clement Willoughby) that Lord Orville thinks her "'pretty modest-looking,'" "'*silent*'" and "'weak,'"[1] Evelina instantly feels demoralized. She writes to Mr Villars: "What mortifying words! I am resolved, however, that I will never again be tempted to go to an assembly. I wish I had been in Dorsetshire."[2] Jane Austen's Elizabeth, on the other hand, facing very much the same mortification, only more directly, appears amused, and she spreads, rather than suppresses, the story "with great spirit among her friends" (12). If the comic spirit is, as George Meredith says, "born of our united social intelligence,"[3] then its "*social* signification"[4] here is the intended purging of Darcy's anti-social behaviour by Elizabeth and company. Elizabeth is "delighted in any thing ridiculous" (12); as she acknowledges shortly to Darcy, "'Follies and nonsense, whims and

---

[1] *Evelina, or, The History of a Young Lady's Entrance into the World*, ed. Stewart J. Cooke (New York: Norton, 1998) 28.

[2] *Evelina* 29.

[3] George Meredith, "Prelude" to *The Egoist*, ed. Robert M. Adams (New York: Norton, 1979) 4.

[4] Henri Bergson, "Laughter," *Comedy*, intro. Wylie Sypher (Garden City: Doubleday, 1956) 65.

inconsistencies *do* divert me, I own, and I laugh at them whenever I can'" (57).

At Sir William's ball, shortly after the Meryton assembly, the good-natured host, eager to see everyone happy, tries, without warning, to present Elizabeth to Darcy as his dancing partner, just after the latter has ill-humouredly told him, "'Every savage can dance'" (25). Elizabeth is caught by surprise, for she must have observed Darcy's "silent indignation" (25). But Sir William has already taken her hand and "would have given it to Mr. Darcy," who, "though extremely surprised, was not unwilling to receive it" (26). A similar incident happens in *Evelina* where Sir Clement Willoughby, intending to humiliate Evelina for not agreeing to dance with him earlier, "suddenly" seizes her hand and accosts Lord Orville, who he knows has indicated a low opinion of the girl, "'Think, my Lord, what must be my reluctance to resign this fair hand to your Lordship!'"[1] Although the nature of the two sets of circumstances is different, the embarrassment to the heroine is the same. Orville and Darcy both understand what is going on and try to be gallant like true gentlemen despite the awkwardness caused to themselves. But the reaction from Elizabeth is, again, sharply different from that of Evelina. Evelina, we remember, "coloured violently" and is thrown into great confusion, crying out: "'By no means—not for the world!'"[2] Elizabeth, being similarly trapped, shows considerable presence of mind. She suffers "some discomposure" (26) but quickly recovers. She withdraws her hand before Darcy can catch it—in *Evelina* Lord Orville "took" the hand before the heroine tried to "recover it"[3]—and, smiling, she calmly explains to the slow-witted Sir William: "'Mr. Darcy is all politeness'" (26).[4] The tension is defused, and Elizabeth is victorious: she "looked archly, and turned away" (26)--making a very favourable impression on Mr Darcy.

---

[1][2][3] *Evelina* 38.

[4] Reuben Arthur Brower offers an excellent analysis of Elizabeth's five-word statement; see chapter 9 of *The Fields of Light: An Experiment in Critical Reading* (New York: Oxford UP, 1951) 168 – 169.

The point of these two examples is to stress the dialectical nature of the engagement between the two protagonists in *Pride and Prejudice*. As a result of the dialectical turn the narrative takes, what happens on a social occasion is not simply social. The simplicity of Burney's always well-intentioned but socially incompetent heroine is replaced by the complexity of an always quick-witted and sharp-tongued ironist. The encounter is not lopsided, but one of equal strength, morally as well as intellectually. The action is not monotonously conventional or overbearingly patriarchal but amusingly innovative and instructive, not just for the protagonists involved but also for the readers. ①

2

Fitzwilliam Darcy and Elizabeth Bennet are intelligent and sensitive characters who are capable of discovering and responding to what appear to be the faults in others and also in themselves. However, at first neither seems to care to look inward and reflect on his or her manner of judging people. Both are eager to take positions on issues involving Bingley or Jane or George Wickham. Yet due to the constraint of social decorum and the awkward nature of their respective agendas, neither can very well voice what he or she really thinks in a straightforward manner, so that valid criticism or gross misconception may be accepted or rejected, or

---

① Interesting elements like these account largely for the popularity of this novel, which the author fondly calls: "my own darling Child" (*Letters* [29 January 1813]), among Austen readers today. Austen herself is obviously pleased with her achievement. In her subsequent letter to Cassandra from Chawton, she says of *Pride and Prejudice*:

The work is rather too light & sparkling;—it wants shade;—it wants to be stretched out here & there with a long Chapter—of sense if it could be had, if not of solemn specious nonsense—about something unconnected with the story; an Essay on Writing, a critique on Walter Scott, or the history of Buonaparte—or anything that would form a contrast & bring the reader with increased delight to the playfulness & Epigrammatism of the general stile. — I doubt your quite agreeing with me here—I know your starched Notions.

Austen is clearly indulging, in typical relaxed ironic tone, in her new success. In fact the preceding sentence: "I am quite vain enough & well satisfied enough" rather sets the tone of her own assessment (*Letters* [4 February 1813]).

simply explained.

This situation, which renders their engagement doubly interesting, is compared by Juliet McMaster to what happens in *Much Ado about Nothing*: "[A]s with Beatrice and Benedict, the state that exists between them is war: 'They never meet but there's a skirmish of wit between them' (*Much Ado about Nothing*, I, i.)."① The analogy, however, is not an entirely happy one. For one thing Shakespeare's protagonists wage a battle of wit with each other for no particular reason except for the sake of browbeating the opponent or entertaining the frolicsome friends, whereas Austen's protagonists not only talk at but also talk with each other (civilly, one might add) as they try to put across meaningful messages. Both Darcy and Elizabeth have a good idea of what they are talking about, and neither wastes time, or words, in exposing what one perceives to be the other's foibles. For another, in *Pride and Prejudice* the confrontational zest is not a shared one, because Darcy, being less emotionally involved in the affairs involving Jane and Wickham, is most of the time on the defensive, fending off Elizabeth's aggressive irony and sarcasm.

Darcy's defensive mode is partly due to the discovery, shortly after he has made the unflattering remark about Elizabeth's looks at the Meryton assembly, that his first impression of Elizabeth Bennet is less than accurate; in fact it is quite false: "[N]o sooner had he made it clear to himself and his friends that she had hardly a good feature in her face, than he began to find it was rendered uncommonly intelligent by the beautiful expression of her dark eyes" (23). Yet more "mortifying" (23) discoveries follow suit:

> Though he had detected with a critical eye more than one failure of perfect
> symmetry in her form, he was forced to acknowledge her figure to be light and

---

① "Love and Pedagogy," *Jane Austen the Novelist* 156. McMaster thinks that "[t]he similarity between *Pride and Prejudice* and *Much Ado About Nothing* extends not only to the main plot, where hero and heroine come to accord only after having pointedly singled each other out for abuse, but also to the subplots—the making and breaking of the Hero / Claudio and Jane / Bingley matches being a point at fierce issue between the main characters" (171, note 11).

pleasing; and in spite of his asserting that her manners were not those of the fashionable world, he was caught by their easy playfulness. (23)

As a result, Darcy wants to make amends, and he wishes "to know more of" (24) rather than to wrangle with Elizabeth.

Elizabeth alone, as she later admits, "meant to be uncommonly clever in taking so decided a dislike to him, without any reason" (225). Needless to say, she somewhat exaggerates her guilt in this late sisterly confession to Jane, but her behaviour at the time does show a tendency to excessive antipathy. In this respect Elizabeth does resemble Beatrice; like her, she makes a point of teasing her male counterpart when and where she can, and seems to derive some sort of sardonic satisfaction from her sarcasm, even as Darcy is growing more and more perceptive and tolerant of her as a result of his not disinterested understanding of her.

Nevertheless, we know Elizabeth has a motive in doing so. She has a moral grudge against Mr Darcy and she has pledged to her mother to snub him: "'I believe, Ma'am, I may safely promise you *never* to dance with him'" (20). The promise may imply that Elizabeth does not think that Darcy will invite her to dance, but when he does, she duly declines. Generally speaking, Jane Austen is not interested in re-presenting a battle of the sexes; instead she wishes to show how such human defects as pride and prejudice may prevent one person from understanding another, how they may cause conflicts in ordinary human, to say nothing of romantic, relationships, and how they may, as a consequence, disrupt the harmony of social life. Worse, they give such dubious or devious characters as Miss Bingley or George Wickham a chance to misinform people and carry out their immoral schemes.

The Netherfield scene, where Jane falls ill as a result of being caught in the rain—earlier Mrs Bennet deliberately sent her daughter on horseback for the visit despite plentiful signs of rain (30)—provides some initial insights into the nature of the kind of dialectical narrative that Jane Austen creates. When Elizabeth walks three miles in ankle-deep mud to visit her sister, she provokes a number of interesting reactions. Jane is of course "delighted" (33) by Elizabeth's sisterly anticipation of what she did not fully express in her brief note home for fear of "giving alarm or inconvenience" (33). Petty-minded Mrs Hurst sees impropriety in Elizabeth's sudden appearance with her petticoat "'six inches deep in mud'" (36), in spite of "'the gown which had been let down to hide it'" (36). Miss Bingley intuitively senses in the "intruder" (35) a rival for the man she herself covets and tries to protect her own interest by pointing out to Darcy what "'an abominable sort of conceited independence'" (36) and "'a most country town indifference to decorum'" (36) she finds in the uninvited guest. The ingenuous Bingley, however, has noticed none of the things that his sharp-eyed sisters have spotted; he thinks that "Miss Elizabeth Bennet looked remarkably well" (36), that her prompt visit shows "'an affection for her sister that is very pleasing'" (36). Darcy, who must be in agreement with Bingley, repulses Miss Bingley's insinuation by telling her that his "'admiration'" of Elizabeth's "'fine eyes'" has "'[n]ot at all'" been affected adversely; on the contrary, he thinks that "'they were brightened by the exercise'" (36).

Thus those who judge by the standards of the conduct books or have their own axe to grind find faults with Elizabeth's muddy, "'blowsy'" (36) and "'almost wild'" (35) appearance at an awkwardly early hour; yet those who are capable of perceiving inner qualities appreciate what they see. Elizabeth's appearance is one and the same, but it reflects, like a mirror, the different modes of thinking of the characters at Netherfield; it measures and reveals the differences in their moral capacity. The controversy over Elizabeth's "'fine eyes'" is a significant detail, for it sheds considerable light on the character of Darcy as well as on that of Caroline Bingley. Darcy's compliment was originally made at a gathering at Sir William's. Just after Elizabeth, declining to dance with Darcy, "looked archly" and "turned away," Miss Bingley glided along and complained to him about the "'insipidity,'" the "'noise,'" the "'nothingness'" and "'the self-importance of all these people!'" (27). Unluckily for her, Darcy's mind has just started to change after his brief but intriguing interaction with Miss Elizabeth Bennet. Had Miss Bingley come five minutes earlier, she would have heard Mr Darcy's "'strictures'" (27) on those people. But now she hears something quite unexpected: "'I have been meditating on the very great pleasure which a pair of fine eyes in the face of a pretty woman can bestow'" (27). When Miss Bingley coquettishly presses for the name of the fortunate lady, Mr. Darcy replies "with great intrepidity" (27): "'Miss Elizabeth Bennet'" (27), and he meets Miss Bingley's subsequent jealous sarcasm "with perfect indifference" (27).

Darcy's appreciation of Elizabeth Bennet's wit and intelligence shows his discernment. As a matter of fact Elizabeth has earlier attempted to appear tauntingly tasteless: like flippant Lydia, she asks Darcy if he does not find her expressing herself "'uncommonly well'" when she is "'teazing Colonel Forster'" to give a ball (24); like aphoristic Mary, she informs him, with a mocking gravity, before playing the piano: "'There is a fine old saying, which every body here is of course familiar with—"Keep your breath to cool your porridge,"—and I shall keep mine to swell my song'" (24). However, her assumed vulgarities fail to detract from her unassuming character. Darcy may have misread Elizabeth's archness, which is meant to be ironic and critical, but he has read her general character correctly. He will not let appearance obscure his vision, nor will he allow Miss Bingley's insinuation to influence his judgment. His reaffirmation of his positive estimation of Elizabeth at Netherfield in the teeth of the Bingley sisters' condemnation proves his moral conviction as well as his imperturbable interest in Elizabeth Bennet.

In short Darcy's prompt revision of his earlier hasty judgement reveals his capacity for dialectical thinking. Jane Austen shows a keen sense of the moral as well as aesthetic importance of eyes as she takes pains to describe their quality and movement, a technique which George Eliot will adopt to great advantage in her novels. If, as Shakespeare says, "Beauty is bought by the judgment of the eye, / Not utt'red by base sale of chapmen's tongues,"[①] Darcy's "judgment of the eye" both precedes

---

① *Love's Labour's Lost* 2. 1. 15 – 16.

and is complemented by his compliments to Elizabeth's comeliness and elegance. Elizabeth, too, will demonstrate her understanding of the importance of eyes. Later when reluctantly accompanying her uncle and aunt on a visit to Pemberley (since she wishes and expects to avoid all contact with Darcy) in the opening chapter of the third volume, Elizabeth will seek those familiar eyes of Darcy from his porfrait and through them become totally convinced of his virtues.

But for now, at this point, Elizabeth Bennet does not yet have the vision to see the real merits of Fitzwilliam Darcy, or has too much of her own vision to see beyond her prejudice—an ironic situation worthy of the Shakespearean metaphor: "Light, seeking light, doth light of light beguile."[①] Elizabeth has grossly misread Darcy's genuine interest in her. Darcy's earlier bias has primarily been against "the less polished'" (25) Meryton society as a whole, exemplified by, say, the pompous but slow-witted Sir William and the vain and self-conceited Mary Bennet (25), not to mention Elizabeth's own mother and her other younger sisters; it is not against Elizabeth Bennet in particular, despite the fact that she happens to have overheard one particular remark about her looks.

Consequently, although Darcy's view of Elizabeth has substantially changed, Elizabeth's view of Darcy has not. It is not so much because she is not privy to Darcy's compliments to her as because her mind is set rigidly and negatively against Darcy regardless of what he says or does. Elizabeth simply cannot erase her first impression of the inordinately proud man; she insists that that single initial image represents the whole character of Mr Darcy. Whereas Darcy follows the Lockean empirical approach and tries to see Elizabeth beyond her appearance, Elizabeth is bent on casting him as a morally deficient man, thus ironically mirroring the earliest Darcy who refuses to mingle with the Meryton folk because of their apparent unsuitableness. As a result, the hero's rational urge for interaction is being vigorously opposed by the heroine's taste for pungent satire. Darcy's self-portrait: "'My temper would perhaps be called

---

① *Love's Labour's Lost* 1. 1. 77.

resentful. —My good opinion once lost is lost for ever'" (58) is ironically apt for Elizabeth as well. When she playfully tells Darcy while dancing with him: "'I have always seen a great similarity in the turn of our minds'" (91), she is unconsciously making a point doubly ironic.

There is an interesting debate in chapter 10 of the first volume between Elizabeth and Darcy over "'the influence of friendship and affection'" (50) while the two are in frequent contact with each other at Netherfield due to Jane's illness. The chapter begins with a familiarly simple dialectical scene, which then switches to a fully dialectical tableau that features two participants who do not share an equal interest in the dialectical discussion in which they are engaged. It is evening: Darcy is writing a letter to his sister, and Miss Bingley is sitting near him. While "watching the progress of his letter" (47), the lady is constantly showering him with lavish praises "either on his hand-writing, or on the evenness of his lines, or on the length of his letter" (47), but the gentleman remains impassive:

> "How delighted Miss Darcy will be to receive such a letter!"
> ... He made no answer.
> "You write uncommonly fast."
> "You are mistaken. I write rather slowly."
> ...
> "How can you contrive to write so even?"
> He was silent.
> ...
> "But do you always write such charming long letters to her, Mr. Darcy?"
> "They are generally long; but whether always charming, it is not for me to determine." (47 – 48)

This is "a curious dialogue" (47) indeed! —it reminds us of the equally curious dialogue between Mr and Mrs Bennets at the opening of the novel, though there are some marked differences between the two. Mr Darcy, who is perfectly aware of Miss Bingley's interest in him, tries rather hard, yet not impolitely, to escape the onslaught of her focused and purposeful flattery. However, Miss Bingley, governed by her *idée fixe* of marrying this single man of large fortune, is unabashedly determined to attract him. She simply will not let the quarry slip away. The seemingly intimate dialogue in fact constitutes two separate monologues going right past each other. The two speakers are poles apart in mental occupation despite their close physical proximity.

This initial dialogue is soon replaced by one more intrinsically dialectical when Elizabeth, who is doing her needlework nearby yet also watching with interest the scene unfolding in front of her, joins in. Elizabeth compliments Mr Bingley: "'Your humility must disarm reproof'" (48). The chat takes an analytical turn when Darcy explains that "'the appearance of humility'" can mean two things: "'carelessness of opinion'" or "'an indirect boast'" (48). He then cites the example of Bingley's telling Mrs Bennet that if he ever resolves on quitting Netherfield he "'should be gone in five minutes'" (49), questioning the point of such "'a precipitance which must leave very necessary business undone, and can be of no real advantage to [himself] or any one else'" (49). Apparently, Darcy, like Henry Tilney, Elinor Dashwood, Fanny Price, and George Knightley, pays close attention to the correct use of language because "[p]roper words in proper places" is an issue not only of style[1] but also of morality. As Locke says, words are "the Marks of the *Ideas* of the Speaker."[2] One of the glaring faults of Catherine Morland, Mr Thorpe, Miss Thorpe, Mrs Dashwood and her daughter Marianne, Lucy Steele and Mary Crawford is their misuse or abuse of language. Clearly, Darcy esteems precision and substance—virtues of his creator's own prose.

Darcy's style contrasts not only with Mr Bingley's fuzziness and Miss Bingley's inaneness but also with Elizabeth's looseness. When Elizabeth suggests:

> You appear to me, Mr. Darcy, to allow nothing for the influence of

---

[1] Jonathan Swift, "Letter to a Young Clergyman," *The Writings of Jonathan Swift*, ed. Robert A. Greenberg and William Bowman Piper (New York: Norton, 1973) 473.

[2] *Essay* 2.21.

friendship and affection. A regard for the requester would often make one readily yield to a request, without waiting for arguments to reason one into it. I am not particularly speaking of such a case as you have supposed about Mr. Bingley. We may as well wait, perhaps, till the circumstance occurs, before we discuss the discretion of his behaviour thereupon. But in general and ordinary cases between friend and friend, where one of them is desired by the other to change a resolution of no very great moment, should you think ill of that person for complying with the desire, without waiting to be argued into it? (50)

Darcy counters rhetorically: "'Will it not be advisable, before we proceed on this subject, to arrange with rather more precision the degree of importance which is to appertain to this request, as well as the degree of intimacy subsisting between the parties?'" (50). Darcy sounds like a lawyer, but the legalese is necessary. Unless one identifies who the "'requester'" is and the nature of the "'request,'" there is no clearing up the issue. For example, when Mr Bingley shortly after leaves for London on Darcy's advice, Elizabeth, who speculates (correctly as it turns out) that Darcy is the "'requester'", becomes upset on behalf of her elder sister, leaving her own "principle" in shambles. Elizabeth in fact does exactly the opposite of what she preaches to Darcy.

It is this kind of discrepancy between vision and action that makes Elizabeth appear, at times, hypocritical. For another example, while she argues, justifiably, with Darcy that "'people themselves alter so much, that there is something new to be observed in them for ever'" (43), she refuses to apply the principle generally and allow Darcy to change and herself to look at him in a new light, for no apparent reason other than the determination to apply to him some of her father's "'set downs'" which Mrs Bennet earlier wished "'to have given him'" (13) at the assembly ball. At Netherfield Elizabeth behaves in a single-mindedly confrontational manner by interpreting every friendly move by Darcy negatively. When he observes her admiringly, she imagines that he is criticizing "something about her more wrong and reprehensible, according to his ideas of right" (51). When Darcy repeatedly and good-naturedly invites her to dance to the tune of "a lively Scotch air" (51), as she is by nature a lively person, she, after much reflection, responds:

> I heard you before; but I could not immediately determine what to say in
> reply. You wanted me, I know, to say 'Yes,' that you might have the pleasure
> of despising my taste; but I always delight in overthrowing premeditated
> contempt. I have therefore made up my mind to tell you, that I do not want to
> dance a reel at all—and now despise me if you dare. (52)

Elizabeth has become a symbol of negativity to Darcy. Her careful
deliberation merely produces the same old negative response.

What is thematically suggestive is that many of Darcy's remarks to
Elizabeth at this point, which she invariably misinterprets, seem to have
been made with George Wickham in mind, such as: "'Nothing is more
deceitful than the appearance of humility'" (48) or, more incisively and
extensively, "'My temper I dare not vouch for.—It is I believe too little
yielding—certainly too little for the convenience of the world. I cannot
forget the follies and vices of others so soon as I ought, nor their offences
against myself.'" (58). The timing of these remarks is interesting, for
George Wickham is merely three short chapters away.

Elizabeth's decidedly prejudicial inclination makes her an easy prey
to George Wickham's dark half-truths and wicked lies about Darcy's
character which are smoothly introduced by his flattering manner of
conversation. It does not strike her as odd and suspicious that someone
should have lodged, in the very early stage of their association, so many
pernicious complaints against a mutual acquaintance. Earlier when the two
men met by accident in the street, there was a telltale change of
countenance: Wickham's face, presumably, turned "white" and Darcy's
"red" (73), which Elizabeth did observe and register in her quick mind.
But there was no follow-up investigation or serious reflection on the odd
occurrence by Elizabeth. She is content to make a superficial comparison
between Wickham and Darcy. Her first impression of the "most
gentleman-like" (72) former is contrasted with her tenaciously
remembered impression of the latter, which excites "no very cordial
feelings" (12). Wickham's "fine countenance" and "good figure" (72)
exert great influence, but what seduces her judgment most decisively and

swiftly is Wickham's flattering manner of conversation.

The narrator draws our attention to the contrast between the disarmingly flattering manner of speech and the ominously subversive content of the speech. She shows through two successive examples how George Wickham manages to ingratiate himself in Elizabeth's favour, not so much by what he says as by how he says it, and how he skilfully controls the timing and substance of his speech in order to achieve optimum effect. In the first example, as all the Bennet daughters except Mary are walking on the street in Meryton, "the attention of every lady was soon caught by a young man" who turns out to be Mr Wickham, a friend of Mr Denny, an officer with whom Lydia is on familiar terms. "The introduction was followed up on his side by a happy readiness of conversation—a readiness at the same time perfectly correct and unassuming" (72). Whereas Wickham's physical appearance, which is "greatly in his favour" (72), does not call for comparison with that of Darcy, who is after all "fine," "tall," and "handsome" himself (10), his "very pleasing address" (72) certainly does. Should it not have occurred to Elizabeth that such sharp contrast exists between Wickham and Darcy in terms of their manners, especially their manner of speaking, the hated man himself appears on the scene at this very moment to urge and facilitate a necessary comparison. Tall Mr Darcy mounted high on his horse intrudes, as it were, upon the congenial little group "talking together very agreeably" (72). This is the point at which Elizabeth spots the colour change on both men's faces and observes Darcy's curt acknowledgement of Wickham's "salutation"—which he "just deigned to return" (73).

In the second example, all five Bennet girls are at their aunt's house in Meryton; Wickham, who happens to be returning Mr Philips' call, is also in the house, and, again, "almost every female eye was turned" (76) towards him. However, Wickham chooses to honour Elizabeth by seating himself beside her and by conversing "immediately" with her (76). Wickham's marked attentions give the impression that he is courting Elizabeth; the charming effect of his speech makes Elizabeth, an able talker herself, "feel that the commonest, dullest, most threadbare topic might be rendered interesting by the skill of the speaker" (77).

It is under these circumstances that Wickham begins to attack Darcy's character. But not before Elizabeth has attacked it first. At Wickham's rather suggestive but nonetheless neutral comment on their chance meeting the day before and "'the very cold manner of [their] greeting'" (77), Elizabeth "warmly" informs him that she thinks Darcy "'very disagreeable'" (77). Thus Wickham's pleasant manner of speech has rendered his unpleasant experience with Darcy credible. The apparently truthful eyewitness report by Wickham, which should have alerted Elizabeth to the "impropriety of such communications to a stranger" (207), is listened to by a "very willing" (77) ear because she has been seduced by his flattering manners and because his misinformation rather conforms to her own fixed mode of thinking. Elizabeth's confidence in her own character-reading skills, boosted by a series of genuine successes in identifying the insensible Mr Collins and the supercilious Miss Bingley, seems reaffirmed by Wickham's corroborative evidence against Mr Darcy. Conversely, the fact that Darcy does not insidiously flatter her seems to give rise to Elizabeth's assumption that he must be suffering from "'such abominable pride'" (81).

3

Darcy's understanding of Elizabeth, though much improved as a result of his conscious and deliberate studying of her, remains incomplete. He is attracted to her mainly by her wit and intelligence, which are on a par with his. Taking her moral capacity for granted, Darcy interprets Elizabeth's teasing as what Jane Austen calls "light & bright & sparkling" and is brought "with increased delight to the playfulness & Epigrammatism" of her speech. [1] What Darcy is not aware of is that Elizabeth's teasing, so naturally and inimitably graced by her

---

[1] *Letters* 4 February 1813.

arch smiles, is also a weapon which she wields to put down Darcy's perceived arrogance, as well as to resist his attention.

Darcy's illusion of where he stands in terms of his understanding of Elizabeth is shattered at Hunsford rectory by the fiery reaction of the object of his desire. This second proposal scene is the single most significant and exciting dialectical event of the novel, in which the two opponents, fully incensed, attack each other in a gloves-off engagement. This second proposal scene bears resemblance to the first involving Mr Collins and Elizabeth. Both men ignore clear signals of discouragement and insist on making their feelings known to the woman in question. In Mr Collins' case, Elizabeth tries to run away; in Darcy's case she responds to his enquiry after her health "with cold civility" (189). Both men assume that their superior status, social as well as financial, speaks for itself; both presume that their condescension to make the proposal is by itself a gallant service to the less fortunate young woman, not to speak of her gentle but less well-to-do family; both therefore are convinced that they have made an offer too good to be refused—even though Elizabeth has negative feelings towards both of them.

But the similarities also highlight the dissimilarities. To begin with, Darcy represents a vastly more desirable match than Mr Collins, not only in terms of income but also in terms of intelligence and appearance. Secondly, Darcy's mind is not made up until he has come to know Elizabeth for quite some time: snubbing her, watching her, talking with her, dancing with her, debating with her and disagreeing with her. He has turned the matter over in his mind many times, carefully weighing the pros and cons, struggling and overcoming "'the scruples that had long prevented [his] forming any serious design'" (192). In short his proposal is a logical step because it is primarily based on moral understanding and compatible temperament, at least from his point of view. Mr Collins, on the other hand, has only just met Elizabeth when he makes the proposal. He hardly knows her and has no idea of her moral and intellectual qualities. In fact he proposes to her mainly because Miss Bennet, his first choice (a barely appropriate word), is no longer available ("'likely to be very soon engaged'" according to his "complaisant" hostess who however directs his attention to "her *younger* daughters" [71]).

The significant differences underlying the two equally presumptuous proposals account for the different reactions from Elizabeth. In the first instance Elizabeth's " feelings " are " divided between distress and diversion," and, as Mr Collins continues the comic proposal, she is "so near laughing" that she is unable to tell him to stop (105). Elizabeth eventually interrupts him and curtly refuses him. Although she tells Mr Collins that she is "'very sensible of the honour of [his] proposals'" (107), Elizabeth is never interested in his offer and is actually intent on rejecting him even before he begins his preamble.

Although Elizabeth's determination to decline is implicit in the second instance as well, given her hostile attitude towards Darcy leading to the proposal scene, the nature of her decision is quite different. Her feelings are divided between appreciation and resentment. Although she "[can] not be insensible to the compliment of such a man's affection" (189), she is nevertheless angered by Darcy's talk of "[h]is sense of her inferiority—of its being a degradation—of the family obstacles which judgment had always opposed to inclination" (189) to form the connection. At this stage, Elizabeth cannot tolerate Darcy's finding faults with her family because she thinks the man himself is full of faults. She acknowledges his "tenderness" but rejects his "pride" (189). In short Elizabeth rejects Darcy on moral grounds over issues involving Wickham, Bingley and Jane, and Darcy's own character; she rejects Mr Collins on the grounds of his plain foolishness.

The styles of the two proposal scenes are also dialectically complementary in terms of the actual speechs of the parties involved. Mr Collins' proposal is lengthy and preposterous, conventional and punctilious. The reasons for his proposal are itemized, and the suggestion by Lady Catherine de Bourgh that he should marry is emphasized. Mr Darcy by contrast comes straight to the point. The succinct and emotional proposal made by him bespeaks his sincerity and love:

> In vain have I struggled. It will not do. My feelings will not be repressed.

You must allow me to tell you how ardently I admire and love you. (189).

Paradoxically, Elizabeth's reply to Mr Collins is short and direct:

> Accept my thanks for the compliment you are paying me. I am very sensible
> of the honour of your proposals, but it is impossible for me to do otherwise than
> decline them. (107)

Yet her reply to Mr Darcy is formal, conventional and long-winded—the style reminds one of Mr Collins, and is particularly taunting and punishing to the proposer. Elizabeth is making a point of informing Mr Darcy that she is not being coy—as Mr Collins thinks elegant females usually are—and that she is rejecting him absolutely. But what might have been suitable for Mr Collins seems distasteful for Mr Darcy:

> In such cases as this, it is, I believe, the established mode to express a sense
> of obligation for the sentiments avowed, however unequally they may be
> returned. It is natural that obligation should be felt, and if I could *feel* gratitude,
> I would now thank you. But I cannot—I have never desired your good opinion,
> and you have certainly bestowed it most unwillingly. I am sorry to have
> occasioned pain to any one. It has been most unconsciously done, however, and I
> hope will be of short duration. The feelings which, you tell me, have long
> prevented the acknowledgement of your regard, can have little difficulty in
> overcoming it after this explanation. (190)

There is little doubt that Jane Austen's narrator means to provide a dialectical scenario by alluding to the parallel features in the two proposals so that the readers may compare and draw their own conclusions.

Although the directly negative outcome of the second proposal is the same as that of the first, its short-term and long-term values are immensely positive. Unlike what happens in the first proposal scene, where there is no real communication of thoughts between Mr Collins and Elizabeth, where the latter feels it "absolutely necessary" to stop the former's exuberance of verbosity about "'one thousand pounds in the 4 per cents'" and the inane declaration of "'the violence of [his] affection'" (106), what has been verbally transacted through the face-to-face engagement in the second proposal scene is meaningful and enlightening for both Darcy and Elizabeth. It is an indispensable step in the long process toward their mutual understanding. Therefore Darcy's words to Elizabeth: "'I thank you for explaining it so fully'" (192) are not entirely ironic. Darcy's pride in his superior social status which he thinks also entails his moral superiority is exposed and humbled by Elizabeth's pointed and swift rejection: "[W]hy with so evident a design of offending and insulting me, you chose to tell me that you liked me against your will, against your reason, and even against your character?'" (190). What Elizabeth fails to acknowledge properly is that Darcy's confession of his feelings is the result of his belief that "'disguise of every sort is [his] abhorrence'" (192), that he is really opening his heart to her.

Meanwhile Elizabeth, by being on the offensive most of the time during the proposal scene, has exposed herself completely and become vulnerable to a counter-attack, which is soon launched in the form of Darcy's long letter. If Darcy is unconscious of his pride, even as he points to its existence in Elizabeth's own character ("'these offences might have been overlooked, had not your pride been hurt by my honest confession of the scruples'" [192]), Elizabeth is equally unconscious of her prejudice: "'From the very beginning, from the first moment I may almost say, of my acquaintance with you, your manners impressing me with the fullest belief of your arrogance, your conceit, and your selfish disdain of the feelings of others, were such as to form that ground-work of disapprobation, on which succeeding events have built so immoveable a dislike'" (193). This evidence confirms our suspicion that Darcy's unflattering remark on Elizabeth's looks at the Meryton ball did wound as well as amuse Elizabeth.

All in all, the confrontation between the two protagonists serves as the basis for later rethinking by these intelligent characters. The truth is: the more earnestly the two parties engage each other, the more thoroughly they understand each other, and the more clearly they perceive each other's inner-self behind the curtain of appearance. They may not realize it at the moment, but the very act of their soul-to-soul clash forces both of them to drop their complaisance and to reflect and readjust their existing views. This is a crucial step in their dialectically informed moral transformation. Mr Darcy will have to turn over in his mind the blunt criticism of his overbearing pride, insulting condescension, self-importance, egotism, smugness and insensitivity, all of which he has unconsciously brought out with his proposal. Elizabeth will have to consider if her attack is entirely justified.

Once the facts are known and once they have been studied and reflected upon, Elizabeth realizes that she has been "blind, partial, prejudiced, absurd" (208). Elizabeth has rightly seen the root cause of her moral blunder: courting "prepossession" (208) of knowledge upon partial understanding of appearance, and relying on insufficient evidence without carrying out proper investigation and evaluation. In short she has failed to think dialectically. Now she realizes that pride is not just a problem that tarnishes Darcy's character; she has a fair share of it as well, not just family pride but also personal pride, pride in her own ability to detect pride in others—"'I, who have prided myself on my discernment!'" (208). Elizabeth's intelligence and quickness, which have attracted Darcy's attention yet also distracted, to a certain extent, his perspicacity, have been misdirected and become the means of promoting and completing her own foolishness. Her self-criticism: "'Till this moment, I never knew myself'" (208) is a fair statement, though complete understanding is yet to come.

4

The lesson learnt in the epistemological process forces Elizabeth to balance her own point of view with that of Darcy and make adjustments through objective induction rather than subjective deduction. In so doing she begins to acquire a dialectical understanding not only of herself but also of the reality around her. However, it is important to realize that Elizabeth's change of mind does not happen overnight. Darcy's epistle, hand-delivered in Rosings Park, no doubt marks the turning point in her outlook, but the event by itself means merely the beginning of a new stage in the epistemological process. The letter itself, despite its length—taking up almost the entire twelfth chapter of volume 2—clearly fails to reconcile everything. In fact, part of it turns out to be a constant source of irritation. Elizabeth is of course no longer "'determined to hate'" (90) Darcy, but she is not ready to like him either. She still "could not approve him; nor could she for a moment repent her refusal, or feel the slightest inclination ever to see him again" (212) in spite of, or perhaps because of, her careful study of "every sentence" of the epistle, to the extent of being "in a fair way of soon knowing [it] by heart" (212).

Mary Lascelles does not find Darcy's letter "plausible:"

> The manner is right, but not the matter: so much, and such, information would hardly be volunteered by a proud and reserved man—unless under pressure from his author, anxious to get on with the story. And perhaps it may be the same pressure that hastens Elizabeth's complete acceptance of its witness; for there is no time to lose; she must have revised her whole impression of him before her visit to Pemberley. ①

Lascelles's point seems out of place not only because the matter of probability or inevitability is something that depends on an individual's taste but, more importantly, because Jane Austen, as the architect of her narrative, must have felt the necessity of adding the letter-episode here, which initiates the process of closure at the middle point of the novel. If, as Aristotle says, "[a] middle is that which follows something else, and is itself followed by something," ② then Jane Austen cannot be faulted.

It seems to me that the epistolary "part" fits rather nicely into the "whole." Given the fact that Darcy and Elizabeth have just confronted each other and parted in anger, it would be improbable for them to meet cordially and discuss calmly their differences in a constructive way. However, Darcy, who is shaken by Elizabeth's scathing criticism, is still in love with his critic. He realizes that Elizabeth's moral indignation must be dealt with if he wants to

---

① Lascelles 162.

② *On the Art of Poetry*, *Classical Literary Criticism*, trans. T. S. Dorsch (Harmondsworth: Penguin, 41). Paul Goodman elaborates on Aristotle's notion of plot in *The Structure of Literature* (Chicago: U of Chicago P, 1954) 12–17.

win her affection. The fairly presented details about Wickham's wickedness in his letter are meant to clarify the issue for Elizabeth so that she cannot fault him in that regard, but the intimate family details involving his younger sister, Georgiana, can only mean an invitation to Elizabeth to form a special relationship, especially when the writer decides to take the sole reader of his letter into confidence: "'Having said thus much, I feel no doubt of your secrecy'" (201). Mr Darcy's letter is surely an indication of his intent to show Elizabeth that his feelings for her have not changed, as he will later inform directly the woman who receives and reads his letter. It is also a mark of his maturity. Mr Darcy chooses to delay the detailed explanation of his side of the story precisely because he was sanely aware, even at the height of their debate in the rectory, that he "'was not then master enough of [himself] to know what could or ought to be revealed'" (202).

Claudia Brodsky Lacour makes an excellent point explaining the rationale of the epistolary device: that "something fixed—something with which she can have no conversation, which cannot be made light, bright, and sparkling by the lively translating power of her mind" is deployed for the simple reason that "there is nothing transformative one can say back to a written letter, nothing, in any case, that can change the writing on the page."①, Nevertheless the dialogue is continued despite the physical impossibility of talking back to the letter; it has simply taken another form. Every time the letter is retrieved by Elizabeth, Darcy's voice will ring forth and his remarks will be, as it were, heard. When those remarks have been more or less committed to memory by Elizabeth, the dialogue becomes internal and even permanent in her mind. It is true that the wording of the epistle cannot be changed, but the comprehension of it can. Elizabeth's constant recapitulation and reflection of the contents of the letter, either appreciating or rejecting any part of it, have created an inward dialectical debate which coincides with the outward investigation and verification of Darcy's testimony in the form of her subsequent visit to Pemberley.

---

① Lacour 615, 616.

While approaching Darcy's estate with her London uncle and aunt, Elizabeth experiences sensuous and aesthetic satisfaction at seeing "natural beauty" so little "counteracted by an awkward taste" (245). Not only does the layout of the estate appeal to her taste, but the interior corroborates her impression of the outside. The rooms are "lofty and handsome;" the furniture is "neither gaudy nor uselessly fine," showing, by comparison with what she has seen at Rosings, "more real elegance" and "less of splendor" (246). Darcy's home is, in Alistair Duckworth's words, "a natural analogue of his social and moral character."[1] From the housekeeper, Mrs Reynolds, Elizabeth learns that Darcy is a good brother, excellent landlord and considerate master. At one point during the visit at Pemberley the old housekeeper shows them the family gallery where there is a large portrait of Mr Darcy:

> Elizabeth walked on in quest of the only face whose features would be known to her. At last it arrested her—and she beheld a striking resemblance of Mr Darcy, with such a smile over the face, as she remembered to have sometimes seen, when he looked at her. She stood several minutes before the picture in earnest contemplation, and returned to it again before they quitted the gallery. (250)

Watching the likeness of Darcy closely, and reflecting on the warm praise she has just heard from the amiable and good-natured Mrs Reynolds,[2] Elizabeth is able to vision, or revision, Darcy's moral rectitude.

Elizabeth "stood before the canvas, on which he was represented, and fixed his eyes upon herself" (251). This vicarious encounter sought by Elizabeth implies her wish to see the real Darcy again and her eagerness to form a friendship. The point about their "eye-contact" is significant. It echoes an earlier point at which Darcy's view of Elizabeth begins to

---

[1] Duckworth 123.

[2] Samuel Johnson in *Rambler* 68 maintains: "The highest panegyrick, therefore, that private virtue can receive, is the praise of servants. For, however vanity or insolence may look down with contempt on the suffrage of men, undignified by wealth, and unenlightened by education, it very seldom happens that they command or blame without justice" (*The Yale Edition of the Works of Samuel Johnson*, ed. W. J. Bate and Albrecht B. Strauss [New Haven: Yale UP, 1969] vol. 3, 361). All references to Samuel Johnson's works are to this edition.

change, i.e., when he discovers Elizabeth's "'pair of fine eyes.'"
Elizabeth's gesture exhibits the essential quality of the Wordsworthian
"spots of time" or the Joycean epiphany, as though the attentive observer
had caught a glimpse of the intrinsic quality of the observed through the
window of his "eyes." But neither "spots of time" nor "epiphany" would
accurately or satisfactorily characterize this high point in Elizabeth's
understanding, which is not achieved until she has done a substantial
amount of moral and intellectual thinking. Elizabeth's re-vision at
Pemberley reveals what her earlier vision has missed: "[S]he thought of
his regard with a deeper sentiment of gratitude than it had ever raised
before; she remembered its warmth, and softened its impropriety of
expression" (251). The word "regard" is a nice pun: it pays tribute to
Darcy's vision and esteem of the observer. Instead of monopolizing the
vision by fixing her eyes on his, Elizabeth is now willing to perceive
reality through the sight of her sometime antagonist and make due
allowance for a noble nature's "impropriety of expression."

The new understanding, reached through a long process of dialectical
transformation, is the basis of a possible new relationship between Darcy
and Elizabeth. Darcy puts into practice his argument that "'[t]o yield
without conviction is no compliment to the understanding'" (50), now
that he is convinced by Elizabeth's reproach that his attitude of aloofness
and superiority has erected barriers between himself and others. At
Pemberley, where he accidentally comes across Elizabeth and the
Gardiners, an enlightened and amiable Darcy makes a point of
overcoming his natural shyness—no longer using it as an excuse—and
"seeking the acquaintance of some of those very people [Mr Gardiner
being a businessman and a brother of Mrs Bennet's], against whom his
pride had revolted" (254–255). Instead of "decamping as fast as he could
from such disgraceful companions" (255) once he is told who and what
they are, he entertains them with a warmth and considerateness befitting
old friends (say, Mr Bingley). Upon learning Mr Gardiner's hobby,
Darcy invites him to fish, "offering at the same time to supply him with
fishing tackle, and pointing out those parts of the stream where there was

usually most sport" (255). Of course the Gardiners' own merits, especially those of Mr Gardiner—"every expression, every sentence of her uncle marked his intelligence, his taste, or his good manners" (255)— account for the note of congeniality that has been struck, but Darcy's decided admiration for Elizabeth, as her aunt quickly senses, is perhaps a more dominant factor.

It is a much stronger kind of admiration, too. Elizabeth's outright, thorough and sound rejection of him on moral grounds, partly prejudiced as it may have been, has shaken him to the core, and forced him to reflect on his own behaviour and to resolve to rid himself of the moral deficiencies pointed out by Elizabeth. The change in Darcy impacts dialectically on Elizabeth in turn; her own moral transformation, jump-started by what Oliver MacDonagh calls "the exculpatory letter" from Darcy,[1] is sustained and facilitated by what she has observed during her visit to Pemberley. Last but not least, discovering Darcy's indispensable and material assistance, very discreetly offered, in solving the Bennets' family crisis caused by Lydia's elopement with the deceitful Wickham, who does not intend to marry her, Elizabeth fully realizes Darcy's extraordinary sense of responsibility and delicacy. He has proved himself a true and improved gentleman. The epistemological process has come full circle wherein "[w]hat is for understanding an object in a covering veil of sense, now comes before us in its essential form as a pure notion."[2] Darcy "knew" that his letter "'must'" give Elizabeth "'pain'" but deems it "'necessary'" (368). Elizabeth, on the other hand, shows true flair in her summary of the epistemological experience: "'The conduct of neither, if strictly examined, will be irreproachable; but since then, we have both, I hope, improved in civility'" (367).

---

[1] *Jane Austen: Real and Imagined Worlds* (New Haven: Yale UP, 1991) 90.

[2] Hegel, *The Phenomenology of Mind*, trans. J. B. Baillie, 2nd ed. (1910; London: George Allen, 1949) 211. Baillie's translation is here preferred for its fluency (arabic numerals being page numbers). For comparison see Miller's translation, *Phenomenology of Spirit* 102.

5

The morally transformed Elizabeth Bennet shows her remarkable ability in her skirmish, in chapter 14 of the third volume, with the well-seasoned matriarch Lady Catherine de Bourgh, one of the hopelessly unenlightened characters in *Pride and Prejudice*. When the intimidating lady unexpectedly drops in at Longbourn and rudely interrogates Elizabeth about the nature of her relationship with her nephew, Elizabeth is able to meet her overbearing insolence with civility and sobering reason. In spite of her self-claimed "'sincerity and frankness'" (353), Lady Catherine de Bourgh will not at first come clean with the main issue that brings her over from Rosings in such a great hurry. Instead of going to London (where Darcy is apparently staying) and asking her nephew to clarify his relationship with Elizabeth, she comes to Longbourn to intimidate the woman in question. Instead of admitting that she is very much afraid that her nephew will not marry her daughter, she emphasizes that "'it must be a scandalous falsehood'" (353) that "'Miss Elizabeth Bennet, would, in all likelihood, be soon afterwards united to my nephew, my own nephew, Mr. Darcy'" (353). Elizabeth astutely and fearlessly points out the illogical contradictions between her ladyship's actions and intentions. She calmly exposes the inconsistency between her ladyship's subjective notion and the objective reality, and has all but told Lady Catherine that she is powerless in controlling either her or her nephew, whatever hollow threats she may choose to make.

In short throughout the heated engagement Elizabeth manages to be polite without servility, assertive without stubbornness, and witty without insincerity. She is like Catherine Morland towards the end of *Northanger Abbey* who is able to write that well-balanced Johnsonian letter to Miss Tilney under great personal distress (*NA* 235) but with admirable presence of mind. In a dialectical sense, her ladyship's visit to Longbourn, as Elizabeth points out on the spot, "'will be rather a confirmation'" of the rumour of a possible union between Darcy and

Elizabeth, and the fruitlessness of her visit will be a clear signal to her nephew, as Darcy later reveals to Elizabeth (367), that his hope is not unilateral. Hence Lady Catherine's negative intent meets a negative end, and the double negatives must produce a positive result—the inevitable union of Darcy and Elizabeth.

For Lady Catherine de Bourgh, Miss Caroline Bingley, Mr Collins, Mrs Bennet and Mrs Hurst, whose thinking is non-dialectical, appearance is all that they will see, and all that they think they need to see. Their minds are controlled by fixed ideologies, and their actions directed accordingly. So far as Lady Catherine de Bourgh can see, there is nothing beneath Elizabeth's appearance but the "'upstart pretensions of a young woman without family, connections, or fortune'" (356), who is seeking a superior marriage in order to advance herself socially and financially and, in the process, cause the "'ancient'" (356) and "'noble'" (356) blood to become "'polluted'" (357). Lady Catherine's nosiness ensures that she is well-informed, but the kind of information that she eagerly and impertinently collects invariably concerns such material yet superficial facts as age, looks, accomplishments, whether one is out or not, marital status, mother's maiden name, type of carriage owned, financial situation, relations, connections, and scandals. She bases her understanding upon evidence of social appearance and pecuniary worth. She holds the notion of class and status, rank and fortune, as the *only* basis of marriage and will not "have her judgment controverted" (163).

Miss Caroline Bingley is a subtle version of Lady Catherine. While high-handed Lady Catherine uses intimidation in her attempt to have Elizabeth surrender Darcy to her sickly daughter, Miss Bingley resorts to underhanded tactics to discredit Elizabeth and her relations, behind her back but in front of Darcy. She keeps reminding Darcy (as well as her own brother) of the ignominious relations the Bennets have and what "'a charming mother-in-law'" (27) Darcy, or Bingley, would get. When the notorious Mrs Bennet and her two ill-mannered younger daughters come to Netherfield to see Jane, Miss Bingley mischievously and insidiously invites them away from the bedroom where the subject of their visit is lying sick in bed, to the breakfast parlour where Darcy and Bingley may watch their vulgarities in full display.

Lady Catherine at least allows Elizabeth to be "pretty" (163); Miss Bingley not even that:

> I must confess that I never could see any beauty in her. Her face is too thin; her complexion has no brilliancy; and her features are not at all handsome. Her nose wants character; there is nothing marked in its lines. Her teeth are tolerable, but not out of the common way; and as for her eyes, which have sometimes been called so fine, I never could perceive any thing extraordinary in them. They have a sharp, shrewish look, which I do not like at all; and in her air altogether, there is a self-sufficiency without fashion, which is intolerable. (271)

Miss Bingley implies that she is all that Elizabeth is not. Her subjective and dogmatic way of thinking little prepares her for the shock when she learns that Darcy prefers Elizabeth to her. Her closed mind does not improve in the entire duration of the narrative; it remains the same at the end of the story as it was at the beginning, though she is compelled to modify her behaviour towards Elizabeth after her marriage to Darcy so as "to retain the right of visiting at Pemberley" (387). These characters are wilfully blind to the inner quality of the hero and the heroine. They exemplify Hegel's metaphor of the person with sight put in a room in absolute darkness and therefore seeing absolutely nothing even though the room may be full of objects. The mere appearance of darkness convinces them that there is nothing there to be seen.

There is one little interesting case to mention before we close this chapter. Charlotte Lucas, Elizabeth's sometime bosom friend, gives her own opinion, early in the novel (volume 1, chapter 6), about the institution of marriage, which differs from that of Elizabeth. Charlotte, who is about twenty-seven years old, believes that a woman should actively—"'make the most of every half hour'" (22)—seek a well-to-do husband first and foremost, because "'[h]appiness in marriage is entirely a matter of chance'" and therefore "'it is better to know as little as possible of the defects of the person with whom you are to pass your life'" (23). Elizabeth's view is sharply different. She does not believe in catching a man by accident, nor does she believe, as Charlotte Lucas does, that "'the desire of being well married'" (22) should govern a woman's action. Her own successful marriage, as it turns out, is based on mutual understanding and mutual affection built up over a relatively long period of time.

This discussion between two intimate friends is genuine but it is not dialectically helpful because their different views on marriage are irreconcilable. Both make good their respective theories: Charlotte marries the foolish but comfortable (and potentially well-to-do) Mr Collins though she scarcely knows him;[①] Elizabeth refuses first Mr Collins and then Mr Darcy—even though she is tempted by the latter's status and wealth. While viewing the grounds of Darcy's estate Elizabeth cannot help thinking that "to be mistress of Pemberley might be something!" (245). The exclamation mark reveals the excited state of Elizabeth's mind regarding the material reality of society which one has to face in life one way or the other. Although Elizabeth will never compromise her principles even in face of the massive temptation offered by Darcy's wealth, she is not ignorant of or indifferent to the economic benefit an advantageous marriage entails.

Pride and Prejudice marks an important milestone in Jane Austen's writing career. It shows clear signs of maturity as the author ceases reacting to the romantic or Gothic tradition and starts concentrating instead on fulfilling her own intellectual and artistic design. The narrative shows a consciously constructed intricate pattern of dialectical events. In particular the engagement between Elizabeth and Darcy has been consistently and significantly portrayed in light of the dialectical principle. This I consider to be the essence of *Pride and Prejudice*.

---

① There seems to be, however, some modification in Charlotte's view after her marriage. At Rosings Park Elizabeth observes that her sometime best friend does not appear to prefer her husband's company (168).

This is also precisely the point which Marilyn Butler and Mary Poovey fail to notice. Butler, for example, ignores Jane Austen's conscious and systematic delineation of the protagonists' thought processes; she observes:

> The trouble with *Pride and Prejudice* is that many readers do not perceive just how critical the author is of Elizabeth's way of thinking. The meaning is obscure partly because Elizabeth's thoughts are insufficiently characterized, and partly because no character within the novel effectively criticizes her. ①

Such observation ignores the persistent engagement between the two protagonists throughout the novel. The problem is the critic's insistence on applying her notion that Austen is a religiously conservative writer who is committed to "a view of human nature that derives from orthodox Christian pessimism, not from progressive optimism."② Consequently, any narrative symptom that cannot be logically explained by the application of this line of argument will be deemed some sort of deviation on the part of Jane Austen. In fact, Butler speculates that "in *Pride and Prejudice* Jane Austen might have appeared to err from orthodoxy, not wilfully, but through a fault in the execution," because "it has no clear message," "and she never made the same mistake again."③ But Austen would make the same "mistake" again, as Butler will once again have us believe, in her next novel.

Poovey, on the other hand, applies a modified version of a nonetheless rigid feminist approach to *Pride and Prejudice*. To begin with, she finds the book depicting a polarity between "feeling and imaginative energy" and "moral authority," and she sees Elizabeth Bennet as a serious threat to "both the social order, which demands self-denial, and the moral order, which is based on absolute Christian principles."④ Poovey's general argument is in format very similar to Butler's except for standing

---

① Butler 216.
② Butler 212.
③ Butler 218.
④ Poovey 194.

Butler's on its head from time to time. As I have illustrated in earlier chapters in general and in chapter 3 in particular, Butler tends to see Austen's novels in terms of a negative individualism against a positive society, with Austen taking the side of society. Poovey, however, sees a positive individualism in contradiction with a negative society. For example, she talks about "Elizabeth's lively wit" in terms of a "pretentious and repressive society;" she argues: "That Miss Bingley despises Elizabeth for what she calls 'conceited independence' simply enhances our sympathy for conceit and independence, if these are the traits Elizabeth embodies."[1]

Poovey suggests that Austen relies on a couple of strategies to bridge the gap. First she uses the "notion of the family," a "patriarchal" vehicle, to accommodate "the proper coexistence of the individual and society."[2] Second she constructs a romantic "model of private gratification" which "seems to promise to women in particular an emotional intensity that ideally compensates for all the practical opportunities they are denied," even though "romantic relationships, by their very nature, cannot materially affect society."[3] What such strategy achieves therefore is a "kind of temporary and imaginative consolation that serves to defuse criticism of the very institutions that make such consolation necessary."[4] In other words, "[b]y such narrative magic, Austen is able to defuse the thematic conflict between sense and sensibility—or reason and feeling, or realism and romance—that troubled her earlier works."[5]

Ironically, by narrowly focusing on women's role as romantic angels housed in "those fairy-tale marriages that stop realism dead in its tracks"[6] and by ignoring the intellectual and philosophical capacity that Austenian heroines actually enjoy and exercise, often to their advantage, as particularly clearly shown in *Pride and Prejudice*, Poovey is in fact

---

[1] Poovey 195.

[2] Poovey 203.

[3][4] Poovey 237.

[5] Poovey 194.

[6] Poovey 238.

perpetuating the patriarchal myth of which she has been all along critical in her book. Instead of paying close attention to the moral and intellectual engagement between Elizabeth and Darcy that proves mutually stimulating and beneficial, Poovey falls for the superficial romantic plot and insists that Austen is offering such "romance in the service of propriety."[1] Thus she contends that "by forcing her reader to participate in creating the moral order that governs the novel's conclusion, Austen is able to make this aesthetic 'solution' seem, at least momentarily, both natural and right."[2] The assertion is self-contradictory. If Austen had to force her readers to agree to a certain point of view to begin with, what would be the point of talking about her aesthetic prowess? By putting "solution" in quotation marks and by using the ambiguous verb "seem" Poovey re-casts her doubts about deriving any real meaning from the conclusion, even though she regards *Pride and Prejudice* as one of "Austen's mature novels."[3]

Pride and Prejudice, "so full of contradictions and varieties" (279), bears powerful witness to the philosophical working of the dialectical process essential to the shaping of a rational moral being. The moral of the story is this: only when one considers reality from multiple perspectives and thinks dialectically can one expect to judge people or situations objectively and achieve knowledge and self-knowledge. What Darcy is most grateful to Elizabeth for is not only requited love but the fact that she has taught him "'a lesson, hard indeed at first, but most advantageous'" (369) in the end, which has made him a better person. The same is true of Elizabeth. Humbling, she is humbled; teaching, she is taught. Jane Austen, albeit residing in the political and social backwater of Steventon and Chawton, focuses on the activity and improvement of the mind. A sound mind is a dialectical one which will induce moral transformation. A fixed mind is often the source of all that is fallacious, injudicious, and vacuous.

---

[1][2]   Poovey 194.
[3]   Poovey 238.

In *Mansfield Park* the dialectical process of the heroine's moral development is rendered in an even more sophisticated form due to her humble status and economic dependency. The narrative is more inward yet no less intense. Consequently, the task of cultivating her own moral consciousness and combating rampant corrupt influences around her is a much more formidable and arduous one for Fanny Price than for Elizabeth Bennet. Fanny does not have the kind of freedom and manoeuvrability that Elizabeth Bennet enjoys, but her limited physical movement does not prevent her from ranging freely in the realm of her own mind. In fact she has made the most of her moral and intellectual scope in a less than propitious environment.

5 *Mansfield Park*:
The Dialectics of Moral Growth

To talk about the dialectics of moral growth in *Mansfield Park* is to disagree with a number of eminent Austen critics. It seems that these critics, instead of appreciating Jane Austen's complexity, are committed to the view of her simplicity. Their deprecating conclusions about the novel seem to derive from their preoccupation with prescriptive criticism and their inattention to the fluidity of the text. But if disagreement is, as F. R. Leavis suggests in *The Common Pursuit* (and I think he is right), a form of collaboration, then the following may be perceived as an effort to join in what T. S. Eliot calls "the common pursuit of true judgment."[1] In this chapter I will first give a synopsis of the mostly negative critical reception of *Mansfield Park* in general in the twentieth century; I will then present a dialectical analysis of the novel, which is consistent with my reading of the rest of Jane Austen's work. I will demonstrate in particular how Fanny Price benefits from a seriously flawed but nonetheless indispensable educational scheme at Mansfield, and how, as a result, her learning process is dialectical.

1

Mansfield Park is often referred to as a unique work, not, however, in any complimentary sense but in the sense of its being problematic. As R. W. Chapman long ago put it, "it is there hardest to be sure of the

---

[1] *The Common Pursuit* (London: Chatto, 1952) v. The title of Leavis's book is derived from a phrase in T. S. Eliot's essay, "The Function of Criticism" (1923).

writer's general intention."① The task of interpretation is further
complicated by the famous ambiguity of Jane Austen's reference to
"Ordination" in her blithe letter to Cassandra on 29 January 1813.② That
"Ordination" is not being announced as *the* subject of *Mansfield Park* is
clear; although it remains a crucial point of moral contention between
Edmund Bertram and Mary Crawford. Indeed *Mansfield Park* forms a
stark contrast in many respects with its predecessor, *Pride and Prejudice*,
which is deemed by Austen herself, not without some well-deserved
complacency, as "rather too light & bright & sparkling," needing
"shade".③ Chapman, after the hesitation noted above, declared that
"[t]he ostensible moral" of *Mansfield Park* is "almost blatantly didactic,"
though he did find some consolation in the supremacy of Austen's art:

---

① R. W. Chapman, *Jane Austen: Facts and Problems* (Oxford: Clarendon, 1948) 194.

② *Letters*; see also note 7 on page 411. Commentators have consistently assumed that Jane
Austen refers to the theme of her new novel, i. e., *Mansfield Park*, when she says "Now I will
try to write of something else;—it shall be a complete change of subject—Ordination." A recent
book on Austen shows that its author is still under the impression that "[t] he subject of
Mansfield Park is indeed, as Jane Austen says, or seems to say, 'ordination'" (see Edward
Neill, *The Politics of Jane Austen* [Houndmills: Macmillan, 1999] 87). R. W. Chapman
perhaps bears chief responsibility for this interpretation as he comments that Jane Austen "wrote
to her sister, at the outset, that she was 'going to take a new subject, ordination'" (*Jane
Austen: Facts and Problems* [194]). However, Chapman himself has reservations about his own
interpretation. Earlier in the same book he writes: "Jane's statement cannot mean what it seems
to mean, that she was about to begin a new book. For we know from herself that *Mansfield
Park* was begun two years earlier; and allusions in a letter written a few days before the letter
just quoted show that Cassandra was already familiar with parts of the second volume" (82). The
letter of a few days before is that of 24 January 1813 where Jane tells Cassandra: "I learn from
Sir J. Carr that there is no Government House at Gibraltar. —I must alter it to 'the
Commissioner's'" (see *MP* vol. 2, ch. 6, 235). Chapman even muses that "Ordination" would
not be the word "we should choose, if we had to describe the theme in a word or a phrase"
(194). Charles E. Edge seems to have been the first to challenge the traditional assumption (so
to speak); he argues that the announcement of "a complete change of subject" is simply a
"transitional device" emitting "a kind of stylistic humour," something to do with "her
characteristic manner of writing her letters" rather than the subject of *Mansfield Park* (*NCF* 16
[1961] 269–274). J. F. Burrows follows this new interpretation (see "Jane Austen's *Emma*: A
Study of Narrative Art." Diss. U of London, 1967; app. A, 284–287). My own enlightenment
came on the heels of Oliver MacDonagh's painful discovery (see *Jane Austen: Real and
Imagined Worlds*, 1).

③ *Letters*, 4 February 1813.

What she tells us of her persons is vitiated by this one-sided theory. But the persons themselves act and talk naturally, exhibiting just that share of original sin with which nature—helped or hindered, no doubt, by their upbringing—had endowed them. ①

Chapman's assessment of the novel seems to have given impetus, if not license, to a barrage of objections to *Mansfield Park* ever since.

Lord David Cecil is among the first to echo Chapman's negative view; he asserts that "[o]nly once, in *Mansfield Park*, did Jane Austen try another type [of heroines]; and she failed."② He also regrets that "Fanny is a little wooden, a little charmless, and rather a prig."③ Then D. W. Harding suggests that the novel is a "*reductio ad absurdum* of the Cinderella theme;"④ C. S. Lewis regards it as rigidly moral with an exemplary prig as its heroine who is endowed with "really nothing except rectitude of mind."⑤ A. Walton Litz calls the book "a strategic retreat from the exposed position of *Pride and Prejudice*, a retreat which is not— in terms of narrative structure—wholly successful," and attributes the "bald didacticism" to a conscious reaction on Austen's part "against the confident irony of her early fiction, against that which is 'light, and [sic] bright, and [sic] sparkling' at the expense of decorum and sense."⑥ "To invite Mr and Mrs Edmund Bertram round for the evening," opines

---

① Chapman, *Facts*, 194.

② *Jane Austen* (Cambridge: Cambridge UP, 1935) 11.

③ Cecil 12.

④ "Regulated Hatred: An Aspect of the Work of Jane Austen," *Scrutiny* 8 (1940) 358. David Daiches agrees that "*Mansfield Park* employs a simple Cinderella theme" but adds that its working out shows "subtlety and complexity" (*A Critical History of English Literature* [New York: Ronald, 1960] vol. 2, 755). Glenda A. Hudson recently comments that "[a]t the core of all of Austen's novels lies the Cinderella story, or, rather, several mutations of the popular fairy tale" (*Sibling Love and Incest in Jane Austen's Fiction* [New York: St. Martin's, 1992] 97). Juliet McMaster, more recently, maintains that "Austen is often happy to follow the Cinderella plot ("Class," *The Cambridge Companion to Jane Austen*, eds. Edward Copeland and Juliet McMaster" [Cambridge: Cambridge UP, 1997] 117).

⑤ C. S. Lewis, *Selected Literary Essays*, ed. Walter Hooper (Cambridge: Cambridge UP, 1969) 182.

⑥ Litz 113, 116, 115.

Kingsley Amis, "would not be lightly undertaken."① Clearly, Fanny Price has become the lightning rod for various kinds of harsh criticism.

Feminist critics also focus on the heroine's passiveness and priggishness, only to draw different conclusions. Sandra M. Gilbert and Susan Gubar, for example, think that Fanny "resembles Snow White not only in her passivity but in her invalid deathliness, her immobility, her pale purity;" so that she "seems unable fully to actualize herself as an authentic subject" and "is destined to become the next Lady Bertram, following the example of Sir Thomas's corpselike wife."② Claudia L. Johnson regards Fanny as "a grateful slave" who "lets particular and small acts of kindness overshadow a larger act of cruelty." The irony, she finds, is that the enlightened slave-owner—meaning Sir Thomas—shows "breathtaking impercipience" by attributing "radical agendas and ungovernable passions to the dutiful and mild Fanny." Such a twist, she maintains, makes *Mansfield Park* "a bitter parody of conservative fiction" since it helps to "turn conservative myth sour."③ Mary Poovey finds it "difficult to understand" how "the qualities of passivity, reserve, and self-depreciation" enable Fanny to "overcome either the Bertram's [sic] moral inertia or the Crawfords' anarchic power." She concludes that Fanny is "so passive" that "our sense of triumph comes not from Fanny but from the tone and machinations of the narrator, whose vitality is far closer to Mary Crawford's energy than to Fanny's passivity."④

Marilyn Butler, apparently even more frustrated, pronounces that "Fanny is impossible," that she "is a failure," and that "*Mansfield Park* is at its best when her part is smallest." Consistent with her conservative, i.e., anti-Jacobin, reading of the Jane Austen canon, Butler speculates that Austen is of the Jacobin party without knowing it; that is, she "inadvertently lets in the enemy, subjectivism," without being

---

① Kingsley Amis, *What Became of Jane Austen? and Other Questions* (London: Jonathan Cape, 1970) 14.

② Gilbert and Gubar 165, 166.

③ Johnson 108, 105, 96, 97.

④ Poovey 223.

sufficiently careful while writing *Mansfield Park*, in which Fanny's consciousness takes centre-stage. "In an anti-jacobin novel," she advises, "'consciousness' must be treated critically."[①] Butler further explains that "[w]hen her consciousness succeeds the Bertrams' as the *locus* of the important action, there is a movement from the plane of what could happen to the plane of what should happen, from the actual observable world to the ideal."[②] The implication of Butler's surmise is that Austen's desire for "shade" has got the better of her judgment since she makes a morally impeccable Fanny decide the issue of the day.[③]

Butler's analysis in fact echoes that made by Lionel Trilling, who as early as 1950 declared that "all the other novels of Jane Austen are, in essential ways, of our modern time" but "*Mansfield Park* is the exception, and it is bitterly resented."[④] The reason, Trilling argues, is that:

> It scandalizes the modern assumptions about social relations, about virtue, about religion, sex, and art. Most troubling of all is its preference for rest over motion. To deal with the world by condemning it, by withdrawing from it and shutting it out, by making oneself and one's mode and principles of life the very center of existence and to live the round of one's days in stasis and peace thus contrived—this, in an earlier age, was one of the recognized strategies of life, but to us it seems not merely impracticable but almost wicked.[⑤]

A decade or so later, Trilling continues the discussion and tries to vindicate philosophically the unhappiness of the disgruntled critics and commentators:

> Alone among Jane Austen's novels, *Mansfield Park* is pledged to the single vision of the 'honest soul'. It knows that things are not what they will become

---

① Butler 248.

② Butler 245.

③ Butler's evaluation of Fanny here seems to contradict her evaluative statement about Austen's moral principle in her following chapter on *Emma*: "Jane Austen does not present stupid characters as really good, since she thinks of goodness as an active, analytical process, not at all the same thing as passive good nature" (271).

④ *The Opposing Self* (1950; New York: Viking, 1955) 210.

⑤ Trilling, *Opposing Self* 210–211.

but what an uncorrupted intelligence may perceive them to be from the first. Seven years after the publication of the *Phenomenology* this novel tells us in effect that Hegel is quite wrong in the method of judgement he propounds and exemplifies. ①

Trilling argues that "our commitment to the dialectical mode of apprehending reality is outraged by the militant categorical certitude with which *Mansfield Park* discriminates between right and wrong"② because the novel, in his view, "ruthlessly rejects the dialectical mode and seeks to impose the categorical constraints the more firmly upon us. "③

Trilling obviously wants to see some dialectic in *Mansfield Park* but fails to identify anything close to it. He has looked in the right direction but come up with an inadequate answer. Indeed, the questions that haunt *Mansfield Park* remain inadequately answered. What is the matter with Fanny Price? What is after all going on in her mind? Why does Jane Austen create a heroine whom she obviously cherishes, fondly calling her "My Fanny" (461), yet many Austen critics love to hate, or hate to love?④ Why has this particular novel incensed so many critics?

---

① The earliest English translation of Hegel's philosophical works was made in 1855 (see *Dictionary of Philosophy and Psychology*, ed. James Mark Baldwin [New York﹔Macmillan, 1905] vol. 3, pt. 1, 243 – 244). J. B. Baillie's English translation of *Phenomenology* was made in 1910 (George Watson's *NCBEL* gives the wrong date [1821] whereas Bateson's *CBEL* gives the correct one).

②③ Trilling, *Sincerity* 79.

④ There have been from time to time dissenting voices﹔for example, D. D. Devlin discusses Fanny's "freedom of spirit" and moral growth in his excellent chapter on *Mansfield Park* (see *Jane Austen and Education* [London﹔Macmillan, 1975] 76 – 126). However, these voices are sporadic and sometimes indistinct. Avrom Fleishman, for example, rightly argues that Fanny is not presented "as a paragon of virtue," that Fanny's "morality continually proves inadequate to the complexities of mature experience and must therefore continually be bolstered with fresh supplies of hostility, greater indignation." Yet he then argues that "Edmund's rejection of Mary is not, strictly speaking, moral, for Mary does nothing immoral," so that Mary Crawford is entitled to blame Fanny's moral fortitude for Henry's immoral act. All in all, Fleishman wants to suggest that "Fanny's morality . . . is to be neither affirmed nor rejected but understood" (see *A Reading of* Mansfield Park [1967, U of Minnesota P﹔Baltimore﹔Johns Hopkins, 1970] 44, 46, 53).

In order to answer these questions properly we need to review carefully the moral and epistemological process of Fanny's development throughout the novel as a whole and, more importantly, to heed the dialectical nature of such process. *Mansfield Park* is about moral education, its success and, more significantly, its failure. The complexity of the moral education lies in the fact that Fanny is subject, on the one hand, to a Mansfield educational system that has a built-in double standard discriminating against her as a pupil, and on the other to a group of "educators" —Sir Thomas, Mrs Norris, Edmund, the Crawfords and even Lady Bertram—who each have different expectations of her. Fanny's willingness to go through such an educational process without surrendering her faculty of rational thinking enables her to graduate with a sound understanding of herself and the people around her. Sir Thomas, Lady Bertram and Mrs Norris may have absolute mastery of Fanny's physical movement, but they can not limit her mental scope and never succeed in controlling her thoughts. Eventually, not even Edmund, her mentor, can influence her moral judgment as he used to.

Fanny is engaged in a dialectical relationship with her "educators," and she learns by observing, reflecting, reasoning and, above all, acting. A common misconception, a by-product, so to speak, of the mistakenly presumed Cinderella-theme, is that Fanny never acts. For example, Bernard J. Paris argues that, as "a variation of the Cinderella story," Fanny "does not grow up, just being good, helpless, totally passive," while succeeding in "getting her wishes" as well as "her due."[①] Juliet McMaster, in one of her essays on Jane Austen, thinks that Fanny is "morally admirable from the beginning" and "remains morally static" so that the progress she makes is "rather a social than a moral one."[②]

---

① *Character and Conflict in Jane Austen's Novels* (Detroit: Wayne State UP, 1978) 24.

② Juliet McMaster, "Emma Watson: Jane Austen's Uncompleted Heroine," *Critical Reconstructions: the Relationship of Fiction and Life*, eds. R. M. Polhemus and R. B. Henkle (Stanford: Stanford UP, 1994) 215. Robyn Warhol echoes McMaster's view by grouping Fanny Price with Elinor Dashwood and Anne Elliot whose "character seems fully formed at the beginning of the novel" ("the look, the body, and the heroine of *persuasion* [sic]: A Feminist-

But Fanny does act, even unexpectedly at times. She cries, she smiles, she reads, speaks (agrees, disagrees, argues, compromises, coaches, advises, etc.), she walks, she rides, she dances, she visits, she loves, and she would even have acted in *Lovers' Vows* (but for Sir Thomas's unexpected return); not to mention all kinds of household errands that she runs for either Mrs Norris or Lady Bertram. More importantly, Fanny acts throughout as a moral agent, and she exerts herself to the full extent of her limited capacity, given her social circumstances. The progress Fanny makes is not just a social one but indeed a moral one as well. Fanny's learning experience spreads over a number of years: she comes to Mansfield Park at the age of ten, and she is between eighteen and nineteen years old towards the end of the novel. There are different stages in her moral maturity, just as physically she grows bigger and taller and even prettier—Sir Thomas, returning from his prolonged trip abroad, has noticed all those changes (178); so does Henry Crawford a little later (229).[1] Therefore, temporal and spatial factors figure in Fanny's learning process which, not surprisingly, involves committing errors as well as deriving truths.

2

The issue of education has been dwelt upon even before Fanny Price

---

Narratological View of Jane Austen," *ambiguous* [sic] Discourse: *Feminist Narratology and British Women Writers*, ed. Kathy Mezei [Chapel Hill: U of North Carolina P, 1996] 36).

[1] After looking at Fanny closely "nearer the light," Sir Thomas, who has just returned from a lengthy trip abroad, feels that "he was justified in his belief of [Fanny's] equal improvement in health and beauty" (178). At the beginning of chapter 6 of volume 2, Henry the capable connoisseur cavils about Mary's insensitivity to Fanny: '"You do not seem properly aware of her claims to notice. When we talked of her last night, you none of you seemed sensible of the wonderful improvement that has taken place in her looks within the last six weeks. You see her every day, and therefore do not notice it, but I assure you, she is quite a different creature from what she was in the autumn. She was then merely a quiet, modest, not plain looking girl, but she is now absolutely pretty'" (229).

arrives at Mansfield Park. In fact it is discussed when the possibility of adoption is first raised by Mrs Norris, who loves to be charitable at others' expense. Even at this early planning stage there already exist dialectically positioned views in regard to Fanny's education. Although it is Mrs Norris who produces the idea of having the nine-year-old eldest daughter of Mrs Price adopted—by the Bertrams of Mansfield Park—she is the least prudent about her education, for she merely regards it as a way of learning manners and receiving social benefits:

> Do not let us be frightened from a good deed by a trifle. Give a girl an education, and introduce her properly into the world, and ten to one but she has the means of settling well, without farther expense to any body. A niece of our's, Sir Thomas, I may say, or, at least of *your's*, would not grow up in this neighbourhood without many advantages. I don't say she would be so handsome as her cousins. I dare say she would not; but she would be introduced into the society of this country under such very favourable circumstances as, in all human probability, would get her a creditable establishment. (6)

Mrs Norris, seemingly prophetic here, is clearly thinking of Fanny's education in social terms: living with the eminent Bertrams will give Fanny "'many advantages,'" not the least of which are the opportunities of being favourably perceived and the ensuing possibility of securing for herself a good marriage. Besides, the arrangement will also be "'the only sure way of providing against the connection'" (6–7) between the Bertrams and the Prices, since the brother-and-sister-like relationship will defeat the romantic possibility of her marrying either of the Bertram sons.

Sir Thomas, while acknowledging the soundness of Mrs Norris's argument—"'There is a great deal of truth in what you say'" (7), prudently ponders his future responsibility for a dowry—"'the provision of a gentlewoman'" (7)—adequate enough to secure Fanny a "'creditable'" establishment (7), should they decide to undertake the project. Sir Thomas is considering the matter not only in social terms but also in financial terms. He is as considerate and shrewd as Mrs Norris is rash and mean; the latter soon makes clear that she has never meant to commit any resources to the "joint venture" which she has so enthusiastically launched.

However, Sir Thomas is also concerned with a possible moral contamination of his own girls by Fanny:

> Should her disposition be really bad we must not, for our own children's sake, continue her in the family. Had my daughters been *younger* than herself, I should have considered the introduction of such a companion, as a matter of very serious moment; but as it is, I hope there can be nothing to fear for *them*, and every thing to hope for *her*, from the association. (10)

Thus Fanny is going to benefit from her stay in Mansfield Park not only socially, but financially and morally. The educational scheme will work well only if a "balance," or an invisible distinction, is tactfully but strictly maintained between Fanny and her cousins, as Sir Thomas clearly envisions and blandly expresses:

> There will be some difficulty in our way, Mrs. Norris ... as to the distinction proper to be made between the girls as they grow up; how to preserve in the minds of my *daughters* the consciousness of what they are, without making them think too lowly of their cousin; and how, without depressing her spirits too far, to make her remember that she is not a *Miss Bertram*. (10)

What Sir Thomas implies is a two-tiered educational system. While he aims at propriety in the conduct of the girls, he stresses their difference, worldly difference at that. He is projecting a parochial concept of education, reducing learning—the cultivation of the mind—to taking the right estimate of one's "'rank, fortune, rights, and expectations'" (11). What Sir Thomas asserts in the apparently fair statement is that Fanny and the Bertram girls cannot be equals, either in terms of worldly possessions or in terms of moral capacities. A Miss Bertram is not just rich, she is also by definition moral. Her overall superiority is guaranteed, only she should refrain from showing it off. The words "'preserve'" and "'remember'" connote Sir Thomas's desire to maintain the status quo and to keep intact what Burke refers to in the *Reflections* as the "*hereditary right.*"①

What Sir Thomas's discretion prevents him from fully discussing, Mrs Norris makes a point of emphasizing: "'It will be an education for the child ... only being with her cousins; if Miss Lee taught her nothing, she would learn to be good and clever from *them*'" (10). Mrs Norris is clearly flattering Sir Thomas and implicitly denigrating Miss Lee in the process. The implication for Fanny, however, is that her prospects have been decided even before she makes her appearance at Mansfield Park. It is not that she cannot improve herself but that she can never expect to reach the level of elegance to which her cousins were already born. Clearly, both Sir Thomas and Mrs Norris prejudge the moral being of their poor niece. External factors are allowed not only to reflect but also to represent internal qualities. Hegel describes this kind of fixed thinking as the unreasoning "conceit" that "relies on truths which are taken for granted and which it sees no need to re-examine; it just lays them down, and believes it is entitled to assert them, as well as to judge and pass sentence by appealing to them."②

That Fanny has eventually become a morally conscious and competent individual bespeaks the falsehood of the expectations of Sir Thomas and Mrs Norris. Mansfield may teach good manners, but manners alone do not ensure morality; Portsmouth may not be competent in teaching manners, but that does not mean the Prices cannot be virtuous.③ Indeed Fanny at the beginning of the novel is rather like young Catherine

---

① Burke, *Reflections* 26.

② Hegel, *Phenomenology* 41.

③ The Prices are, on the whole, a virtuous group with inadequate manners, which have been unfortunately equated to signs of an evil nature. Some critics have tried, with more ingenuity than insight, to read Freud into Mr. Price's justifiable sentiment upon reading Henry and Maria's elopement in the local paper: "'[I]f she [Maria] belonged to me, I'd give her the rope's end as long as I could stand over her" (*MP* 440). For example, Claudia L. Johnson senses a certain "sexual undercurrent" (118), whereas Roger Sales detects "a sadistic sexual fantasy" (123); Edward Neill, more recently, echoes the same Freudian reading by supposing that "[t]his happy vision of the punitive knout comes close to invoking that very 'aggressive' sexuality which has been the character note of Henry Crawford himself" (73).

Morland in being "ignorant and uninformed" (*NA* 18); but, like her counterpart, she is also capable of discerning and reasoning. Fanny is not a Regency paragon; her moral maturity is the result of a process of vigorous learning. In the following sections, I will trace a number of distinct stages in the process of Fanny's moral growth and illustrate how each stage is different from the other, and how each higher stage marks an improvement in Fanny's moral consciousness and, above all, how dialectics performs a crucial role in the depiction of Fanny's moral growth.

3

When Fanny first arrives at Mansfield Park as a young girl, she is all feeling and sensibility, emotionally registering what she senses from the household hierarchy:

> She was disheartened by Lady Bertram's silence, awed by Sir Thomas's grave looks, and quite overcome by Mrs. Norris's admonitions. Her elder cousins mortified her by reflections on her size, and abashed her by noticing her shyness; Miss Lee wondered at her ignorance, and the maid-servants sneered at her clothes. (14)

In this initial encounter the chief "educators" are put to their first test, and both Sir Thomas and Mrs Norris, despite the latter's assurance that between them the business of Fanny will be "easily managed" (11), instantly fail for all their vision and prowess. Sir Thomas's "most untoward gravity of deportment" (12) frightens rather than pacifies the ten-year-old niece, even though he tries his best to be "conciliating" (12). Mrs Norris, however, puts great pressure on little Fanny, urging her to make an impressive début and show an "extraordinary degree of gratitude" (13); yet all her "officious prognostications ... that she would be a good girl" (13) are sadly punctured by Fanny's constant crying and then dozing off. Even Lady Bertram's smile, which instantly makes her "the less awful character" (12) in Fanny's eyes, cannot achieve more than that. This initial encounter is brief, but its implication is

significant. It points to a barrier between the pupil and her educators,
whose insensitivity to the psychology of the newly-arrived child and
whose inability to make her relax hint at their failure to understand the
moral need of the children at Mansfield in general.

Fanny's real mentor turns out to be Edmund Bertram who "knew her
to be clever, to have a quick apprehension as well as good sense, and a
fondness for reading, which, properly directed, must be an education in
itself" (22). However, she is soon to learn that moral struggle is as much
a private test as it is a matter of respecting a mentor's opinion. The first
disagreement that Fanny has with Edmund is over the character of Mrs
Norris. When the Mansfield living is presented to Mr Grant upon Mr
Norris's death, Mrs Norris is to vacate the parsonage and live in the
"White house" in the neighbouring village, and Fanny is intended by the
Bertrams to be removed with her. Fanny is shocked when Lady Bertram
breaks the news to her, for she "had never received kindness from her
aunt Norris, and could not love her" (25). But when Fanny relays the
distressing information to Edmund, he thinks that it is an "'excellent'"
(25) arrangement and automatically assumes that Mrs Norris "'is acting
like a sensible woman in wishing for [Fanny]'" (26). When Fanny
assures him that it is not the case at all and reminds him "'how
uncomfortable'" (26) he knows she has been with her, Edmund becomes
condescending and begins to make assertions:

> I can say nothing for her manner to you as a child; but it was the same with
> us all, or nearly so. She never knew how to be pleasant to children. But you are
> now of an age to be treated better; I think she *is* behaving better already; and
> when you are her only companion, you *must* be important to her. (26)

The truth is that Mrs Norris does not treat Fanny "'the same'" as she does
her cousins. It is only too obvious that Maria and Julia are spoilt by "their
considerate aunt" (18), for they report to her about their impressions of
Fanny's oddity and stupidity, such as her lack of interest in "'either
music or drawing'" (19) and her poor knowledge of geography—for
example, little Fanny thinks that one must cross to the Isle of Wight in
order to get to Ireland (18). Mrs Norris, wrong-headed, then encourages

the Bertram girls to take their privilege of "early information" (19) for intelligence of the mind. She will praise her endeared nieces—carefully using either "'my dear'" (18) or "'my dears'" (19) depending on whether she speaks to one or both—for their "'wonderful memories'" (19), and she will degrade Fanny for having "'probably none at all'" (19).

Memory, according to Locke, is an important component in the operations of the mind because it must precisely retain the sensations received and, when required, recall them and present them for the next steps of comparison, discernment, abstraction, and so on.[1] However, memory by itself is not the same as intelligence. As Locke, again, points out, it is worth little if people just read useful books and simply "lodge ... opinions or some remarkable passages in [their] memories."[2] Locke emphasizes that "it is thinking makes what we read ours."[3] Confusing memory with intelligence is a serious moral defect. Fanny's intelligence should not be judged by what her memory has never been acquainted with. Conversely, the Bertram girls' wonderful memories cannot guarantee that they can make intelligent judgments. That last involves not only memory (recalling) but also rational thinking (analysing). Mrs Norris, by making false generalizations: "'There is a vast deal of difference in memories, as well as in every thing else, and therefore you must make allowance for your cousin, and pity her deficiency'" (19), encourages a flawed comparison and persuades the proud Bertram girls that they are superior not only in memory but also in everything else.

Mrs Norris clearly brings out the worst in Sir Thomas's educational scheme, inherently imperfect as it is, by carrying it to the extreme. The ill-effects of her mismanagement affect equally the favoured and the disfavoured. The indulged Bertram sisters go on fancying that they are

---

[1] Locke, *Essay* 2. 9 – 12.

[2] Locke, *Conduct* 24.

[3] Locke, *Conduct* 20.

almost perfect—"Their vanity was in such good order, that they seemed
to be quite free from it, and gave themselves no airs; while the praises
attending such behaviour, secured, and brought round by their aunt,
served to strengthen them in believing they had no faults" (35), while
the intimidated Fanny, "'the lowest and last'" (221), is so afraid of
becoming an example of what Mrs Norris calls "'[t]he nonsense and folly
of people's stepping out of their rank and trying to appear above
themselves'" (221) that she does not dare to share her acute feelings with
her cousins. An invisible wall is being built between them, and any
dialectical engagement is out of the question. The social distinction turns
education into isolation.

To come back to the point, if Edmund is oblivious of Mrs Norris's
gross indulgence of his sisters at the expense of Fanny Price, often
publicly displayed in "the drawing-room" (18), he should at least notice
that, unlike Sir Thomas or Lady Bertram, Mrs Norris never addresses
Fanny with any form of endearment, for there has never been sufficient
warm feeling to warrant a simple affectionate "dear." It is insensitive of
Edmund to misread Mrs Norris, who demands both service and servility
from her humble niece and returns the favour by being a major source of
constant "alarms or embarrassments" (35). Edmund is even "'quite
convinced that [Fanny's] being with Mrs. Norris, will be as good for
[her] mind, as riding has been for [her] health—and as much for [her]
ultimate happiness, too'" (27–28). Although Fanny, who has
personally suffered for five years, by this time, from Mrs Norris's
censoriousness and petty cruelties, disagrees with Edmund completely,
she decides to heed his "wisdom," just as Catherine Morland initially
gives her brother James the benefit of the doubt about the character of
John Thorpe. Sighing, Fanny says: "'I cannot see things as you do; but I
ought to believe you to be right rather than myself'" (27). The irony is
heightened when Fanny tells Edmund: "'I am inclined to hope you may
always prophesy as well'" (27). We later realize that the son's blindness
and peremptoriness serve as a foreshadowing of the father's to come.

If this serious discussion between Fanny and Edmund marks the beginning of a series of morally-weighted dialectical engagements, what happens three years later, during Sir Thomas's extended absence from Mansfield Park, reveals a marked increase in Fanny's moral awareness, while the moral stakes are considerably higher. The departure of the authoritarian moral figure not only grants Mrs Norris an opportunity to prove her prowess in executing the educational plan but also gives others a chance to act according to his or her free will, properly or improperly. A crisis is brewing, though not of a financial nature,[1] for Edmund is ably taking care of the day-to-day management of the Mansfield estate (34). The crisis is a moral one, for a foreign legion, the Crawfords, has arrived and is later reinforced by Tom Bertram's dandy friend, the Honourable John Yates.[2] Charming, liberal ideas start to invade the tranquil, regulated domain of Mansfield Park.

James Thompson, observing that "Fanny Price is the least autonomous of Austen's heroines," that "she is the most subject to persuasion, having, as a dependent female, to agree and to obey," contends that "Fanny cannot exert her will until she develops a voice to speak it, a process that begins in Portsmouth with Fanny's interaction with Susan and then is completed upon her return to Mansfield Park."[3] However, the narrative evidence suggests that Fanny has found her voice much earlier: if not at the time of her imminent removal from Mansfield Park to the custody of her eldest and odious aunt—discussing her character with Edmund and finding him lacking in moral understanding—then

---

[1]   The overall financial picture of the Bertrams is of course not rosy, what with the poor returns of Sir Thomas's investment in the West Indies—prompting him to go to Antigua—and Tom Bertram's gambling debts—leading to the sale of the reversion of the Mansfield living to Dr Grant instead of its being kept for Edmund.

[2]   Sales discusses the rise of dandyism in Regency England, the Prince Regent being one of the prominent dandies, in his innovative as well as informative study, where he notes: "Dandyism was inextricably linked with gambling since it was the ultimate game of chance in which it was crucial both to have a nerve and to know how to hold it." He also discusses the private theatricals at *Mansfield Park* in the context of the Regency scandals involving well-known actresses and members of the aristocracy (see 65 – 83 and 116 – 131).

[3]   Thompson 59, 57.

definitely at the time when she visits Sotherton with her cousins and vocally expresses her moral concern, and unmistakably during the private theatricals at Mansfield Park when she opposes the dubious project.

At Sotherton, while the restless Maria and Henry walk with the romantic Edmund and Mary Crawford along "'a very serpentine course'" (94) in the wood in their tireless search of "all the sweets of pleasure-grounds" and "air and liberty" (90), Fanny decides to sit still. Her excuse is that she is "'tired'" (94), which distinguishes her physically from Mary who is "'not at all tired'" (94), and metaphorically from what the narrator terms the "feminine lawlessness" (94) that Mary is promoting. The bench on which Fanny is seated is strategically situated. It stands near the iron gate, overlooking the ha-ha into the park.

The lack of physical movement does not prevent Fanny from carrying out mental operations. Vigilantly, she discerns the wantonness of Henry, and she warns the infatuated Maria in the only way she possibly can, given the occasion and her situation:

> "You will hurt yourself, Miss Bertram," she cried, "you will certainly hurt yourself against those spikes—you will tear your gown—you will be in danger of slipping into the ha-ha. You had better not go." (99 – 100)

Maria, however, gives no heed to Fanny's warning and escapes into the wilderness of the park with Henry, the pleasure-seeking dandy, without the company of Mr Rushworth, her future husband, who has been dispatched with the task of fetching the key.

However, Fanny's moral action is not always pure. There may be nothing complicated in her warning to Maria, who is trying to escape with Henry into the wilderness of the park, but in the case of Mary and Edmund there is something that taints her moral judgment: sexual jealousy. Fanny has been jealous of Mary Crawford since the latter's arrival, and her jealous behaviour has been consistently recorded throughout the novel. In fact the intensity of Fanny's jealousy grows in direct proportion to the growth of her moral consciousness.

Both begin at an inchoate stage but gradually reach the level of consciousness and then that of self-consciousness. An interesting passage in chapter 7 of volume 1 describes the earliest symptoms of Fanny's jealousy as she is anxiously waiting for her turn to ride—because Mary Crawford has cut into her riding time—under the supervision of her sometime "personal" riding instructor Edmund:

> The houses, though scarcely half a mile apart, were not within sight of each other; but by walking fifty yards from the hall door, she could look down the park, and command a view of the parsonage and all its demesnes, gently rising beyond the village road; and in Dr. Grant's meadow she immediately saw the group—Edmund and Miss Crawford both on horseback, riding side by side, Dr. and Mrs. Grant, and Mr. Crawford, with two or three grooms, standing about and looking on. A happy party it appeared to her—all interested in one object—cheerful beyond a doubt, for the sound of merriment ascended even to her. It was a sound which did not make *her* cheerful; she wondered that Edmund should forget her, and felt a pang. (67)

Fanny observes every single detail of their intimate movement, from quite far away, and imagines "what the eye could not reach" (67). Her pathetic logic that "if she were forgotten the poor mare should be remembered" (68) vividly reveals the envy of an ardent eighteen-year-old girl who is just beginning to savour the possibilities of love, yet whose humble social and economic status prevents her from even hinting at her genuine passion. [1]

Fanny's love for Edmund is based on mutual friendship and moral understanding; her disapproval of Mary, however, is based mainly on her antipathy to Miss Crawford's loose London morals but also on her displeasure towards her appropriation of Edmund's attention. Fanny's almost irrepressible jealousy, lasting right to the end of the novel, contributes to the complexity of Fanny's moral growth. Indeed the coupling of morality with sexuality severely tests Fanny's effort to stay morally upright. That she self-consciously separates herself from Edmund at Sotherton is partially due to her being jealous of the warmth between him and Miss Crawford. Later, just before the Mansfield ball, Fanny

---

[1]   Claudia L. Johnson, who thinks Fanny is "like a grateful slave," interprets her remark as evidence of her genuinely "[b]elieving the grey mare more entitled to consideration than she is herself" (108).

will have to struggle to reconcile herself to the fact that she is one of "'the two dearest objects'" (264) to Edmund Bertram, and not even that shortly afterwards. But before we examine those later developments we need to look at Fanny's performance during the private theatricals at Mansfield, which serves as a watershed in her overall moral and intellectual maturity, as well as her heightened sexual awareness.

4

Fanny's association with the private theatricals at Mansfield Park is a complicated issue. Edmund's report to Sir Thomas, concerning the acting scheme, the morning after his return from Antigua, that "'Fanny is the only one who has judged rightly throughout, who has been consistent'" (187) is an acknowledgement of her reluctant role in the ill-fated theatrical project. Edmund is guilt-ridden about pressuring Fanny into doing what he knew to be wrong; he wants to protect Fanny from any possible censure, for he is acutely aware that, of all the people who have participated in or connived at the theatrical scheme, Fanny is the least blameable because of her peripheral participation in the project yet most vulnerable because of her profound timidity, her acute sensibility, and her humble social position. When Julia makes the dramatic announcement, at the very end of volume 1, that Sir Thomas "'is come! He is in the hall at this moment'" (172), ① Fanny's "agitation and alarm exceeded all that was endured by the rest" [176]), even though her guilt is the least. She has yielded because she is pressured by all in general and by Edmund in particular to fill in for Mrs Grant who cannot come and

---

① Julia's using verb "to be," rather than "to have," as the auxiliary verb—in announcing "'My father is come!'"—changes the nature of the full verb, from past participle to predicative adjective. This functional change makes it possible to emphasize what K. C. Phillipps calls "the result of a motion rather than the movement itself" (*Jane Austen's English* [London: Andre Deutsch, 1970] 110), which is exactly what self-exiled Julia wants to deliver to the preoccupied theatrical participants. Fanny's alarm epitomizes the desired effects this linguistic construct is meant to achieve.

play the role of "Cottager's wife," a " ' most trivial, paltry, insignificant'" (134) role in the play with " ' not above half a dozen speeches altogether' " in " ' only two scenes' " (145, 146). Edmund defends Fanny because he realizes that Fanny has indeed judged uprightly.

The choice of Kotzebue's play poses a problem, ① though it would attach too much importance to the play itself by deeming it ideologically "crucial." ② Edmund opposes the idea of acting as soon as it is floated by Tom, well before the issue of choice of play presents itself (125 - 127), though he is later amazed to learn that *Lovers' Vows*, which he thinks " ' exceedingly unfit for private representation' " (140), has been agreed upon as the play to be put on. The significance of this sentimental piece lies rather in the fact that it panders perfectly to the different inclinations of the active amateur players: Henry, Mary, Maria, Julia (later quitting out of jealousy), Tom and Yates. In the words of the last, " ' [T]there is nothing that will suit us altogether so well' " (139).

Under the joint direction of Maria, Henry and Tom, the amateur actors and actresses are cast according to their individual characters, even to their intentions in certain cases. Once the play is in rehearsal, it is all too clear what opportunities the plot of the play provides for certain enterprising characters. As A. Walton Litz judiciously points out, "With its emphasis on feeling and disregard for traditional restraints, with its contempt for social form, *Lovers' Vows* stands as an emblem of those forces which threaten the neoclassical security of Mansfield Park." ③ The play allows those with loose morals to act out their indulgences. Indeed even as the play is still in the casting stage, the illicit pleasure is already

---

① Kotzebue's plays were the rage of London theatre beginning with the 1798 - 1799 season. *Pizarro*, adapted by Sheridan from *The Spaniards in Peru*, became "one of the most successful plays of the entire century" and ran "thirty-one nights" at Drury Lane, accounting for "about a quarter" of what the theatre took in for the entire season. However, *Lovers' Vows* had a run of forty-two nights in the same season at Covent Garden (see *The London Stage 1660 - 1800*, ed. and intro. Charles Beecher Hogan [Carbondale: Southern Illinois UP, 1968] Pt 5: 1776 - 1800, 2097, 2102).

② Butler 233.

③ Litz 125.

being anticipated and looked forward to by the sophisticated Mary, who is going to play Amelia. She naughtily enquires, in her capacity of actress: "'Who is to be Anhalt? What gentleman among you am I to have the pleasure of making love to?'" (143). Litz again is right in pointing out that even the casting has "prophetic overtones."[①]

The whole thing amounts to a painful test for Edmund Bertram. Edmund is determined to take orders and be dedicated to the sacred role of cleansing souls, as we learn from his conversation with Mary at Sotherton (91 – 94), but he is at the same time strongly attracted to the charming Mary, who is against his ordination. Mary is in favour of the theatricals and wishes in particular for Edmund to play her amorous object, Anhalt. She "archly" insinuates the seeming appropriateness for him to join the cast: "'If *any* part could tempt *you* to act, I suppose it would be Anhalt for he is a clergyman you know'" (144 – 145). By a remarkable paradox, Mary is distracting Edmund by what precisely attracts him. She is luring Edmund away from the holy profession that he is determined to pursue by enticing him to play, rather than perform, the clerical role. Ironically, if Edmund agrees to play the part of the clergyman, he will be sacrificing his morals and abasing himself to the object of Mary's unprincipled love-making. By refusing to play the role of the theatrical clergyman, Edmund will be immunized, at least for now, from being corrupted by subtle influences of depravity from the sexually exploiting Miss Crawford. Although Edmund tells Mary resolutely at this point: "'*That* circumstance would by no means tempt me'" (145), other circumstances will collude to trap him.

Whereas Edmund is forced to deliberate dialectically about the pros and cons regarding the erection of the theatre at Mansfield in general and his own participation in it in particular, Fanny is simply drafted to act. She, unlike Edmund, does not have the option to be or not to be part of what she does not want to. It is a matter of offering her "'services'" as required (145) —not "'*present* services'" (145) for their physical

---

① Litz 124.

comforts, as Tom tells her, but future services for their mental indulgences. Although Fanny protests against the request in her own way, she is fighting a losing battle.

Nevertheless the complex situation causes Fanny to conduct an intense internal dialectical debate. The strain on the eighteen-year-old, who would be the youngest of the cast, is tremendous, for the business of acting affects her in many ways: moral, social, sexual and psychological. Fanny's moral attitude is clear: she trusts Edmund's moral judgement and supports his initial prudent position without having read the play. But when she does read it, she is equally shocked that "it could be proposed and accepted in a private Theatre!" (137):

> Agatha and Amelia appeared to her in their different ways so totally improper for home representation—the situation of one, and the language of the other, so unfit to be expressed by any woman of modesty, that she could hardly suppose her cousins could be aware of what they were engaging in; and longed to have them roused as soon as possible by the remonstrance which Edmund would certainly make. (137)

Clearly, Fanny is alarmed, but it is also clear that she cannot single-handedly stem the stampede of the theatrical troupe. The main action of "remonstrance" must be taken by Edmund, the vanguard of their shamefully outnumbered moral resistance. Therefore when Fanny pronounces to all: "'I really cannot act'" (146), she means more than is understood. But Fanny, who is acting morally, is also acting in a theatrical sense (at least auditioning), being "the only speaker in the room" and with "almost every eye upon her" (145 – 146); and Tom, in his capacity as "'Mr Manager,'" is already showing appreciation of one of the talents of his company: "'Yes, yes, you can act well enough for *us*'" (146).

Fanny is in a bind, a different one from Edmund's, however. If she resists the request "now backed by Maria and Mr. Crawford, and Mr. Yates" (146), she will suffer the dire consequence of becoming, in the words of Mrs Norris who urges her to do as required, "'very ungrateful indeed, considering who and what she is'" (147). If she agrees to the request, she will be acting against her better judgment and sacrificing her moral principles. This is the first time that she has been openly accused of being ungrateful, a charge she is especially afraid of deserving given her dependent status. Fanny is forced to ponder. She goes into her East room, her personal and moral space, to deliberate.

However, even her home-room turns out to be an environment of a dialectical nature, which mirrors the see-sawing in her mind. Fanny looks at the "profile" of Edmund, "her champion and her friend," hoping to "catch any of his counsel" (152). But there are other objects in the room, and the associations they rouse increase the pressure on the young girl; "the sight of present upon present that she had received from [her cousins]" reminds her of "the debt" she owes them and makes her wonder if she has done "her duty" (153):

> ... she had begun to feel undecided as to what she *ought to do*; and as she walked round the room her doubts were increasing. Was she *right* in refusing what was so warmly asked, so strongly wished for? What might be so essential to a scheme on which some of those to whom she owed the greatest complaisance, had set their hearts? Was it not ill-nature—selfishness—and a fear of exposing herself? And would Edmund's judgment, would his persuasion of Sir Thomas's disapprobation of the whole, be enough to justify her in a determined denial in spite of all the rest? (152 – 153)

Ironically, just as Fanny begins to doubt her own and even Edmund's judgment and is in urgent need of some moral reaffirmation from his favourite cousin, Edmund appears to ask for her support. However, Edmund does not come to gather moral support; he is not even here to ask for Fanny's real "opinion" (153). Rather, he wants to solicit Fanny's approval of his newly-conceived plot of convenience, i.e., throwing his lot with the "players" and acting the part of Anhalt. In fact he has more or less decided to concede the "'triumph to the others'" (155); he has even rationalised his "'*appearance* of such inconsistency'" (154) with himself and hopes to have Fanny on his side who has been lending him staunch, if less vocal, moral support. Edmund's policy of appeasement: sacrificing his personal integrity in exchange for "peace" at

Mansfield, offering himself as a "player" to the company in order to thwart the ill-advised attempt to enlist a "stranger" from outside, is ingenious but for two fatal flaws.

Although he is right in taking measures to prevent an outsider from entering Mansfield, he is wrong in overlooking the fact that outsiders have not only arrived but also ensconced themselves within: Yates and the Crawfords have already, for all purposes and intents, infiltrated the "citadel."[①] Together they are about to sabotage Sir Thomas's moral and physical establishment. Although Edmund shows good judgment by foreseeing the unwelcome "'excessive intimacy'" (153)—even dangerous "'familiarity'" (154)—which Tom's original plan of recruiting either Tom Oliver or Charles Maddox would breed, he does not consider, perhaps he cannot imagine, what intimacy and familiarity, given the nature of *Lovers' Vows*, the frequent rehearsals will inevitably beget amongst the young ladies and gentlemen already on the premises. These two serious oversights more than offset the insignificant gain which Edmund imagines his "'concession'" (155) would secure, for the subversion will be carried out from within, under the cover of legitimacy.

There is no doubt that Fanny understands the predicament in which Edmund finds himself, but she is reluctant to give her blessing to Edmund's dubious plot. Edmund senses Fanny's reservation and realizes that he "'still has not [her] approbation'" (155). Yet without changing his mind, he pleads for it: "'Give me your approbation, then, Fanny. I am not comfortable without it'" (155). Upon meeting further

---

① There is some indication that Jane Austen is alluding to the larger conflict going on at the time, i. e., the war between England and France. At the time about the writing of *Mansfield Park* (February 1811-June 1813), two of Austen's brothers, Francis and Charles, were serving in the Royal Navy. About nine years earlier, the husband of Austen's cousin Eliza de Feuillide, was found guilty by the Committee of Public Safety in Paris and was subsequently guillotined. The Crawfords noticeably resort to using French expressions from time to time, which reminds the readers of the political and military context. However, French expressions are also used to describe Fanny's sentiment. For example, Fanny's "happiness" on the day of Mansfield ball "was very much *à-la-mortal*" (274). For an informative discussion of the association between the Crawfords and French manners and mannerisms, see Roberts 33 – 37.

resistance, Edmund resorts to the low stratagem of exploiting Fanny's generosity, which in effect, from Fanny's point of view, amounts to sexual manipulation. Edmund mentions that Fanny should think of "'Miss Crawford's feelings'" (155), which forces Fanny to show her magnanimity.

He also reminds Fanny of Mary's kindness to her the previous night when Mrs Norris accused her of being "'very ungrateful,'" the implication being that it is time for Fanny to pay back. Fanny is forced to admit that Miss Crawford "'*was* very kind indeed'" and that she is "'glad to have her spared'" (156). ① But she is at the same time astute enough to be conscious of the need of not saying more than is necessary because her cousin is desperately hoping to grasp anything remotely positive from her mouth: "She could not finish the generous effusion. Her conscience stopt her in the middle" (156). Nevertheless, Edmund arbitrarily takes satisfaction from Fanny's innocent words and hastens to carry out his ingenious plot, which eventually backfires.

This is perhaps the most traumatic incident throughout the whole theatrical sequence. For the second time, she has learned the lesson that she cannot rely on external guidance for her own moral struggle. Although she tends to blame Mary for her cousin's fault—"Alas! It was all Miss Crawford's doing" (156)—it is only too apparent to her that Edmund is capable of being "so inconsistent" in moral judgment— submitting to his (or their) opponents "[a] fter all his objections— objections so just and so public!" (156).

One other dialectical aspect in Fanny's moral growth is her ambivalent approach to the theatricals once it becomes a certainty. Morally speaking, Fanny is opposed to staging *Lovers' Vows* during these

---

① Again, Austen exploits the ambiguity of the present tense, which may indicate future actions. What Fanny says to Edmund is: "'I am glad to have her [Mary] spared,'" but what he wishes to hear is: I will be glad to have her spared, or I am glad that she will be spared. A future tense would mean categorically that Fanny wishes him to go ahead with his plan of appeasement. Nevertheless, Fanny's linguistic inadequacy, reflecting her inner struggle, does not prevent Edmund from interpreting a neutral message the way he wants to.

uncertain and delicate times. Aesthetically speaking, however, she is able "to derive as much innocent enjoyment from the play as any of them" (165). "[I]nnocent enjoyment" is the key phrase here—after all, this is what private theatricals are about, and Jane Austen and her own family would certainly understand and appreciate her conduct. Fanny is a normal human being, not at all the perfect heroine that many critics perceive her to be, with nothing but a "superlative moral rectitude."① This is an example of the intrinsic beauty of Jane Austen's realistic narrative.② Fanny is no allegorical Virtue borrowed from morality plays or an extraordinarily moral figure transplanted from late eighteenth-century conservative novels like, say, Mrs West's fiction. She is human and her morality does not override or displace her humanity. Once the theatricals are under way (with Mrs Grant playing "Cottager's wife"), it is "a pleasure to her to creep into the theatre" (165) to watch the rehearsals and closely observe the quality of acting of all the actors and actresses—in her opinion Henry Crawford is "considerably the best actor of all" (165). Fanny is also generally useful, when called upon, in helping the cast to rehearse and in listening to their complaints about one another. In particular; she takes great pains to teach Mr Rushworth how to learn "his two and forty speeches" (165 – 166), "giving him all the helps and directions in her power, trying to make an artificial memory for him, and learning every word of his part herself" (166). Practically, Fanny's good nature and work habit compel her to be useful in producing a successful play even though, morally, she "must condemn [it] altogether" if only on account of her uncle (160).

---

① Roger Gard, *Jane Austen's Novels: the Art of Clarity* (New Haven: Yale UP, 1992) 131.

② Jane Austen has a personal dislike for anything "perfect" in fiction. Talking about "ideas of Novels &. Heroines," Austen states that "pictures of perfection as you know make me sick &. wicked" (*Letters* 23 – 25 March 1817).

5

The single most important dialectical debate in which Fanny Price participates in *Mansfield Park* is over her rejection of Henry Crawford's marriage proposal. Fanny's action is such a momentous one that almost every one around her is shaken. Just consider what a comfortable life style she has managed to lose! Henry is worth a clear £ 4,000 a year from his solid estate at Everingham in Norfolk, and he has the resources to rent a house in London for the social season. This wealth, staggering to Fanny, would enable her to live very comfortably for the rest of her life. Besides, the combination of social elevation and financial security would enable Fanny to assist, in various ways, her poor Portsmouth family. When the stakes are so high, a hasty decision could mean a life-time regret. ① But Fanny resolutely refuses to become "'the perfect model of a woman'" (347), which Edmund suggests she should, when she senses that her conscience would suffer should she marry this morally questionable man. The resolute refusal is no doubt the clearest sign of Fanny's moral maturity.

Fanny's estimation of Crawford is a complex one; it is affected by a number of factors, not all having to do with the man himself. Fanny does not dislike Henry: he is intelligent, witty, well-mannered, and, above all, he has helped William, Fanny's favourite elder brother, to be promoted to the rank of lieutenant in the Navy. But Fanny has serious reservations about Henry's virtue. Her decision is not lightly taken, as Sir Thomas and Edmund tend to assume; it is based on her observation of the man's character: Fanny has watched with her own eyes how he tempts Maria into the wilderness at the Sotherton estate, leaving her would-be

---

① We may recall that in November 1751 Jane Austen's aunt, Philadelphia, tried to avoid the fate of "becoming a penniless dependant" by possibly inventing a white lie in order to board the *Bombay Castle* to go to India "with the object of finding a husband amongst the European community there; she did find a surgeon twenty years her senior" (see Le Faye, *Family Record* 4 - 5).

husband behind, how he continues to flirt with Maria at Mansfield Park, rehearsing together the first scene of *Lovers' Vows* "so needlessly often" that even dim-witted Mr Rushworth begins to complain (165), ① and how at the Grants' house he insidiously grumbles about Sir Thomas's early return and the subsequent ruining of the immoderate pleasure of the theatricals. Fanny's refusal to give her hand to Henry Crawford is an effort to preserve her moral integrity. It is the result of rational deliberation. It is especially poignant when we consider that she has little tangible to gain by her action.

Nevertheless, Fanny cannot very well tell Sir Thomas about his children's bad behaviour in general and Maria's impropriety in particular. But Sir Thomas's grave authority, which has made him generally a distant and unapproachable figure, is another factor. Fanny is afraid of him from the very beginning; not even his own children, say, Tom and Maria, feel comfortable enough to confide their intimate thoughts to him. The third factor is Fanny's secret love for Sir Thomas's second son. These factors combine to overwhelm Fanny's timid nature and compel her to be less than straightforward on why she cannot accept Mr Crawford's proposal.

Consequently, Fanny's rational act of refusal is overshadowed by her seemingly irrational failure to justify it. The lack of apparent motive makes Sir Thomas suspect that Fanny has given her heart to another. Fanny, being interrogated by her uncle as to why someone who has "'every thing to recommend him'" (315 – 316) should not be acceptable, is on the point of lying when Sir Thomas "eyed her fixedly" and "saw her lips formed into a *no*, though the sound was inarticulate, but her face was

---

① According to the stage directions for Act 1, Scene 1, Maria (Agatha) at one point would be "*rising and embracing*" Henry (Frederick) while saying: "My dear Frederick! The joy is too great—I was not prepared—" and at another would be "*press[ing] him to her breast*" while saying: "Where could be found such another son?". Also, Maria would confess to Henry: "I was intoxicated by the fervent caresses of a young, inexperienced, capricious man" and ask him why he has not "written to [her] this long while;" both of those acts, needless to say, Henry Crawford is capable of performing (see *Lovers' Vows*, MP, 483 – 489).

like scarlet" (316).

This is a deliberate, dramatic and dialectical scene. Sir Thomas reads Fanny's "scarlet" face as a sign of innocence and modesty—"so modest a girl" can know nothing but "innocence" (316). In fact there is no reason for him to suspect anything of an alarming nature afoot at well-secluded Mansfield Park. Sir Thomas's enquiry of Fanny reminds one of his enquiry of Maria. Indeed, it is almost a case of *déjà vu* in that financial considerations have again overridden all other considerations. In Maria's case, Sir Thomas is "too glad to be satisfied" about the advantageous "alliance" to "urge" his daughter "quite so far as his judgment might have dictated" (201). In Fanny's case, Sir Thomas is solely concerned with the financial implications of Mr Crawford's proposal. He is rather anxious to hear Fanny, who has no dowry, say yes rather than no to Henry's extraordinary offer. This is why he has asked Fanny three times in succession if she really means no. Fanny, of course, has to convince him three times that her no does not mean yes.

Sir Thomas ignores Fanny's feelings even though he has seen her reacting in a detached manner to Henry Crawford on a number of occasions. For example, at Dr Grant's dinner party, Sir Thomas notices that "Fanny's reception" of Henry's gallant address is "proper and modest," "calm and uninviting" (246). A little later, he observes that his niece "did not thank him for what he had just done" (280), i.e., inviting Mr Crawford over for breakfast on the morning of William's departure from Mansfield Park. Finally, he has heard from Fanny herself that Mr Crawford's proposal is "'very disagreeable,'" and that it is "'quite out of [her] power'" to accept him (314).

Nevertheless, Fanny Price is not in any sense a symbol of innocence, let alone a reincarnation of Snow White or Cinderella. There is no question that her decision to refuse to give her hand to Henry Crawford is based on her strict moral criteria, but the sticking factor of her being in love with Edmund can not be overlooked. Fanny may have been acutely conscious of the conflict between the firmness of her mind and the weakness of her pretext: "'I—I cannot like him, Sir, well enough to marry him'" (315). She may also have been mortified by the impurity of her motive and the ambiguity of her reply. Christopher Ricks, quoting Thomas H. Burgess's line that "'there is a physiology of the mind as well as of the body,'" once directed our attention to the "consideration of blushing and embarrassment as a moral and social matter (involved in friendship and love) because blushing" may be an acknowledgement of error. [1] Fanny's situation here clearly invites such consideration because she is being less than truthful.

Fanny, at the same time, may have been flustered by the possible detection by her uncle of her unspeakable thoughts. The emphatic "*no*" that Sir Thomas derives from Fanny's "lips" is fallacious, and her face's being "like scarlet" tells the tale. Jane Austen's choice of the two seemingly innocuous words is felicitous. The preposition "like" introduces a simile which is a form of metaphorical language; but the use of simile is based on the essential fact that the two things in comparison are not the same. Sir Thomas takes "scarlet" for innocent embarrassment—we, like Fanny, know better.

The noun / adjective "scarlet" invokes a rich biblical context which corresponds precisely to this particular narrative situation. The word appears in both the Old and New Testaments. In the Book of Isaiah the prophetic messages are delivered at a time of crisis, as is the case here in Austen's novel. One of the messages which Isaiah is spreading to the belligerent states around Judah reads:

> Come now, and let us reason together, saith the LORD: though your sins be as scarlet, they shall be as white as snow; though they be red like crimson, they shall be as wool. If ye be willing and obedient, ye shall eat the good of the land:
>
> But if ye refuse and rebel, ye shall be devoured with the sword: for the mouth of the LORD hath spoken *it*. [2]

---

[1] *Keats and Embarrassment* (Oxford: Clarendon, 1974) 19, 20, 21.

[2] The Bible, Authorized King James Version, ed., intro. and notes Robert Carroll and Stephen Prickett (Oxford: Oxford UP, 1997) OT, Isa. 1. 18 – 20. All references to The Bible are to this edition.

Fanny is faced with a similar dilemma; she is under tremendous pressure from her uncle; she has to reason hard as to whether she should obey or disobey his obvious wish. If she is "willing" and "obedient," she will enjoy "the best from the land" provided by Henry's estate; otherwise she will suffer the wrath of Sir Thomas and be stamped with the stigma of "'*ingratitude*'" (319). The problem is that Fanny is being less than truthful, and, as a devout Christian (shown in the chapel scene at Sotherton [86]), she may remember the line "'your sins are like scarlet,'" even though she is certain that her moral character is "as white as snow.'"

In the Book of Revelation John relates that one of the seven angels took him to the spot where "the great whore" was being punished:

> So he carried me away in the spirit into the wilderness: and I saw a woman sit upon a scarlet coloured beast, full of names of blasphemy, having seven heads and ten horns.
>
> And the woman was arrayed in purple and scarlet colour, and decked with gold and precious stones and pearls, having a golden cup in her hand full of abominations and filthiness of her fornication. ①

"[S]carlet" as a sign of embarrassment embodies Fanny's complicated thoughts, virtuous and tainted. It may also be read as a sexual image which is not irrelevant in Fanny's case here because her inner self is confronted with the dilemma of a spiritual choice in Edmund and a material one in Henry. She is determined not to prostitute her body to a sinner. Fanny's will is strong—she is determined to resist any penetration by Mr Crawford, who is equally determined "'to make Fanny Price in love with [him]'" (229)—but her flesh is weak—her "lips" begin to fail her, betraying their mistress as if practising a form of prostitution. The "scarlet" that Sir Thomas perceives signifies in fact the admission of guilt and dishonesty. Such are the intricate circumstances under which Fanny judges, acts and reacts. It is rather obvious that she is caught in a myriad human factors as she tries to make a moral decision. It is almost

---

① NT, Rev. 17.3–4.

imperative that her mind work in a dialectical manner.

6

A persistent moral weakness in Fanny Price, which Jane Austen has taken pains to portray in the novel, is her jealousy. Ironically, Fanny's sexual jealousy has developed side by side with Henry's sexual depravity. Whereas at the time of the horse-back riding incident, a jealous Fanny is displeased with the fact that Miss Crawford has encroached upon her instruction time with Edmund; whereas during the tour of Sotherton Fanny awakes to the potent charm of Miss Crawford that mesmerizes Edmund; whereas at the time of the private theatrical rehearsals, Fanny begins to feel the threat of Mary's sexual manipulation of Edmund's virtuous mind; by the eve of the Mansfield ball Fanny has more or less conceded that Edmund has been won by Mary. Fanny has heard Edmund speaking "so openly" (264) in favour of Mary Crawford for the first time while trying to persuade her to keep Mary's necklace that she comes to the conclusion that "[he] would marry Miss Crawford" (264). Fanny feels "a stab" (264) to her heart; she even imagines that Edmund has already proposed to Mary during his "errand" (268) to Dr Grant's house—he was there to engage Miss Crawford for the two first dances (268)—and the very thought "turned her too sick for speech" (268). Fanny is doubly hurt: both emotionally and morally.

Whereas her earlier rationale that "the poor mare" should not be put to "such double duty" (68) seems a comically feeble pretext, her present "agitation" over the "deception" (264) which Mary practises on Edmund embodies much moral urgency. Fanny regrets very much the sad fact that Edmund is "deceived in her" (264) and is in every danger of losing, to quote Milton, "his upright shape" and turning "into a grovelling swine. "[1] Fanny's maturity is no longer what it was; her sexual jealousy is incorporated into her moral outlook. She feels that she would probably not suffer as much—"how far more tolerable!" (264)—if Mary proved to be virtuous. As it is, the psychological damage to her moral being hurts much more than any to her emotional being. She cries bitterly but her tears are shed over her keenly felt moral loss, and her "fervent prayers" (264) are really for Edmund's spiritual safety.

Nevertheless, even at this high moral altitude, Fanny is acutely conscious of the danger of using morality as a mask to disguise her own romantic urge. She feels it "to be her duty, to try to overcome all that was excessive, all that bordered on selfishness in her affection for Edmund" (264). She is determined "to be rational, and to deserve the right of judging of Miss Crawford's character and the privilege of true solicitude for [Edmund] by a sound intellect and an honest heart" (265). Fanny has been more or less true to this pledge. However, human nature being what it is, burying her romantic feelings for Edmund is virtually impossible for Fanny. Consequently, her rational judgment is often mixed with her romantic feelings, especially when Edmund reveals that he still has reservations about Mary's moral stand. For a time it seems that those reservations are serious enough to block his total emotional commitment to Mary. Although he tells Fanny that Mary is someone who "'does not *think* evil'" but "'speaks it'" (269), Edmund has to admit, at Fanny's prompting, that "'it does appear more than manner; it appears as if the mind itself was tainted'" (269).

Edmund's wavering mind is handily exposed by his ambiguous language—the emphatic auxiliary verb "'does'" reinforces the impression

---

[1]   *A Masque of the Same Author*, *Presented at Ludlow Castle*, *1634*, *Before the Earl of Bridgewater*, *Then President of Wales*, ["*Comus*"], *John Milton*, ed. Stephen Orgel and Jonathan Goldberg (Oxford: Oxford UP, 1991) ll. 52 - 53, 46. Austen apparently knows Milton's works well, as there are references to him or his works in her letters (14 October 1813, 9 September 1814) and her novels—*Northanger Abbey* (37), *Mansfield Park* (43), *Emma* (308) (Chapman, "Of Literary Allusions," NA *and* P, 324).

("'appear'") of deficient morality, but the duplicity of the full verb
"'appear'" leaves room for an alternative view. The subjunctive mood
and the reappearance of "'appear'" in the parallel sentence that follows
are in perfect synchronization with the inconclusive nature of the
preceding sentence. Edmund's language now undermines his earlier
pronouncement regarding the disjunction between mind and speech in the
case of Mary Crawford. The agreement between the vacillation in the
mind and the contradiction in terms prove that Locke is right about
"Words" being "sensible Marks of Ideas,"[1] and that Hegel is right in
recognizing language as the medium whereby "the inwardness is as
external as the externality is inward."[2] Fanny, sensitive to the nature of
language as well as her delicate situation, hastens to warn Edmund:
"'Excuse the liberty—but take care *how* you talk to me'" (269).

Meanwhile Edmund's physical posture, while he is making all those
contradictory speeches, indicates, rather unambiguously, where his
affection truly lies. He takes Fanny's "hand" (268) and continues to hold
it in a loving gesture through the duration of his speeches. What is more,
"pressing her hand to his lips" as he winds up, Edmund cries passionately:
"'Dearest Fanny!'" (269). The signals that Edmund sends are mixed; he
seems to be wavering between two choices. The telltale past perfect tense
in the adverbial phrase—"pressing her hand to his lips, with almost as
much warmth as if it had been Miss Crawford's" (269)—suggests the
possibility that he has performed something similar with Mary Crawford.
Edmund's kissing of Mary's hand may have occurred in a theatrical
context during their rehearsal of *Lovers' Vows*.[3] If so, a theatrical gesture
is placed in contrast with a spontaneous act. The contrast and the wavering
are reaffirmed in Edmund's parting remark: "'I have almost given up

---

[1]   Locke, *Essay* 3.2.1.

[2]   *Phenomenology* 729 (Baillie).

[3]   It would appear that Edmund has turned the tables on Mary by making her the object of
his love-making instead of being the object of her love-making. Yet Edmund's seeming
improvement signifies his real degeneration since he comes close to identify with the moral values
of Mary Crawford.

every serious idea of her'" (270). The lame affirmative, which is handicapped by the crippling adverb "almost," shows Edmund's reluctance to close the door on Mary; at the same time, it implies in effect that the door is still left ajar for Fanny. No wonder Edmund's speeches and his body language inject into Fanny "some happier feelings than she had lately known" (270).

As a result, in terms of her relationship with Edmund in general, Fanny is well aware that to "think of him as Miss Crawford might be justified in thinking, would in her be insanity" (264); yet in regard to the relationship between Edmund and Mary she is not sure if the moral differences between them can be removed in time for their marriage, especially when she has witnessed Edmund's scrupulous mind and floundering conscience. This complex situation leaves Fanny with a lingering hope that Edmund may eventually, and in time, find out that he and Mary are morally incompatible. Jane Austen's narrator, who is acutely aware of the intricacies of human hearts, takes care to hint to us, towards the end of the novel, that Edmund's account of his final break-up with Mary may have just possibly given Fanny "'more pleasure than pain'" (455), because it allows her to savour "'the retrospect of what might have been—but what never can be now'" (455).

Edmund's account of his final meeting with Mary shows how he has eventually come to realize, as Fanny has more sensitively felt earlier, that he and Mary do not share the same value system. This is a rather dialectical and dramatic scene in that it constitutes in effect two scenes— one recalled, one unfolding—that coalesce to seal, finally, the moral bond between Edmund and Fanny. Edmund has gone to see Mary at her request, thinking that she must be feeling the same "'shame and wretchedness'" and understanding that it will be their "'last, last interview of friendship'" (454). But Mary's characterization of Maria's elopement with Henry as "'the folly of our two relations'" (454) stuns Edmund, who regards the incident as no less than a "'dreadful crime'" (457). Mary's cavalier manner of speech is as shocking to Edmund as the news of the elopement is to Fanny (440). Edmund has at last realized that the "'difference in [their] opinions'" (457) is of a fundamental kind; he admits to Fanny that he "'had never understood her before'" (458).

However, even during this parting conversation of "'[f]ive and twenty minutes'" (456), there is a traceable dialectical movement going on in Edmund's mind. Emotionally, he is extremely reluctant to give Mary up as a potential marriage partner; morally, he realizes that he must make a clean-break in that respect. Twice he mentions the pain of "'losing her'" or "'parting'" with her, but his resolution becomes increasingly firm as he sees more and more clearly the darkness of Mary's contaminated mind. Suppose we compare the two sentences in question:

> Gladly would I submit to all the increased pain of losing her, rather than have to think of her as I do. I told her so. (456)

And a little later:

> [C]ould I have restored her to what she had appeared to me before, I would infinitely prefer any increase of the pain of parting, for the sake of carrying with me the right of tenderness and esteem. This is what I said. (458)

Whereas "'Gladly'" and "'submit'" may suggest some still lingering tenderness of a forlorn lover in the first instance, in the second, the sometime lover is painfully aware that he no longer has even the "'right'" to any "'tenderness and esteem'" for his once beloved.

The accompanying manner of speech is suggestive too. Whereas "'I told her so'" implies at least some form of engaged conversation, "'This is what I said'" makes it clear that the conversation is so disengaged that the speaker does not care what effect it will produce on the listener. His mind is firmly made up, and the parting will be for ever. This is why quick-witted Mary is "'exceedingly astonished'" at hearing this, and her face "'turned extremely red'" (458). But Mary's red face differs in nature from Fanny's. Mary is more embarrassed than ashamed, as Edmund has correctly divined, because her "'charm'" is broken.

It is to Edmund's credit that he is able to analyze Mary's moral being dialectically under such extraordinary circumstances. For example, when Fanny refers to Mary's speaking lightly of the serious crime as "'[a]bsolute cruelty'" (456), Edmund explains that the "'evil lies yet deeper'" (456): "'Her's are faults of principle, Fanny, of blunted delicacy and a corrupted, vitiated mind'" (456). When Fanny tactfully suggests that "Tom's illness" is also a factor in Mary's "wish for a complete reconciliation" (459), Edmund's "vanity" makes him resist the validity of the point; "but his vanity was not of a strength to fight long against reason" (459). Yet even then he concludes that Mary "'had certainly been *more* attached to him than could have been expected, and for his sake been more near doing right'" (459 – 460).

It is worth dwelling upon Fanny's revelation of Mary's mercenary motive here. We know that Fanny has observed for some time that Mary's love for Edmund is impure. However, Fanny has long resisted the temptation to disclose to him what she knows about her, not only because she realizes that it is not for her to tell Edmund whom he should choose but also because she takes great care to be disinterested in her own regard for her cousin. Earlier, when Tom suddenly becomes seriously ill, Mary breaks a long silence and writes to Fanny at Portsmouth. She minces no words about the purpose of her letter: "'I want to know the state of things at Mansfield Park'" (433). What she is really interested in, however, is whether "'poor Mr. Bertram has a bad chance of ultimate recovery'" (433). Mary paints her selfish motive as "'philanthropic and virtuous'" because it is "'natural,'" and she urges Fanny, whom she takes to be equally selfish, to ignore conscience: "'And now, do not trouble yourself to be ashamed of either my feelings or your own'" (434).

Fanny knows that Tom has got over the worst and is "so far pronounced safe" (429). She would, presumably, love to put to rest Mary's "'agitated'" (434) state of mind by telling her bluntly that Tom is safe and sound, that the dream of a Sir Edmund (434) is premature. But Fanny's jealousy is not a factor: she will not "'trifle'" (434) with Mary's "'anxiety'" (434) one way or the other—as Mary suspects she might; "[h]er representation of her cousin's state at this time, was exactly according to her own belief of it, and such as she supposed would convey to the sanguine mind of her correspondent, the hope of every thing she was wishing for" (436). This is an important moral victory for Fanny, considering that she had been vexed to learn quite recently from Edmund that he was on the verge of proposing to Mary (421 - 423). Fanny does not disclose the seamy side of Mary to Edmund until she is certain of her own disinterestedness and "felt more than justified" (459) to do so.

As for the relationship between Henry Crawford and Fanny Price, there is a similar albeit much less emotionally charged dialectical complexity. It is crucial to understand that Fanny's turning down the offer from Henry does not mean that she has seen through him and written him off as an incarnation of evil, as many critics seem to conclude (apart from the fact that her feelings for Edmund will continue until he marries Mary Crawford). Fanny is simply unwilling, at this stage, to commit herself to someone who has proved, so far, to lack moral principles, or whose only principle is to gratify his own appetite for pleasure. Henry's remark to Fanny: "'Your judgment is my rule of right'" (412) is of course gallantry, but it is also a candid admission of his own deficiency in judgment. Henry has seen the virtue of Fanny and is deeply attracted to it. During his hot pursuit of Fanny, Henry clearly tries to close the moral gap between them by acting in accordance with her criteria. At Portsmouth, Fanny is quick to notice the "wonderful improvement" in Henry (413) and is prepared to be reacquainted with his character. This kind of open-mindedness is a prerequisite to dialectical thinking, as it allows one to keep making sense of what one feels and perceives. Moreover, Fanny is subject to the same emotions as one of her age and education is likely to be, and in the face of Henry's romantic offensive, she proves just as vulnerable as her female cousins.

While Fanny is back at her Portsmouth home, to cool off her "overheated" vanity as far as Sir Thomas is concerned, Henry visits her and tells her how he has worked actively to preserve the welfare of his deserving tenants and how he goes out of his way to make acquaintance with the cottages on his estate (404). Indeed, "he had been acting as he ought to do" (404) and his deeds undeniably qualify him, however temporarily, as "the friend of the poor and oppressed!" (404). Fanny's response, conveyed through interior monologue, carries a positive note: "It was pleasing to hear him speak so properly" (404); she feels that "[n]othing could be more grateful to her" (404). In fact the narrator goes as far as to tell us that Fanny is "on the point of giving him an approving look" (404). Interestingly enough, neither Butler nor Poovey comments on this "ideological" incident, which seems a rather apt example for their respective arguments. But the incident is in fact revelatory of Jane Austen's own dialectical stance. Any attempt by Henry to be an upright landowner and perform his Christian duty is valued by Fanny. Henry's effort to assist and protect "a large and (he believed) industrious family" (404) from an unjust steward is welcomed by Fanny. However, the ulterior motive of Henry in carrying out the action undermines the philanthropic nature of the act itself. Fanny is "on the point of giving him an approving look when it was all frightened off by his adding a something too pointed" (404): he hopes to have "a guide in every plan of utility" who will make his estate "a dearer object than it had ever been yet" (404 – 405).

There is little doubt that Fanny is conscious of the arrival of a new Henry displaying "good qualities" (405), and she reacts appropriately to the perceived changes. Marilyn Butler sees Fanny as "the champion of Christianity" and argues that "she is never even really tempted by Henry."[1] This rigid religious-cum-conservative view allows the heroine too much wisdom and gives the resourceful Henry too little credit. As a matter of fact, another British critic, whose study was published in the same year as Butler's, calls Fanny Price "the greatest rhapsodist in Jane Austen."[2] If this assessment of Fanny's sensitivity to nature sounds excessive in itself—for Marianne Dashwood may be a more deserving candidate—it is nonetheless important to recognize Fanny's capacity for

---

[1]   Butler 246.

[2]   Barbara Hardy, *A Reading of Jane Austen* (London: Peter Owen, 1975) 58.

emotions. Fanny reacts romantically not only to natural objects but also to human beings. Barbara Hardy's analysis of Henry's courtship of Fanny at Portsmouth in chapters 10 and 11 of volume 3 does justice to this important aspect of Fanny's character. ① On the other hand, Henry's easy charm and pleasant manner must be credited as well.

An instance of the magic potency of such power is vividly illustrated in the walk that Mrs Price, Fanny and Henry take on the ramparts as they enjoy the "uncommonly lovely" weather and the "beautiful" scenery (409). Before she knows it—"somehow or other—there was no saying how—Fanny could not have believed it" (409)—she finds Mr Crawford "walking between them with an arm of each under his" (409). The "combination of charms"—the "mild air, brisk soft wind, and bright sun" and "the ever-varying hues of the sea now at high water, dancing in its glee and dashing against the ramparts with so fine a sound"—gradually renders Fanny "almost careless of the circumstances under which she felt them" (409). But credit must also go to Henry Crawford who has skilfully mingled his personal charm with the natural charms and managed to have Fanny, quite imperceptibly, accept his arm as well as company while drinking in the beauty of nature.

It is also possible that Henry Crawford, standing on the ground that is William's home base and watching the ships like those on which William is serving, may have recalled his earlier wish to emulate Fanny's favourite and moral brother who has shown to him "[t]he glory of heroism, of usefulness, of exertion, of endurance" (236). At the time he did, albeit briefly, feel ashamed of "his own habits of selfish indulgence" and "wished he had been a William Price" (236)! It is apparent that Henry Crawford does have a clear sense of right and wrong, morality and immorality, but his faulty education and early independence have cultivated a deeply-rooted "selfish indulgence" which is almost ineradicable. It is a fair assessment when the narrator later observes that "[w]ould he have persevered, and uprightly" (467) in his suit of Fanny

① Hardy 37 - 65.

in the manner he had shown at Portsmouth, it would be hard to imagine
that Fanny could have done otherwise than accept him—"Fanny must have
been his reward" (467). Things would, and could, have worked out
"within a reasonable period from Edmund's marrying Mary" (467).

We should not forget, however, that Fanny is by no means in a
position to control her own destiny, let alone those of others. In the final
analysis "'rank, fortune, rights, and expectations'" (11) matter in terms
of her finding a husband. Sir Thomas's ball in her honour has no doubt
raised her profile in the Mansfield neighbourhood, but Fanny is still in no
position to find an ideal marriage partner, as Mary Crawford apparently
is. [1] To put it bluntly, she is there to be chosen by Henry or Edmund,
though she does have the right to refuse or accept. Therefore we should
not exaggerate Fanny's moral strength to the point of suggesting, as some
critics have enthusiastically done, that she has usurped altogether the
moral, social, and geographical realm of the Bertram children (despite
Tom Bertram's recovery and reformation) and has become "the true
inheritor of *Mansfield Park*"[2] and "virtually its mistress."[3] As F. T.
Flahiff judiciously reminds us,[4] Fanny, even after her marriage with
Edmund, lives, according to the text, "within the view and patronage of
Mansfield Park" (473). What Fanny has achieved, really, is a quiet but
steady moral influence which is seen at Mansfield Park as well as at
Portsmouth.

In conclusion, what is unique about *Mansfield Park* is not the myth
of its ultra-morality, or the groundless claim that Fanny is "never, ever,

---

[1]   In their analysis of *Mansfield Park*, Gilbert and Gubar curiously characterize Mary and
Fanny as typical Austenian "sisters" who "have much in common .... Both are relatively poor,
dependent on male relatives for financial security" (164). The fact is that Mary has £20,000
under her name, or £1000 a year (double the £500 a year on which the four Dashwood women
have to eke out their living), whereas Fanny has hardly any money.

[2]   Tony Tanner 157.

[3]   Trilling, *Opposing Self* 212.

[4]   See "Place and Replacement in *Mansfield Park*," *University of Toronto Quarterly* 54
(1985): 226.

wrong,"① but the illumination of the empirical and dialectical mode of thinking that characterizes a young person's moral growth. That dialectical process is marked by its gradualness and tortuousness. The process yields Fanny Price a salutary experience; she comes to know more about herself and the reality around her.

Fanny's dialectical example proves to be "medicinal" (369) for a few others as well. Sir Thomas, for example, has learned that "hereditary distinction"② can only help so much, that distinction in "elegance and accomplishments" may have "no moral effect on the mind" (463), that there is indeed "no necessary correspondence between class and morality."③ *Mansfield Park* in general, then, should not be taken as "a strategic retreat from the exposed position of *Pride and Prejudice*" and a conscious reaction on Austen's part "against the confident irony of her early fiction."④ The novel may in fact be more appropriately seen as a daring advance into the philosophical realm of moral being which has always interested Jane Austen. It is also yet another comprehensive example of illustrious irony, which Sir Thomas eventually comes to see yet certain others do not. ⑤

In the next chapter we are going to see a different mode of dialectical

---

① Tanner 143.

② Burke, *Reflections* 51.

③ Raymond Williams, *The Country and the City* (London: Chatto, 1973) 145.

④ Litz 113, 115.

⑤ Marvin Mudrick, for example, regrets that *Mansfield Park* "has nothing of ... the sustained shaping irony of *Pride and Prejudice*" because it is dominated by "inflexible and deadening moral dogma" (for details see 155 – 180). Lionel Trilling declares that "there is one novel of Jane Austen's, *Mansfield Park*, in which the characteristic irony seems not to be at work. Indeed, one might say of this novel that it undertakes to discredit irony and to affirm literalness, that it demonstrates that there are no two ways about anything" (*Opposing Self* 208). Apparently, the young Northrop Frye also misses the irony in the novel. In the diary entry for August 23, 1942, Frye indignantly writes: "I can't forgive Jane for the vulgarity and Philistinism of *Mansfield Park*: if she hadn't written that absurd book I could enjoy her without reservations. But her explicit preference for her dim-witted Fanny to her intelligent and sensible Mary Crawford means that in the long run she accepted her county families, and had no positive basis for her satire of Lady Catherine or Collins or Sir whatsisname in *Persuasion*" (*Robert D. Denham, Northrop Frye Newsletter* 7.1 [1996]: 17).

thinking occurring in the mind of Emma, who is in almost all aspects the opposite of Fanny Price. Granted that every heroine in Jane Austen's fiction is unique, Emma as a community leader has the rare power and opportunity to set a moral example for others; yet the fact that she is actually using what she is endowed with to subvert the stability and harmony enjoyed by Highbury is disturbing. It is not that Emma is not morally intelligent but that there is always something that interferes with her moral awareness so that she tends to come to a subjective conclusion about an objective reality. Why it happens so persistently and what effect it produces on Emma and other characters will be the focal point of the next chapter.

6 *Emma*: The Dialectics of Moral Judgment

Emma brings to a new height Jane Austen's art of dialectic. What seems special here is the way Austen expertly accommodates two centrally dialectical actions in one narrative, namely, the dialectical contention between Mr Knightley and Emma Woodhouse, and the dialectical conflict within the mind of Emma herself. The focus of the two dialectical strands is the process of making rational, moral judgments. Technically, *Emma* has a closer affinity with *Mansfield Park* than with *Pride and Prejudice* in that interior monologue, or free indirect speech, is the major medium in conveying to the readers Emma's decision-making process, which is itself more dialectically similar to that of Fanny than to that of Elizabeth. In other words, the inward turn of dialectics, begun in *Mansfield Park*, continues in *Emma*, and earmarks the heroine's inner life as she sets about making moral judgments. Indeed Emma's trade mark, so to speak, is the seemingly endless train of conflicting thoughts that she entertains as she reacts to other people's opinions in general and to Mr Knightley's judgement in particular.

Emma, almost twenty-one years of age at the beginning of the novel, is a different kind of heroine from the naïve Catherine Morland and Marianne Dashwood in terms of intellectual maturity; she is also significantly different from Elizabeth Bennet and Fanny Price in terms of fortune, status and consequence. Emma has social and economic power and also the power to think. It is the process of her thinking that matters. Hence Jane Austen's theme is philosophical rather than political, and hers is neither "the classic plot of the conservative novel" nor "an ingeniously comic revamping of the anti-jacobin plot," as Butler is inclined to think. ①

On the other hand, radical feminist critics equally misread this mature novel by either seeing the heroine and the female characters in general as trapped in a male-dominated world and suffering from the phallic psychology it forces upon them, or by seeing Emma as someone independent and rebellious and even successful in turning the tables upon the patriarchy and dominating male desires. Daniel Cottom, for example, argues that "in [Austen's] novels women do not have the power of interpretation that men have, even when that interpretation applies to their own psychological condition. "② Cottom asserts:

> Generally speaking, then, when a man's judgment runs contrary to a woman's, he has the power to presume that his judgment finds confirmation within her, even if he must allow that confirmation to be unconscious. Consequently, the minds of women may be said to be colonized by an unconsciousness that is always agreeable to men. And that will be forced into consciousness by the power of men if the women should ever seem to differ from their judgment. This overruling of the minds of women is so powerful that even when a woman simply makes a mistake in judgment or comes to be threatened by an ambiguity or an actual danger in the world around her, she may be held responsible for her situation if she has not been perfectly passive, projecting an image of total unconsciousness, ceding all interpretation to those men who have the authority in her world. ③

Cottom's argument about men's "overruling of the minds of women" and their effective silencing of female voices clearly contradicts what *Emma* tells us, where the heroine never seems to be shy of doing anything, least perhaps of voicing her opinions, and obviously doing so according to her own understanding, as her counterpart Mr Knightley does according to his. Mr Knightley, forthright as he is in pointing out

---

①   Butler 250.

②   *The Civilized Imagination: A study of Ann Radcliffe, Jane Austen, and Sir Walter Scott* (Cambridge: Cambridge UP, 1985) 73.

③   Cottom 73.

Emma's errors, is unable to sway Emma's judgment, either in the case involving Harriet and Martin or in the case involving Harriet and Elton, either in the case concerning the marriage of the Westons or in the case involving Frank Churchill and Jane Fairfax. This gives the lie to what Cottom claims to be "the rule of Austen's novels" by which "the minds of women ... will be forced into consciousness by the power of men if the women should ever seem to differ from their judgment."[1] Mr Knightley's last words to the headstrong Emma indulging in "'the pride of the moment'" (375) at Box Hill, before his withdrawal to London, are: "'I will tell you truths while I can'" (375) rather than anything remotely resembling the wielding of "the power of men."

Precious few examples from *Emma* are selected by Cottom to illustrate his large and sweeping claims,[2] yet when they appear they tend to discredit rather than enhance his central argument. For example, while trying to illustrate the novel as a lesson for women to stay humble, Cottom cites the instance of Harriet's failed romance with Mr Elton: "Harriet is unable to become another Pamela not because she is the bastard daughter of a tradesman ... but because she is brought to approach a higher social rank through the incentive of pride rather than through the deference of humility and abject imitation."[3] This really sounds like a backhanded ridiculing of Harriet who has nothing but deference and humility for Mr Elton. Cottom's ideologically-driven criticism lends itself to the view that it is unhelpful to read Jane Austen's novels along the dividing line of male and female constructs, for the philosophical nature of her novels defies such simplistic, politically motivated, measuring. One must have gravely misread the characters of Catherine Morland, Elinor Dashwood, Elizabeth Bennet, Fanny Price, Emma Woodhouse and Anne Elliot, and given little attention to the kind of moral struggle they wage in order to argue that "women in Austen's

---

[1]   Cottom 73.

[2]   *Emma*, widely regarded as the most finished novel of the Austen canon, is conspicuously absent from Poovey's discussion of Jane Austen in *The Proper Lady*.

[3]   Cottom 104.

novels are entrapped in a world of meaning beyond their control, and they have to learn to live with it, all the while maneuvering around the central institution of marriage."[1] It is ironic that this type of feminist criticism will have to demean Austen's female characters so as to score a political point.

At the other extreme of the feminist spectrum, Claudia L. Johnson regards the novel as an experiment "to explore positive versions of female power," and she argues that "in *Emma* woman *does* reign alone."[2] "Woman, Lovely Woman Reigns Alone" is the title of Johnson's chapter on *Emma*. The recycling of the line in Mr Elton's charade is, however, ironic: by glorifying Emma's short-lived success in prodding Mr Elton to make advances (alas, not to Harriet) and proving Mr Knightley wrong, Johnson actually highlights Emma's failure to see that she is a vainglorious yet ill-informed match-maker whose folly is rudely stopped in its tracks by Mr Elton's surprise proposal in the dark cold carriage.

This perhaps unintended irony in criticism matches the intended irony in the narrative. Emma's intelligence enables her to decipher quickly the message cleverly hidden in Mr Elton's charade—whereas stupid Harriet can only think of "'a mermaid'" or "'a shark'" (73)—but her misguided intelligence also makes her miss the real target of Mr Elton's courtship. Emma's lone "dominion" is the result of her being ruled by vanity and misconception. Emma likes to think herself outside the marriage game and above it, but she is not, as the Westons, and even Miss Bates, can see. Similarly, Emma likes to think that she is instrumental in making things happen, such as the marriage of Miss Taylor and the "would-be" marriage between Mr Elton and Harriet, but she really is not. She deceives herself by believing in such "evidence" as she herself creates. Emma presumes that she can read Mr Elton like a book, but the man proves to be a "crux." In fact Emma cannot even read Harriet correctly all the time.

---

①　Cottom 81.

②　Johnson 126.

Sticking, as Cottom does, to the gender line in her critique, Johnson commends Emma's bid for "independence and power—power not only over her own destiny, but, what is harder to tolerate, power over the destinies of others,"[1] without mentioning what harmful effects and dire consequences Emma's power, or abuse of power, has caused in the lives of others. She then offers two marginal examples—Emma's inviting George Knightley to dine with them against the inclination of Mr Woodhouse for one, and Emma's serving more food to the guests than Mr Woodhouse wishes for another—and insists that they contribute to what is "remarkable" about *Emma*, since both examples illustrate that "[t] he excellence of Emma's rule is disclosed tactfully," and not "vaunted brusquely à la Mrs. Elton."[2] A more significant example that Johnson uses as proof of Emma's triumphant rule over the patriarchy is the fact that toward the end of the novel the Knightley couple decides to live at Hartfield, during Mr Woodhouse's lifetime, instead of at Donwell. Johnson then emphatically concludes: "In moving to Hartfield, Knightley is sharing *her* home, and in placing himself within her domain, Knightley gives his blessing to her rule."[3] What Johnson forgets to mention is that Emma does so to please Mr Woodhouse as she is afraid of disturbing "her father's comfort" (448),[4] and Mr Knightley kindly and sensibly agrees on account of "her father's happiness" (449). One could equally and easily argue that this is an example of patriarchy internalized (along the line of Cottom's argument) since Emma has after all chosen to reside at her father's home. [5]

---

[1] Johnson 125.

[2] Johnson 130.

[3] Johnson 143.

[4] Emma is the only heroine in Jane Austen's fiction who does not travel as a tourist, despite the many references to trips and journeys in the self-same novel. Emma admits that she has never seen the sea (101), and it is hinted that her trips to London are solely for the sake of seeing Isabella and her family (7).

[5] Julia Prewitt Brown thinks that the arrangement makes Mr Knightley "a kind of father to [Emma's] own father" (*Jane Austen's Novels: Social Change and Literary Form* (Cambridge: Harvard UP, 1979) 15.

It is apparent that neither radical nor conservative viewpoints are conducive to a fruitful reading of *Emma*, a highly complex novel in Jane Austen's canon. In the following pages I will attempt to shed light on the complexity of this novel by focusing on some significant dialectical elements, especially those moments where the working of dialectics seems most prominent in the heroine's judgment-making process.

1

Emma is a complex character, "'whom no one,'" remarked Jane Austen, "'but myself will much like.'"[1] To the contrary, the heroine's attractive personal qualities have long been recognized by readers of this novel. Kenneth L. Moler, for example, has observed that "Emma is witty and intelligent, and has a sort of intellectual vitality that is appealing," that "there is a magnanimity, a lack of pettiness and selfishness in some of her actions."[2] For many readers, it is these qualities, which offset those that are not so attractive, that make Emma endearing. What has not much caught the attention of critics, however, is the way Emma's virtues co-exist with her faults, the way her subjective vision interacts with her objective understanding, and the way her moral intelligence battles her faulty judgment.

At the opening of *Emma* Jane Austen follows her usual empirical approach to characterization by giving us the necessary background information about Emma Woodhouse, that is, the essential facts about her early education and her domestic circumstances. Emma's family is "first in consequence" in "the large and populous village" (7) of Highbury, and her social and financial advantages are registered by the special status she enjoys. Emma is "nearly twenty-one" (5) at the opening of the novel;[3]

---

[1] *Memoir* 157.

[2] Moler 171.

[3] Age is, again, of importance here, as elsewhere in Jane Austen's novels. Emma is, strictly speaking, still in apprenticeship, i. e., has not quite come of age when the novel begins, though she will do so at some point in the course of the novel.

for sixteen years since the death of her mother, she has been the favourite pupil and bosom friend of Miss Taylor, the family governess, who is "particularly" fond of Emma (5) because, in the words of Mr Knightley, she is "'always quick and assured,'" and at ten could "'answer questions which puzzled her sister at seventeen'" (37). Emma's undeniable talent might have developed into healthy intelligence had it been properly guided and trained. But the lack of firm discipline and direction—Mr Woodhouse indulges his daughter, and Miss Taylor's mild temper "had hardly allowed her to impose any restraint" (5) on Emma—has allowed her quickness to degenerate into mere cleverness.

The problem of Emma's early training as a pupil is best illustrated by the way she conducts her reading. As I have previously remarked, reading is a touchstone in the Austenian assessment of a character. To read or not to read, to read rationally or to read irrationally, serve as crucial indicators in the moral diagnosis and prognosis of a character. On this test Emma definitely scores low. George Knightley, who has seen Emma growing up, wryly observes that ever since she is twelve Emma "'has been meaning to read more'" (37) but never does, that she is capable of drawing up "'very good lists'" of books that are "'very well chosen, and very neatly arranged—sometimes alphabetically, and sometimes by some other rule'" (37) but never able to maintain "'any course of steady reading'" (37). Here we have a significant glimpse of the root cause of Emma's later vicissitudes and fluctuations in arriving at moral decisions. Clearly, Emma is aware of the means to cultivate a moral character: "'very good lists'" and "'very well chosen'" bespeak her intelligence. Yet equally clear is her lack of moral stamina to follow through what she knows will be morally beneficial. Thus Emma's cleverness, the essential quality spelt out in the opening line of the novel,[1] is dangerously compounded by her lack of moral perspectives. Even if Emma wants to judge judiciously, she lacks the means to do so.

---

[1] Of the three epithets—"handsome, clever, and rich" (5)—that describe the heroine, only the centrally placed "clever" refers to the inner quality of Emma.

These serious flaws in moral training give rise to Emma's habit of "doing just what she liked" and "having rather too much her own way" (5). Emma has been "'mistress of the house'" since she was twelve (37). Her excessively lax education and early freedom prove fertile soil for the growth of conceit. Her doting father comments—and she must be inclined to agree—that whatever she says "'always comes to pass'" (12). Mr Woodhouse is of course mistaken—as the novel shows us repeatedly— but within the Woodhouse household Emma is accustomed to having her own way and winning praises for doing so.

But outside Hartfield, it is a different matter. As a public figure in the Highbury community, Emma is a trouble-maker as she wields her social power to make whatever she thinks right come to pass. Her subjectively-powered vision not only causes her to miss what she should have seen but also induces her to see what is not in the field of normal vision. If Miss Bates can only see what is before her (176), Emma sees what is not before anyone else. In this respect Emma resembles Catherine Morland, who alone is able to envision a horrid murder or at least some cruel immurement inside the peaceful Northanger Abbey.

2

Emma's association with Harriet Smith illustrates vividly the uncomfortable co-existence of the rational and irrational qualities that dog and trap her. Emma embraces Miss Smith as her new friend "on account of her beauty" (22) which is "of a sort which Emma particularly admired" (23). But the essential qualities of Harriet's "beauty" turn out to be quite unimpressive: "short, plump and fair" (23). What seem to have caught Emma's eyes are actually her manners. Harriet is "very engaging" and "so pleasantly grateful;" she also shows "great sweetness" as well as "so proper and becoming a deference" (23). Needless to say, she makes a useful companion for walks now that Miss Taylor is gone. In a nutshell Harriet poses no challenge to Emma in any higher category of feminine beauty such as elegance, nor does she demonstrate "any thing

remarkably clever in [her] conversation" (23). In fact, Harriet
represents, as we are soon to learn, all that Jane Fairfax is not.

Harriet's lack of moral judgment or, to be more exact, judgment of
any kind, is shown in a variety of situations, from the least significant to
the most consequential. Her "business at Ford's" (233) serves a very clear
example of the kind of blandness of her mind. Harriet is "always very
long at a purchase" because she is "tempted by every thing and swayed by
half a word" (233). Emma tries to divert herself by going "to the door
for amusement" (233); but when she returns she finds Harriet still doing
what she was doing before—"hanging over muslins and changing her
mind" (233). Emma has to "convince her that if she wanted plain muslin
it was of no use to look at figured; and that a blue ribbon, be it ever so
beautiful, would still never match her yellow pattern" (235). It is very
frustrating for Emma that "all the force of her own mind" (235)
produces precious little effect on her protégée, who cannot decide where
her parcel should be sent once the few items have at last been bought.

Emma's decisiveness is clearly contrasted with Harriet's indecision,
but the contrast is not all in Emma's favour, for it contains multiple
layers of meanings. Emma's insistent patronage of someone so immature
and unpromising points to her misplaced intelligence. The fact that
Harriet's inferior physical and intellectual condition dovetails with
Emma's superior physical and intellectual condition results in a lop-sided
relationship between the two, which yields, not infrequently, double
irony. For example, while cajoling her into thinking of Mr Elton instead
of Robert Martin as her matrimonial partner, Emma urges Harriet to pay
more attention to external features that give good impressions rather than
internal qualities that account for real worth:

> What say you to Mr. Weston and Mr. Elton? Compare Mr. Martin with
> either of *them*. Compare their manner of carrying themselves; of walking; of
> speaking; of being silent. You must see the difference. (33)

Based on her own very brief observation of Robert Martin in a
chance encounter, Emma determines that Mr Martin is no gentleman-
farmer because he is "'remarkably plain'" (32), "'totally without air'"

and "'so very clownish'" (32). From these external features alone she concludes that there is an "'entire want of gentility'" (32) in Robert Martin. Emma further predicts that when Martin reaches "'Mr Weston's time of life'" he "'will be a completely gross, vulgar farmer—totally inattentive to appearances, and thinking of nothing but profit and loss'" (33).

However, just as Emma is poised to succeed with her "'pretty good guessing'" (33), she is confronted by Robert Martin's well-written letter of marriage proposal, which constitutes an unmistakable sign of the man's worth, even intellectual worth at that, and thus flatly contradicts her preconceived notions about the farmer. Emma is "surprized" (50) by the impressive letter of proposal which Robert Martin has written to Harriet Smith:

> The style of the letter was much above her expectation. There were not merely no grammatical errors, but as a composition it would not have disgraced a gentleman; the language, though plain, was strong and unaffected, and the sentiments it conveyed very much to the credit of the writer. It was short, but expressed good sense, warm attachment, liberality, propriety, even delicacy of feeling. (50 – 51)

The high intellectual quality of the letter is totally unexpected; in fact it causes Emma to pause and ponder. The black-and-white evidence of the letter clearly separates the superior Martin from the inferior Harriet, who, while anxiously expecting her mentor to pronounce a judgment, badgers Emma: "'Is it a good letter? Or is it too short?'" (51). That Harriet easily and totally misses the point is no surprise, given her very limited moral and intellectual capacity. What is surprising is the remarkable pattern of similarity between Harriet and Emma's method of making judgments. Harriet's measuring the marriage proposal by its length is a reductive imitation of Emma's identifying a gentleman by the way he looks or walks. The stupidity of one mirrors the wrong-headedness of the other.

Yet Emma, morally misguided rather than morally flaccid, is no Harriet. Emma is a thinking individual and she has certain moral criteria

to rely on when making moral judgments. Emma is compelled to admit—
"rather slowly" (51)—to her protégée that Martin's is "'indeed, a very
good letter'" (51). However, she decides that the letter is too good to be
true: "'[S]o good a letter,'" she tells Harriet, who is all ears, "'that
every thing considered, I think one of his sisters must have helped him'"
(51). Emma, suppressing the truth literally in her hand, seeks what
Locke calls "not the evidence of truth, but some lazy anticipation, some
beloved presumption."[1]

But, again, Emma's sense of justice intervenes: although she "'can
hardly imagine'" that Robert Martin could "'express himself so well, if
left quite to his own powers,'" she frankly acknowledges the
unfoundedness of her own presumption: "'[Y]et it is not the style of a
woman; no, certainly, it is too strong and concise; not diffuse enough
for a woman'" (51). Emma even goes further to contradict her own
prejudice against Mr Martin, granting that "'[n]o doubt he is a sensible
man'" (51). It is important to realize that Emma has made these just
comments while she is trying to substantiate her favourite notion that
Robert Martin is a country bumpkin, and while she is under no pressure
from her particular friend to be fair and just. It is Emma's own honesty,
taste and moral instincts that make it hard for her to reach a "verdict"
about Martin's letter and, by extension, the man himself. Her moral
sense tells her one thing; her royal fancy another.

Emma's dialectical struggle boils down to the philosophical choice of
being subjective or objective. Emma's subjective judgment dies hard. As
a last-ditch attempt to explain away the contradiction, she tries to limit
the significance of the evidence as much as she can. She hastens to add:
"'I suppose [he] may have a natural talent for—'" (51). The sentence is
broken off, but it is not because Emma is at a loss for words. What she
has intended to say, presumably, is that Martin has a talent for writing
good, grammatical letters. The awareness of the natural connection
between character and style (as is invariably the case in Jane Austen's

---

[1] Locke, *Conduct* 10.

fiction) must have made it difficult for Emma to pronounce an untruth to her protégée, even though the latter is quite ignorant of the nature of their association and completely oblivious to the dialectical debate going on in her patroness's mind. Holding the physical evidence of Martin's well-written letter, Emma's instinctive moral judgment compels her to make favourable comments about the letter and the man who wrote it and prevents her from denouncing Robert Martin out of hand.

When the broken sentence is resumed, its subject has changed. In fact the whole original sentence structure is given up. What is substituted is a strong succinct assessment adopting the simple present tense, which is usually reserved for a statement of universal truth: "'—thinks strongly and clearly—'" (51). The substitutive predicate voids the sentence beginning with "'I suppose'" and is logically extrapolated to its proper subject, i.e., Mr Robert Martin. Emma subsequently confirms her hesitant verdict by informing Harriet: "'Yes, I understand the sort of mind. Vigorous, decided, with sentiments to a certain point, not coarse. A better written letter, Harriet, (returning it,) than I had expected'" (51). At last it seems that justice has prevailed over prejudice.

Emma's back-and-forth movement here is an ironic mirror image of Harriet's at Mrs Ford's; it is in reality a stark contrast to that mindless floundering. Whereas Harriet speaks without thinking or thinks without understanding, Emma, to borrow her own words on Mr Martin, "'thinks strongly and clearly,'" and her "'thoughts naturally find proper words'" (51). The beauty of Jane Austen's depiction of the dialectics in the heroine's decision- or judgment-making process is that it catches every flicker of thought in the context of a broad range of significant details. The process of making moral judgment often follows a zigzag pattern. The resolution of one issue does not mean the automatic solution of another. Emma's eventual realization that Martin is a man of superior qualities does not mean that she is going to give up Mr Elton, whom she has already designated as the ideal marriage partner for Harriet. As Locke says, "[H]e who can reason well to-day, about one sort of matters, cannot at all reason to-day about others. "① Unless Emma realizes that there is something fundamentally wrong with her mode of thinking and takes immediate and effective measures to rectify it, she is unlikely to make sound moral judgments.

During the remaining part of this long dialogue, Emma keeps infusing her own prejudice against Robert Martin into Harriet's head. However, the dialogue between the two turns into one of cross-purposes because of the mixed signals—signs of her inner dialectical conflict—that Emma is sending to an imperceptive recipient. The apparently clear prose begins to lose its clarity and the message it carries becomes double. Harriet is waiting for a final verdict from her superior. When her soliciting signals—"'[W] ell ... well—and—'" (51)—fail to draw one, she directly asks Emma "'what shall I do?'" (51). Emma, unperturbed by Martin's good letter and determined as ever to prosecute her secret plan, offers a rhetorical question as her definitive answer: "'But what are you in doubt of?'" (51). However, what is clear to Emma is not clear to Harriet. The linguistic degeneration is Emma's sole responsibility since Harriet remains dim-witted and, as a protégée, she looks up to her patroness for guidance. The simple girl is gratified by being the object of Robert Martin's desire, at whose Abbey-Mill farm she had just spent two very happy months (27), and is more than inclined towards requiting his love. However, she is confused by Emma's flip-flop assessment of Martin's letter. For a moment Emma seems to be playing verbal tricks like the dubious as well as devious Iago, driving at something but refusing to be explicit, even though it has never occurred to Emma to adopt Iago's method of sowing seeds of doubts.

Emma cannot say much against Mr Martin as a result of the evidence she has just examined, but she is still in favour of Mr Elton. The hesitation creates a limbo that makes not only Emma but also—and more so—Harriet very uncomfortable. The presence of the obtuse Harriet adds humour to the double dramatic irony yet it also highlights Emma's

---

①   Locke, *Conduct* 6.

inner-conflict.

Emma has earlier heard Harriet's enthusiastic talk about Mr Martin, but she is determined that "her poor little friend" must not "sink herself for ever" (28) by marrying the clown of a yeoman-farmer. Emma never bothers to investigate her particular friend's genuine feelings for Mr Martin, let alone understand them. Mr Martin's good letter makes her pause but does not induce a purge of her preconceptions.

When Harriet, still in the dark, pleads with Emma for some specific advice: "'But what shall I say? Dear Miss Woodhouse, do advise me,'" Emma replies:

> Oh, no, no! the Letter had much better be all your own. You will express yourself very properly, I am sure. There is no danger of your not being intelligible, which is the first thing. Your meaning must be unequivocal; no doubts or demurs: and such expressions of gratitude and concern for the pain you are inflicting as propriety requires, will present themselves unbidden to *your* mind, I am persuaded. *You* need not be prompted to write with the appearance of sorrow for his disappointment. (51 – 52)

Emma is confidently setting the tone of Harriet's letter of refusal, a fact which she later hides from the inquisitive Knightley. By now even the dull-witted Harriet comes to sense the drift of Emma's intent: "'You think I ought to refuse him then'" (52). Only now does Emma realize that she has been "'under a mistake'" (52), and she promptly apologizes to a disappointed Harriet. But Emma's mistake is not simply "'misunderstanding'" (52) Harriet. Hers is a slavish adherence to her own subjective notions while disregarding all other factors, including Harriet's feelings and Martin's good character.

A similar dialectical conflict is seen in Emma's judgment of Jane Fairfax. Jane is not favoured by Emma even though they have known each other from childhood and "their ages were the same" (166). Mr Knightley suggests that the cool relation between the two is the result of Emma's seeing in Jane "the really accomplished young woman, which she wanted to be thought herself" (166). But another reason is that Jane does not flatter Emma, who is "first in consequence" at Highbury, the way

Harriet and Churchill do. That gives rise to the third reason: Emma is unable to manage, let alone manipulate, Jane who possesses "higher powers of mind" (165), as she does Harriet and apparently Frank Churchill. Miss Fairfax is not prepared to let Emma think for her, as Harriet invariably does and Churchill pretends to. Emma is never sure of Miss Fairfax; her hankering for some inside knowledge is always frustrated by Jane's reticence, a necessary defence for someone in her position. It is therefore logical that Emma would feel gratified if she could prove that "[t]his amiable, upright, perfect Jane Fairfax was apparently cherishing very reprehensible feelings" (243).

What interests us is the fact that Emma is often aware of her unfair judgment of Jane Fairfax and even tries from time to time to curb her prejudice. She aptly sums up her relationship with Jane as "always doing more than she wished, and less than she ought!" (166). Although Emma flatly rejects Mr Knightley's suggestion of envy as the main reason for their lukewarm relationship, on reflection she acknowledges, albeit transiently, that there is a grain of truth in his diagnosis. However, whatever Emma rationally realizes during "moments of self-examination" (166) tends to be quickly overcome by her jealousy of Jane who is "made such a fuss with by every body!" (166). Emma even cites the fault of Miss Bates as part of Jane's problem—"her aunt was such an eternal talker!" (166). Nevertheless, when Emma meets Jane again "after a two years' interval" (167), she is "particularly struck with the very appearance and manners" (167) of her competitor. What is of particular significance here is that Emma gives full credit to Jane's elegance: from her "height" to her "figure" and to her "size," from her "face" to her "eyes" and to her "skin" (167). This is indeed striking, especially when we consider that Emma "had herself the highest value for elegance" (167) and that she is known to have "a dislike so little just" (167) for Jane Fairfax. The fact that Emma is able to sanction Jane's elegance unreservedly, though not without some reluctance—she "must, in honour, by all her principles, admire it" (167), once again rehabilitates and redeems part of Emma's less than perfect character.

This triumph of honesty and justice is without doubt the shining part of Emma's character. Miss Bingley, we recall, denies that Elizabeth Bennet has any beauty at all, not even her fine eyes which have attracted Darcy and won his admiration. Emma's honesty, a prerequisite for moral improvement, is consistently depicted throughout the novel. We have seen that she will not even take advantage of Harriet's ignorance to aggrandize herself. [1] Emma will not knowingly falsify truth or fabricate evidence. Calling a spade a spade whenever she is able to helps to establish Emma as a redeemable character. This is essentially why Emma's learning process could have been a dialectical one.

3

Emma's judgment of Frank Churchill is fraught with dialectical twists bearing far-reaching effects. The fluctuations, consistently illustrated in the last third of the first volume, where her thinking fluctuates between rational and irrational, vividly demonstrate the moral complexity of the heroine and her interesting relationship with Mr Knightley. Emma suffers from vanity and undue pride. These moral deficiencies are masterfully exploited by Frank Churchill who has apparently perfected his skills through his managing and appeasing his rich, odd and arrogant aunt, Mrs Churchill—"'no small credit'" (121) in the opinion of his father. Shortly after they have made acquaintance with each other, Frank Churchill sets to work on Emma's weaknesses for his own gain.

Emma does not know much about Frank Churchill's character. However, she is predisposed in such a way that what she has heard from the Westons about him convinces her that he is an unfortunate young man at the mercy of an "'odd woman'" (120) whom he has to "'please'"

---

[1]   Elsewhere Emma would not allow Harriet to rate her piano skills on a par with those of Jane Fairfax: "'Don't class us together, Harriet. My playing is no more like her's, than a lamp is like sunshine'" (231). The graphic language is no doubt for the benefit of Emma's slow-witted friend who, however, remains unconvinced (231-232).

(120). Isabella Knightley must have expressed her sister's feelings well when she sentimentalizes about the uncertainty of Frank Churchill's pending visit to his parents:

> I am sure I never think of that poor young man without the greatest compassion. To be constantly living with an ill-tempered person, must be dreadful. It is what we happily have never known any thing of; but it must be a life of misery. What a blessing, that she never had any children! Poor little creatures, how unhappy she would have made them! (121 – 122)

These remarks, coming from Isabella Knightley, who has successfully escaped from her hypochondriac and self-centred father, contain a shade of irony at the speaker's expense. However, the indignation at the selfish control of Mrs Churchill is shared and welcomed by Emma who is likewise used to the indulgence of their insipid father and surrogate "mother," i.e., Miss Taylor turned Mrs Weston, who refers to Emma and Isabella as "'my two daughters'" (121).

Nevertheless, Emma's moral consciousness tells her that it is Frank Churchill's duty, his domestic difficulty notwithstanding, to visit his newly-wed parents. Emma thinks that Frank Churchill "'ought to come'" and doubts "'a young man's not having it in his power to do as much as that'" (122). In fact she "'cannot comprehend a young *man*'s being under such restraint, as not to be able to spend a week with his father, if he likes it'" (122). Emma's moral position is in fact very similar in nature to that of Mr Knightley which is clearly stated, during their quarrel, in the last chapter of the first volume. Mr Knightley argues the same point only in more concrete terms, if in a more irate tone as well:

> If Frank Churchill had wanted to see his father, he would have contrived it between September and January. A man at his age—what is he? —three or four-and-twenty—cannot be without the means of doing as much as that. It is impossible. (145)

However, underneath the almost identical moral sentiment lie differences of moral commitment. Emma's moral judgment is coalesced

with her romantic illusions about Frank Churchill. She subsequently
defends Frank Churchill on the ground of mitigating circumstances
surrounding the event. Mr Knightley, on the other hand, will argue
strictly along moral lines, though his motive may be tainted by some
other considerations as well. Mr Knightley does not believe that external
factors are important in this case and he lays the blame squarely on Frank
Churchill. He argues that "'a young man, brought up by those who are
proud, luxurious, and selfish'" is more likely to be "'proud, luxurious,
and selfish too'" (145).

Emma's ambivalent attitude towards Frank Churchill is a natural
reflection of her mixed feelings about him. She is not disinterested.
Frank Churchill has always attracted Emma who has been hearing
favourable things about him from the Westons who think that the two
young people are ideal for each other. Emma keenly remembers Frank
Churchill's age and has in fact "frequently" contemplated his candidacy as
a bridegroom, "if she *were* to marry" (119). Without knowing his moral
character, Emma imagines that Frank Churchill is "the very person to suit
her in age, character and condition" (119). So when Emma tells Mrs
Weston that she thinks Frank Churchill "ought to come," her moral
sentiment is not unmixed with some private thoughts. Emma's last words
to Mrs Weston, at the end of chapter 14, about Frank Churchill's planned
visit are a tell-tale sign of the selfish aspect of her moral opinion: "'I shall
not be satisfied, unless he comes'" (123). The tone of Emma's voice
implies that she is personally interested in the young man's visit; she
needs to satisfy her own curiosity; and she would be sorely disappointed
if the announced visit should fizzle out. Such is Emma's psychological
state when Mr Knightley corners her and urges her to dwell upon the
moral implications of Frank Churchill's failure to visit Randalls.

4

Chapter 18 of volume 1 sees one of the most intriguing dialectical
engagements in Jane Austen's fiction. Mr Knightley's swift condem-

nation of Frank Churchill's procrastination irks a wavering Emma trapped between her romantic fancy and her sense of rectitude. Emma has a soft spot for Frank Churchill, which gives rise to her facile sympathy for the man. But Emma's affection is secret and should not—as she well knows—figure in her counter-argument against Mr Knightley. This situation creates complications. Whereas she may agree that Frank Churchill's now confirmed absence is reprehensible, Emma does not think that he deserves the kind of severe censure Knightley unleashes. Emma tries to save Frank Churchill's bacon by attacking his rich and domineering aunt while hiding, unsuccessfully—at least to Mr Knightley—her questionable sentimentality.

As the moral debate goes on, Emma finds her slipping into the same argument which the Westons have either tactfully or candidly presented in defence of their son, which she herself has earlier dismissed. Indeed Emma herself is surprised by what she is actually doing to Mr Knightley, "taking the other side of the question from her real opinion, and making use of Mrs. Weston's arguments against herself" (145). Mr Knightley is incensed by Emma's facetious argument and tries to convince her that it is the man's character—not the extenuating circumstances—that is at issue (earlier Emma blames Mr Elton—"so blind" and "most provoking" [136]—for her match-making fiasco). But his direct refutation of her moral relativism achieves little effect because Emma is not being morally serious: she is "acting a part" (145) with "great amusement" (145).

Emma is reputed to have "a mind delighted with its own ideas" (24), but it is clear that the "imaginist" (335)① is not simply engaged in imagination pure and simple. Her imaginings are often motivated by some selfish considerations: be it jealousy, vanity or self-gratification. They are anything but abstract and they usually carry social and moral consequences. Mr Knightley, on the other hand, is no representative of pure morality either, as Emma has smartly perceived—a small yet not

---

① Tave alerts us that, according to the *OED* (205), the nonce word "imaginist" is actually invented by Jane Austen for Emma.

insignificant credit to her ability to judge. Thus Emma's rejection of Mr Knightley's criticism of Frank Churchill not only reveals her own moral weaknesses but also challenges the absolute integrity of Mr Knightley's moral judgment.

Mr Knightley's refutation of Emma's moral relativism is entirely justified. He takes into account the role of the Churchills—"'very likely in fault'" (145)—but he will not condone the tepid, if also shiftless, young man on that account. Mr Knightley notes that Frank Churchill is well over the age of majority and that he had the time to fulfil his obligation—he had actually managed to loiter "' for ever at some watering-place or other'" as well as "'at Weymouth'" (146) where he first met Miss Fairfax. It is clear to Mr Knightley that Frank Churchill lacks "' vigour and resolution '" yet is good at "' manœuvring and finessing'" (146). Such reasonable analysis makes Emma's complaint that it is "' very unfair to judge of any body's conduct, without an intimate knowledge of their situation'" (146) appear spurious and even downright silly. Mr Knightley further points out:

> It is Frank Churchill's duty to pay this attention to his father. He knows it to be so, by his promises and messages; but if he wished to do it, it might be done. A man who felt rightly would say at once, simply and resolutely, to Mrs. Churchill—'Every sacrifice of mere pleasure you will always find me ready to make to your convenience; but I must go and see my father immediately. I know he would be hurt by my failing in such a mark of respect to him on the present occasion. I shall, therefore, set off to-morrow.'—If he would say so to her at once, in the tone of decision becoming a man, there would be no opposition made to his going. (146)

Mr Knightley's argument is as forceful as it is valid; it is also consistent. It is reassuring too to hear him alert Emma to the feelings of Mrs Weston, which must have been hurt as a result of "'the omission'" (149) caused by Frank Churchill's repeated delays of his filial visit.

However, Emma does not focus upon the gist of Mr Knightley's moral judgment; instead she fusses about the manner in which it is expressed. She accuses Mr Knightley of being "' odd.'" (145) and

"'singular'" (149) and "'prejudiced'" (150). Emma's choice of words
is interesting. The negative adjectives poorly characterize Mr Knightley's
moral intent, but they seem to hint at Emma's penetration into the depth
of the man's mind. Emma has sensed that Mr Knightley is attacking
Frank Churchill with extra zest and her spontaneous reaction leaves no
doubt about how she feels. Although the narrator coyly suggests that
Emma "could not comprehend why he should be angry" (150), the
narrative evidence she artfully supplies seems to advise otherwise. Mr
Knightley, as if a sore point had been touched, refuses to admit that he is
"'prejudiced;'" yet the more Emma talks about Frank Churchill's
apparent virtues, the more incensed Mr Knightley becomes, and the more
antagonistic he turns towards the younger man. He seems to find Emma's
veiled and inchoate suspicion provoking and, despite his normally
balanced judgment, appears momentarily to let something obscure "the
real liberality" of his "mind" and allow himself to be "unjust to the merit
of another" (151). The narrator will eventually confirm that Mr
Knightley, "for some reason best known to himself," has "certainly taken
an early dislike to Frank Churchill" (343).

　　It is also interesting to observe that, even in the heat of their
argument, Emma seems to be aware where the line between right and
wrong is drawn. When she feels that she can no longer argue sensibly, she
shifts her ground. She tells Mr Knightley that if Frank Churchill has
"'nothing else to recommend him'" he will still "'be a treasure at
Highbury'" (149). The reason she offers is again facetious: "'We do not
often look upon fine young men, well-bred and agreeable. We must not
be nice and ask for all the virtues into the bargain'" (149). [1] Emma is in
effect calling *touché* but her loaded remarks are no less irritating to an
already fuming Knightley.

　　What seems absent for the moment is the possibility of any romantic
relationship between Emma and Mr Knightley. That does not mean,

---

　[1]　Roberts discusses the differences between English and French values that seem to be the
subtext in this passage (37 – 40).

however, that there is a lack of mutual sexual awareness; it merely intimates that Emma's sexual awareness of Mr Knightley's manly presence is subdued by her wilful opposition to his just criticism of Frank Churchill, with whom she thinks she could fall in love, and that Mr Knightley's sexual appeal suffers as a result of his insistence upon principles. In a sense Mr Knightley is filling in that part of the paternal role which Mr Woodhouse fails to fulfill whereas Emma is attempting to play the "wife" that Mr Woodhouse no longer has.

Generally speaking, though, Mr Knightley's jealousy does not detract from his moral judgment whereas Emma's fancy gets the better of hers. There is no denying of Mr Knightley's superior moral vision and his genuine concern for Emma's moral well-being; yet there is also no denying that Emma's sharp perception and supreme articulation have put his morality in perspective and, at the same time, proved him human. Mr Knightley's prediction that Emma "'could not endure such a puppy when it came to the point'" (150) is in the end borne out by her moral indignation at Frank Churchill's shady behaviour and the man's own admission of being "'an impudent dog'" (478). However, Emma's suspicion that he is jealous of Frank Churchill is also vindicated by Mr Knightley's own admission that he does envy him (428), and by the possibility that "he might have deemed" his feared competitor "a very good sort of fellow" (433) the moment Emma is securely his.

This passionate moral engagement between Emma and Mr Knightley makes yet again clear that Emma does not lack the ability and acumen to make a moral judgment, though she lacks the moral seriousness or maturity to make such judgments on a regular and consistent basis. Emma has "'qualities which may be trusted'" (40) but she cannot be trusted to tap those trusted qualities all the time. Her moral outlook is in constant danger of being undermined by her deviating fancy. The incident once more makes apparent Jane Austen's dialectical narrative design; she wants her readers to think dialectically of her novels, and she provides them with abundant, if also unobtrusive, details to work with.

5

A less discernible yet no less revealing dialectical relationship, important to the understanding of Emma's judgment-making process, is that between Emma and Miss Bates. Although Emma never deigns to acknowledge the relationship and is in fact inimical to any idea of an association between her and the loquacious spinster, the shadow of Miss Bates never seems far behind her and even threatens to claim some sort of kinship. For example, the way these two characters are introduced, respectively in chapters 1 and 3 of the first volume, seems to set them up as point and counterpoint. Their separate "portraits" seem to echo and comment upon each other. Let us review Miss Bates' narrative debut:

> [Mrs. Bates's] daughter enjoyed a most uncommon degree of popularity for a woman neither young, handsome, rich, nor married. Miss Bates stood in the very worst predicament in the world for having much of the public favour; and she had no intellectual superiority to make atonement to herself, or frighten those who might hate her, into outward respect. She had never boasted either beauty or cleverness. Her youth had passed without distinction, and her middle of life was devoted to the care of a failing mother, and the endeavour to make a small income go as far as possible. And yet she was a happy woman, and a woman whom no one named without good-will. It was her own universal good-will and contented temper which worked such wonders. She loved every body, was interested in every body's happiness, quick-sighted to every body's merits; thought herself a most fortunate creature, and surrounded with blessings in such an excellent mother and so many good neighbours and friends, and a home that wanted for nothing. The simplicity and cheerfulness of her nature, her contented and grateful spirit, were a recommendation to every body and a mine of felicity to herself. She was a great talker upon little matters, which exactly suited Mr. Woodhouse, full of trivial communications and harmless gossip. (21)

The quotation seems excessive only because the narrator's cataloguing of details is repetitive and redundant, catching the letter and spirit of Miss Bates' linguistic style.

Upon first reading, Miss Bates seems in every respect the opposite of

Miss Woodhouse who is young, "handsome, clever, and rich" (5) and has "a comfortable home" (5). Whereas Emma seems "to unite some of the best blessings of existence" (5), Miss Bates seems to muster the rottenest luck and can only count her blessings in such an excellent mother and so many good neighbours and friends. Whereas Emma enjoys her life in a world that has "very little to distress or vex her" (5), Miss Bates must eke out a humble living—striving "to make a small income go as far as possible." The two characters seem to be situated at the opposite ends of the same pole. In Emma's mind, if there is any woman in Highbury that she does not want to be, it has to be Miss Bates.

However, just as this impression of two opposing selves begins to take hold, striking resemblance between the two starts to emerge and challenge our easy credulity and quick classification. Both women are unmarried; both have lost one parent and both look after the other. Both have a happy disposition; both enjoy a high level of popularity; and both are interested in the welfare of others; and, last but not least, both are well informed of the Highbury gossip. Interestingly enough, Emma's "ingenious and animating suspicion" (160) of Miss Fairfax's romantic involvement with Mr Dixon is the direct result of Miss Bates' profuse talk of Jane's being with the man in question (159–60). The resemblance linking the two women, despite the willingness of one and the reluctance of the other, is in fact misleading, for it camouflages the fundamental differences between them.

Whereas Miss Bates is always well-meaning, Emma does not hesitate to criticize anyone if he or she does not conform to her way of seeing things. Whereas Miss Bates is genuinely "interested in every body's happiness," Emma's interested participation in the social life of Highbury embodies an urge to satisfy her fancy and sense of power. She wants public recognition of her goodness, usefulness and, sometimes, even contriteness. For example, the day after the Box Hill incident, Emma is "determined" to call on Miss Bates "early" in the morning so that "nothing might prevent her" (377) from making apologies to Miss Bates. This is of course the right thing to do except that Emma wishes that "she might see Mr. Knightley in her way; or, perhaps, he might come in while she were paying her visit" (377).

It is dialectically interesting that, of all the people surrounding Emma, Harriet turns out to be the one that points out Emma's fellowship with Miss Bates at a hilarious moment in their otherwise droll conversation about marriage and celibacy in chapter 10 of volume 1. Emma passionately asserts her desire to stay independent and never to marry, at least for now:

> Fortune I do not want; employment I do not want; consequence I do not want: I believe few married women are half as much mistress of their husband's house, as I am of Hartfield; and never, never could I expect to be so truly beloved and important; so always first and always right in any man's eyes as I am in my father's. (84)

The confessional declaration prompts Harriet, who is used to literal rather than dialectical thinking, to exclaim: "'But then, to be an old maid at last, like Miss Bates!'" (84). Emma is annoyed and sarcastically replies:

> That is as formidable an image as you could present, Harriet; and if I thought I should ever be like Miss Bates! so silly—so satisfied—so smiling—so prosing—so undistinguishing and unfastidious—and so apt to tell every thing relative to every body about me, I would marry tomorrow. (84 – 85)

Harriet, capable of drawing the most superficial comparison due to her limited intellect and shallow understanding, has inadvertently touched a sore subject with Emma and spoiled her indulgence in self-righteousness. Emma is stung by the analogy because her superior power of intellect makes her fully understand the potential truth that Harriet has unwittingly pronounced. Her denial is swift, decisive and vehement. There is no commonality whatsoever between Miss Bates and her. The irony is: the harder Emma tries to distance Miss Bates from her, the closer she seems to become. Emma's characterization of Miss Bates is too sweeping to be accurate, too derogatory to be credible, and too desperate—six emphatic adverbs are used in one sentence to drive home the point—to be objective. Miss Bates appears, and perhaps is, silly, but at Box Hill she is sensitive enough to feel embarrassed and hurt by Emma's quip—"'only three at once'" (370), and intelligent enough to voice her uneasiness about the moral turpitude of such treatment of her. Although she does not know it herself, Miss Bates is instrumental in bringing on Mr Knightley's ultimate censure of Emma's misbehaviour. ① Emma is perhaps right after all in identifying Miss Bates as her nemesis because she really turns out to be just that.

6

Emma's wilfulness and preconception are contrasted with Mr Knightley's reason, caution and objectivity in their respective judgments of characters. For example, in regard to the secret relationship between Frank Churchill and Jane Fairfax, Mr Knightley shows patience in collecting evidence to build a solid case. He has initially observed certain symptoms: at the Eltons' he has "seen a look, more than a single look, at Miss Fairfax, which, from the admirer of Miss Woodhouse, seemed somewhat out of place" (343 – 344); at the Woodhouses' he is strategically seated so that he is able "to see them all" (347)—Emma, Frank and Jane—"and it was his object to see as much as he could, with as little apparent observation" (347). By contrast, Emma builds her case without proper investigation. When she tries to investigate, she is either easily misled by the scheming Frank Churchill or readily guided by the ill notion of her rival, Jane Fairfax. At one point during Mr Cole's house party, Emma's view is literally, and metaphorically, blocked by Frank, who "had improvidently placed himself exactly between [Emma and Jane]" so that she "could absolutely distinguish nothing" (222).

---

① Tara Ghoshal Wallace perhaps goes too far in arguing that Miss Bates is a manipulator, though not "a reincarnation of Lucy Steele and Mrs Norris" (93). She regards Miss Bates' reaction on the Hill—"'I must make myself very disagreeable, or she would not have said such a thing to an old friend'" (371)—as a "brilliant" piece of "rhetorical manipulation" because it highlights "Emma's rudeness" and compels her to be "doubly attentive to her victim" (92).

Mr Knightley is Emma's dialectical opposite. His careful observation enables him to draw the correct conclusion. When he tells Emma: "'I have lately imagined that I saw symptoms of attachment between [Frank and Jane]'" (350), he is using the word, "'imagined,'" advisedly. He has seen the two in question engaging in a number of surreptitious activities and, most recently, exchanging "'certain expressive looks, which [he] did not believe meant to be public'" (350); only then does he begin to wonder what they can mean. This is legitimate Lockean mental operation, essentially different from the kind of *a priori* imagination in which Emma indulges. It is one thing to turn the evidence over in one's mind and then offer some tentative diagnosis, as a good detective often does; it is another to contrive a sensational plot of secret romance and gossip about it. As Stuart Tave aptly puts it, Mr Knightley's "imagination begins neither in an internal emptiness nor with a superfluity of sensation. His imagination does not create the truth he wants, nor any other for that matter; it does not wander but has a concentrating effect that helps lead him to the truth."[1]

The vigorous and persistent engagement between the two protagonists not only shows how a morally firm mind may withstand the test of reality and how a morally infirm mind must struggle to avoid pitfalls, it also conveys the notion that truth seldom appears in black and white, and that it is often more complicated than one thinks. Through much of the narrative it is apparent that Mr Knightley's moral position is constantly under siege by Emma, and there are moments when the attacking Emma seems to have got the upper hand and forced her opponent to retreat. For example, the positions of Emma and Mr Knightley are worlds apart on the issue of match-making. Emma's romantic notions clash with Mr Knightley's down-to-earth approach. Emma enjoys match-making as a game, "the greatest amusement in the world!" (12). The whole point of the game for Emma is to identify the prospective partners and divine the matrimonial possibility before anyone else has sensed or thought of it. If a

---

[1] Tave 234 – 235.

match, say, the one between Mr Elton and Harriet, is "only too palpably desirable, natural, and probable, for her to have much merit in planning it" (34 – 35), since "every body else must think of and predict" (35) it, Emma will take the credit for outmatching others "in the date of the plan" (35). It is this kind of vainglorious romantic conceit that cripples Emma's ability to judge morally, and it is to this fault that Mr Knightley, who does not "'pretend to Emma's genius for foretelling and guessing'" (38), tries to alert Emma.

Emma professes that she has single-handedly promoted the match between Mr Weston and her governess Miss Taylor—"'I made the match myself'" (11). She takes great pride in this achievement especially because the public opinion of Highbury had been set against such a possibility:

> Every body said that Mr. Weston would never marry again. Oh dear, no! Mr. Weston, who had been a widower so long, and who seemed so perfectly comfortable without a wife, so constantly occupied either in his business in town or among his friends here, always acceptable wherever he went, always cheerful—Mr. Weston need not spend a single evening in the year alone if he did not like it. Oh, no! Mr. Weston certainly would never marry again. Some people even talked of a promise to his wife on her death-bed, and others of the son and the uncle not letting him. All manner of solemn nonsense was talked on the subject, but I believed none of it. (12)

For a moment it would rather seem that Emma has scored a point. The marriage of the Westons appears to be a personal triumph that proves Emma's extraordinary vision and ingenuity. But Mr Knightley disagrees; he coolly suggests that a "'straight-forward, open-hearted man, like Weston, and a rational unaffected woman, like Miss Taylor, may be safely left to manage their own concerns'"(13). "'You are more likely to have done harm to yourself, than good to them, by interference'" (13), he tells Emma.

Narrative evidence suggests that Mr Knightley's reservation about Emma's role in Mr Weston's marriage is well grounded in reality. The truth does not even lie somewhere between Knightley's outright disavowal of Emma's involvement in and contribution to her best friend's marriage and Emma's insistence that she has played a big role in the event. In point of fact, the marriage of Miss Taylor and Mr Weston is a thoroughly calculated event, not at all as romantic as Emma chooses to see it. As Mr Weston is well into his middle age, "the tyrannic influence of youth on youth" (16) is not a factor. Although Miss Taylor had been romantically attached to her man for "some time" (16), Mr Weston had his own economic plan to follow. His "determination of never settling till he could purchase Randalls" (16) would not be shaken. It was not until he "had made his fortune, bought his house" (17), felt that he had realized affluence "enough to marry a woman as portionless even as Miss Taylor, and to live according to the wishes of his own friendly and social disposition" (16), that he "obtained his wife" (17). Emma's energetic promotion of the marriage, however effective she may have supposed, has not been indispensable or even relevant.

7

An old Chinese saying goes: never trip over the same stone twice. That, however, seems to be what Emma has been doing in the story; not because she is too slow, as Harriet undoubtedly is, but because she is too quick. Emma places too much trust in her own quick judgment, and has been mostly impervious to caution and advice by Mr Knightley, "one of the few people who could see faults in Emma Woodhouse, and the only one who ever told her of them" (11). What she actually does is trying to modify reality to suit "[t]hat very dear part of Emma, her fancy" (214). Such misuse of mind Johnson is highly critical of in *The Vanity of Human Wishes* (1749), *Rasselas* (1759) and many of his *Rambler* essays; for example: "[W]hat men allow themselves to wish they will soon believe, and will be at last incited to execute what they please themselves with contriving."[1] Emma's indulgence in fanciful thinking prevents her from

---

[1]   *The Rambler* 8, vol. 3, 42.

looking at things dialectically.

In *Of the Conduct of the Understanding* Locke has repeatedly warned about the harm which fancy may do to understanding:

> [I] f the fancy be allowed the place of judgment at first in sport, it afterwards comes by use to usurp it; and what is recommended by this flatterer (that studies but to please), is received for good. There are so many ways of fallacy, such arts of giving colours, appearances, and resemblances by this court dresser, the fancy, that he who is not wary to admit nothing but truth itself, very careful not to make his mind subservient to any thing else, cannot but be caught. ①

Emma's moral capacity to think rationally and dialectically, which she clearly demonstrates in the novel, has been seriously undermined, if not usurped, by her indulgence in fancy. The corollary is, as Emma herself acknowledges, "'One might guess twenty things without guessing exactly the right'" (217). In hindsight Emma admits: "'[W]ith common sense ... I am afraid I have had little to do'" (402). When she belatedly compares Frank Churchill with George Knightley—dialectical thinking would have suggested it earlier—her flawed way of thinking suddenly becomes crystal-clear to her: "'[H]ad it—oh! had it, by any blessed felicity, occurred to her, to institute the comparison'" (412)! Emma also regrets her manipulative yet unprofitable relationship with Harriet—"'Oh God! that I had never seen her!'" (411).

To give her credit, once Emma sees the real character of Frank Churchill, she will not condone him on any account. Emma is ruffled by Mrs Weston's glossing over her step-son's "'impropriety'" (397):

> Impropriety! Oh! Mrs. Weston—it is too calm a censure. Much, much beyond impropriety! —It has sunk him, I cannot say how it has sunk him in my opinion. So unlike what a man should be! —None of that upright integrity, that strict adherence to truth and principle, that disdain of trick and littleness, which a man should display in every transaction of his life. (397).

Emma is definitely thinking of Mr Knightley here, and very positively

---

① *Conduct* 33.

too, now that she realizes that he has been judging rightly and she wrongly. Mrs Weston, however, continues to take Frank Churchill's part and tries to exonerate him from the serious charge that Emma thinks fits him—as Emma has previously done in her debate with Mr Knightley. But Emma will not compromise, just as Edmund Bertram would not budge while facing his sometime beloved Mary Crawford who called her brother's immoral act "'folly'" rather than "'crime'" (*MP* 454, 457).

Emma is a very complex novel from a technical point of view, not the least because of the nuances and gradations in the narrative as a result of the play of dialectics. Yet it is also a very realistic novel, if only because of Emma's constant demonstration of her deficiency in moral understanding and her trouble with making moral judgments. It is rather reassuring that in the end Emma's assertion: "'I cannot really change for the better'" because "'it is not my way, or my nature'" (84) turns out to be untrue. Emma is capable of learning although it has taken her longer to learn. The dialectical twists in her learning process distinguish Emma as a rather modern protagonist—neither the run-of-the-mill heroine in what Butler calls the "classic plot of the conservative novel" nor the ultramodern feminist rebel as Johnson will have her—who must play by the stringent rules of reality. She must think, not one-sidedly but dialectically.

The closure of the novel seems to indicate that Emma's dialectical thinking process will go on. D. A. Miller points out that Emma has yet to make a clean breast of all her embarrassing secrets to Mr Knightley. [1] Indeed there is a degree of difference in the closure of *Emma* as opposed to Austen's closures elsewhere. But the few instances of unfinished business should not take us by surprise, for it illustrates precisely Jane Austen's philosophical point: "Seldom, very seldom, does complete truth belong to any human disclosure; seldom can it happen that something is not a

---

[1]   Miller mentions such things as Emma's failure to inform Mr Knightley of Harriet's romantic feelings towards him; see *Narrative and Its Discontents: Problems of Closure in the Traditional Novel* (Princeton: Princeton UP, 1981) 89.

little disguised, or a little mistaken" (431). Given the nature of her character, it is not unexpected that Emma should remain a little imperfect at the end of the novel, as she will likely be in the conceivable future. Emma still needs to cultivate, in the words of the eighteenth-century educationist Isaac Watts, "this Habit of conceiving clearly, of judging justly, and of reasoning well" because such habit "is not to be attained merely by the Happiness of Constitution, the Brightness of Genius, the best natural Parts, or the best Collection of logical Precepts. It is Custom and Practice that must form and establish this Habit."[1]

We will next discuss Jane Austen's last completed novel, *Persuasion*, where the hero seems to share some of Emma's problems. The story shows how Captain Wentworth, who seems unlikely to change his mind about Anne Elliot, gradually allows his moral discernment to break through the clouds of anger, doubts, and wilfulness in the constant, though not intrusive, moral presence of Anne Elliot. The readers equally feel the strong impact of Anne's moral influence, not because she takes every opportunity to spread the truth, as Mr Knightley does—"'I will tell you truths while I can'"—but because each of her thoughtful actions truthfully reflects her dialectical thinking. In this last finished novel Jane Austen's art of dialectic has gone even more deeply inward.

---

[1] *Logick: Or, The Right Use of Reason in the Enquiry after Truth* (1726); quoted in Peter A Schouls, *Reasoned Freedom: John Locke and Enlightenment* (Ithaca: Cornell UP, 1992) 327.

7 *Persuasion*: The Dialectics of Love

Jane Austen's art of dialectic achieves new subtlety in presenting the love-story of Anne Elliot and Frederick Wentworth in her last completed novel, *Persuasion*. As some critics have recognized, Anne's consciousness, conveyed through interior monologue,[①] is the most salient feature of the novel.[②]

The prevalence of this particular narrative technique has, however, prompted such critics as Marilyn Butler and Mary Poovey to draw certain dubious conclusions. Butler thinks that "the exclusively subjective viewpoint of *Persuasion*" exemplified "so consistently in the presentation of Anne" implies "that the senses have a decisive advantage over reason and fact."[③] To prove her point, Butler cites one instance of Anne's interior monologue: "Alas! With all her reasonings, she found, that to retentive feelings eight years may be little more than nothing" (60). Here we witness Anne's loss of composure when she encounters her former lover for the first time in eight years; this is not unexpected since Anne is no personified Reason. It is an apt example demonstrating, as I will argue in this chapter, the dialectical struggle between reason and emotion within the heroine; it does not mean that Anne will embrace feeling at the expense of reason.

Butler polarizes what is presented through interior monologue and

---

① Norman Page remarks that, "[t]o an unprecedented extent, the narrative style has left behind the formal eighteenth-century sentence, with its elaboration of subordinate clauses and its emphatic patterning, and has moved towards a more relaxed and conversational manner, with a quiet intimacy which is in tune with the heroine's nature" (49).

② Jocelyn Harris's rather convincing argument that Chaucer's "Wife of Bath"—its theme of transformation—thoroughly diffuses *Persuasion* is relevant here, too; see *Jane Austen's Art of Memory* 188 – 212.

③ Butler 277.

what is not. As a result, she is puzzled by the fact that what she sees contradicts what she claims to be. Butler thinks, for example, that Anne Elliot is guilty of making a "selective view of external 'reality,'"① and she asserts that "there is no organic relationship between the novel's manner, style, and language, and the element which in the last resort must express a novel's meaning—which elsewhere *does* express Jane Austen's meaning—the form."② Hampered by her self-imposed "conservative" viewpoint, Butler seems unable to make sense of *Persuasion*. Reluctantly, she concedes:

> If *Persuasion* cannot rightly be described as a conservative novel, this is because it neither takes up an intelligible new position, nor explicitly recants from the old one. It is the only one of Jane Austen's novels that is not whole-heartedly partisan, and it is none the better for it. ③

On the other hand, Mary Poovey, insisting on a narrowly defined feminist point of view, thinks that "*Persuasion* takes us beyond the subduing of desire to its struggle against social restraint."④ Poovey constructs a bipartite model for this feminist "struggle" that consists of two contrasting spheres, "'private'" and "'public,'"⑤ and she traps Austen in one of them. Poovey implicates Jane Austen (in a backhanded way) in a feminist drive for power when she argues that "Austen's novels now alert us to yet another liability of romantic love: its illusion of personal autonomy."⑥"In retaining the premises and promises of romantic love" in the "private" plot, she warns, "Jane Austen perpetuates one of the fundamental myths of bourgeois society. For the model of private gratification that romantic love proposes can disguise the inescapable system of economic and political domination only by foregrounding the few relationships that flatter our desire for personal autonomy

---

①   Butler 277.
②   Butler 290.
③   Butler 291.
④⑤   Poovey 228.
⑥   Poovey 237.

and power. "①

Poovey further argues that the "private" plot actually provides women with a "kind of temporary and imaginative consolation that serves to defuse criticism of the very institutions that make such consolation necessary. "② In other words, Jane Austen is offering, through *Persuasion*, some sort of anaesthetic drug to women that induces "the immediate gratification of believing that this single moment of apparent autonomy will endure, and that the situation in which a woman seems most desirable when she is most powerful will continue on in marriage and in society. "③

While there is no reason not to expect that the marriage between Anne Elliot and Captain Wentworth will be a lasting success, like those of Elinor Dashwood, Elizabeth Bennet and Fanny Price, there is every reason to question the validity of Poovey's sweeping generalization and radical claim, for which she supplies no narrative evidence. It is curious to hear Poovey's gratuitous pronouncement that "Austen's novels contain almost no examples of marriages that the reader would want to emulate. "④ There is no telling whether this is true or false unless we know what kind of reader Poovey is assuming. The pronouncement seems patently false at least on one occasion, because it contradicts her subsequent statement that "freezing the narratives precisely at the height of emotional intensity endorses the promises of romantic love and, in doing so, enjoins the reader to imitate the moral love the hero and heroine promise to bring to fruition in society. "⑤

Poovey's feminist interpretation creates a socially, as opposed to Butler's politically, oriented polarity, one that sets romantic love against social repression. Poovey states that "the fundamental assumption of romantic love—and the reason it is so compatible with bourgeois society— is that the personal can be kept separate from the social, that one's 'self'

---

①②③　Poovey 237.

④⑤　Poovey 239.

can be fulfilled in spite of—and in isolation from—the demands of the marketplace. "[1]

The problem with the Butlerian and Pooveyesque interpretations of *Persuasion* is very similar to what we have found in our earlier discussion of *Northanger Abbey*. There is the same tendency, either from the right or from the left, to reduce Austen's fiction to a neat political formula, dampening its moral, intellectual and philosophical spirit. Poovey's analysis is especially unconvincing because it is often without supporting argument and frequently without supporting evidence. Although both critics have sensibly pointed out the place of emotion or feeling in *Persuasion*, neither bothers to investigate the significance of its counterpart, intellect, which exists in abundance in the same novel. Consequently, neither notices the dialectical interplay between feeling and reason, the two most important qualities in the character of the two astute protagonists, and neither touches upon the key issue of this novel, that is, the moral nature of Anne's romantic relationship with Captain Wentworth against the intricacies of persuasion in complicated social circumstances.

Both Anne Elliot and Frederick Wentworth make difficult moral choices even in what Poovey calls the "private" plot, and the issues they deal with are frequently dialectical in nature, such as the crucial question of firmness in regard to their romantic choices. The dialectics of their romantic love is kept in the foreground of the narrative by the verbal interchanges, such as Wentworth's ludicrous conversation with Louisa in the vicinity of Winthrop in which Anne makes an unseen third participant and Anne's luminous conversation with Captain Harville in which Wentworth participates silently, and by the actions of the characters, such as Louisa's fall and the resulting consequences, and Anne's performance during the accident at Lyme and her active engagement with Wentworth later at Bath. Besides, Jane Austen employs a variety of narrative techniques such as irony, imagery, contrast, and parallel structure to

---

[1] Poovey 236.

effect the working of dialectics in the narrative speech and action.

Indeed the framing of the romantic story is dialectically striking. The first three chapters of *Persuasion* fail to introduce the central romantic interest into the story; instead what is least romantic—vanity, snobbery, social distinction and economic calculations—fill the pages. Yet Sir Walter's double hatred for the Navy—denouncing the profession for allowing people to rise by merits (rather than by birth) and seeking satisfaction by disparaging the looks (19) of naval personnel—poses a special problem for the romantic protagonists, a would-be Navy couple. How they are going to negotiate and reconcile their romantic attachment—which itself has to be negotiated and reconciled in the first place— with the social reality constitutes the dialectical drama of *Persuasion*. An investigation of some of the most significant dialectical situations, speeches, imagery and structural arrangements may help us understand the dialectical patterning behind the moving love story.

1

In *Persuasion* the breaking-off of the engagement, which happened long before the narrative action begins, is the painful *primum mobile*. How to evaluate the traumatic experience in the past and deal with its aftermath at present becomes an urgent philosophical issue in the lives of Anne Elliot and Frederick Wentworth. ① The challenge is enormous. Both must learn to analyze the painful event rationally, rather than just remember it emotionally, so as to turn the negative experience into a positive one. Both must come to a dialectical understanding of the complex issue of persuasion in their troubled romance.

Persuasion, as the title which Henry Austen had decided upon, is as

---

①   Daniel P. Gunn believes that "[i]t is Wentworth, not Anne, who revises his values during the course of the novel" ("In the Vicinity of Winthrop: Ideological Rhetoric in *Persuasion*," *NCL* 41 [1987]: 411). Although such belief is basically sound, it overlooks Anne's on-going inner conflict and her continuing change of view regarding both Lady Russell and Captain Wentworth.

good as, if not better than, the title of *The Elliots* which would nonetheless forebode conflicts of different values among members of the Elliot family. ① The present title, however, wades right into the middle of a topical debate in the society at the time; that is, the "[c]onflict between a parent who wishes his child to make a marriage that is socially and economically acceptable and a child who wants to follow the inclination of his heart."② So the word "persuasion" is suggestively open-ended. It pertains to the kind of matrimonial contention Moler points out; yet it also alludes, in a larger sense, to a contest of two philosophical modes.

Captain Wentworth, to whom the word "persuasion" brings a nightmare, errs by considering only one part of the equation. As a typical military man normally would, he strongly believes in "'resolution,'" "'fortitude,'" "'strength of mind,'" "'decision and firmness'" and "'powers of mind'" (88). However, his belief is narrowly sustained by his personal disgust with the way he had been treated by Anne Elliot eight years before. His is therefore a private value system disguised as having a public appeal. He wishes that Anne could have been firm as he had wanted her to be, not as her sense of moral right had directed her to be.

Anne Elliot, on the other hand, has given serious considerations to her part in the broken engagement and arrived at a rational conclusion about the painful affair by the time the novel opens in the year 1814. Anne believes that she has done the right thing under the circumstances.

---

① Claudia Brodsky Lacour has once observed that "[t]he very titles of Austen's completed novels reveal the division between notional and concrete language in her understanding of narrative realism, dividing, as it happens evenly, between abstract nouns (*Sense and Sensibility*, *Pride and Prejudice*, and *Persuasion*) and the names of particular people and places (*Northanger Abbey*, *Mansfield Park and Emma*)." Lacour is commenting on Austen's maneuvering between "abstract and representational language by way of narration and thus of representing an abstraction, truth, in fiction," and the shrewd observation makes perfect sense for the point she is trying to make except that the titles of two of the six novels are not Jane Austen's (*ELH* 59 [1992]: 603, 604).

② Moler 193. Moler's chapter on *Persuasion* (187–223) gives a helpful historical background of the term "persuasion" and the literary relationship between this work and relevant works in Austen's time.

She could not but acknowledge that there was nothing wrong in a nineteen-year-old's heeding the advice of an older and more experienced mentor, whose "fair interference of friendship" is out of "almost a mother's love" for her (27). Anne could not but admit the prudence of Lady Russell's opposition: "[S]o young; known to so few, to be snatched off by a stranger without alliance or fortune; or rather sunk by him into a state of most wearing, anxious, youth-killing dependance!" (27). Though the advice she relied on caused her much grief and distress—including an "early loss of bloom" (28)—Anne sees no reason to "blame Lady Russell" or "herself for having been guided by her" (29).

Anne's point of view, crucial in *Persuasion*, is treated dialectically. Her sacrifice of immediate romantic gratification in order to fulfil her filial duty and social obligation is affirmed strongly but also nicely. By not giving in to her own romantic urge at the age of nineteen, Anne showed great moral courage. That Commander Wentworth has turned out very successful, proving himself a worthy choice, does not pertain to the crucial moral thinking of Anne Elliot at the age of nineteen, though it may prove that Lady Russell is overly cautious and Sir Walter and Elizabeth utterly wrong. Captain Wentworth eventually comes to see the root problem of his error of judgment when he admits to Anne: "'I too have been thinking over the past, and a question has suggested itself, whether there may not have been one person more my enemy even than that lady [Lady Russell]? My own self'" (247). This is hitting the nail on the head, but it comes very late in the novel. When the novel opens, it is completely uncertain whether Frederick Wentworth will ever see the moral sense in Anne Elliot's termination of the engagement or the fact that though she broke off the engagement she had continued to love him.

It should perhaps be noted that the collapse of the engagement between Anne and Wentworth, from seeing "highest perfection" (26) in each other to a unilateral suspension of the passionate relationship, is not brought about by Lady Russell's counsel alone, as has been widely believed and argued. Her opposition represents only the external social pressure applied to Anne; the domestic pressure coming from her only living parent, Sir Walter, as well as her elder sister, Elizabéth, is no less significant, emotionally and financially. [1] Sir Walter, who "had been constantly exceeding [his income]" (9), gave the engagement "all the negative of great astonishment, great coldness, great silence, and a professed resolution of doing nothing for his daughter" (26). In addition to the parental scorn and financial threat, Anne had to suffer the psychological blow delivered by her elder sister who sided with the cold-hearted father and refused to give her younger sister "one kind word or look" (27). At this point, under the pressure of a concerted opposition from within, Lady Russell's disapproval from without became the last straw. Lady Russell, who had "prejudices on the side of ancestry" and "a value for rank and consequence" (11), thought it was "a throwing away" (27) for Anne to "involve herself at nineteen in an engagement with a young man" (26) who had "no fortune" and "no connexions" (27). We recall at this point Miss Frances, Fanny Price's mother, who "did it very thoroughly" by marrying "a Lieutenant of Marines, without education, fortune, or connecxions" (*MP 3*).

Lady Russell's mainly positive persuasion differs from Sir Walter's mainly negative persuasion. To Sir Walter, a man who has "nothing but himself to recommend him" (26) is worth nothing. To Lady Russell, birth and wealth are important, but equally important is character. Wentworth's "confidence," "wit," "sanguine temper, and fearlessness of mind" suggest "a dangerous character" (27) to Lady Russell. That Anne eventually agrees that the engagement is "a wrong thing" (27) does not signify, however, her sanction of Sir Walter's haughty, snobbish and egotistical view, though it does mark her compliance with a prudent attitude towards the institution of marriage. The narrator has carefully explained what is behind Anne's concession: "Had she not imagined herself consulting his good, even more than her own, she could hardly

---

[1]   Claudia L. Johnson, for example, thinks that "the crisis in *Persuasion*—Anne's decision to break off her engagement—has little to do with Sir Walter's paternal displeasure" (146).

have given him up" (28).

The significant word in the above quote describing Anne's thought process is "imagined," which suggests a lack of conclusiveness. But Anne has made her decision based on what information is available to her, and it is therefore the most prudent position she is able to take at the time. Wentworth is a junior naval officer who had yet to save his prize money and establish himself as an eligible gentleman. He could be killed in action at any time, leaving Anne a penniless widow, perhaps with a child too. A wife, if he were to take that responsibility seriously, would be a hindrance in his professional career at this stage. ① Anne was also worried that she could not bring him money enough for decent housekeeping. So their marriage would have been imprudent in both senses of the word (in fact Jane Austen's own real-life attitude is very similar to Anne's). ② However, Commander Wentworth felt "himself ill-used by so forced a relinquishment" (28) and failed to see that the "relinquishment" was not "a merely selfish caution" (27). It is rather obvious that the young Wentworth was at this point being both selfish and self-centred. He was so engrossed in his own ideal that he did not, or would not, try to understand Anne's motives: he was "totally unconvinced" at "parting" (28), believing that their romance had come to an end.

The pressing issue for now, however, is whether the hindsight of both the hero and the heroine can develop into a vision of their future. Unless both can see the past in a dialectical light, there is no hope for their reunion. The narrative evidence suggests that Anne Elliot has done just that, and Frederick Wentworth has not. To begin with, Anne does not close the book on the past; instead she dwells upon the connection

---

①   Robert Southey relates that Nelson nearly made an imprudent marriage while he was in Quebec, only to be persuaded by his friend, Alexander Davison, to stay in the Navy rather than seek his "'utter ruin'" (*The Life of Horatio Lord Nelson* [1813; London: Dent, 1906] 22).

②   Jane Austen once said, "Single Women have a dreadful propensity for being poor— which is one very strong argument in favour of Matrimony" (*Letters* 13 March 1817), but elsewhere she warns, "Anything is to be preferred or endured rather than marrying without Affection" (*Letters* 20 November 1814), and a little later reiterates that "nothing can be compared to the misery of being bound without Love" (*Letters* 30 November 1814).

between the past and the present, and the future. She uses her memory of the past as the basis of a diligent effort towards a rewarding future. Secondly, Anne does not stop reflecting upon the ethics of the decision she had made earlier, even though it was regarded by all, including herself, as the correct one at the time. As a result, she is able to review the event from a point of view more sophisticated than that of Captain Wentworth. Anne recognizes the validity of Lady Russell's argument against the early marriage, but she also comes to see that the normally judicious Lady Russell is not immune from misjudging. The "nice tone of her mind" (28) persuades Anne that she should continue to value her own feelings and judgement, which have gained new depth and maturity from her life experience, while giving appropriate consideration to whatever advice she receives. Anne's feelings for Wentworth have been refined. She has been closely following "navy lists and newspapers" (30) and has remained up-to-date on Wentworth's personal success and marital status. She wishes to re-engage Captain Wentworth's affection.

As a result of her reflection and deliberation, taking account of the mitigating circumstances, Anne Elliot has become aware of the complications of her romantic relationship with Wentworth. Whereas it would have been imprudent had she decided to marry against Lady Russell's advice, the "marriage" would probably have turned out all right. As things stand now, Commander Wentworth seems to have been denied a chance to prove his worth in both senses of the word. Therefore when Frederick Wentworth reappears in her life in the present world of *Persuasion*, Anne cannot but experience a variety of complicated feelings. Nevertheless, she is ready to meet the challenge of engaging him under the new circumstances. Anne's philosophical contemplation has transmuted her traumatic experience into a source of quiet strength; it has also transformed her into a new personage whose fortitude will match Wentworth's prowess and whose alacrity will surpass even Wentworth's when the occasion arises. On social occasions, Anne neither joins the Miss Musgroves in pursuit of the glamorous and attractive naval officer nor discourages positive gestures from him. She is generally able to maintain her composure, whatever turbulent feelings she may have, neither aloof or superior nor submissive or obsequious (these characteristics are found in Sir Walter first at Kellynch and then at Bath).

In a sense we have already witnessed Anne Elliot in action before Captain Wentworth's arrival at Kellynch. As if to remedy the injustice she has done to Frederick, Anne Elliot declines the offer of marriage from Charles Musgrove. As "the eldest son of a man, whose landed property and general importance, were second, in that country, only to Sir Walter's" (28), Charles satisfies the requirements of land and status, conditions first and foremost in the mind of Sir Walter; his "good character and appearance" (28) to boot easily carry Lady Russell as well. By refusing to accept the candidate for marriage whom they fully endorse, Anne makes it clear that she is faithful to her first love and that she wants to think for herself—leaving "nothing for advice to do" (29). Indeed Anne begins to learn, from this point onwards, that "she and her excellent friend [Lady Russell] could sometimes think differently" (147). Anne's newly acquired moral and intellectual capacity differs sharply from the Shaftesburian worship of natural feelings and from the Jacobin tendency of self-sufficiency. Her moral position incorporates society's traditions and beliefs but does not allow them to dictate her own conscience, her sense of right.

2

When Captain Wentworth revisits Kellynch Hall in early October of 1814, after an interval of about eight years, he is riding high in glory both from a victorious war against France and from personal successes. Captain Wentworth is in possession of a good fortune gained by capturing enemy ships, and he has not suffered a single wound from the naval battles. He has truly beaten the odds. Physically, he looks healthy and handsome as ever. Understandably, Captain Wentworth is quickly surrounded by the Miss Musgroves and the Miss Hayters—every one of whom is much younger than Anne—and soon relishes being "a little spoilt by such universal, such eager admiration" (71).

Wentworth dismays Anne when they finally meet again. This encounter throws sensitive Anne into a painful mental turmoil. Anne appears to be at a physical disadvantage in competition with the Musgrove and Hayter girls for the eye of the man she still loves deeply. But her feelings are strong, and they even threaten to offset the rational position she has formulated over the years: "Alas! With all her reasonings, she found, that to retentive feelings eight years may be little more than nothing" (60). Jane Austen takes care to convey Anne's emotionally charged inner struggle through an extensive use of interior monologue.

On the one hand, Anne feels "the utter impossibility, from her knowledge of his mind, that he could be unvisited by remembrance any more than herself" (63) when "'the year six'" is referred to by Captain Wentworth himself. She is confident that he remembers the time when "there could have been no two hearts so open, no tastes so similar, no feelings so in unison, no countenances so beloved" (63–64). On the other hand, Anne assumes that "the same immediate association of thought" cannot be expected to bear "equal pain" (63); in fact Anne is "very far from conceiving it" (63) to be the case. Anne has stayed in the same place, whereas Captain Wentworth has travelled widely and gained wide experience (a point which she later will stress in her debate with Captain Harville). The question remains as to what Captain Wentworth now thinks of both Anne Elliot and their former attachment. At this point he is an enigma to Anne just as she is to him.

We learn from the narrator that "[i]t was now his object to marry" (61), but we are not sure which of all the women Captain Wentworth desires. The omniscient narrator further details that his readiness "to fall in love" is conditional on what "a clear head and quick taste could allow" (61). At the same time, however, the narrator informs us that although he "had a heart for either of the Miss Musgroves," it is not certain "if they could catch it" (61). Oddly enough, as we know more about Captain Wentworth's criteria for a wife, we get the impression that he is a man perplexed by the dilemma he is setting up for himself. He is ready to offer his heart to "any pleasing young woman who came in his way" (61), yet he will exclude Anne Elliot—"excepting Anne Elliot" (61)— from his range of choices even if she is undoubtedly pleasing. The description he gives to Sophia Croft, his sister, of the kind of woman he wishes to meet: "'A strong mind, with sweetness of manner'" (62), surprisingly fits Anne Elliot in spite of his determination not to consider her.

Captain Wentworth is being self-contradictory here: he is being irrational by imposing a limit to his choices even as he tries rationally to define those choices. It seems that the more he tries to forget Anne Elliot and ignore what she represents, the more he is drawn to her, against his skewed determination. Wentworth's wilful mode of thinking forms a contrast with Anne's level-headed attitude. For example, although she is hurt by Wentworth's indifferent comment about her altered appearance— thanks to an equally insensitive Mary Musgrove who reports it to Anne (60)—Anne is not bitter and will not take offence at the remark or belittle Captain Wentworth out of revenge. Anne has always loved him, and she broke off the engagement with his future in mind. Indeed, she has retained her favourable impression of him:

> [H]e was not altered, or not for the worse. She had already acknowledged it to herself, and she could not think differently, let him think of her as he would. No; the years which had destroyed her youth and bloom had only given him a more glowing, manly, open look, in no respect lessening his personal advantages. She had seen the same Frederick Wentworth. (61)

Anne is not simply being magnanimous; she lets her intellect rather than her emotion take charge. Despite her strong emotions, she tries to look at things as they are. However, as we are soon to learn, it is all she can do to maintain a dialectically balanced attitude when she finds herself in more taxing situations.

For Captain Wentworth, the process of dialectical thinking is a difficult one, perhaps unavoidably so. As the injured party, Captain Wentworth bears grudges against the people who he thinks have misjudged him. He has successfully vindicated himself by making his mark in the Navy, but emotionally and psychologically he is still suffering from well-remembered humiliation and devastation. Captain Wentworth sees the past event in a fixed light. He views the present in terms of the negative past. As a result, he is unable to turn the past into something constructive for the present, let alone for the future. His head-strong individualism, which was rather offensive to Lady Russell earlier, proves indeed to be his moral weakness,[1] and this weakness threatens to turn the advantages that he has at present into disadvantages, into liabilities, because they intoxicate him and induce him to commit errors of judgment.

What is dialectically interesting about *Persuasion* is that neither Anne Elliot nor Frederick Wentworth is able to stick to her or his game plan, so to speak. Although Anne Elliot has philosophically come to terms with the severance of her engagement with Captain Wentworth and is at peace with herself, believing that "time had softened down much, perhaps nearly all of peculiar attachment to him" (28), she is catapulted into emotional stress once she is face to face with Frederick Wentworth again. She is "electrified"[2] by Mrs Croft's happy recognition that it is her rather than Elizabeth that her brother "'had the pleasure of being acquainted with'" even though the brother being referred to is Edward, her clergyman brother (49). Even Anne herself finds it "absurd to be resuming the agitation which such an interval had banished into distance and indistinctness!" (60). Although Frederick Wentworth has resolved to

---

[1] Daniel P. Gunn confuses the moral differences between Captain Wentworth and Mr Elliot by speculating that "there is a sense in which Wentworth's vigorous individualism, for all its attractiveness, leads us finally to William Elliot's morality, which is simply 'to do the best for himself' [*P* 202]" (417).

[2] Roger Gard speculates that "'Electrified' must have been a very strong word in an age not familiar with electricity" (193). One might as well assume that the unfamiliarity may precisely be the reason that the word might not have been stronger in Austen's time than in ours. The fact, however, is that electrical machines were widely used at the time for medical purposes (relief of various complaints) and were found even in villages. Cowper, while nursing his melancholia at Weston Lodge in 1792, borrowed one from his neighbour to treat Mrs Unwin's paralytic stroke. William Hayley, who happened to be visiting Cowper and who had one at home, installed the machine and conducted the treatment (*The Letters and Prose Writings of William Cowper*, vol. 4, 1792–1799, eds. James King and Charles Ryskamp [Oxford: Clarendon, 1984] 80).

forget about Anne Elliot, who, he thinks, "deserted and disappointed him" (61), he cannot help noticing her and commenting upon her and even wanting to dance with her during the party at Uppercross (72). It seems that, once his "natural sensation of curiosity" (61) at seeing Anne is satisfied, something deeper than what he will allow himself to admit has developed. Captain Wentworth begins to show a renewed interest in the welfare of his ex-fiancée—releasing her from the burden of little Walter Musgrove (80) and assisting her into Admiral Croft's gig (91) are two of the most obvious signs of his solicitude towards her.

These gallant actions—happening in short order—are especially encouraging to the sensitive Anne because they offset Mary's earlier report that "'Captain Wentworth is not very gallant by her'" (60). Though neither of these actions, strictly speaking, goes beyond the call of good manners, that they have happened at this point and in rapid succession means a great deal to a taut Anne. More importantly, they contradict Wentworth's reported remarks of indifference about Anne Elliot's altered appearance and the difficulty of recognizing her. Captain Wentworth not only renews his acquaintance with Anne but also ably perceives her needs. Seeing Anne moving in front of him and doing useful things for others persuades Captain Wentworth to pay attention and react appropriately. In fact he is enough interested in Anne to pursue the topic of her turning down Charles Musgrove's proposal. His earlier self-claimed superficial curiosity in Anne has given way to a new round of "feeling and curiosity" (89), which gives Anne, who happens to have heard his conversation with Louisa, "extreme agitation" (89).

Wentworth's gallantry towards Anne also makes nonsense of Anne's early impression that Wentworth has come back to spite her (60 – 61). In fact Anne has been somewhat self-deluded about her ex-fiancé's inner feelings about her as she keeps imagining negative innuendoes of Captain Wentworth's positive actions. For example, when she hears from Mary and Charles that he will come for breakfast, but not at the Cottage where she is lending a hand in nursing the injured little Charles, Anne thinks that Captain Wentworth is deliberately trying "to avoid seeing her" (59);

but then Captain Wentworth turns up at the Cottage after all, having had his breakfast at the Great House (59), and manages to effect their first meeting in eight years. For another example, when she hears the reported words by Wentworth about her much altered appearance, Anne self-consciously dwells upon them and interprets them as evidence of Wentworth's decided antagonism, as meaning that he "had no desire of meeting her again" (61); but then we learn that "Captain Wentworth and Anne Elliot were repeatedly in the same circle," that "[t]hey were soon dining in company together at Mr. Musgrove's," and that "this was but the beginning of other dinings and other meetings" (63). It is safe to assume that Wentworth does not mind meeting Anne at all.

Indeed, Anne's inferiority complex seems excessive and even becomes the source of amusing irony. At the aforementioned "merry, joyous party" at Uppercross, Anne Elliot, observing a female quartet vying for the attention of her former lover while she herself is dutifully playing the piano—"her eyes would sometimes fill with tears" (71)—is lost in self-pitying thoughts. When she feels that Wentworth is looking at herself, she imagines that he is "observing her altered features, perhaps, trying to trace in them the ruins of the face which had once charmed him" (72). Anne is so absorbed in self-deprecation that she misses hearing Wentworth inquiring whether she dances or not (72)—apparently contemplating asking her to dance with him. This is followed by another suggestive gesture, which is Wentworth's sitting down in the chair—as if he were to pick out a tune on the piano—which has just accommodated Anne. Wentworth's gesture will assume greater significance in hindsight when in the climactic scene towards the end of volume 2 Anne is seen "sinking into the chair which he had occupied, succeeding to the very spot where he had leaned and written" (237). However, all these significant acts, Anne, trapped in her particular state of mind, interprets negatively as his "cold politeness" and his "ceremonious grace" (72). This is perhaps one of the lowest points in Anne's life, but it is mostly the result of her own one-sided thinking. Apparently, it is one thing to reconcile herself dialectically with her disrupted relationship with Wentworth; it is another to conduct herself the way she thinks she should, once the direct contact is made. At one point Anne whimsically thinks that Wentworth's indifference to her "must make her happier" (61) since it should cut off the source of her agitation; but actually it troubles her and makes her unhappy.

3

As Anne Elliot and Captain Wentworth renew their acquaintance under awkward circumstances, their frequent contacts give them ample opportunities to observe, hear and respond to each other. Being intelligent characters, Anne and Frederick gradually re-discover their past happy experience. However, Anne Elliot knows that the damaging effects of the broken engagement will not wear off easily. When Captain Wentworth helps her to get into Admiral Croft's gig, towards the end of their long walk in the environs of Winthrop, Anne gratefully acknowledges his "perception of her fatigue" (91), yet she remains cautious. She believes that, whereas Captain Wentworth "could not forgive her," he "could not be unfeeling" either (91). Anne's inner feelings and thoughts are aptly conveyed by the following interior monologue:

> Though condemning her for the past, and considering it with high and unjust resentment, though perfectly careless of her, and though becoming attached to another, still he could not see her suffer, without the desire of giving her relief. It was a remainder of former sentiment; it was an impulse of pure, though unacknowledged friendship; it was a proof of his own warm and amiable heart, which she could not contemplate without emotions so compounded of pleasure and pain, that she knew not which prevailed. (91)

There is good reason for Anne to be cautious even as she is excited, judging from what she has overheard from the intimate conversation between Wentworth and Louisa. Nevertheless, as the last sentence of the above interior monologue reveals, Anne is not absolutely sure of her own emotions despite her calm analysis of Wentworth's gallant overtures.

Captain Wentworth, on the other hand, uses his past humiliation as a guide in his present search for happiness, focussing on firmness as the primary, if not the only, virtue in a prospective fiancée. His is a typical case wherein, as Locke says, "[m]atters, that are recommended to our thoughts by any of our passions, take possession of our minds with a kind of authority, and will not be kept out or dislodged; but, as if the passion that rules were, for the time, the sheriff of the place, and came with all the posse, the understanding is seized and taken with the object it introduces, as if it had a legal right to be alone considered there."① By fixing his mind on one issue, in one direction, Captain Wentworth, under the influence of passion, is in danger of losing his moral bearings. As a self-made professional, he does not think highly of Sir Walter and Lady Russell. However, it is unjust of him to dwell solely upon his own agony and ignore the factors of time, place and circumstances surrounding the very personal and regrettable incident. Being parochial-minded and preoccupied with his own suffering does not contribute to the healing process, nor will it help him to establish a set of sound criteria for choosing his wife. Worse, his error of judgment will mislead the immature Louisa in a dangerous direction and encourage her to practise what is morally, even physically, dangerous.

Captain Wentworth feels gratified when Louisa tells him that, if she loves a man, she will never leave him and that, if he were a poor gig-driver, she "'would rather be overturned by him, than driven safely by anybody else'" (85). He assures her of his absolute agreement:

> It is the worst evil of too yielding and indecisive a character, that no influence over it can be depended on. —You are never sure of a good impression being durable. Every body may sway it; let those who would be happy be firm. (88)

In the heat of the "love-in," so to speak, Wentworth thinks that he has found a soul-mate. When Louisa tells him that it is she who has made the wavering Henrietta go and visit her fiancé Charles Hayter, Wentworth

---

① *Conduct* 45.

congratulates her: "'Your sister is an amiable creature; but *yours* is the character of decision and firmness'" (88).

But the truth is much more complicated than Captain Wentworth's principle of firmness can measure. Henrietta is attracted by Captain Wentworth, who seems a more romantic and dashing match than her fiancé, the Rev. Charles Hayter, who is looked down upon by the snobbish Mary, her sister-in-law. Mary's exclamation: "'Bless me! here is Winthrop—I declare I had no idea! —well, now I think we had better turn back; I am excessively tired'" (85) is a thinly-veiled disgust with such less than glamorous relations,① which dissuades Henrietta, "conscious and ashamed" (85), from making the descent. Louisa, who wants to keep her older sister out of the competition for Captain Wentworth, insists that Henrietta should go and visit her fiancé. As "the principal arranger of the plan" (86), Louisa even takes the trouble to go "a little way" with her sister and brother "down the hill," while "still talking to Henrietta" (86), to make sure that the plan is executed to her satisfaction.

Both Mary's firmness in not going down the hill (discouraging Henrietta from going down as well) and Louisa's firmness in persuading her sister to go are tainted by their respective ulterior motives. Only Charles Musgrove's firmness is disinterested—"declaring his resolution of calling on his aunt, now that he was so near" (86). Captain Wentworth, governed by his self-righteous principle of firmness, detects the moral fault in Mary—giving her a thoroughly deserved "contemptuous glance" after she tells him: "'It is very unpleasant, having such connexions! But I assure you, I have never been in the house above twice in my life'" (86)—but misses the dangerous headiness in Louisa.

Captain Wentworth's narrow understanding of firmness is further

---

① Mary's pride here echoes exactly her father's. In chapter 3 of volume 1, Sir Walter blames Mr Shepherd for misleading him by describing the Rev. Mr Wentworth as "'gentleman'" (23): "'Mr Wentworth, the curate of Monkford. You misled me by the term *Gentleman*. I thought you were speaking of some man of property: Mr. Wentworth was nobody, I remember; quite unconnected; nothing to do with the Strafford family'" (23).

revealed in the metaphor he chooses to illustrate his dubious principle.
While still on the same subject with Louisa, Wentworth catches a hazel-
nut "down from an upper bough" (88) and goes on with his pseudo-
philosophical discourse:

> To exemplify,—a beautiful glossy nut, which, blessed with original
> strength, has outlived all the storms of autumn. Not a puncture, not a weak spot
> any where. —This nut ... while so many of its brethren have fallen and been
> trodden under foot, is still in possession of all the happiness that a hazel-nut can
> be supposed capable of. (88)

The metaphor seems arbitrary, gratuitous and also comic. While there is
no denying that the hazel-nut is known for its hard shell, it is also
common knowledge that it is rich and fragrant inside and has a not so hard
kernel. The hardness represents merely the external character of the hazel-
nut, hence an incomplete representation. Besides, the fact that some nuts
have fallen to the ground and others have not does not lend support to the
idea that some nuts are intrinsically better or harder than others. It is more
a matter of chance that some have fallen earlier than their brethren. Thus
by promoting firmness indiscriminately, almost illogically, Wentworth is
misleading both Louisa and himself.

Captain Wentworth may not realize it at the moment, but he has
planted some dangerous seeds in the head of an impetuous Louisa. His
promotion of firmness and his description of it in such absolute yet
misleading terms prepare his eager admirer for an act of serious
imprudence. At the same time he is laying a trap for himself, since the
two of them stimulate each other in a mutually indulgent relationship.
Wentworth's dubious ideal inspires Louisa's intractable will, while her
credulousness, compliance and adoration (characteristics opposite to
firmness) supply him with a false sense of rectitude and infallibility. It is
clear, again, that Captain Wentworth's high-sounding principle of
firmness lacks a firm moral basis. It is simply another way of venting his
frustration while nursing his anger over the failed engagement with
Anne. His talk of "'circumstances'" that require "'fortitude and strength
of mind'" and his calling for "'resolution enough to resist idle

interference in such a trifle as this'" (88) are selfishly driven. He has his own axe to grind even though he himself may not be sensible enough to realize it.

Anne's reflection on Louisa's accident clearly shows her dialectical judgment: "[F] irmness of character" may be an attractive, even admirable, quality in a human being, but, "like all other qualities of the mind, it should have its proportions and limits" (116). Ironically yet fittingly, the accident at Lyme happens at precisely the moment when Captain Wentworth caves in to Louisa's headstrong bid to act resolutely and firmly. Such words as "'Had I done as I ought! But so eager and so resolute!'" (116) reveal the state of confusion Captain Wentworth is in over the true meaning of firmness. Louisa Musgrove, who is of the same age as Anne Elliot was when she broke off the engagement, behaves in exactly the opposite way in a rather less momentous matter. Louisa must do what she "'knew to be right'" (87); if Louisa wants to be jumped down the steep flight of steps, then "she must be jumped down them by Captain Wentworth" (109). Her motto "'I am determined I will'" (109) is a form of regurgitation of Captain Wentworth's " hazel-nut " philosophy. ①

4

Since she overheard the conversation between Louisa and Wentworth concerning her refusal of Charles Musgrove, Anne Elliot has grown increasingly confident of herself, of her dialectically informed attitude. This self-confidence of being in the right soon manifests itself on a number of occasions during a subsequent trip to Lyme Regis, culminating in Anne's heroic performance on the Cobb. For example, Anne finds it less difficult now to associate with Captain Wentworth and his naval

---

① Louisa's wrong-headedness is perhaps metaphorically implied when the narrator explains that her fall on the Cobb causes "no wound, no blood, no visible bruise" but "a severe contusion" (112) in the "head" (109); Admiral Croft's remark later at Bath that Wentworth and Louisa "'must wait till her brain was set to right'" (171) seems likewise suggestive.

friends:

> Anne found herself by this time growing so much more hardened to being in
> Captain Wentworth's company than she had at first imagined could ever be, that
> the sitting down to the same table with him now, and the interchange of the
> common civilities attending on it—(they never got beyond) was become a mere
> nothing. (99)

She strikes up a conversation with Captain Benwick who has recently
lost his fiancée, Fanny Harville, and "was well repaid the first trouble of
exertion" (100). Indeed, during her conversation with Captain Benwick,
Anne is sufficiently "emboldened" that she even feels "in herself the right
of seniority of mind," and ventures "to recommend a larger allowance of
prose in his daily study" (101), "such works of our best moralists, such
collections of the finest letters, such memoirs of characters of worth and
suffering" (101), in order to combat his over-indulgence in the romantic
poetry of Scott and Byron (100).

Captain Benwick's pathetic example matches dialectically Captain
Wentworth's passionate one: both show a loss of perspective and
judgment, albeit in different ways, as a result of their succumbing to
understandable but immoderate and unjustifiable emotions. Whereas Anne
is hindered by personal circumstances from speaking directly and
explicitly to Captain Wentworth, she is able to give Captain Benwick
advice in regard to his unhealthy absorption in romantic poetry. The
dialectical irony is that, while she is able "to preach patience and
resignation" to Captain Benwick, Anne realizes that "she had been
eloquent on a point in which her own conduct would ill bear
examination" (101)! But the very fact that she is aware of the danger of
being overcome by one emotion, one mode of thinking, bespeaks her
dialectical mind; such superior understanding prevents her from being
dragged into an emotional impasse or extreme, unbalanced thoughts.
Captain Wentworth will learn to see firmness in appropriate contexts the
hard way; he will in time learn that "a persuadable temper might

sometimes be as much in favour of happiness, as a very resolute character" (116). ①

The dialectical engagement between Anne Elliot and Captain Wentworth in the wake of Louisa Musgrove's accident at Lyme (occurring in the last chapter of the first volume) becomes an increasingly conscious act with a near-reverse in their respective attitudes. Captain Wentworth's policy of firmness has proved both imprudent and impracticable. Anne's swift action and presence of mind in the emergency afford an ultimate demonstration of what rational fortitude and firmness really are. But even before the ultimate lesson is delivered in the form of the terrible (though avoidable) fall, the balance of power, so to speak, has already started to shift in Anne Elliot's favour.

When Anne Elliot overhears Louisa Musgrove relating to Captain Wentworth how Anne had refused Charles Musgrove when he proposed to her and how the senior Musgroves thought that "'it was her great friend Lady Russell's doing,'" and that it was Lady Russell who "'persuaded Anne to refuse him'" (89), she must have felt psychologically relieved. The Musgroves, who are not noted for their thinking and understanding, manage to discredit Lady Russell when Anne should have been credited for the persuasion. The authorial commentary: "The listener's proverbial fate was not absolutely hers; she had heard no evil of herself" (89) is perhaps the biggest understatement in the novel. Anne must have realized that Louisa's information constitutes a vital though unintended

---

① Anne's mocking tone here matches Wentworth's satirical facial expression when Mrs Musgrove talks about her wayward son Dick:

"Ah! it would have been a happy thing, if he had never left you. I assure you, Captain Wentworth, we are very sorry he ever left you. "

There was a momentary expression in Captain Wentworth's face at this speech, a certain glance of his bright eye, and curl of his handsome mouth, which convinced Anne, that instead of sharing in Mrs. Musgrove's kind wishes, as to her son, he had probably been at some pains to get rid of him; but it was too transient an indulgence of self-amusement to be detected by any who understood him less than herself. (67)

Clearly, the two characters, as designed by Jane Austen, keep the same mental pace and are both consummate ironists.

clarification of her character, and that it is too clear a signal for quick-minded Captain Wentworth to miss. If Charles Musgrove, perfectly eligible by worldly criteria in addition to his good character, could not be accepted by Anne a few years after the breaking-off of the engagement, ①
it might well mean that Anne still loved Wentworth. It also compels Frederick to acknowledge that Anne is firm in following her own notion of love and romantic relationship. ② Not even Lady Russell could persuade Anne to marry Charles Musgrove.

The fact that Captain Wentworth has come to know about Anne's refusal of Charles Musgrove, and the fact that Anne knows that he knows, opens a new phase in their current relationship. Anne's increasing confidence in her rectitude is in proportion to her decreasing anxiety about Wentworth's misunderstanding of her. Her mental tranquillity inevitably gives rise to her improved physical appearance:

> She was looking remarkably well; her very regular, very pretty features,
> having the bloom and freshness of youth restored by the fine wind which had been
> blowing on her complexion, and by the animation of eye which it had also
> produced. (104)

It is at this point that Mr William Walter Elliot encounters Anne and shows great admiration for her fine looks, which in turn spurs Captain

---

① We learn from Sir Walter's addition in his favourite book, the *Baronetage*, that Mary "'married, Dec. 16, 1810, Charles, son and heir of Charles Musgrove, Esq. of Uppercross, in the county of Somerset'" (3).

② Wentworth must have done some quick calculation after he asked Louisa for the specific date of Anne's refusal of Charles Musgrove. Louisa could not tell for sure but she believed it happened "'about a year before he married Mary'" (89). If she is right, that puts 1809 as the likely date because Charles married Mary in December 1810. The year 1809 must be the most approximate date because Anne's age that year, "about two-and-twenty" (28), presupposes that when she met Commander Wentworth "in the summer of 1806" (26) she must have been "nineteen" (26). Wentworth mentions "'the year six'" (63) as the beginning of his naval adventures and the very mentioning of the year gives Anne "pain" because it is "the year of their engagement" (63) and also of its termination. Therefore when Captain Wentworth "'returned to England in the year eight'" (247), Anne was available, being of age and free to marry even if her father disapproved. If Captain Wentworth had made the right move, "'[s]ix years of separation and suffering might have been spared'" (247).

Wentworth to "'see something like Anne Elliot again'" (104).

Anne's bodily change originates from her inner peace with herself which can be traced back to Louisa's unwitting attestation of Anne's sterling and steadfast character even as the girl is eagerly promoting herself; but seeing her lover again may also have contributed to her rejuvenation. This psychological sequence, only too natural yet no less interesting, is similar to but different from what happens in *Pride and Prejudice* where the inner change of Darcy induces the external "change" of Elizabeth. ① But in *Persuasion* things are more complicated. There is the inner change that must have rejuvenated Anne; there is also the inner change that must have prepared Wentworth to mark the physical changes in Anne once they are pointed up by William Walter Elliot's "earnest admiration" (104) on the steps of the Cobb. Wentworth's jealousy as a result of Mr Elliot's keen regard is doubtless significant, but the absence of the mental block accounts for more—after all only a few weeks earlier Wentworth was reported to have said that Anne was so altered he should not have known her again (60). ②

5

The Lyme episode, at the middle of the novel, represents the turning point in the relationship between Anne Elliot and Captain Wentworth. However, the turning of their relationship is not without dialectical twists and turns. The process of reconciliation is complicated by Mr Elliot's appearance on the scene and by the change of locale from the country to the city. The extended Bath scene, beginning in chapter two of the second volume, consists of a dialectical reversal of the Somerset scenario involving Anne and Wentworth. At Kellynch and Winthrop

---

① Mr Darcy upgrades Elizabeth Bennet's appearance from "'tolerable'" to "'pretty'" in short order and eventually to "'loveliest'" (*PP* 12, 27, 369).

② When they have happily engaged each other, Captain Wentworth earnestly avows that "'to my eye you could never alter'" (243), which contradicts what he is purported to have said earlier. But Anne thinks that "[i]t was too pleasing a blunder for a reproach" (243).

Captain Wentworth is undoubtedly the centre of attention. He is well liked and cordially invited to dinner at Uppercross where his talk of naval feats monopolizes the attention of the female company (the Miss Hayters and the Miss Musgroves)—even Anne, who has heard similar heroic adventures before, must do all she can to keep her "shudderings" (66) to herself. Like Othello speaking to Desdemona "of most disastrous chances: / Of moving accidents by flood and field / Of hair-breadth scapes i' th' imminent deadly breach," Wentworth thrives in the general esteem and adoration of his female audience who, like Desdemona, devour up his discourse. ① But at Bath, the focus is shifted to Anne as Wentworth tentatively and unwillingly joins Mr Elliot as a rival for her hand. Whereas Captain Wentworth is resolutely gallant in his matrimonial search in Somersetshire and has got into a tangle with Louisa, he withdraws into a state of irresolution while at Bath. His courtship of Anne is marked by timidity and uncertainty, in sheer contrast to his rival's suavity and complacency.

Captain Wentworth's task of re-engaging Anne is not an easy one, though it is made relatively easy by Anne's active engagement with him. He has learned two object lessons from two different engagements—one explicit, the other implicit—and has taken each to heart. His modified romantic ideal tells him that Anne Elliot is the woman he both desires and wants, but his pride and self-respect will not suffer him to be hurt a second time by the same woman. In addition, as a gentleman, Captain Wentworth hesitates to compete with Mr Elliot as a suitor, especially because her marriage to Elliot would make Anne the titled mistress of her old home in due course. Wentworth knows what he wants, but he hesitates to say it because of the circumstances, whereas earlier at Somersetshire he spoke freely about what he wanted without really knowing the implications of what he wanted. To complicate the matter even further, Captain Wentworth is deterred by the heavy presence at Bath of the conservative forces of Sir Walter, Elizabeth and Lady Russell,

---

① *Othello* 1. 3. 134 – 136, 150.

joined by the aspiring Mr Elliot and the scheming Mrs Clay, reinforced by the Dowager Viscountess Dalrymple and the Honourable Miss Carteret. This group, by virtue of its social distinction and its claimed kinship from within, creates an impression of cohesiveness and exclusiveness.

The situation at Bath imposes restraints upon both Wentworth and Anne Elliot and erects a formidable barrier between the two sometime lovers. The challenge for Anne Elliot is how to disarm Frederick Wentworth of his jealousy and mistrust without alienating either him or herself from the social circle in which she now moves. The challenge for Wentworth is how to distinguish Anne Elliot nicely and properly from the rest of her family without committing the same error of going to extremes as he did eight years ago. In other words, he has to suspend his collective contempt for the Elliots and Lady Russell and be prepared to join them, if not mingle with them, on social occasions. There is an interesting play of the dialectic of place here. Whereas in the dull country Captain Wentworth seems most active, at glamorous Bath he seems most inactive or lacking initiative. Dialectically juxtaposed with the change in Wentworth is the change in Anne, who shows that, put in a similarly advantageous position as Wentworth once was at Kellynch, she is able to act graciously. She will not compromise the principled understanding she has reached over eight years of reflection, yet she will not refrain from intimating her genuine affection to the man she loves. Her dialectical approach to Captain Wentworth indicates that, while she remains the same Anne Elliot as far as her attachment to him goes, she is not the same Anne Elliot morally and intellectually. She is the regenerated Anne Elliot whom he must learn to appreciate anew. [1] Anne is acutely aware of the evil of some of the social values which she does not share with the rest of her family; she is also sharply aware of the negative perception which the

---

[1]   By contrast Jay Gatsby tragically imagines that Daisy's love for him can transcend the reality of time and decay, that love is immortal in the teeth of materialism. What is retrievable in Austen through the working of dialectics is irretrievable in Fitzgerald.

people she associates with day in, day out are capable of giving. Hers is a tricky and trying undertaking, as subsequent events will prove.

During the encounter with Captain Wentworth in Molland's on Milsom Street, Anne notices that Elizabeth, who is with her at the time, "would not know him" (176), even though she "saw that he saw Elizabeth, that Elizabeth saw him, that there was complete internal recognition on each side" (176). Although this "did not surprise" Anne, it "grieved" her (176). A subsequent incident, where Anne, riding with Lady Russell down Pulteney Street, spots Captain Wentworth "at such a distance" (179) whereas Lady Russell misses him for some fancy window-curtains at close range, seems to confirm the difficulty of Anne's task of initiating a reconciliation with Captain Wentworth. R. W. Chapman has made some shrewd observations about this particular incident in his notes to the text, [1] and the sequence of events in question bears out the subtlety of Jane Austen's art of dialectic.

To begin with, there is a sense of contrast between Anne's total preoccupation with such a living person as Captain Wentworth and Lady Russell's seeming absorption in such trivial materials as window-curtains. The narrator does not confirm or deny whether Lady Russell's looking at the curtains in some private windows is a prevarication—"Anne sighed and blushed and smiled, in pity and disdain, either at her friend or herself" (179). A. C. Bradley has rightly observed a "touch of comic irony" here in that Anne is induced to measure in vain Lady Russell against her own passionate feelings. [2] But there is also a touch of indifference, if not hostility, here. It could be that Lady Russell is intent on giving Wentworth what she thinks he deserves. Earlier when she was informed by Anne of "the attachment between him and Louisa" (125), Lady Russell's heart "revelled in angry pleasure, in pleased contempt, that the man who at twenty-three had seemed to understand somewhat of

---

[1] NA *and* P 294 – 295.

[2] "Jane Austen," *Essays and Studies by Members of the English Association*, 2 (1911): 33; quoted by Chapman in his notes to *Persuasion* (N *and* P 294).

the value of an Anne Elliot, should, eight years afterwards, be charmed by a Louisa Musgrove" (125). It could also be that Lady Russell, having more recently been surprised by the news that Louisa is to marry not Captain Wentworth but Captain Benwick, may have harboured "another shade of prejudice against him," as Anne quite reasonably suspects, due to "her imperfect knowledge of the matter" (178). In any case, Anne is alarmed by the apparent or perceived indifference of the people she closely associates with and is concerned that what she has observed threatens to thwart her attempt to engage and enlighten Captain Wentworth.

This is why Anne gathers nerve and courage to make a significant overture to Captain Wentworth at the concert, under the camouflage of observing standard social obligations, in order to counter the fact that "Elizabeth had turned from him, Lady Russell overlooked him" (180). ①
As soon as she sees Frederick walk into the concert hall alone, Anne greets him with a "gentle 'How do you do?'" (181). But before she speaks, she has made "yet a little advance" towards him even though she is "the nearest to him" (181) already. The physical movement away from her own social group toward the solitary man whom she loves draws a line between them and her. By doing so she has turned the negative family background, consisting of "the formidable father and sister" (181), to positive effects: her gesture of rapprochement gains significance. Anne's conscious move sets her apart from the rest of the Elliots and also Lady Russell; the distance between them and her symbolizes the moral gap between a dialectical mind and a mind (or minds) transfixed by the traditional trappings of birth, money and status.

While the two are engaged in conversation, Anne's dialectical point of view, cultivated in years of suffering and reflection, is subtly yet unmistakably compared and contrasted with the honest but simplistic view of Captain Wentworth. Reflecting on the horrible incident at Lyme,

---

① Chapman notes that the word "overlooked" would suit unintentional at least as well as intentional lack of recognition (295), but he wonders "why should the failure be thought of as a slight?" I think that in the context of Elizabeth's contemptuous behaviour, Lady Russell's ambiguous action carries more negative than positive implications.

Wentworth laments, "'I am afraid you must have suffered from the shock, and the more from its not overpowering you at the time'" (181). As he reminisces, the terrible scene seems to have loomed again in front of him. He has a painful memory of it all: "'It was a frightful hour ... a frightful day!'" (182). Then he remembers what a crucial role the accident has played in his release from Louisa Musgrove: "'The day has produced some effects however—has had some consequences which must be considered as the very reverse of frightful. —When you had the presence of mind to suggest that Benwick would be the properest person to fetch a surgeon, you could have little idea of his being eventually one of those most concerned in her recovery'" (182).

Captain Wentworth seems to have at last realized the dialectical nature of things. Lyme is where his wrong-headed romanticism both peaked and crashed, where he foolishly got himself tangled in a relationship that he regretted and was later freed from it by a stroke of good luck. But what he has managed to come to grips with can only be credited as reaching the initial and intuitive stage of philosophical thinking. His train of thought is still primarily affected by his emotions. This is apparent in his incredulous reaction towards Benwick's swift attachment to Louisa:

> "A man like him, in his situation! With a heart pierced, wounded, almost broken! Fanny Harville was a very superior creature; and his attachment to her was indeed attachment. A man does not recover from such a devotion of the heart to such a woman! —He ought not—he does not." (183)

It is also seen in his response to Anne's saying that she "'should very much like to see Lyme again'" (183):

> "Indeed! I should not have supposed that you could have found any thing in Lyme to inspire such a feeling. The horror and distress you were involved in—the stretch of mind, the wear of spirits! —I should have thought your last impressions of Lyme must have been strong disgust." (183)

Wentworth's direct, passionate observations are genuine and understandable, but they lack depth and perspective. Anne's eloquent rejoinder shows a remarkable contrast in philosophical maturity:

> The last few hours were certainly very painful ... but when pain is over,
> the remembrance of it often becomes a pleasure. One does not love a place the
> less for having suffered in it, unless it has been all suffering, nothing but
> suffering—which was by no means the case at Lyme. We were only in anxiety
> and distress during the last two hours; and, previously, there had been a great
> deal of enjoyment. (183 – 184)

Anne's speech, though brief and spontaneous, carries a profound
philosophical point. It manifests her dialectical approach to life, which
seems a customary practice by now. She is at once consoling Captain
Wentworth and opening his eyes to the positive side of things. If he were
a quick and imaginative learner, he might have applied Anne's principle
to their own eventful relationship: when pain is over, the remembrance
of it often becomes a pleasure; one does not love a person the less for
having suffered in the relationship, unless it has been all suffering,
nothing but suffering.

Indeed misery is not the whole story about their love. For Anne the
unfortunate past has also been a source of strength and guidance. Once emotion
is reined in by intellect, memory of "the tenderness of the past" will more than
balance any "anger" or "resentment" (185). Anne's simple, brief yet
thoughtful and soothing words—"'when pain is over, the remembrance of it
often becomes a pleasure'"—speak volumes for a serene and superior mind.
Captain Wentworth, now under the therapeutic influence of Anne Elliot, is
beginning the dialectical process of turning the bitter past into something
medicinal and constructive.

The philosophical point which Anne Elliot brings forward is stressed
during her friendly debate with Captain Harville over the comparative
degrees of men and women's romantic devotion. Countering Harville's
argument that "'as our bodies are the strongest, so are our feelings'"
(233), [1] Anne gently points out the fallacy of using gender as the basis of

---

[1] This sounds like one of the sexist sentiments which Mary Wollstonecraft criticizes in her
Vindication of the Rights of Woman (1792).

emotion: "'Your feelings may be the strongest ... but the same spirit of analogy will authorise me to assert that ours are the most tender. Man is more robust than woman, but he is not longer-lived'" (233). However, Anne, at the same time, assures Captain Harville that she by no means supposes that "'true attachment and constancy were known only by woman'" (235). Nevertheless, Anne is sure that she has every reason to declare: "'All the privilege I claim for my own sex (it is not a very enviable one, you need not covet it) is that of loving longest, when existence or when hope is gone'" (235).

As a matter of fact, this debate between Captain Harville and Anne Elliot is part of the reflection on the broken engagement between Anne and Wentworth, and a vivid expression of its tortuous and dialectical process of reconstitution. Jane Austen's revised ending allows the dramatic climax to emerge rather appropriately out of a very pertinent dialogue which forms the audible part of an intensely emotional and philosophical exchange in the consciousness of the two people who are understanding each other better daily, even hourly. It is highly significant that Captain Wentworth quietly but resolutely joins in Anne's passionate discourse on women's enduring love—"'in some respect saying what should not be said'" (234)—with an equally passionate discourse on men's constancy by offering himself, in writing this time, to the woman he dearly loves "'with a heart even more [her] own, than when [she] broke it eight years and a half ago'" (237). The unspoken dialogue takes place at the same time and within the same space as the spoken one. The fact that the two forms of discourse—oral and written—are proceeding simultaneously, [1] tuning into each other and interpenetrating each other's thoughts and emotions, endeared by their earnest tones of voice, audible or inaudible, and made poignant by such words of sincerity, uttered or lettered, epitomizes the glorious triumph of the dialectics of love. Their

---

[1] I disagree with James L. Kastely's interpretation that "[t]he greater significance behind Wentworth's writing is that he consciously gives up control of his discourse," and "to give up such control is his ultimate act of faith in Anne" ("*Persuasion*: Jane Austen's Philosophical Rhetoric," *Philosophy and Literature* 15 [1991]: 86).

early romantic relationship which was formed by chance—"he had nothing to do, and she had hardly any body to love" (26)—has graduated to a spiritual fusion through philosophical persuasion and understanding.

6

Anne Elliot's romance is fraught with affliction and reflection, but it is also marked by action. She probably would not like to see other young lovers undergo similar trials, but she likely would not exchange her memorable experience for any of their quick successes either. The kind of love she has eventually won is more precious because it has cost her over eight years of wretchedness and uncertainty, more dependable because it has already withstood a series of severe tests, and more virtuous because it is not hinged on mundane considerations① but built upon solid moral and philosophical understanding.② This is the ultimate form of love human beings may aspire to and hope to realize in real life. Their marital happiness is all but guaranteed.③

The triumph of romantic love in *Persuasion* is the triumph of dialectics. It is dialectical thinking that has helped both protagonists to acquire new, rational attitudes towards their genuine yet complicated and

---

① The couple is not poor either—what with captain Wentworth's "five-and-twenty thousand pounds" and Anne's "small part of the share of ten thousand pounds which must be hers hereafter" (248). Chapman's note about the Elliot sisters' having "10,000 l. each" ("Notes," NA *and* P 314) is incorrect: there is £10,000 to be shared among the three sisters, and Anne's third will amount to £3,333.33. However, Sir Walter is only able to give her a small part of this share, for the remainder of which his heir will be responsible.

② Duckworth, however, thinks that Anne's union with Wentworth comes about "not, as before, through the rational enlargement of the hero or the heroine or of both, but through an emotional rapport that goes beyond rational processes" (183).

③ Mary Poovey curiously supposes that "Anne's happiness is less complete than Elizabeth's, Fanny's, or Emma's" because she "had no Uppercross-hall before her, no landed estate, no headship of a family" (250). But these are the thoughts of the jealous Mary who takes consolation in the fact that none of the three worldly symbols will be attached to her sister Anne; "and if they could but keep Captain Wentworth from being made a baronet, she would not change situation with Anne" (250). For Austen's heroines, happiness is not contingent upon those worldly symbols.

convoluted attachment. To be more exact, it is Anne's exemplary conduct under the direction of her dialectical mind that eventually convinces Captain Wentworth of his erroneous ways of thinking. Therefore *Persuasion* is not at all a case where "the senses," according to Butler, "have a decisive advantage over reason and fact;" nor is the novel a soothing anodyne that tricks women to believe that they can be safe from the very public "repressive social conventions" by indulging in their private romantic desire. [1] *Persuasion* is a fine piece of work, more positive than negative, more optimistic than pessimistic. It demonstrates rather convincingly that approaching a problem, such as that which has plagued Anne Elliot and Captain Wentworth, in a dialectical way—as they have respectively learned to do, sooner or later—is well within the power of human beings so long as they know how to put their most valuable asset, i. e., moral intellect, to work.

Jane Austen's dialectical attitude is also reflected in her way of treating the social structure in the novel. *Persuasion* is perhaps a very appropriate title after all for Jane Austen's last completed novel, for the abstract but substantive noun not only denotes, as Kenneth L. Moler explains, the "rather specialized sense in Jane Austen's day" in matters of engagement and marriage, [2] but also connotes, in a larger ideological context, the necessity of revamping the outmoded thinking and behaving of the gentry. In the world of *Persuasion* in general, it is clear that Jane Austen is less than sanguine about a spiritual regeneration of the members of the gentry existing on a hereditary basis. Virginia Woolf, among others, has noticed that Jane Austen "has almost ceased to be amused by the vanities of a Sir Walter or the snobbery of a Miss Elliot." [3] The criticism of these members of the gentry is indeed made harsher by ridicule and contempt. The snobbishness and moral inertia of Sir Walter and Elizabeth Elliot are, for example, upstaged by those of Dowager

---

[1]   Poovey 228.

[2]   Moler 193.

[3]   Southam, vol. 2, 282.

Viscountess Dalrymple and her daughter the Hon. Miss Carteret. ① Sir Walter's ridiculous vanity, sometimes reaching the point of pathological infatuation, reminds one of the foppish coxcomb in the Restoration drama or, as Roger Sales argues, "an ageing dandy" of Regency England. ② He admires his own "good looks" (4) in the many mirrors he keeps at Kellynch—"'rather a dressy man for his time of life'" (128), comments Admiral Croft. At Bath Sir Walter vainly checks the looks of passers-by, once counting "eighty-seven women go by" without managing to discover "a tolerable face among them" (141 – 142).

Sir Walter is fascinated by the smooth surface while ignorant of or oblivious to the rotten core which is the cause of the smooth but blighted surface. If he cannot maintain such a surface at Kellynch he will try to do it at Bath, on an equally ostentatious scale. His obsession with the

---

① Michael Williams has perceptively pointed out that "the fact that the Dalrymples are Irish" further sinks the Elliots who, "[s]ituated as [they] are, and only too anxious to claim the relationship to nobility," are actually "precluded by their particular snobbery from participating in the more general snobbery by which the Irish peerage was regarded as greatly inferior to that of England" (*Jane Austen*: *Six Novels and Their Methods* [Houndmills: Macmillan, 1986] 161). In a note referring back to the point, Williams further suggests that Austen reverts a joke from Maria Edgeworth's novel, *The Absentee* (1812). In the "crush-room" scene, the Duchess of Torcaster mistakes an Irish lord for an English peer because of his excellent "manner" (*The Absentee* [Oxford: Oxford UP, 1988] 3). At the concert scene in *Persuasion* Lady Dalrymple takes Captain Wentworth to be Irish ("'More air than one often sees in Bath. —Irish, I dare say'" [188]). Williams concludes: "Lady Dalrymple has no qualms about her own Irishness, and seems actually to feel that only the best can be Irish. Thus she takes Wentworth by his fine 'air' to be Irish" (196, note 7). However, Jane Austen's intent seems more complex and elusive than Williams suggests. First, it is not clear whether Dalrymple—a Scottish name—is Irish by origin; her unmarried daughter, the Hon. Miss Carteret, has an English name (by a second marriage?). Second, there is no reason for us to trust Lady Dalrymple's judgment. She could be ironic if she were English. Yet if she were Irish and serious, then, Sir Walter's quick correction of her haphazard appraisal—"Captain Wentworth" is English and serves in "the navy" (188) and has a sister who is not only English but also married an English admiral currently renting my house— would surely arouse her displeasure, something Sir Walter would not contemplate. I agree with Williams that there is some echoing of Edgeworth here—the fact that Sir Walter is an absentee landlord of sorts lends support to this view—but I think Austen is probably laughing up her sleeve by creating an amusing situation of double irony.

② Sales points out that "Sir Walter is just two years older than the Prince Regent" but would "probably insist that he looked at least ten years younger" (171).

Baronetage fixes his nostalgia about the good old days, represented by "the limited remnant of the earliest patents" (3). For "the almost endless creations of the last century," he has only "pity and contempt" (3). However, Sir Walter's vain effort to perpetuate what he imagines to be the old way of life seems in vain; the opening chapters not only manifest realistically how his attempt is pitifully failing but also demonstrate figuratively how the frame serves merely to introduce the more substantive content. By looking backward and being absorbed in the surface of things, Sir Walter disqualifies himself from playing an active role in moving society forward. He is without "principle or sense enough to maintain himself in the situation in which Providence had placed him" (248). Jane Austen has made it clear that, with Mr Elliot in line to succeed Sir Walter, possibly abetted by the crafty and obsequious Mrs Clay, the moral prospects of Kellynch are bleak.

As an alternative, Jane Austen—through her heroine Anne Elliot— places her trust for a spiritual reconstitution of the gentry in such morally alert individuals as the Crofts and the regenerated Anne Elliot and Captain Wentworth, whose warm, sincere, moral, thoughtful and practical ambience contrasts sharply with Sir Walter's cold, vain, shameless, thoughtless and spendthrift style, and his heir's hypocritical, scheming and calculating demeanor. It is high time that the old blood, anemic and deteriorating, were infused with, if not replaced by, the new blood, fresh and invigorating. These moral persons rely on individual efforts, "'honourable toils and just rewards'" [247]) rather than hereditary privileges, to gain status and recognition. They are a solid and positive force to be reckoned with. The symbolic act of the Crofts' temporarily taking over Kellynch Hall broadly hints that "they were gone who deserved not to stay, and that Kellynch-hall had passed into better hands than its owners" (125).

We should not, however, read too much into the leasing of Kellynch Hall by the Crofts and interpret the event, or even the whole story, idealistically as a sign of "[t]he decline of the hereditary landed aristocracy and the ascendency of the energetic naval class," nor should we read "renting" for "abdication" and "occupation" for "usurpation."[①] Jane Austen has no intention to sink the gentry and initiate a naval rescue. Her attitude towards the gentry is dialectical, just like her attitude towards the conservative and Jacobin sentiments and practices in the last decade of the eighteenth century. She makes fine distinctions between various members of the gentry. For example, Lady Russell, despite her faults, approves of Anne's visits to Mrs Smith (157) and may ultimately change her opinion of Captain Wentworth.[②] This is why she is treated with gentle irony (whereas Sir Walter with heavy sarcasm). However, Lady Russell has to start learning if she ever wants to keep up with the new reality. She "must learn to feel that she had been mistaken with regard to both [Captain Wentworth and Mr Elliot]; that she had been unfairly influenced by appearances in each" (249). In short, "[t]here was nothing less for Lady Russell to do, than to admit that she had been pretty completely wrong, and to take up a new set of opinions and of hopes" (249). She must try to "become truly acquainted with, and do justice to Captain Wentworth" (249).

Persuasion is one of the precursors to the modern novel not only

---

① See Joseph M. Duffy, Jr. "Structure and Idea in Jane Austen's *Persuasion*," *NCF 8* (1953) 274. The anachronism is perpetuated in more recent Jane Austen criticism. Daniel Cottom, for example, thinks that "[t]he aristocracy" is "still the dominant class in her work," that "the aristocracy still dominates social values in her novels," and that their estate is "in danger of usurpation, as when Anne Elliot admits in *Persuasion*" (95, 96). David Monaghan argues that "[t]he account of Sir Walter Elliot's way of life with which *Persuasion* opens demonstrates very forcibly the decadent condition into which Jane Austen believes the gentry has sunk" (*Jane Austen: Structure and Social Vision* [London: Macmillan, 1980] 146). Poovey talks of "the sphere of influence of the upper classes" in *Emma* as well as in *Persuasion* (235). R. W. Chapman has long ago made it clear, in his curt reply to Duffy's article, that putting Sir Walter in the "aristocracy" would have shocked the man himself, that in 1815 neither aristocracy nor landed gentry were in any danger of supersession, that there was no such thing as an "energetic naval class," and that in fact naval officers were themselves very often younger sons of peers or country gentlemen (see "A Reply to Mr. Duffy on *Persuasion*," *NCF 9* [1954]: 154).

② I think Moler's conclusion that "Lady Russell, the character who is placed opposite Wentworth in *Persuasion*'s antithetical pattern, is also reformed" (218) is a little hasty. The narrator's final comment on Lady Russell is tactful: Anne is satisfied by "Lady Russell's meaning to love Captain Wentworth as she ought" (251).

because of its skilful exploitation of interior monologue as a means to lay bare the heroine's dialectical deliberation but also because of its inspiring philosophical content vividly rendered with realistic details. Admittedly, there are some shortcomings in conception and execution. Butler, for example, has quite rightly pointed out some of the weaknesses in the novel such as the entry of "Mr. William Walter Elliott [sic], the alternative claimant for Anne's hand" and "[t]he manœuvre by which Mr. Elliott [sic] is disposed of, his *affaire*, with Mrs. Clay."[1] But these defects merely suggest that the work is unfinished; they do not detract from its major virtue, i.e., the dramatic presentation of the dialectics of love.

---

[1] Butler 280.

8 Conclusion

Is there such a thing as dialectic in the novels of Jane Austen? Strong narrative evidence suggests that there is. In fact not only is the phenomenon present in Jane Austen's six completed novels, but its pervasiveness in theme, structure, character (and character relations), motif and action bespeak deliberate architecture rather than haphazard attempts on the part of the novelist. Indeed the design is conscious and the application systematic.

Jane Austen's literary achievement reflects her intellectual acumen and the quality of her mind in general. While deeply immersed in the literary productions of her own period and of the preceding half century and more, she manages to maintain critical detachment. Her novels embody her dialectical attitude towards the historical events raging in the tumultuous 1790s, the decade in which she came of age. Her intellectual novels mark a high point since the genre's emergence in the first half of the eighteenth cenfury. They not only offer pleasure and instruction, but also meticulously chart the actual and entire process of the operations of the mind—to use a typically Lockean and also eighteenth-century phrase. What is more, they dramatize and shed light on the dialectical nature and benefit of such operations.

Whereas during the years at the turn of the eighteenth century, the novel, to borrow J. M. S. Tompkins's metaphor, "had for the first time been the arena of a serious war of ideas,"[1] Jane Austen offers a unique point of view that shows her unwillingness to follow exclusively any political faction: neither the reform-minded nor the anti-Jacobin, neither the female Gothic (or Gothic feminist) nor the religious orthodox. She

---

[1] Tompkins 301.

stands at a height that looks beyond what is immediately fashionable or profitable. She sees through the war of ideas in the foreground and focuses her attention on the moral struggle that is commonly experienced by the mind of every thinking individual.

Jane Austen's ability to analyze and subsume the diverging political, religious and literary influences both in the domestic environment and in the wide society bears testimony to her moral and intellectual superiority. Her greatness lies in her capacity to create characters that are, in Hegel's words on epic heroes, "total individuals who magnificently concentrate within themselves what is otherwise dispersed in the national character, and in this they remain great, free and noble human characters."[①] Jane Austen's novels reflect the important social concerns of her time, and her ideological sensitivity (without being ideologically committed one way or the other) is clearly and consistently set forth in the moral battle of ideas recurrent in the daily lives of her characters. Jane Austen is not the spokesperson of any political camp, but the proponent of what is worthy in humanity. It is from this perspective that we should approach her novels.

This book has expressed reservations about conservative and feminist readings of Austen that are based on premises which do not originate in Austen's fiction. Although those readings have alerted us to some of the concerns present in Jane Austen's novels, they do not recognize the dialectical elements in her novels, and consequently tend to obscure, even as they try to illuminate, many of the salient features of Jane Austen's works. I have raised issues throughout this study with such (as I believe) misplaced emphases in order to indicate how they are at variance with Jane Austen's texts. Jane Austen's novels, like her personality, are extraordinarily complex and part of the reason must be attributed to the prevalence of a variety of well-conceived and artfully rendered dialectical elements.

---

①   Quoted by Georg Lukács in *The Historical Novel*, trans. Hannah and Stanley Mitchell (1937; Harmondsworth: Penguin, 1976) 36.

Jane Austen's art of dialectic itself reveals stages of transformation as well as layers of sophistication. From *Northanger Abbey* through *Sense and Sensibility* to *Pride and Prejudice* (the novels known—thanks to Cassandra's note—to have been originally conceived and written in the 1790s), Jane Austen's practice is to set up characters and actions as dialectically opposed and unfold their development with a strain of dialectics undercutting their opposition. In the three later novels, written since the success of her first publication in 1811, Jane Austen's narrative mode assumes an inward tendency as dialectical meditation becomes more prominent than dialectical movement. In *Mansfield Park* Fanny's thoughts and feelings are central to the narrative; indeed Edmund's moral growth taking place in the background is enveloped and sustained by Fanny's intense moral deliberation in the foreground. In *Emma* dialectic governs the heroine's entire thinking process, and provides for her moral attractiveness even as she commits all those morally alarming acts. In *Persuasion* Anne Elliot is engrossed in a dialectical evaluation of her past self in juxtaposition to her present self, which yields the guiding principle for her admirable engagement with Captain Wentworth. These main characters (and even some secondary ones)—neither revolutionarily feminine nor conservatively docile—all go through some painfully dialectical experiences before they mature enough to achieve a higher level of knowledge and self-knowledge. Although such dialectical process is common in our own life experiences and no less prominent in many of the nineteenth- and twentieth-century novels, Jane Austen was the first who consistently and masterfully presented it, using dialectic both as a reigning strategy and as a successful technique.

I believe that there is no single "theoretical" key to unlock the complexity of the Jane Austen canon. Only when we consciously and patiently trace the authorial intent from the narrative evidence, taking into account the social and cultural as well as personal and domestic situations of the time, will we have some right to say what her novels mean. Identifying the dialectical elements in her novels and seeing them as part of her comprehensive response to a dynamic historical and philosophical environment will help us appreciate Jane Austen as a person of her times.

Jane Austen's dialectical outlook gives rise to the persistent irony that is found throughout her novels; and in order to appreciate that rhetorical *tour de force*, we need to keep in mind the classic tension between dialectic and rhetoric which the Greek philosophers long ago discovered and pondered. Plato's dialogues demonstrate clearly how in reality we find unity in opposition and generality in particularity; similarly, Jane Austen's novels have vividly illustrated how "a truth universally acknowledged" can only make adequate sense when it is understood in its dialectical context. Resorting to one form of rhetoric or another that appears fashionable for the moment is not going to unravel Jane Austen. It is time to consider Jane Austen's rhetoric in light of her dialectic so as to gain a deeper awareness of Austen's philosophical meanings.

I should stress in closing that discussing Jane Austen's novels in light of dialectic is not in any way to assert that the author is a philosopher in literary disguise. Rather, it is an attempt to discern the special attraction which her work holds, an attempt to appreciate its quintessential instruction which its exquisite pleasure tends to tuck away—in short, an attempt to see the basis and shape of her imagination. If we cannot declare that by best representing her time Jane Austen has, like Shakespeare, become timeless, we must say that she has offered us one of the best literary representations of the Age of Enlightenment. Her imaginative and artistic creations naturally recall and amply justify those celebrated couplets by one of her favourite eighteenth-century poets:

True Wit is Nature to advantage dress'd,

What oft was thought, but ne'er so well express'd.

Something, whose truth convinc'd at sight we find,

That gives us back the image of our mind. ①

---

① Alexander Pope, *An Essay on Criticism*, ll. 297 – 300; *Pope: Poetical Works*, ed. Herbert Davis (London: Oxford UP, 1966).

Bibliography

Aarsleff, Hans. *From Locke to Saussure: Essays on the Study of Language and Intellectual History.* Minneapolis: U of Minnesota P, 1982.

Anti-Jacobin; or, Weekly Examiner, The. London. 1797 – 1798.

Aristotle. *The Complete Works of Aristotle.* Trans. J. L. Ackrill, et al. Ed. Jonathan Barnes. 2 vols. Bollingen series LXXI. 2. Princeton: Princeton UP, 1984.

Austen, Caroline. *Reminiscences.* GB: Jane Austen Society, 1986.

Austen, Henry. "Biographical Notice of the Author." *The Novels of Jane Austen.* Ed. R. W. Chapman. 3rd ed. Vol. 5. Oxford: Oxford UP, 1933. Rpt. 1988.

Austen, James. *The Loiterer.* Oxford, 1790. Ed. Li-Ping Geng. Ann Arbor: Scholars' Facsimiles & Reprints, 2000.

Austen, Jane. *The Novels of Jane Austen.* Ed. R. W. Chapman. 3rd ed. 5 vols. Oxford: Oxford UP, 1932 – 1934. Rpt. 1988.

—. *Minor Works.* Ed. R. W. Chapman. Vol. 6. Oxford: Oxford UP, 1954. Rpt. with further rev. B. C. Southam, 1988.

—. *Jane Austen's Letters.* 3rd ed. Collected and ed. Deirdre Le Faye. Oxford: Oxford UP, 1995.

—. *Jane Austen's Manuscript Letters in Facsimile.* Ed. Jo Modert. Carbondale: Southern Illinois UP, 1990.

Austen-Leigh, James Edward. *A Memoir of Jane Austen.* Intro., notes and index. R. W. Chapman. Oxford: Clarendon UP, 1926.

Austen-Leigh, Mary Augusta. *Personal Aspects of Jane Austen.* London: Murray, 1920.

Austen-Leigh, William and Richard Arthur Austen-Leigh. *Jane Austen: A Family Record.* Rev. and Enl. Deirdre Le Faye. Boston: G. K.

Hall, 1989.

Bage, Robert. *Hermsprong: or, Man As He Is Not*. Ed. Peter Faulkner. 1796; Oxford: Oxford UP, 1985.

Bakhtin, M. M. *The Dialogic Imagination: Four Essays by M. M. Bakhtin*. Ed. Michael Holquist. Trans. Caryl Emerson and Michael Holquist. Austin: U of Texas P, 1981.

Beckwith, Mildred Chaffee. "Catharine Macaulay: Eighteenth-Century English Rebel. " Diss. Ohio State U, 1953.

Bergson, Henri. "Laughter. " *Comedy*. Intro. Wylie Sypher. Garden City: Doubleday, 1956.

The Bible. Authorized King James Version. Ed. Robert Carroll and Stephen Prickett. Oxford: Oxford UP, 1997.

Boswell, James. *Boswell's Life of Johnson*. Ed. George Birkbeck Hill. Rev. and enl. L. F. Powell. 6 vols. Oxford: Clarendon, 1934.

Boulton, James T. *The Language of Politics in the Age of Wilkes and Burke*. Toronto: U of Toronto P, 1963.

Bradbrook, Frank W. *Jane Austen and Her Predecessors*. Cambridge: Cambridge UP, 1966.

Bradley, A. C. *Oxford Lectures on Poetry*. London: Macmillan, 1909. Rpt. 1926.

Bredvold, Louis, I. *The Natural History of Sensibility*. Detroit: Wayne State UP, 1962.

Brodsky, Claudia J. "Austen: The Persuasions of Sensibility and Sense. " *The Imposition of Form: Studies in Narrative Representation and Knowledge*. Princeton: Princeton UP, 1987. 141 – 187.

Brower, Reuben Arthur. "Light and Bright and Sparkling: Irony and Fiction in *Pride and Prejudice*. " *The Fields of Light*. New York: Oxford UP, 1951. 164 – 181.

Brown, Julia Prewitt. *Jane Austen's Novels: Social Change and Literary Form*. Cambridge: Harvard UP, 1979.

—. "The Feminist Depreciation of Austen: A Polemical Reading. "

Novel: A Forum on Fiction. 23 (1990): 303 – 313.

Burke, Edmund. *Burke's speeches* on American Taxation, on Conciliation with America *and* Letter to the Sheriffs of Bristol. London: Macmillan, 1956. Rpt. Westport: Greenwood, 1974.

—. *Reflections on the Revolution in France and Other Writings.* Pref. F. W. Raffety. London: Oxford UP, 1907. Rpt. 1958.

Burney, Francis. *Evelina, or, The History of a Young Lady's Entrance into the World.* Ed. Stewart J Cooke. 1778; New York: Norton, 1998.

—. *Cecilia, or Memoirs of an Heiress.* Ed. Peter Sabor and Margaret Anne Doody. 1782; Oxford: Oxford UP, 1988.

—. *Camilla or A Picture of Youth.* Ed. Edward A. Bloom and Lillian D. Bloom. 1796; London: Oxford UP, 1972.

Burrows, J. F. "App. A." "Jane Austen's *Emma*: A Study of Narrative Art."Diss. U of London, 1967. 284 – 287.

Butler, Marilyn. *Maria Edgeworth: A Literary Biography.* Oxford: Clarendon, 1972.

—. *Jane Austen and the War of Ideas.* Oxford: Clarendon, 1975. Reissued with new intro. 1987.

—. *Romantics, Rebels and Reactionaries: English Literature and Its Background 1760 – 1830.* Oxford: Oxford UP, 1981.

Cecil, David. *Jane Austen.* Cambridge: Cambridge UP, 1935.

—. *A Portrait of Jane Austen.* London: Constable, 1978.

Chapman, R. W. *Jane Austen: Facts and Problems.* Oxford: Clarendon, 1948.

—. *Jane Austen: A Critical Bibliography.* 2nd ed. Oxford: Clarendon, 1969.

—. "A Reply to Mr Duffy on *Persuasion.*" NCF 9 (1954): 154.

Cohen, Paula Marantz. "Jane Austen's Rejection of Rousseau: A Novelistic and Feminist Initiation." *Papers on Language and Literature* 30 (1994): 215 – 234.

Copeland, Edward and Juliet McMaster. *The Cambridge Companion to Jane Austen.* Cambridge: Cambridge UP, 1997.

Cottom, Daniel. "Jane Austen." *The Civilized Imagination: A Study of Ann Radcliffe, Jane Austen, and Sir Walter Scott.* Cambridge: Cambridge UP, 1985: 71 – 123.

Cowper, William. *The Letters and Prose Writings of William Cooper.* Vol. 4. Letters 1792 – 1799. Ed. James King and Charles Ryskamp. Oxford: Clarendon, 1984.

DNB, The. Ed. Leslie Stephen. London, 1886.

Darvall, Frank Ongley. *Popular Disturbances and Public Order in Regency England.* Oxford: Oxford UP, 1934.

De Rose, Peter, L. *Jane Austen and Samuel Johnson.* Washington, D. C. : UP of America, 1980.

—. and S. W. McGuire. *A Concordance to the Works of Jane Austen.* 3 vols. New York: Garland, 1983.

Denham, Robert D. *The Northrop Frye Newsletter* 7. 1 (1996).

Devlin, D. D. *Jane Austen and Education.* London: Macmillan, 1975.

Drew Philip. "Jane Austen and Bishop Butler." *NCF* 35 (1980): 127 – 149.

Duckworth, Alistair M. *The Improvement of the Estate: A Study of Jane Austen's Novels.* Baltimore: Johns Hopkins UP, 1971.

Duffy, Jr. , Joseph, M. " Structure and Idea in Jane Austen's *Persuasion.* " *NCF* 8 (1953): 272 – 289.

Dussinger, John A. *In the Pride of the Moment: Encounters in Jane Austen's World.* Columbus: Ohio State UP, 1990.

Earl of Shaftesbury, Anthony. *Characteristics of Men, Manners, Opinions, Times, etc.* Ed. John M. Robertson. 2 vols. Gloucester, Mass. : Peter Smith, 1963.

Edge, Charles E. "*Mansfield Park* and Ordination. " *NCF* 16 (1961): 269 – 274.

Edgeworth, Maria. *Letters for Literary Ladies: to Which is Added, an Essay on the Noble Science of Self-justification.* 4th ed. 1796; London: 1814.

—. *Belinda*. Ed. Kathryn J. Kirkpatrick. 1801; Oxford: Oxford UP, 1994.

—. *The Absentee*. Ed. W. J. McCormack and Kim Walker. 1812; Oxford: Oxford UP, 1988.

—. *Patronage*. Intro. Eva Figes. 1814; London: Pandora, 1986.

The Encyclopædia Britannica. 11th ed. 29 vols. Cambridge: Cambridge UP, 1910 – 1911.

Engels, Frederick. *The Dialectics of Nature*. Trans. Clemens Dutt. New York: International, 1940.

Favret, Mary A. *Romantic Correspondence: Women, Politics and the Fiction of Letters*. Cambridge: Cambridge UP, 1993.

Fischer, David Hackett. *Historians' Fallacies: Toward a Logic of Historical Thought*. New York: Harper, 1970.

Fitzgerald, F. Scott. *The Great Gatsby*. New York: Scribner's, 1925.

Flahiff, F. T. "Place and Replacement in *Mansfield Park*." *University of Toronto Quarterly* 54 (1985): 221 – 233.

Fleishman, Avrom. *A Reading of* Mansfield Park: *An Essay in Critical Synthesis*. Baltimore: Johns Hopkins UP, 1967.

Freed, Lewis. "The Sources of Johnson's *Dictionary*." Diss. Cornell U, 1939.

Gard, Roger. *Jane Austen's Novels: The Art of Clarity*. New Haven: Yale UP, 1992.

Geng, Li-Ping. "*The Loiterer* and Jane Austen's Literary Identity." *Eighteenth Century Fiction* 13. 4 (2001): 579 – 592.

Gilbert, Sandra, M. and Susan Gubar. *The Mad Woman in the Attic: The Woman Writer and the Nineteenth-century Literary Imagination*. New Haven: Yale UP, 1979.

Gilson, D. J. "Jane Austen's Books." *The Book Collector*. 23 (1974): 27 – 39.

Godwin, William. *Caleb Williams*. Ed. David McCracken. 1794; London: Oxford UP, 1970.

—. *Enquiry Concerning Political Justice and Its Influence on Morals and Happiness*. Ed. F. E. L. Priestley. 3 vols. 1798; Toronto:

U of Toronto P, 1946. Rpt. 1969.

Goodman, Paul. *The Structure of Literature*. Chicago: U of Chicago P, 1954.

Grey, J. David. *Jane Austen's Beginnings: The Juvenilia and Lady Susan*. Ann Arbor: UMI Research P, 1989.

Gunn, Daniel, P. "In the Vicinity of Winthrop: Ideological Rhetoric in *Persuasion.*" NCL 41 (1987): 403 – 418.

Hamilton, Elizabeth. *Memoirs of Modern Philosophers*. 3rd ed. 3 vols. 1800; London, 1801.

Hampson, Norman, *The Enlightenment*. The Pelican History of European Thought 4. Harmondsworth: Penguin, 1968.

Harding, D. W. *Regulated Hatred and Other Essays on Jane Austen*. Ed. Monica Lawlor. London: Athlone, 1998.

Hardy, Barbara. *A Reading of Jane Austen*. London: Peter Owen, 1975.

Hays, Mary. *Memoirs of Emma Courtney*. Ed. Eleanor Ty. 1796; Oxford: Oxford UP, 1996.

Bamberg Hegel, G. W. F. *The Phenomenology of Spirit*. Bamberg, 1807. Trans. A. V. Miller. , analysis and fwd. J. N. Findlay. Oxford: Oxford UP, 1977.

—. *The Phenomenology of Mind*. Trans. J. B. Baillie. 2nd ed. London: George Allen, 1949.

—. *Hegel on Tragedy*. Ed. Anne and Henry Paolucci. Garden City: Doubleday, 1962.

—. *Hegel's Lectures on the History of Philosophy*. Trans. E. S. Haldane and Frances H. Simson. London: Routledge, 1896. Rpt. 1955.

Hoeveler, Diane Long. *Gothic Feminism: Professionalization of Gender from Charlotte Smith to the Brontës*. University Park: Pennsylvania State UP, 1998.

Hogan, Charles Beecher. *The London Stage 1660 – 1800*. Pt 5: 1776 – 1800. Carbondale: Southern Illinois UP, 1968.

Holmes, Richard. *Footsteps: Adventures of a Romantic Biographer*.

London: Hodder, 1985.

Honan, Park. *Jane Austen: Her Life*. London: Weidenfeld, 1987.

Hone, J. Ann. *For the Cause of Truth: Radicalism in London: 1796 – 1821*. Oxford: Clarendon, 1982.

Howell, Wilbur Samuel. *Logic and Rhetoric in England*, 1500 – 1700. Princeton: Princeton UP, 1956.

—. *Eighteenth-Century British Logic and Rhetoric*. Princeton: Princeton UP, 1971.

Hume, David. *An Enquiry Concerning Human Understanding*. 1748. Ed. Charles W. Hendel. Indianapolis: Bobbs-Merrill, 1965.

Inchbald, Elizabeth. *A Simple Story*. Ed. and intro. Pamela Clemit. 1791; London: Penguin, 1996.

—. *Nature and Art*. Ed. Shawn L. Maurer. 1796; London: Pickering, 1997.

Johnson, Claudia L. *Jane Austen: Women, Politics, and the Novel*. Chicago: Chicago UP, 1988.

Johnson, Samuel. *The Rambler, Poems, and Rasselas and Other Tales. The Yale Edition of the Works of Samuel Johnson*. Ed. W. J. Bate et al. 16 vols. New Haven: Yale UP, 1958 – 1990.

Kaplan, Deborah. *Jane Austen among Women*. Baltimore: Johns Hopkins UP, 1992.

Kastely, James, L. "Persuasion: Jane Austen's Philosophical Rhetoric." *Philosophy and Literature* 15 (1991): 74 – 88.

Kelly, Gary. *The English Jacobin Novel: 1780 – 1805*. Oxford: Clarendon, 1971.

—. *English Fiction of the Romantic Period: 1789 – 1830*. London: Longman, 1989.

—. *Revolutionary Feminism: The Mind and Career of Mary Wollstonecraft*. Houndmills: Macmillan, 1992.

Koppel, Gene. *The Religious Dimension of Jane Austen's Novels*. Ann Arbor: UMI Research P, 1988.

Kotzebue, August von. *Lovers' Vows: A Play in Five Acts*. From the German of Kotzebue by Mrs. Inchbald. 5th ed. London, 1798.

Lacour, Claudia Brodsky. "Austen's *Pride and Prejudice* and Hegel's Truth in Art': Concept, Reference, and History." *ELH* 59 (1992): 597 – 623.

Laërtius, Diogenes. *Lives of Eminent Philosophers*. Trans. R. D. Hicks. 2 vols. 1925; rev. and rpt. London: Heinemann, 1959.

Lascelles, Mary. *Jane Austen and Her Art*. London: Oxford UP, 1939.

Leavis, F. R. "The Great Tradition." *The Great Tradition: George Eliot, Henry James, Joseph Conrad*. London: Chatto, 1948. Harmondsworth: Penguin, 1962. 9 – 38.

Leavis, Q. D. "A Critical Theory of Jane Austen's Writings." *Scrutiny* 10 (1941): 61 – 294.

Lennox, Charlotte. *The Female Quixote, Or; The Adventures of Arabella*. Ed. and intro. Margaret Dalziel. 1752; London: Oxford UP, 1970.

Leyden, W. von. *John Locke: Essays on the Law of Nature*. Oxford: Clarendon, 1954.

Litz, A. Walton. *Jane Austen: A Study of Her Artistic Development*. New York: Oxford UP, 1965.

Locke, John. *An Essay Concerning Human Understanding*. Ed. Peter H. Nidditch. Oxford: Oxford UP, 1975. Rpt. with corrections, 1985.

—. *Of the Conduct of the Understanding*. Vol. 3 of *The Works of John Locke*. London, 1823. Rpt. Aalen: Scientia Verlag, 1963.

—. *Political Essays*. Ed. Mark Goldie. Cambridge: Cambridge UP, 1997.

—. *Some Thoughts Concerning Education*. Ed. John W. and Jean S. Yolton. Oxford: Clarendon, 1989.

Lukács, Georg. *The Historical Novel*. Trans. Hannah and Stanley Mitchell. Harmondsworth: Penguin, 1969.

—. *The Theory of the Novel*. Trans. Anna Bostock. Cambridge, Mass.: MIT P, 1971.

MLA International Bibliography, The. 1963-present.

Macaulay, Catharine. *Letters on Education with Observations on Religious and Metaphysical Subjects*. Intro. Gina Luria. 1790; New York: Garland, 1974.

MacDonagh, Oliver. *Jane Austen: Real and Imagined Worlds*. New Haven: Yale UP, 1991.

Mack, Peter. "Humanist rhetoric and dialectic." *The Cambridge Companion to Renaissance Humanism*. Ed. Jill Kraye. Cambridge: Cambridge UP, 1996. 8 – 99.

MacLean, Kenneth. *John Locke and English Literature of the Eighteenth Century*. New Haven: Yale UP, 1936.

Macleod, Emma Vincent. *A War of Ideas: British Attitudes to the Wars Against Revolutionary France 1792 – 1802*. Aldershot: Ashgate, 1998.

McMaster, Juliet. *Jane Austen the Novelist: Essays Past and Present*. New York: St. Martin's, 1996.

Meredith, George. "Prelude" to *The Egoist*. Ed. Robert M. Adams. New York: Norton, 1979.

Miller, D. A. "The Danger of Narrative in Jane Austen." *Narrative and Its Discontents: Problems of Closure in the Traditional Novel*. Princeton: Princeton UP, 1981.

Mingay, G. E. *English Landed Society*. London: Routledge, 1963.

Moler, Kenneth, L. *Jane Austen's Art of Allusion*. Lincoln: U of Nebraska P, 1968.

Monaghan, David. *Jane Austen: Structure and Social Vision*. London: Macmillan, 1980.

Morgan, Susan. *In the Meantime: Character and Perception in Jane Austen's Fiction*. Chicago: U of Chicago P, 1980.

Mudrick, Marvin. *Jane Austen: Irony as Defense and Discovery*. Princeton: Princeton UP, 1952.

Neill, Edward. *The Politics of Jane Austen*. Houndmills: Macmillan, 1999.

Nordell, Robert. "Confrontation and Evasion: Argument Scenes in *Mansfield Park* and *Pride and Prejudice*." *English Studies in*

Africa 36 (1993): 17 – 27.

Oxford English Dictionary, *The*. Prepared J. A. Simpson and E. S. C. Weiner. 2nd ed. 20 vols. Oxford: Clarendon, 1989.

Page, Norman. *The Language of Jane Austen*. Oxford: Basil, 1972.

Paine, Thomas. *Collected Writings*. Selected Eric Foner. New York: Literary Classics, 1995.

Paris, Bernard J. *Character and Conflict in Jane Austen's Novels*. Detroit: Wayne State UP, 1978.

Paul, C. Kegan. *William Godwin: His Friends and Contemporaries*. 2 vols. London: 1876.

Phillips, K. C. *Jane Austen's English*. London: Andre Deutsch, 1970.

Plato. *The Collected Dialogues of Plato*, *Including the Letters*. Trans. R. Hackforth et al. Ed. Edith Hamilton and Huntington Cairns. Bollingen series LXXI. New York: Bollingen Foundation, 1963.

Poovey, Mary. *The Proper Lady and the Woman Writer: Ideology as Style in the Works of Mary Wollstonecraft*, *Mary Shelley*, *and Jane Austen*. Chicago: U of Chicago P, 1984.

Pope, Alexander. *Pope: Poetical Works*. Ed. Herbert Davis. London: Oxford UP, 1966.

Price, Richard. *A Discourse on the Love of our Country*. 1789.

Radcliffe, Ann. *The Castles of Athlin and Dunbayne*. Ed. and intro. Alison Milbank. 1789; Oxford: Oxford UP, 1995.

—. *The Romance of the Forest*. Ed. and intro. Chloe Chard. 1791; Oxford: Oxford UP, 1986.

—. *The Mysteries of Udolpho*. Ed. Bonamy Dobrée; intro. Terry Castle. 1794; Oxford: Oxford UP, 1998.

Rice-Oxley, L. , ed. *Poetry of the Anti-Jacobin*. Oxford: Blackwell, 1924.

Ricks, Christopher. *Keats and Embarrassment*. Oxford: Clarendon, 1974.

Roberts, Warren. *Jane Austen and the French Revolution*. London: Macmillan, 1979.

Roth, Barry. *An Annotated Bibliography of Jane Austen Studies:* *1984 -1994* Athens: Ohio UP, 1996.

—. *An Annotated Bibliography of Jane Austen Studies: 1973 -1983* Charlottesville: UP of Virginia, 1985.

—. and Joel Weinsheimer. *An Annotated Bibliography of Jane Austen Studies: 1952 -1972* Charlottesville: UP of Virginia, 1973.

Sales, Roger. *Jane Austen and Representations of Regency England.* London: Routledge, 1994.

Schacht, Richard. *Classical Modern Philosophers: Descartes to Kant.* London: Routledge, 1984.

Schouls, Peter A. *Reasoned Freedom: John Locke and Enlightenment.* Ithaca: Cornell UP, 1992.

Shakespeare, William. *The Riverside Shakespeare.* Ed. G. Blakemore Evans et al. Boston: Houghton, 1974.

Smith, Charlotte. *Emmeline, The Orphan of the Castle.* Ed. Anne Henry Ehrenpreis. 1788; London: Oxford UP, 1971.

Sophocles. *The Three Theban Plays: Antigone, Oedipus the King, Oedipus at Colonus.* Trans. Robert Fagles. Harmondsworth: Penguin, 1984. Rpt. with revisions 1984.

Southam, B. C. , ed. *Jane Austen: The Critical Heritage.* 2 vols. London: Routledge, 1968.

—. *Jane Austen's Literary Manuscripts: A Study of the Novelist's Development through the Surviving Papers.* London: Oxford UP, 1964.

Southey, Robert. *The Life of Horatio Lord Nelson.* London: Dent, 1906.

Steele, Richard and Joseph Addison. *The Spectator.* Ed. Donald F. Bond. 5 vols. Oxford: Clarendon, 1965.

Stephen, Leslie. *History of English Thought in the Eighteenth Century.* 3rd ed. 2 vols. London: Smith, 1902.

Stokes, Myra. *The Language of Jane Austen: A Study of Some Aspects of Her Vocabulary.* Houndmills: Macmillan, 1991.

Sulloway, Alison G. *Jane Austen and the Province of Womanhood.*

Philadelphia: U of Pennsylvania P, 1989.

Tanner, Tony. *Jane Austen*. Houndmills: Macmillan, 1986.

Tave, Stuart M. *Some Words of Jane Austen*. Chicago: U of Chicago P, 1973.

Thompson, James. *Between Self and World: The Novels of Jane Austen*. University Park: Pennsylvania State UP, 1988.

Thomson, James. *The Seasons*. Ed. James Sambrook. Oxford: Clarendon, 1981.

Tompkins, J. M. S. *The Popular Novel in England: 1770 – 1800*. London: Methuen, 1932.

Trilling, Lionel. *The Opposing Self*. New York: Viking, 1955.

—. *Sincerity and Authenticity*. Cambridge, Mass. : Harvard UP, 1972.

Vickers, Brian. "Territorial Disputes: Philosophy versus Rhetoric." *Rhetoric Revalued*. Binghamton: Center for Medieval & Early Renaissance Studies, 1982.

—. *In Defence of Rhetoric*. Oxford: Clarendon, 1988.

Waldron, Mary. *Jane Austen and the Fiction of Her Time*. Cambridge: Cambridge UP, 1999.

Wallace, Tara Ghoshal. *Jane Austen and Narrative Authority*. New York: St. Martin's, 1995.

Warhol, Robyn. "The Look, the Body, and the Heroine of *Persuasion*: A Feminist-Narratological View of Jane Austen." *Ambiguous Discourse: Feminist Narratology and British Women Writers*. Ed. Kathy Mezei. Chapel Hill: U of North Caroline P, 1996. 21 – 39.

West, Jane. *A Gossip's Story*. 5th ed. 2 vols. 1796; London: Longman, 1804.

Williams, Michael. *Jane Austen: Six Novels and Their Methods*. Houndmills: Macmillan, 1986.

Williams, Raymond. *The Country and the City*. London: Chatto, 1973.

Wimsatt, Jr. , W. K. *Philosophic Words: A Study of Style and Meaning in the* Rambler *and* Dictionary *of Samuel Johnson*. New

Haven: Yale UP, 1948.

Wollstonecraft, Mary. *A Vindication of the Rights of Men*, *A Vindication of the Rights of Woman*, and *An Historical and Moral View of the French Revolution*. *The Works of Mary Wollstonecraft*. Ed. Janet Todd and Marilyn Butler. 7 vols. London: Pickering, 1989.

Woolf, Virginia. *A Room of One's Own*. London: Hogarth, 1929.

Wordsworth, William. *The Prelude*: *1799*, *1805*, *1850*. Ed. Jonathan Wordsworth et al. New York: Norton, 1979.

Wright, Walter Francis. *Sensibility in English Prose Fiction*: *1760 – 1814*: *A Reinterpretation*. Urbana: U of Illinois P, 1937.

Yolton, John W. *John Locke*: *Problems and Perspectives*. Cambridge: Cambridge UP, 1969.

Young, Arthur. *Travels in France during the Years 1787, 1788 and 1789*. Ed. Jeffry Kaplow. 1792; Garden City: Doubleday, 1969.

Index